ALSO BY TIM HEALD

John Steed: An Authorized Biography
The Making of Space 1999
It's a Dog's Life
Unbecoming Habits
Blue Blood Will Out
Let Sleeping Dogs Die
Deadline
Just Desserts
HRH: The Man Who Will Be King (co-author)

CAROLINE

CAROLINE

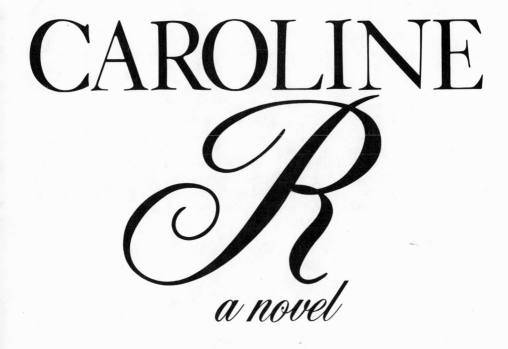

a novel

by Tim Heald

ARBOR HOUSE
New York

It is customary for the Kings and Queens of England to sign themselves by a single Christian name followed by the letter "R." In the case of a Queen, this stands for the Latin word "regina."

T.H.

"My marriage has to be forever"
—PRINCE CHARLES

CHAPTER

1

*J*T WAS a grand day for a wedding.

All along the Mall spectators had camped, curled in sleeping bags, to be sure of a good view of the processions, and at 8:45, as Henderson walked to work, they were eating breakfast. Above them, banners fluttered brightly from specially erected flagpoles, and the sun caught the gold of the ornamental crowns designed for the occasion by the Department of the Environment. There had been a heavy dew, and mist hung over the grass of Green and St. James's Park. At the end of the avenue the palace, white from its recent cleaning, looked appropriately like a wedding cake.

At the roundabout under the memorial to Queen Victoria, a photographer was posing a group of middle-aged tourists clutching small Union Jacks. Beside him a companion was scribbling into a lined notebook. He glanced up as Henderson passed.

"Hello Maurice," he said. "Your big day."

Henderson smiled and gave a little shrug of the shoulders.

"Hardly," he said, "It's *their* day, after all."

Henderson made to move on. He had never much cared for

the man when they were on the staff of the same paper and had let it show. Now he had to be civil. "You going to be in the Abbey later?" he asked.

The reporter grimaced. "Color piece," he said. "Mingling with the crowd. Glenda's doing the Abbey, pulling out all the stops as usual. Silly bitch." He laughed sourly.

Henderson laughed with him and used the laughter to camouflage his getaway. "Must rush," he said. "Busy day."

The policeman at the gate saluted and gave him a cheery "Morning, sir" as he passed through. Normally he would have gone in the back way, past the picture gallery, but he was late now and he saved five minutes by using the front. The man on the Privy Purse Door saw him coming and opened it. He had the half respectful, half domineering manner of a Brigade of Guards sergeant-major, which was what he had once been.

"Morning, Sir" he said.

"Morning, Fox," said Henderson, noticing with a mild satisfaction that the use of the man's name had pleased him. It was a minimal piece of flattery but worthwhile. All the more effective because he had only met him once before, when he was shown around on his first day at work.

Henderson had been the King's press secretary for a fortnight. It was not a job he would have considered when he entered Fleet Street as a tea boy on the *Daily Express*, but after almost twenty-five years of low pay and late nights, constantly disrupted plans and occasional discomforts, he had finally opted for something a bit more civilized. He had covered royal tours before, of course, and had exchanged odd words with royalty at the press cocktail parties which traditionally herald such visits, but this spring in Canada it had been different. He had been the only old hand on the trip and had turned in a couple of long pieces which had found royal favor; and Donnelly, the previous press officer, had boobed badly in Quebec, gratuitously upsetting the French press just when they had been thawing out. The King was livid. Then, in Vancouver, just before journey's end, he'd been taken aside by Sir Evelyn Blackrock, the Private Secretary, and sounded out. A week later, after a cosy chat at Windsor Castle, the job was his.

"Sir Evelyn was looking for you, Mr. Henderson," Deborah smiled. She was exactly the sort of secretary he had anticipated. Nice, pretty in an antiseptic way, irredeemably upper middle class. Everyone in the palace, except for the footmen, was like that. Henderson reckoned ruefully that he was the only state-educated man in the place. He gazed at the pale China tea in its large bone china cup. He had once asked if he might have it with a slice of lemon, and with a slice of lemon it came, every morning, arriving seconds after he had come through the door. The well-oiled sense of gracious living was a long way from the *Daily Express.*

"Oh. Does he want to see me?"

"As soon as you got in."

"Right." Henderson took a mouthful of tea, then got to his feet and straightened his tie. He was a good-looking man, heavy but not yet fat, his dark hair barely touched with grey. In his black tailcoat and grey striped trousers he looked every inch the courtier, and the fancy dress gave him extra confidence—something he badly needed when dealing with Blackrock, whose special talent was making others feel ill at ease in the most charming manner imaginable.

"Henderson, my dear chap," he said, as the press secretary entered. "Do sit down. I'll be with you in just a moment."

Henderson sat and watched, irritated, as Blackrock finished writing, signed whatever it was with a neat signature and blotted it fussily on the outsize sheet of blotting paper in front of him. He too was in morning dress, but whereas Henderson's tie was an anonymous, mass-produced grey, Blackrock's was the midnight blue and double white stripe of Harrow. Even in uniform, men like Blackrock knew how to make men like Henderson feel inferior.

"Now," Blackrock said, putting the paper into an envelope, "everything all right?"

"Yes thank you."

"No problems?"

"Not that I'm aware of." Henderson smiled. "All the foreign

3

magazines seem to think they can have exclusive photo sessions with the bride and groom before *and* after. But our chaps are no problem."

"Our chaps know the form," said Blackrock, fingering his moustache, which was grey and spare. He had been a colonel in the cavalry, one of the youngest in World War II. "His Majesty didn't much care for this." He pushed across a cartoon from one of the mass circulation dailies. It showed the King and his bride at the altar. He was in robes and crown, she in a cheerleader's outfit, with stars on her bottom and stripes across her breast. It wasn't a very good cartoon.

"You might have a quiet word with the proprietor. And in general terms get them to lay off a bit could you? *He* can take it, but she's not used to it. And above all I don't want any damned paparazzi hanging around the yacht. It is their honeymoon after all, and they are human."

"I've already made that clear," Henderson said. "I think they'll play ball . . . except for the Italians and the French; but I've told them there'll be trouble if they step out of line."

"Good," Blackrock said. "I'm sure the navy will do the proper thing."

He stood, signalling the end of the meeting, a small man, but lean and leathery and hard as teak. Not to be taken lightly. Henderson had heard stories about Blackrock, and he was inclined to believe them.

"Well, good luck then," Blackrock said, "and let me know if there's anything I can do. We're all here to help."

"Thank you, sir. You too."

Back in his office he took a call from the New York *News,* who wanted to know if they could witness the signing of the register. With the greatest tact and patience, he explained that the signing was a private affair and in any case the St. Edward the Confessor Chapel was very small, and that frankly the *News* were very lucky to have their single seat in the Abbey. It was more than some English papers had. Then he checked on progress with his two assistants and took a car over to the Savoy. He had to touch base with the bride.

In his study at Buckingham Palace, the King flicked imaginary dust from his shoulders, glared back at the mirror and wished that rank and protocol did not require quite so many medals. At times such as this he felt like a Christmas tree, and although he knew that his subjects were supposed to want a king who looked every inch the part, he could not help wondering. Would they really object if he were to marry in a plain black tailcoat with striped trousers? Did he really have to wear the full gear, as if he were taking the Trooping the Color on Horse Guards? He pulled in his stomach and expanded his chest. No question about it, a uniform flattered the figure, though his figure was the least of his worries. For a man in early middle age he was remarkably fit.

And in love. Yes, he was bloody lucky. He knew that. Girls like Caroline didn't grow on trees. For years now he had been looking for a queen, and it had not been easy. He was damned if he was going to be fobbed off with some European princess who looked like the back end of a bus and was probably a Catholic to boot. Duty came into it, of course, and he was only too well aware that it was his duty to marry and sire children, but there was more to it than *just* duty. He had to have someone he could love. He had had those, all right. Plenty of them and nearly all impossible—divorcees and actresses and adventuresses and older women—beddable, biddable but not, for a King of England, marriageable. Then last year when his parents had been thrown into exile in New Zealand—after what he still insisted was a wretched misunderstanding, a national failure of communication, a ghastly avoidable nonsense—after that the pressure had become still more intense. The monarchy had tottered. More than tottered. He himself had hung on by his fingertips and the Machiavellian scheming of the invaluable—the unavoidable—Colonel Blackrock, but it had been born in on him that if it was to be more than a temporary reprieve from a similar fate or worse, he had to find the right wife in double quick time. The prospect had been daunting and depressing. Then, suddenly, against all the odds, the miracle that was Caroline . . .

He looked at his watch. In a few moments his groomsman would join him and this solitary minute of contemplation would be over. From now on his solitariness would be permanently diminished, and Caroline would be there to take some of the strain. She was strong enough, he was sure. Some had been dubious, pointing out, with a plodding insistence that angered him, her unfamiliarity with the demands of the job. In the last analysis heart, or at least instinct, had to rule head. No one could predict the future with confidence but his hunch was that Caroline was going to turn up trumps. She was a diplomat's daughter. She had the pedigree, the education, the strength of character. She certainly had the looks. And he loved her. He smiled now at his reflection and rubbed a palm thoughtfully across his chin. He felt lucky, he felt elated; and when the knock on the door announced that the rituals were about to begin he felt a surge of confidence and gratitude. Someone up there loved him.

Just as Henderson's car moved gracefully down the Mall, the television broadcast began. In the small scruffy second-floor office of the People's Revolutionary Crusade, Julian Locke winced at the bland preamble of the British Broadcasting Corporation's Man in the Studio. The camera followed the black limousine past the streetliners, men from the Coldstream Guards, the Welsh Guards, the Royal Regiment of Wales and the King Edward VII's Own Gurkhas. It paused briefly at the Royal Winnipeg Rifles, while the BBC men dwelt sonorously on the glory of the old Empire and the magnificence of the New Commonwealth. Then the camera dipped under Admiralty Arch and followed Henderson across Trafalgar Square and up the Strand to the Savoy Hotel. Everywhere there were crowds of flag-waving people, as many, said the commentator, as there had been during the Jubilee in 1977—far more than had turned out for last year's lugubrious coronation.

"Look at them," said Julian Locke, sipping instant coffee from his enamel mug, "Where *do* they come from? And why, for God's sake?"

He took a Gitane from the breast pocket of his denim jacket

and lit it with a cheap disposable lighter, then blew smoke through his nose. "I mean, what *is* it all about?"

At the other desk, leaning heavily on the old manual Remington, Samantha didn't answer. There was nothing to say. She was as perplexed and frustrated as Julian by the stupidity of ordinary people. Every election the Crusade contested ended in tears and lost deposits. They had never attracted a four figure vote, and more often than not they polled less than a hundred, yet as far as Sam could see, the evils of capitalism were self-evident. People seemed willing to live under the tyranny of big business, dominated by inherited wealth which had survived untouched despite years of so-called socialist government. And at the top of the corrupt pyramid which ruled Britain there was the monarchy, the epitome of all that was wrong with society as viewed from the PRC's headquarters in Camden Town.

"Do we have to watch?" she asked, finally, as the outside cameras yielded to the ones in the wedding studio. The master of ceremonies announced a fifteen minute documentary about the new Queen, and the screen was filled with scenes of a white clapboard mansion set in rolling parkland whose fiery golden trees announced the New England fall. "For nigh on two hundred and fifty years," intoned the mellifluous voice of the BBC's chief of bureau in New York, "this has been the home of the Knight family." The film cut to a small churchyard and zoomed in on the gravestones, panning slowly along the line of Henry Knight, and Arthur Knight, and Henry Knight and Arthur Knight, alternating remorselessly with the generations, each one at rest with the "much loved" wives they had taken through the centuries.

"It's too much," said Sam, getting to her feet and snapping the set off. "I can't stand it."

"No," said Julian. "I want to watch it. The more we know about them the easier it will be to get rid of them."

In her suite on the fifth floor of the Savoy, the next Queen of England was echoing Sam's sentiments. She sat, red-eyed in the window seat with her back to the sluggish flow of the Thames.

"Joanne," she said, "for God's sake turn that damn thing off." She crushed another half-smoked cigarette into the ashtray and began pacing again. "I wish I'd never gotten into this whole . . . this whole ludicrous business." She picked another cigarette from the pack of Marlboro King Size. "All I'm doing is getting married," she said, "and it's being beamed by satellite to goddamn China."

Joanne Hollis, sitting very upright on the edge of the deep chintz sofa, sipped brandy and said nothing. There was little she could say. She had been against it from the start, but now was hardly the time to say that she had told her so. She had known Caroline since childhood, had been through school with her, and college, had travelled the hippy trail in Greece and North Africa. Together they had got drunk for the first time on vodka and orange juice in a chalet outside Aspen, Colorado. They'd even lost their virginity together on the same beach on vacation in Southern California. And now this adorable, beautiful, impossible friend of hers was marrying the King of England. It was crazy.

The trouble was that it didn't look impossible to anyone else. Caroline Knight was the nearest Americans get to aristocracy in the British sense. As the BBC film made clear, her family were old money. They had been prosperous since the middle of the eighteenth century, rich since the middle of the nineteenth. Her father was a millionaire several times over, owned a string of racehorses, and had recently completed a term as U.S. Ambassador to Australia. He had been on a first name basis with every president since Eisenhower (with the happy exception of Richard Nixon), and he had prudently married a rich woman from one of the oldest families in Boston.

And Caroline. Even now with her moist eyes and her Marlboro and wearing only a Japanese silk bathrobe, she looked the part. She was tall and leggy and slim and blonde, with high cheekbones and eyes the color of newly melted ice. There was a suggestion of the young Grace Kelly about her, except that she looked more real, less packaged. There was also a squareness about the jaw and a habit of narrowing her eyes when piqued which should have warned anyone seeking to mold her into a neat conforming shape. A girl of spirit and independence one would say on meeting her. Clever too. She had passed all her exams easily, if not summa cum laude, and she was above all nobody's fool. Good qualities for a queen, although who could say what a queen would really need to stay on the throne after what had happened to the last royal couple?

She had first met the King in Dublin during the Irish state visit. They had danced at the ball in Dublin Castle, and a week later she had had an invitation to stay at Balmoral. She disliked the castle's heavy Germanic paneling, its oppressive reminders of Prince Albert, but she was enraptured by the Highlands and by the King's knowledge of them. He took her on day-long treks into the hills, and they shared romantic picnics at the Shiel of Altnaguisach and the Glassalt by the side of Lake Muick. She was no monarchist, no great respecter of tradition or convention and, to her surprise, she found that privately he too had a streak of irreverence and unconventionality. He talked of his flirtation with Buddhism, of the stuffiness of official audiences with government ministers and foreign ambassadors. He mimicked the great and the good, and the old and the bold, and she laughed at the skill and humor with which he did it. When, on the last day of the vacation, he proposed to her, she found that she had come to feel less at odds with the underlying sense of duty which dominated his life.

In her charming, optimistic, possibly naive way she believed that her love would find a way. She realized that love might have thrown her judgment off course, but she had too much confidence in herself to be alarmed. It was a challenge she could relish.

When her parents counseled caution, she protested. "Would you rather have me marry a David or Winthrop, so I can be the wife of a vice-president of the Chase Manhattan Bank or something and have a nice apartment on the Upper East Side, a nice house in Vermont, nice kids?"

Her parents looked at one another. In a way, it was exactly what they both wanted.

"No, dear," her mother said, "your father and I just want you to be happy—"

"But I *am* happy, mom. I am deliriously happy. I'm not only marrying a man I adore, I'm taking on a job, a whole career, which is difficult, I know, but which I can make really fulfilling and meaningful. It's a fantastic opportunity, don't you see that?"

"Caro," said her father very seriously, in the voice he reserved for his little lectures on world affairs, "I wonder if you understand what all this is going to involve you in. You've spent enough time with the English to know that they're not like us. They see things differently, and the closer you got to it the more acutely you'd feel it. And you'd not just be going to live among them, you'd be going to live as their Queen. That means that you'd not only have to conform, you'd have to do more than conform. You'd have to be a goddess almost. Given the political situation over there, they have to love and respect you, practically worship you. Otherwise this could be a very uncertain business."

"Jesus, dad, this is the twentieth century. I'm not trying to be Queen Elizabeth the First. I know it's going to be tough, but God and Bunny willing, I know I can do it, and do it well."

. . .

But now that "D" day had arrived she was not so sure. Ever since the announcement, she had been hounded by journalists wherever she went. There was a permanent squad of photographers stationed at the gates of the ancestral home, and a similar team squatted on the sidewalk in Manhattan until the police department cleared them away with nightsticks. She had been given a twenty-four-hour security guard, but they were no protection against the telephoto lens. Bunny (as she called the King in private on account of his enormous ears) had said it would be different in England, where his subjects were accustomed to royalty and took them for granted; but when she stayed at Sandringham, the royal home in Norfolk, she and her fiancé were almost mobbed by a crowd of thousands as they attended morning service at the tiny Church of St. Mary Magdalene. And as she pointed out, irritably, that was on the estate—private property. People should have been kept out. Her future husband had replied equably that such restrictions might have been possible a hundred years ago, but nowadays Britain was a democracy. For the first time in their relationship she had sulked . . .

"Darling, whatever are you thinking of! You're not dressed." Her mother's brittle, anxious voice interrupted her daydreaming. "You're going to be late."

"Isn't that the bride's privilege?" She smiled frostily.

Her mother did not return the smile. "Mr. Henderson's here," she said, "with your father."

"Oh."

"He'd like to see you."

"Well, he'll have to wait a minute."

She went into the bedroom to dress. There had even been appalling pressures over the wedding dress. Princess Anne and Princess Alexandra had always gone to Maureen Baker of Susan Small. Her mother had wanted Dior. The palace had promoted the claims of Norman Hartnell. She had listened politely, and then bought a severely plain white gown off the rack at Harrods. It was a perfect choice. She looked like a cross between a vestal virgin and a Valkyrie, and her family and advisers swallowed hard and put a brave face on it.

Joanne followed her into the bedroom and zipped her up. The dress was on in seconds, and it took her only a quarter of an hour to fix her makeup. The TV companies had proposed a makeup artist of their own, pointing out that she was going out live to hundreds of millions of people the world over and that the lights in the Abbey would be harsh. She had replied that she was the King's bride, not some tacky TV celebrity. No one else had put her makeup on for her, ever. Privately she trusted in her natural complexion and her fine bone structure, and this morning she contented herself with a foundation, a minimum of blusher on her cheeks, a little eye shadow and a lip gloss as near neutral as she could find.

"How do I look?" she asked Joanne.

"Ravishing," replied her friend and chief bridesmaid, "but how do you *feel?*"

"Lousy," she said, grinning.

In the adjoining suite Maurice Henderson was growing nervous. He wanted to brief the bride on the final camera positions, remind her about microphones, but above all check that she would stick to the timetable. It was important, he knew, not to make her feel that the whole event was being staged for the benefit of the world's media, but that was an uncomfortably large part of the truth. Programs everywhere had been adjusted to take account of the timetable. Even a few minutes' delay would throw satellite and microwave networks all over the world into confusion and disarray.

"I don't want to be difficult, Mr. Ambassador," he said to the bride's father, "but I have to get down to the Abbey, and the time is getting on."

Henry Knight smoothed his silver hair with the palm of his hand and tried not to look exasperated.

"When you've served in Dublin," he said, "you tend to lose sense of the importance of timekeeping."

Henderson smiled. "I can understand that sir. Nevertheless . . ."

They were saved further embarrassment by a knock on the door and the arrival of Joanne Hollis.

"Caroline's ready, sir." she said.

Henry Knight glanced at his watch. "That girl leaves *everything* to the last moment," he muttered. "Come on in Henderson. I'd say you had five minutes."

In the event it was ten. Caroline seemed remarkably calm now and beyond a distinctly unregal "Hi, Maurice," on greeting him, she said little as Henderson quickly rehearsed the points he had to make. "Queen Alexandra's State Coach will be waiting at the River Entrance, ma'am, and the camera crews will be to your left as you enter. Of course, you don't have to acknowledge them in any way, but . . . if you could manage to let them get a good shot of your face it would help. And once you're moving it's best if you can lean forward a bit from time to time. If you sit back it's difficult to see inside the coach. And at the Abbey there'll be no cameras until you start up the aisle; so you can relax for a moment, and then you're on parade as soon as you hear the trumpeters' flourish.

She must be nervous, Henderson thought, *she didn't even object to being called "ma'am."*

He was almost back on schedule as he left the hotel but still too hurried to recognize that he was as nervous as the bride. He consulted his clipboard. There was an informal briefing for the foreign press corps at the West door of St. Margaret's, the smaller church next to the Abbey. He had told the nationals and the TV boys that he would be there so that they would have an opportunity to check with him. God knows what they would want to check, but there was always something: "Can you say what His Majesty had for breakfast?" "Has the President sent a wedding gift?" "Why is the Cardinal coming?" "Why hasn't Liza Minnelli been invited?" "Is the gold in the wedding ring really Welsh?" "Will the King and Queen be visiting the Bahamas?" "How tall is she?" On and on, questions, questions. He would be glad when it was over.

The audience at PRC headquarters had grown by one by the time the bride left the hotel. Hermann Schnabel was a Communist from Düsseldorf who had a pair of inordinately thick spectacles which he polished incessantly. His English was immaculate; he had lived more than half his life in London and spent almost half of that at the London School of Economics.

"Very interesting," he said, leaning forward, pudgy fingers revolving fiercely on the bottle-bottom glass of his lenses, "very interesting."

"What's interesting?" Sam asked. "She's just a rich Yankee bitch with an eye for the main chance. What's interesting about that? I don't think groupies are interesting."

"Just look," Schnabel said, still polishing furiously. "Do you see the men on the back of the coach? Eh? Look at the way they hold themselves. See how straight their backs are. And the man on the horse. Look at his buttons, and his boots. Look at those horses. You British always say it is the Germans who pride order and regimentation. But did you ever see such spit and polish?"

"It's the one thing we still do well," Julian said.

The German laughed. "Just like the last days of the Austro-Hungarian Empire. So rotten. So decadent. So doomed. But such uniform! Such bands! Such music! You can always tell when a nation is on the way out—they start writing tunes like the *Pomp and Circumstance March* and the *Radetsky March.*"

"I think it's obscene," said Sam.

Schnabel smiled. "Look at her," he said. "She is magnificent, wouldn't you say?"

Caroline was in the coach now, and she did look every inch a queen, leaning forward slightly and waving to the cameras and crowd as if to the manner born.

"Imagine," Schnabel said quietly, "what that girl is embarking on."

"You mean all that smiling and waving?" Julian laughed.

"No, seriously," said Schnabel. "Most of them are born into that job, and educated for it. They never know anything else. But she . . ." and he paused to consider, "she has tasted the forbidden fruit. She knows that the grass *is* greener on the other side of the fence. It is the difference between an animal that is born into captivity and one that has been captured."

The elegant coach, with its escorting squadron of cavalry, was nearing Westminster Bridge. A dapper Henry Knight waved a gray glove at the crowds lining the Embankment as his daughter smiled radiantly out of the other window. Everywhere there were Union Jacks. The bright red, white and blue waved patriotically from every window and every lamp post and from some there hung the Stars and Stripes—a reminder that this was the first time "the special relationship" had been sanctified by matrimony.

"George III will be turning in his grave," Julian said.

An observant eyewitness would have seen that besides the ceremonial cavalrymen and guardsmen who surrounded the coach and lined the route, there were more plainclothesmen than London had ever known. The English were marginally less obtrusive than their American counterparts, who were easily distinguished by their neat off-the-rack suits, the wires over their left ear and, most obviously, their habit of looking the wrong way through their dark glasses. They were the only eyes in the audience which were not on the bride.

"I wonder how long it will be," Schnabel murmured, more to himself than to anyone else.

"Until what?" Sam asked irritably.

Schnabel smiled distantly. "Until the honeymoon is over," he said.

"Wives," the bishop read in a reedy Church of England voice, "submit yourselves unto your own husbands as unto the Lord . . ."

Caroline blushed and glanced sidelong at the King. He was her husband now. Her lawful wedded husband. She smiled as he noticed her surreptitious look. ". . . for the husband is the head of the wife, even as Christ is the head of the church . . ." Strange words, she mused, because this husband, this man to whom she was tied, was the head of the church in this country. She let his smile warm her, watched the familiar crinkling of the crow's feet at the corner of his eyes, the deepening of the lines that ran from the sides of his nose almost to his chin. She loved that smile. It made her tingle, like rain on naked shoulders or sea-spray on a stormy voyage. "Husbands, love your wives," the bishop continued, robes rustling as he turned the page of the Bible, "even as Christ also loved the church, and gave himself for it . . ."

Caroline cocked an eyebrow, imperceptible to anyone except the King. He, smile fading to an expression of high seriousness, inclined his head in a silent affirmation. Their eyes locked, shutting out the world, the hundreds gathered in the ancient abbey church and the millions more out in the world beyond, trespassing on their privacy through the medium of television. For a moment they were alone in thought, if not in fact. Then the bishop's voice changed tone to announce the ending of the lesson and include the congregation. "Let every one of you in particular so love his wife even as himself; and the wife see that she reverence her husband!"

All around them people shuffled and coughed as the bishop left the lectern and walked back to his place in the pew. Caroline's eyes flicked back to look straight ahead. Her husband's lingered a moment longer on her lustrous beauty, then he too faced front. The intimate little passage was past and they were back on parade once more.

Henderson did not begin to relax until he heard Handel's anthem, "Let their celestial concerts all unite." By then the newly wedded couple were signing the register and the marriage ceremony was over. Dean and archbishop had been word-perfect. The King had said his lines firmly and sonorously, and the bride had sounded demure, relaxed even. As the pure notes of boys' unbroken voices soared towards the majestic Abbey ceiling, Henderson caught the eye of the Abbey's Receiver-General. The two men exchanged the slightest of smiles.

Even the Russian Ambassador had come, surprisingly well tailored (though not in morning dress) and with the Order of Lenin in his buttonhole. In fact the entire diplomatic corps was present, ranging in dress from the drab Mao jackets of the Chinese and the dress military fatigues of the Cubans to the rustling silk robes of the West Africans and the ridiculous Ruritanian uniforms of the new military dictatorship in Iran. Many countries had sent their heads of state: all three Scandinavian monarchs were there, and the elected king of Malaysia, the king of Spain and his daughter, the king of the Belgians, the queen of the Netherlands, though neither the president of the French Republic nor of the German. There were sheiks and sultans from the Persian Gulf and eight Commonwealth prime ministers. The President of the United States had, typically some said, sent her vice-president, her mother, her husband, two sons and a brother but had herself stayed in the White House where she was (it later transpired) watching the ceremony on TV.

The British Establishment was on display in all its finery. The

Earl Marshal, Garter Principal King at Arms, the Constable of
the Tower of London, the Lord Chancellor of England, the
Warden of the Cinque Ports and all manner of mostly elderly
gentlemen in crimson robes with ermine collars, joined queru-
lously in "Immortal, invisible, God only wise" and muttered at
the constant bending and unbending required by the marriage
service of the Church of England. Besides high society, there
was café society. Young Turks and beautiful girls (some of
whom envied the new Queen Caroline and some of whom pitied
her) filled the pews on both sides of the aisle, and made even so
embittered a fatalist as Colonel Sir Evelyn Blackrock think that
perhaps, after all, Britain had a future.

Henderson's eye wandered across the lines of journalists,
many scribbling into small notebooks on their knees, like theater critics at a first night. He knew most of them from the days
when he had been on the other side of the fence and a thorn in
the flesh of every public relations officer he met. He smiled as
the choir started on the Twenty-third Psalm, sung to the tune
of "Brother James's Air." The wedding party reemerged from
the St. Edward the Confessor Chapel, blinking in the TV lights.
The King looked flushed but splendid in his field marshal's
uniform and the vivid blue sash of the Garter across his chest.
The Queen, for Queen she now was, seemed utterly serene.
Henderson felt a surge of emotion which brought a lump to his
throat and—almost—tears to his eyes. They looked, together, so
absolutely right, so entirely appropriate.

"Two years," Schnabel said, glaring at the happy couple as
they came out of the Great West Door of the Abbey.

"I'll take you ten pounds," Julian said, truculently, "I tell you
today means bye-bye republic, bye-bye socialism. It means a
new lease to the Americans, in fact it means more Anglo-Ameri-
can entente than we've had since Macmillan and Kennedy, or
Eisenhower and Churchill for that matter. It puts everything
back to square one. Look at those crowds."

Behind the barricades outside the great Abbey Church of
Saint Peter, people were going discreetly berserk. They were

not dangerous, just jubilant, a mass of cheering, waving, happy, adoring people. High above, the twin towers symbolized the permanence of the English crown. Every English monarch since William the Conqueror had been crowned in the Abbey. A church of sorts was rumored to have stood on this site since the second century A.D. The bells pealed out, mingling with the noise of the crowd, discreetly adjusted by the sound engineers to provide a suitable background to the commentary which was speaking of "the symbolism of this magic moment in the history of two great English-speaking nations, this moment of reason and concord, trust and love as the doors of the historic Glass Coach, traditional wedding coach of the House of Windsor, open now to admit the King . . . and Queen . . ."

"I prefer it without the sound," Schnabel said, "but I'll raise you. Make it one hundred pounds. In two years time the monarchy, the entente, the Conservative Government, it will all be ready for demolition. The discreetest pressure from us and the whole edifice will be as dust."

"You have to be joking," Sam said, "I mean I'd love it to happen but it's just not on. Two years ago maybe, but everything's changed. People here are frightened by what's happened in Italy. I think many of them feel guilty now about sending the last Queen into exile. People here don't dislike kings and queens —only bad ones. They don't want socialism and now they see the King and Queen as the defenders of what they persist in calling 'moderate opinion.' "

"Sam's right," Julian said. "I wish she wasn't, but history's against you this time, Hermann. I'll take your hundred. In two years' time there won't be the slightest hint of things going wrong for the monarchy or the right. We on the left are going to have to fight just to stay alive."

Schnabel smiled. "It's only a honeymoon," he said, "a little euphoria before the end." The camera closed in on Queen Caroline waving from the window, framed by a sovereign's escort of the Household Cavalry. "*She'll* do it for us," he said. After all, he thought to himself, he had seen the files. He *knew*.

There was to be a wedding ball that evening, an affair of magnificence in the Ball Supper Room with its mirrored walls and doorways, but before then there were other rituals. First in the 1844 Room, named after the visit that year of Emperor Nicholas I of Russia, there was champagne for the family. The atmosphere of relief was so electric that the vintage Krug was almost superfluous.

At the business end of the palace, Blackrock poured two glasses of Manzanilla and handed one to the press secretary. "Good show," he said, "In fact, a very good show."

"Yes," Henderson said, looking over Blackrock's shoulder at the chocolate-boxy painting by Fragonard which took up most of the wall, "Pretty good show all round, I should say."

"Let's hope it's only the beginning," Blackrock sipped, then wiped his moustache fastidiously, catlike. "Country needs putting back on its feet," he went on. "People need something to look up to, something to respect. We've got a chance to get our sense of values back."

"Quite," said Henderson.

"Don't care for that word 'image,' but you know what I mean. You and I have to help their majesties create the right *image*. Moderation, decency, all that sort of thing." Blackrock stood up and went to the window, where he tweaked at the net curtain. The view gave on to the palace Quadrangle from which the state coaches and landaus had now all departed. He turned. "I don't mean you should do anything artificial, understand. But now that the marriage is behind us I think we can begin what the trade calls a little creative image building." He smiled. "Or so I believe."

"I'll do what I can," said Henderson. "I agree with you. It's a propitious moment. Last week's Gallup was encouraging." The poll had shown an overall majority in favor of the monarchy for the first time since they had started asking people about the royal family. Over sixty percent in favor and only eleven percent against. It represented an unprecedented reverse.

Blackrock sat down again, and rotated the sherry glass. "Do you know Cathcart?"

"No." Henderson knew who he meant, of course—the government's jack-of-all-trades who sat in the back office at 10 Downing Street, the one George Wigg had used when he was Harold Wilson's paymaster-general. Cathcart had the same title, too, and he used it to cover a multitude of disparate activities. He had a special responsibility for security, reporting direct to the PM. And he had a troubleshooting role which meant that he cropped up from time to time in Zimbabwe or Bermuda or Ulster, skillfully keeping his name out of the headlines and steering clear of the minister nominally in charge. To the public he was a shadowy figure of little or no interest. To insiders he was recognized as the most powerful figure in the government after the Prime Minister. He had carte blanche, deferring only to the PM, and one area that Cathcart had made his own—from a distance, of course—was the royal family. He had seen political advantage in doing so. Besides, he and Blackrock had both been at school in Harrow years before. They still shot together whenever they got the chance, priding themselves on the skill and accuracy with which they dispatched high-flying birds. They killed cleanly, efficiently; it was a matter of pride, and competition.

"You'd better meet Cathcart," Blackrock said, "He's a pretty indispensable part of the scheme of things. Perhaps you'd care to dine one evening?"

Henderson murmured acceptance in principle. "And if there's anyone you'd like to bring along . . ." said Blackrock. This time Henderson shook his head. "No," he said, "there's no one. But thank you all the same." Blackrock frowned and studied his hands. Henderson's wife had died two years ago. Car crash. It was in his report.

They finished their sherry in silence. Then Blackrock pulled a gold watch from his waistcoat. "Better move," he said, "they're due on deck in ten minutes."

The appearance on the Buckingham Palace balcony was part of the ritual of royal celebration. Ever since Queen Victoria had stood there in 1854 as the last Guards battalion marched away to the Crimean War it had been the platform from which royalty showed itself to the people. Today, as so often, there was to be a fly-past by planes from the Royal Air Force's Strike Command but that was just icing on the cake. The real object of the exercise was for the members of the wedding to stand there and be acclaimed, waving while the crowds cheered.

The footmen and flunkeys were lined up in the Balcony Room when Henderson and Blackrock walked in, but the only other man present was Macpherson, the Scotland Yard man in charge of palace security.

"Biggest crowd since the Jubilee, sir," he said to Blackrock.

Blackrock raised his eyebrows. "Let's have a look," he said, and led the way through the open central window. The crowd, mistaking him for a royal personage, gave a roar of greeting which subsided somewhat insultingly when they failed to recognize him. Henderson, following behind, was amazed at the numbers. Now that the processions were over they had been allowed to come out from behind the barricades and they swarmed around the Victoria memorial and even over it, hanging on to bits of ornamentation in the hope of a better view at no matter what risk. They surged against the railings, waving their Union Jacks, happy to be on the fringe of a footnote to history, a vast ocean of people stretching down the Mall towards Admiralty Arch as far as the eye could see.

"Good," Blackrock said, both hands on the balustrade as he gazed out at them. Watching him, Henderson wondered if this sort of adulation corrupted the Royal Family's hangers-on. Already he himself was beginning to feel a reflected glow from it all. Would he start waving and smiling and demanding deference? Would he begin to behave like a minor prince of the blood royal? He hoped not. But looking at Blackrock he couldn't help wondering.

They turned back through the windows to find that the royal party was assembling. Everyone seemed in good spirits. Champagne helped. Royal nephews and nieces and cousins were positively skittish. The King was telling a long joke to his aunt, accompanying the story with much gesture and arm-waving and funny voices. The Queen was in close conversation with Joanne Hollis, the two of them laughing together like the old friends they were. Henderson watched them, pleased. He sensed what an ordeal it must have been for both of them. The others, even young Fitzherbert, the groomsman, were accustomed to this elaborate and public flummery. The Americans were not. He felt like walking over to the Queen and congratulating her, but realized as he saw Blackrock himself hanging back with as much servility as a footman that the gesture would be considered bad form. As it happened, however, the Queen made the gesture herself.

"Hello Maurice," she said, coming across to him and putting a hand on his forearm, "I was all right, wasn't I?"

"Better than all right, ma'am," Henderson said, "you were perfect, if I may say so."

The Queen smiled and fished in her handbag. "Do you have a light?"

Henderson froze. The King did not like smoking. Besides it was only recently that the Royals had allowed themselves to be photographed drinking alcohol. There *were* smokers in the family, but . . . The Queen had taken a Marlboro from the pack and had the cigarette in her mouth.

"I, er . . ." Henderson began.

The Queen looked at him coquettishly. "Don't be absurd, Mr. Henderson. I know you *do* have a light, and I want a cigarette before I go out on to that balcony and wave at all those people down there. Now would you be so kind?"

He hesitated momentarily, then took his gold Dunhill from his trouser pocket. It had been a present from his wife. He fumbled slightly, then flicked his thumb and lit the Queen's cigarette.

"Thanks," she said, and smiled, letting a thin column of grey-blue smoke hover in the atmosphere.

"A pleasure," Henderson was saying when he realized that the King had crossed to where they were standing. At his elbow, a footman.

"Come along, darling," he said. "Time to go outside." And

before anyone had realized what was happening His Majesty had taken the cigarette firmly and adroitly from his wife's fingers and ground it hard into the ash tray carried by the footman. She frowned at him affectionately for a moment before allowing herself to be led by the hand out onto the balcony, where they were greeted by a thunderous cheer of the crowd. Seconds later came a menacing roar as the Royal Air Force's Strike Command's planes tore through the air low overhead, making everyone crane their necks to stare up at the delta-winged fighters silhouetted against the pale blue sky as they streaked over the fluttering royal standard on the roof and disappeared toward the west.

A few miles away, in the office of the PRC, Hermann Schnabel watched the happy couple on the screen and smiled. "Two years," he said, "and then . . ." He smiled again and made a quick slicing movement across his throat. "Kaput," he said.

CHAPTER

$\mathcal{T}$O OUTSIDERS the next two years represented bliss un-
confined. The King appeared relaxed, confident and com-
fortably regal in all that he did. The Queen was obviously doing
him and the country good. She was, in a word, radiant. She
looked like a million dollars and even the most xenophobic
Englishman soon believed that she was worth *more* than a million dollars. In fact the consensus was that she was the best
present the United States had made to the mother country since
Marshall Aid and Lend-Lease in World War II.

Not even keen students of royal life were privy to what went
on behind the palace walls; and even those who lived behind the
palace walls were not sure what the Queen was thinking behind
that immaculately serene expression, but she *looked* happy
enough. She *seemed* happy enough.

"I'm so lucky," she would say to her husband, as they sat
together in the evening, she reading Henry James, he studying
cabinet papers, while Monteverdi's *Vespers* or Elgar or Beetho-
ven's Ninth was playing on the quadrophonic.

"Lucky?" he would say, looking up and smiling. "How come
you're lucky? I'm the lucky one."

And then they would argue about which of them was luckier, until finally the King would throw down his pen, abandon his papers and take her off to bed, where the argument would be adjourned between the sheets . . .

"Interesting?" she would inquire, every week, after the King's weekly meeting with the prime minister.

"Not very," he would say, dispirited. The prime minister both bored and irritated him.

"What did you talk about?"

"Nothing really."

"Oh, come on." And she would put her arms around him and kiss him on the lips, snuggling up warmly. "Nothing really? Nothing really? What is that supposed to mean? You must have talked about something . . . nuclear deterrents . . . the balance of payments . . . the pound . . ."

"Mmmmm." He would stifle the queries with kisses, kisses that, like the argument about luck, led to bed more often than not.

Yet there were the faintest stirrings of unease in their relationship. She wanted him to trust her more fully, more intimately. It was wonderful to be worshipped for one's body and the warmth of one's personality, but she had a mind and she wanted to use it. He, on the other hand, adored her company, was ecstatic about their lovemaking, but was apprehensive about her curiosity, about her anxiousness to be involved in what he saw as the tedious, businesslike, unavoidably male side of his life. It was love all right, but it was not perfect. Neither of them spoke about it; after all, perfection was unreal, and the little imperfections of a young marriage gave them something to work at.

Were they happy? They said so. They thought so. The ripples on the surface of their happiness were, they both believed, no more than ripples. They did not run deep.

A few months after Caroline's marriage an unhappy incident led to an estrangement between her and her oldest friend.

In December, as the damp chill of an English winter descended over London, the Queen began to keep a diary. It was a symbol of her loneliness and isolation—a loneliness and isolation of which, at first, she was barely—consciously—aware . . .

I've never kept a diary before and I'm not sure this is going to be a regular occurrence. I don't know why I'm starting to do it now, but somehow I feel I have to get my thoughts down. It's been a week since Joanne left and for the first time since I came here I feel really dispirited. Bunny is away inspecting some troops in Ulster where Blackrock and the government (and for that matter Bunny) all say it's too dangerous for a woman, especially a pregnant one. I suppose it's mean-spirited of me to feel they're more concerned for the royal foetus than they are for me, but that's exactly how I do feel. The child will be a member of the family by blood, and I'm only a member of the family by accident. He or she will be descended from William the Conqueror or even Egbert or Charlemagne for all I know. No one seems to care that he'll be descended from me too (why does one always assume children are going to be little, boys? Correction—little princes.)

What was it about today that so got me down? I think it was lunch. Nobody had explained the idea of the lunches until just before this one happened. Evidently in the early fifties Queen Elizabeth thought it was time to show the country a human face, so she and the Duke started having little lunch parties for what's laughingly called a "cross section" of society. They've been going ever since, about four a year. We shunt them in, give them an adequate four-course meal, some more than adequate liquor and then shunt them out again after a few sweet informal words. Since the numbers are kept at a dozen, that means ten outsiders at the most. Forty carefully chosen Brits a year to an hour's worth of lunch each strikes me as a somewhat beggarly exercise in meeting Joe Public, but I guess it's better than nothing. Anyway, around one o'clock nice Maurice Henderson tells us the guests are all in the Caernarvon Room being plied with booze so Bunny and I go in and collect our safe abstemious white wine spritzers and start to circulate. Considering they were supposed to represent the cream of British public life they seemed a pretty slow bunch except for a guy from the BBC who was young and bright and who, luckily, I sat next to during the meal. It was in the 1844 Room because it's always been in the 1844 Room which is named after Nicholas I's visit. I don't like the 1844 Room partly because Nicholas I is my least favorite Russian Emperor of all (he tried to rub out the Poles and the Roman Catholics) and partly because it's just too much, decorwise: white and gold and terrible amber pillars and an excruciating 19th-century Axminster carpet—the sort of thing you'd expect to see at the Annenbergs'.

It was the sort of meal you'd get at the Plaza: lobster bisque and filet mignon, only served on pretty Sevres plates. The BBC man was on my right and the one on my left was a physicist from Cambridge, Sir Alfred something, who was about a hundred and five and deaf. It was a square table and the drill was that I sat in the middle on one side, Bunny opposite, Maurice H. on a third and old Gumley, the Master of the Horse, on the fourth. Naturally I tried talking to the old physicist but he was just too much. The broadcaster was witty and entertaining so I spent most of the time talking to him. We were just about through with the beef when I realized Bunny was very ostentatiously trying to draw Sir Alfred into his conversation and in fact managed to get him to utter a few more or less unintelligible words. Then the conversation seemed to get more general for a little but I was busy talking to my BBC man about South East Asia so we didn't join in. Everybody seemed quite happy and I certainly enjoyed myself more than I'd expected until we went back into the Caernarvon Room, Bunny went first of course, with the others well behind so we had a few seconds on our own. When we got in there he turned and said "We're not here to enjoy ourselves. We're here to work." He said it quite viciously and when I asked just what he meant he said "Please talk to all your guests, not just the ones you fancy." I wanted to say that they weren't my guests since no one had even told me who was coming, let *alone asked me, but it was too late since the guests were marching in by then for brandy and cigars and coffee. Later I tried to talk sensibly to Bunny about it but he wasn't really having any. He was in a hurry to go off in the helicopter, so he gave me a kiss and apologized for having snapped at me and we parted on the best of terms. But I'm not happy with it and I've felt like a bear with a sore tooth ever since. Apart from anything else there wasn't a single other woman there and I find that kind of depressing. Rang mom to talk but she doesn't even begin to understand. She puts the slightest hint of depression down to morning sickness and only wants to know who was there.*

It was a bitter winter. There was less snow than Caroline was used to in New England but there was a dampness in the air which depressed her and gave her a head cold which stayed with her for weeks. In the States, people had been organized for the weather just as they were organized for everything else, but in England they seemed to make a virtue of suffering. At the Palace the great fireplaces remained as empty as they were in summer. The King allowed the use of the antiquated central heating system only for a few hours a day. There were old fashioned electric fires, but even the use of these was regulated.

She had been accustomed to wearing light silks and cottons throughout the year at home but now she found herself guided by her helpful if distant dresser and ladies-in-waiting into the thick tweeds and stockings she had always associated with English winter fashions. It seemed grotesque to her that they should practice such stringent economies when it came to their own personal warmth and yet splash out in the most gratuitously ostentatious manner on more public occasions. When the president of an obscure African state came to dinner they ate off gold plate and had caviar and Krug. When she took it up with Bunny, he explained patiently that the president had to be made much of because his country was an invaluable trading partner for Britain. They took Britain's tractors and medical supplies. In return Britain got cut-rate copper. Caroline had not liked the president, thought him autocratic if not fascist, and probably, like Amin and Boukassa, a political cannibal to boot.

"That's all fine," she added, "but remember that they'll throw him over in a year or two and we'll have to explain away our attitude to his successors."

The King smiled wanly and took her to bed.

At Christmas the court decamped, medieval style, to Sandringham, where if anything it was draftier and less comfortable than at Buckingham Palace. At least they were allowed an occasional log fire, but she had assumed, naively perhaps, that the Sandringham visit would be a holiday. It was not, not in any sense that she understood. The boxes, red leather containers full of state papers, continued to arrive for Bunny to sign. The footmen and other servants came with them, dressed in their red, brass buttoned waistcoats, and the house was perpetually full of guests, most of whom she did not know. The King spent much of his time shooting, and at first Caroline accompanied him on these expeditions, standing behind him in the freezing cold as he slaughtered the little birds with a meticulous and seemingly dispassionate efficiency. After a while she found it boring.

No one talked; indeed talking was bad form except over lunch of heavy meat pies, hot consommé and strong whisky. The men talked of little but sport and their wives about the problems of getting staff, of keeping staff, of dealing with staff. Caroline was surprised at this preoccupation. At home they had never had a problem with their servants, nor now that she was married. There was always the marginal concern that some menial might be bribed by a less than scrupulous newspaper into betraying the secrets of royal life, but this did not alarm her. Their marriage was too new for secrets she minded sharing. If the world was interested in what she had for breakfast or what sort of music she enjoyed, then so be it. She didn't care.

But she did care about the mindless prattle of these rich men's wives, and after a while she took to avoiding them. She was not obvious about it but she managed to find other things to occupy her time. The library was full of Victorian novels and on the coldest days she sat in there, well wrapped against the drafts, and read Scott and Mrs. Gaskell. Her pregnancy made this allowable, for nothing must be done to jeopardize the future of the next heir to the throne. The Queen must be pampered and indulged, at least until she had given birth.

Although she did not care for standing around outdoors while the men shot, she liked fresh air. Luckily she discovered a golden Labrador, bred for retrieving fallen birds from the undergrowth or the fields of winter kale. He had proved a failure, hopelessly gun-shy and neurotic, startled even by the crackle of burning logs in the grate, and the keepers talked of having him put to sleep. His name was Oliver and the Queen made a special pet of him, developing the habit of taking him for long solitary walks across the frosty fields. On the whole she preferred his company to that of the house guests.

Not that she disliked everything about her first Sandringham Christmas. There was an intimate, family atmosphere about the estate, and she loved Christmas Eve when all the workers, most of them third- or fourth-generation Sandringham employees, came into the big house for their Christmas presents. It was feudal, she thought, as Bunny handed the men their turkeys and hams and sides of beef, but agreeably so, and there was a bond between these servants and their master which had nothing to do with the county wives' easy talk of "staff."

Morning service was fun too, in the tiny church of St. Mary Magdalene, with its ornate decoration in memory of Edward VII; and afterwards it was amusing to see her husband on television delivering his Christmas broadcast to the nation together with film of the royal year. It was like home movies in Vermont, only rather more public.

Early in the new year she slipped quietly and unnoticed to her parents' for a long weekend. It surprised her how easily the secrecy could be managed. She travelled to Heathrow in one of the unmarked Rolls-Royces, with a single car following close behind in which rode one of the plainclothes police officers assigned to royal security. He was armed, but unobtrusively. At the airport she was driven straight out on to the tarmac and shown up a separate, cordoned off set of steps to the top deck of the British Airways jumbo. The cabin was fitted out as a personal, private apartment. Two security men sat downstairs covering the entrance and exit.

At Kennedy the White House had ordered a black Lincoln Continental, discreetly armor-plated, to meet the plane on the runway. There was no motorcycle escort, but as in England another car with Secret Service agents on board followed behind as the Lincoln drove north through a white countryside to the rural peace of the Green Mountain State and the old house in which she had been born and brought up.

She was surprised at how tired she was. She slept late in the mornings and retired early at night. It was almost like a return to childhood; she stayed in the old nursery with its rocking horse and the wide bed with the patchwork quilt which was still so familiar she could have painted it square by square from memory. The house was quiet, the surrounding countryside muffled by the carpet of snow. She drank hot chocolate thick with cream and snowshoed across the park with her parents. They spoke very little, just enjoyed each other's company.

Returning to Sandringham, Caroline felt she had a new perspective on life. At any rate she felt more able to stand up to those conventions of regal existence which increasingly began to get under her skin.

A disagreement with Bunny. It happens so rarely that I feel I should record it. It was about the bagpipes. I like bagpipes, I really do but not, for God's sake, at breakfast. Or at least not every breakfast. Like everything else, it seems it's been going on since Queen Victoria, who was a sort of Highlands freak. In any event the old bat instituted this custom whereby every morning as she was laying into her kippers and English breakfast tea there was a piper promenading outside the dining room windows playing laments. It was okay at first, but lately it's begun to get on my nerves. So yesterday morning when Bunny was

*away to some reunion for helicopter pilots down in the
West Country, I went outside and asked the pipe major to
pipe down, as it were. He was perfectly civil about it,
saluted and marched off without any trouble but of course
it got back to Bunny and he was furious. First time there
hadn't been piping at breakfast for more than a hundred
years, no respect for traditions, and so on and on and on.
There are times when I wonder things about my husband
and this was one of them. I tried being reasonable. I tried
to argue. I explained it wasn't my favorite music. I even
tried to compromise. I suggested we do without bagpipes
when he's not at breakfast. Or maybe have Tuesdays and
Thursdays off. But no. He just looked whiter and whiter
and became more and more obstinate. Piping at breakfast,
he said, was like ravens at the Tower of London and apes
on the Rock of Gibraltar. He didn't expect me to
understand but he did expect me to do as I was told. And
that was it.
Then an hour later he came into my room and said he was
sorry and would it be all right if the pipers didn't pipe
when he was away. There had to be piping when he was
at breakfast but he thought he could swing a dispensation
for me on account of my being a mere colonial. I said sure
and then he smiled and said that between the two of us he
preferred Berlioz to bagpipes any day of the week. But
there was nothing he could do about it. We laughed and
kissed and made up. I love him very much, but things like
this worry me.*

Buckingham Palace may look to the world like a mausoleum,
but it is well equipped. Most days the Queen swam in the heated
pool. Sometimes she played squash alone or with one of the
more sporting ladies-in-waiting. And gradually she built up a
portfolio of what the staff call "patronages." She became colo-
nel-in-chief of the Devon-Dorset Regiment, patron of the
new South West London General Hospital, president of the
Royal Festival Ballet. Wherever her husband went visiting
(unless it was to someplace dangerous or all-male) she went
with him, hands always ready for the children's bouquets,

smile always poised, ready to flash at those who required it.

Observers, distant and nearer at hand, were visibly impressed. The press ran photographs of her at every imaginable opportunity, using her as happy relief from the gloomy news of politics and economics which filled most of their pages. To those around her at the palace she seemed indefatigable, always optimistic, always managing to suggest by her manner that life was, despite all evidence to the contrary, worth living after all.

This was remarkable, for most of these days of showing herself to her people were similar, to a point of numbing tedium. They certainly bored Henderson, who was responsible for having the itineraries typed up for distribution to the press.

"Arrive Slough Town Hall," the schedule would read. "Presentation of mayor, councillors, local member of Parliament, local dignitaries. Take tea/coffee in mayor's parlor. Proceed by car to Slough swimming baths for display by local schoolchildren (NB: Slough swimming coach is Meriel Smith, Olympic bronze medal winner in women's 100 meter butterfly) proceed to new Slough Arts Center. Unveiling of plaque. Tree planting." And so on.

Privately Henderson wondered whether it was worth the work that went into each trip, but always when she arrived and he saw the faces of people who had come to meet her he revised his opinion. Despite the security problems she went on walkabouts wherever she could. One would think she was running for office, the number of times she shook hands. People loved her. They wanted to touch.

She liked to be liked. That day in Slough, Henderson watched admiringly as she chatted animatedly to the pear-shaped, whiskery mayoress and flirted gently with the local MP, a junior minister whom she had met before. She managed to balance her handbag, a cup of tea, a sandwich and a bouquet of flowers and still look beautifully regal and pleased to be talking to such wonderfully interesting people. Henderson admired this. Local councillors are, he thought, among the most boring and pompous people on earth. But watching her you would never have known.

After the tree planting and plaque unveiling there was a brief tour of the local industrial estate and a visit to a chocolate factory. The royal party donned white overalls and hats and proceeded down line after line of conveyor belts. She was prevailed upon to try packing chocolates into presentation boxes. Cameramen stood on chairs and tables to get a better view. A television crew thrust bazooka-shaped directional microphones at the royal packer. She continued to look radiant and interested as if there was nothing in life that entertained her more enormously than being filmed packing chocolates into a two-pound box. Outside the factory there was a brief hiatus when she was for a moment unescorted.

"Jesus," she murmured to Maurice, "do people actually eat these toffy things?" She made a disgusted face. "Let's cancel their warrant. What's next?"

"Lunch," said Henderson, "in a community center near—"

"Oh God," she exclaimed, "more food. Please let there be someone to talk to."

They returned to their cars and on to lunch, which was inedible and attended entirely by Rotarians and their ladies, many of them wearing chains of office, ribands, medals and other decorations that distinguished them proudly from their fellow men. The Queen sat next to a florid-faced man in his early sixties who turned out to be a dairy farmer. Or, more accurately, he owned dairy farms.

"Breeding, livestock and artificial insemination," she complained to Lady Coker, her lady-in-waiting, as they had a brief private moment in the ladies' lavatory. "For forty-five minutes."

"Bad luck," sympathized Lady Coker. "Mine talked about golf."

And after lunch more walkabout. A spruce drab council estate, a monument to the socialist planning of the 1940s. The crowds were large, mostly schoolchildren, all armed with Union Jacks which they waved frantically. The Queen dutifully talked to as many as possible: "Hello . . . what's your name? . . . Where do you come from . . . how nice . . . no, I left my crown at the Palace . . . yes, it is reather heavy . . ."

One day merged into another, and her hours—if not her mind —were nearly always occupied. Her pregnancy progressed un-eventfully, presided over by a trio of royal gynecologists who examined her every week, sucked their teeth over her continu-ing, though modest, intake of alcohol and tobacco, and pro-nounced her astonishingly fit. She was content. Of course there were irritants, hundreds of them, but during that winter and spring she was too preoccupied to notice them, though another brief holiday, this time with her husband, reminded her of what life, in a normal world, could be like.

The last few days have been so good. We borrowed this island south of Eleuthera. Just us; nobody else but the security guys, who were marvelously unobtrusive, and a million and one servants to mix the rum punches and fix beach barbecues. The doctors were against the trip, but we had the helicopter and they said it would only take fifteen minutes to wing over to Nassau, where the hospital's perfectly able to deal with antenatal problems in normal healthy women under thirty, even Queens!
So we lay on the beach (me feeling like a whale) and sailed a little, and Bunny did some scuba diving and we played Scrabble and read to each other. And there were no boxes for once. All the state papers were being dealt with by a council of regency or something so there were no distractions and we could just concentrate on each other. Reminded me that I married Mr. Right. Felt so well and brown and fit that when we got back I hardly noticed the fog at Heathrow and managed to be quite charming to Colonel Blackrock. I wish we could make a habit of it, but Bunny is wedded to the eternal round of Balmoral and Sandringham for holidays. He thrives on discomfort. Also he says the British like their rulers to have spartan pleasures. They never forgave Princess Margaret for lighting off to Mustique at every opportunity.

Back at home, Caroline attacked her job with renewed vigor. To Maurice Henderson, who, like her, was a stranger to the demands and disciplines of the palace, it seemed that she was almost overanxious to please. It would be stretching a point to say that she confided in him, but as newcomers and outsiders there was a bond between them which both tacitly recognized. His job as press officer did not involve much official contact with her. The Queen did not give interviews or press conferences. She had not, so far at least, made a single speech other than perfunctory and banal thank-yous for flowers and similar favors; but Henderson had been hired for more than speech-writing and the composing of anodyne answers. He was at the palace as an image maker. He was there to make sure that the royal family the public saw was the royal family they wanted to see, a royal family they could admire, respect and even, the next time the chips were down, love and trust. A tall order.

"Your popularity increases with your pregnancy, ma'am," he said one day with uncharacteristic openness, taking coffee with her at eleven in her study.

"With my girth, you mean."

He grinned, affecting a mild embarrassment. "Front page photographs on all your last three public engagements," he said, "in every paper except the *Financial Times*."

"What *will* we do when I'm back to normal?"

"Oh," said Henderson, "I don't think your public will want you back to normal. They like you prettily pregnant. I'm afraid they'll expect you to go on bearing children until you're fifty."

"Ha!" she said, "as far as I'm concerned, childbearing is a phase in my life. I'll give it my all for just so long as is necessary, but it's uncomfortable, rather unsightly and they tell me the worst is yet to come. Before the best, I mean. I know what you all expect of me and you'll get that all right. But no more. And meanwhile I'm going to let it interfere with life as little as possible."

"I was going to suggest," he said, diffidently, "that we call a halt to your public engagements. I've spoken to Sir Evelyn and to Simpson and we don't see anything looming that can't be put on one side quite happily. The doctors agree. They say there's no point in taking any undue risks."

"You're very solicitous," she said, "but I really don't intend to drop out of sight just because I'm having a baby."

That evening she decided to raise the matter with her husband. They had no engagements, formal or informal, so they ate a light supper of scrambled eggs with smoked salmon. Afterward the King said there were boxes to attend to, also some problems over the pheasants at Sandringham. She, however, protested that they could wait till next day, a proposition to which he grudgingly agreed. Instead of work they played Scrabble to a background of Mozart horn concertos.

"I had a talk with Maurice Henderson today," she ventured as the King opened with a high-scoring Z-E-B-R-A.

"Oh, yes. Henderson's good news. The last man was a disaster." He leaned forward and picked up five new letters.

"He wanted to stop my public engagements." She toyed with her letters and made Z-O-N-D-A.

"You can't have trade names," he said. "Not allowed."

"It's not a trade name, silly," she said. "It's a wind, like the mistral, only they have it in Argentina."

"Are you sure?"

"Of course. I lived there, remember?"

"But you were only about five," he protested. "I think you're having me on."

"Nonsense." She picked up more letters. "The zonda blew all the time. Very hot and dusty. We didn't like the zonda. You don't want me to cancel my engagements, do you?"

"Not if you don't want to." He frowned over his letters. "But you mustn't tire yourself. Do you have anything very vital coming up?"

"No," she said, somewhat sharply, and regretted it. "No," she repeated more softly, "I only wish I had."

"Mmmm?" He was not listening. "Do you allow B-I-S-Q-U-E?"

"No. It's foreign. How come you get all the good letters?"

"Luck." He smiled. "I'm a lucky boy. What did you say?"

"I said I was sorry I didn't have anything vital coming up."

"Oh, come on." He was teasing her. "Queens can be seen and

not heard, especially when they're busy being pregnant. The people will adore you because you smile so prettily at them. They think you love them."

"It's not funny, darling. You know I've always wanted to do a decent job of this. I don't want to just be an icon, a figurehead. I want to have more meaning than that."

He abandoned his letters and looked at her thoughtfully. "That's all the meaning there is," he said. "The job *is* being an icon and a figurehead."

"What about your cabinet papers?"

"I only look at them. I can't act on them. Not really."

"But the Prime Minister? Your weekly audience?"

"A charade." He was grim now. "You know as well as I do that we survive on sufferance. We're puppets. Both of us."

She grimaced. "I'd just like a bit more to do, Bunny," she said. "We've talked about it before. I'm an intelligent adult. I know about a lot of things. Okay, so we can't be political, but there are other areas. Women's rights . . . ecology . . . conservation. I could give some leadership there. Be some use."

"Hmmm." The King frowned at the Scrabble board. "I always said you'd find it frustrating," he said, "but I'll see what we can do. I don't want your mind addling through boredom. What about B-A-S-Q-U-E?"

Did an investiture all on my own! Doctors groused because the prince/princess is due in only six weeks but I insisted. It's an hour of standing but I feel strong as an ox and I am determined not to spend the rest of my life at Bunny's elbow, simpering.

Not that it was easy. Knights first, which meant hitting these old codgers on each shoulder with a sword. Hit one of the first far too hard and almost knocked him over.

Luckily he was a general, and leathery even though antique. I apologized and he just said "Not at all, ma'am, all in the line of duty." Very British.

It's one hell of a job finding something different to say to each one of them. They come on and on in an unending stream, endless little men in badly cut grey suits, all scared

*out of their wits and looking even more ludicrous because
of these hooks on their jackets on which I'm supposed to fix
their new gongs. I wish they realized I was as petrified as
they are. And all through it this terrible music played by
an orchestra from the Brigade of Guards—nothing but
Gilbert and Sullivan and Rogers and Hammerstein.
To start with I asked them what they'd won the medals for
but the explanations were so long that I soon stopped and
just said "Congratulations" or "Doesn't it look splendid?"
At least no one complained and most of them looked
pleased and pink.
I wish I could learn how to put people at their ease. They
seem so terribly daunted and so desperately concerned that
they are bowing properly. Also they have to take three steps
backwards after we shake hands and I longed to tell them
not to bother. I was certain someone was going to fall,
though no one did. Dying for a cigarette all the way
through, but not, naturally, possible until afterwards when
I lit up the second I was by myself. The obstetricians say I
shouldn't, but if I believed these doctors I wouldn't get up
in the morning.*

The Queen went into labor at two o'clock in the morning of
June 16th. For half an hour she lay in bed with the lights off
wondering whether it was a false alarm, then as the pains became more severe she got up, put on a dressing gown and
crossed through into her husband's room.

"Bunny," she said, sitting heavily on the bed and putting a
hand gently on his face. "It's started."

Although the child was not technically due for another two
days, the preparations had been made with meticulous
thoroughness. On the first floor, the Buhl Room, where the King
himself had been born, was once more emptied of its ebony and
tortoiseshell furnishings and turned into a maternity ward.
Soon after three, the hastily roused royal gynecologist arrived
by taxi, followed almost immediately by a midwife and two
nurses. The King, after making sure that there was champagne
cooling and ready for imminent use, joined his wife in the Buhl

Room, determined to break with royal tradition and stay with her throughout her labor unless something went wrong and the doctors had to perform a Caesarean. Outside the crowds, alerted by heaven knows what bush telegraph or telepathy—for no announcement had been made—began to gather outside the palace railings. At 4:30 Blackrock, alerted by the King, called Henderson just in time for him to field a call from the British Broadcasting Corporation. Fifteen minutes later one of their large khaki mobile broadcast vans came trundling down Constitution Hill and parked on the corner. It was followed minutes afterward by another from Independent Television News.

Inside the Buhl Room Caroline refused the offer of pain-killing pethedin and breathed hard on the gas every time the pain came. She tried to concentrate on the breathing exercises she had been taught and wondered if it would be unregal to cry out. Bunny sat by her head and dabbed at her forehead with a wet towel. From time to time he tried cheering remarks which, when she heard them properly, she found mildly irritating. After a while he sensed this and just held her hand, wincing as she dug her fingernails into his palm.

On the six o'clock news the BBC announced that Sir Lester Barrowclough, the royal gynecologist, had been called to Buckingham Palace during the night and was still there. "We shall bring you any further news as soon as we have it," the announcer said, not actually saying that the Queen was in labor but making it abundantly clear nevertheless.

The crowd grew. Parts of it began to sing. In the Buhl Room, the Queen was being told to push. "I *am* pushing," she shouted, louder than she realized. The King was sweating almost as much as she was. He was a bad spectator. In fact he wished now that he had not been so damn progressive and had waited somewhere else where he could pace up and down. He hated having to sit still and soothe.

"You're doing just lovely," said the midwife, a buxom middle-aged Londoner, "Just lovely."

"Oh God," cried the Queen, "please let it be over . . ."

At 11:15 Sir Evelyn Blackrock, after a brief and deferential congratulation to his sovereign, telephoned to the Home Secretary. The Home Secretary was in a Cabinet meeting but had left instructions that he was to be interrupted. He took the call in the Cabinet room at 10 Downing Street. "The Prime Minister," he said after relaying the news to the assembled company, "asks me to convey the heartfelt congratulations of His Majesty's Government to His Majesty and Her Majesty."

At almost the same time a military dispatch rider on a Bombardier motorcycle raced away toward the City to give the news formally to the Lord Mayor of London. And at 11:30 Maurice Henderson walked down the corridor and out of the Privy Purse Entrance. In his hand was a large piece of foolscap with the palace crest at its head. On it, in the large typeface of his secretary's IBM Selectric, was the date and below it the words: "Her Majesty the Queen was safely delivered of a daughter at 10:55 A.M. Her Majesty and her daughter are both doing well."

Indoors in the Buhl Room, Queen Caroline sat up in bed, cradling her infant and holding her husband's hand. She looked as tired as she felt, and though she knew that everyone was pleased, and though she knew that she was happy, there was a tiny niggle at the back of her mind, a niggle which spoke of failure.

Over the following weeks, as the palace prepared for its first christening in years, the realization became oppressive. For the succession to be secure, the Queen would have to produce a prince. Her tiny daughter, soon to be named Princess Elizabeth, the Princess Royal, was all very well in her way, but next time she would have to bear a son.

Christening. What a performance! I knew about ceremonial weddings and state funerals but I hadn't realized that we christened our offspring with quite this much ostentation. Poor little girl was surrounded by prelates, including the Archbishop of Canterbury; stifled in a moth-eaten, moth-balled Honiton lace gown which Bunny wore at his christening and which, as far as I can understand, has been

*worn by every babe since Queen Victoria's time (God, that
woman has a lot to answer for!). The water was flown in
specially from the river Jordan, and there were no less than
eight godparents including three ex-kings and queens. All
Bunny's friends and relations were dressed to the nines,
medals and ribbons dangling from every available space,
which made mom and dad look as if they were in their
underwear. Poor things, they seemed subdued by all the
fuss. I never thought I'd live to see them looking homespun.
Mom said she can't wait to get me and Lizzie over to
Vermont and feed us some cherry cake and root beer.
At least I was allowed to hold her for a few minutes, but
as soon as she'd been turned into a little Christian, nanny
whisked her off to the nursery to change her diaper while
we had a single (small) glass of champagne each and made
polite conversation. When I was christened we went to the
village church in the Packard and had our photograph
taken outside, by a little man from Bellingham. It was a
pretty church. In fact I miss the simplicity of white
weatherboard and unvarnished wood. The Music Room is
by Nash and has "eighteen columns of deep blue scagliola
with gilt Corinthian capitals." Too much, too much. And
now I must lie back and conceive again. Bunny must have
an heir.*

She was pregnant again with almost indecent haste. Even the
unbendingly prune-dry Sir Lester allowed himself to express a
mildly amused surprise when he confirmed her condition.
"Congratulations," he said, "if that is the word."

"Naturally," she said, flashing one of the smiles she usually
reserved for a cheering public in the Mall, "I know my duty.
Besides, we Americans don't mess around."

She was pleased to see him blush.

Privately, she was surprised by her fecundity. Perhaps all
those years on the pill were having some effect, perhaps she was
just astonishingly fertile and Bunny amazingly potent. At all
events they worked well together.

"I think we could make babies by just holding hands," she

said, teasing him one morning as they lay naked and entangled in bed.

"I prefer it like this," he said.

She laughed. "So conventional. So traditional. So impossibly British."

"In my family," he said, mock pompous, "we've been making babies like this for over a thousand years. So don't knock it."

"I wouldn't dream of it," she murmured, "It's the best way I know of mixing business with pleasure."

They both wished they could enjoy more of such moments, but their lives were too full of other people. They were always the center of others' attention, even private moments dogged by detectives and equerries and servants.

"You know, Maurice, I have a job just pouring myself a drink in this place," she complained to her press secretary one day as she fixed them both dry martinis. "If I wanted my nose picked," she continued, "I do believe one of the footmen would do it."

"I'm not so sure," Henderson said, bantering, as much as he dared. "There are union rules about that sort of thing. There would have to be a special appointment."

"Gold Nosepicker in Waiting," she said, smiling, "Or Hereditary Grand Nosepicker of England."

Henderson sipped at his drink. "I'm not sure the Civil List would stand a fulltime nosepicker in the palace. I think you'd have to go outside. There must be some suitable place in Jermyn Street longing to have a sign up saying 'By Appointment, Nosepickers to Her Majesty the Queen.'"

Caroline put her hand to her mouth to stop herself spraying martini over the carpet as she choked with laughter. "God Maurice," she said, "that's too much. I've got to put that in my diary."

Henderson looked at her oddly. "I didn't know you were keeping a diary," he said, "I'll be more careful what I say in future."

She smiled as if caught in some misdemeanor. "It's not a real diary," she said, "I just write things down when I feel like it."

She lowered her voice. "Or when I don't have anyone to talk to."

There was a long pause before Henderson, with a forced but sympathetic briskness, returned to practicalities.

"I wonder," he said, "if we might go over the arrangements for Balmoral? I'm taking my own holiday then so I shan't be around."

"We'll miss you," she said.

> *July 30th.*
> *Talk with Maurice Henderson. Or rather did not talk to Maurice Henderson. He's the nearest thing to a human being in this place bar Bunny, but he's paid to do what we say and I daren't compromise him. I already told him I write a diary, which is the sort of thing people consider indiscreet. Someone will steal it, etc. I'd like to be able to talk openly to Maurice but being queen is so . . . distancing.*
> *If this one's a boy I'm going to take some initiatives . . . .*

During the Balmoral holiday she experienced much of the same boredom that had afflicted her at Sandringham. In Norfolk they shot partridge and pheasant. In Aberdeenshire grouse. The scenery around Balmoral was better but the house more sepulchral and depressing. Bunny shot, fished and stalked, and occasionally she stood by him, but she was not allowed to talk, which, she had decided since marriage, was what she enjoyed most. Her husband tried to teach her to cast for salmon but she was a little clumsy at it and not sufficiently interested. She accompanied him on one of his long deerstalks but it was too gruelling for a woman in the early stages of pregnancy and she had to give up early. This prevented him from shooting his quarry, and though he affected to be more concerned for her than the hunt he was quite put out.

Once or twice they went on private picnics to the isolated and beautiful spots where, so recently, they had courted. They even took the infant princess, pried grudgingly from her nanny's arms. But the excursions were not entirely successful. The child cried. Once it rained. They got wet, the Princess Royal included. Nanny was not amused.

Briefly the Prime Minister came to stay. Potter was a high Tory of the old school, much given to country pursuits of a style which had gone out of political fashion during the premierships of Edward Heath and Margaret Thatcher. His wife came too, a stocky tweeded figure whose old-fashioned looks belied a keen mind and a friendly disposition. While their menfolk plunged into the forests in search of deer the two women toured the policies, as the Scots, for some reason, describe their gardens.

"I do hope you realize what a perfectly splendid tonic you've been for us all," said the Prime Minister's wife, swiping at a dandelion with her stout walking stick. Her own frankness, especially when complimentary, embarrassed her, and she did not look at her hostess and Queen. "You've cheered us up no end," she said. "After everything we've been through it's been a real boost to be reminded that there is some spontaneous warmth and generosity left in the world."

Caroline was startled. No one else had said anything like that to her.

"That's very nice of you," she said, and then, realizing that something more was required, she added: "I don't feel as if I've done anything at all really. And people have been very kind." She wasn't sure that this last remark was true but she felt that Mrs. Potter would expect it. They were walking through woodland now, a mixture of oak and spruce through which a stream ran gurgling over stones—the only sound apart from their voices and the snap of twigs under foot.

"Wives don't often 'do' very much, at least not in the sense that their men do things," Mrs. Potter said. "It's being that matters. Being true to yourself. Sometimes doing things actually gets in the way of that. I've never had what normally passes for a job, but I have tried to be myself and I like to think that's been more help to those I love than anything I 'did' could possibly have been."

It was quite dark in the woods, even though the sun shone

outside. Only a few rays penetrated the foliage to make lattice-work light patterns on the ground. Mrs. Potter thwacked at some bracken with the stick.

"You've been a wonderful example of what a young woman should be like," she said, "and I think that's what royalty is all about, don't you?"

Caroline didn't answer for a while, then as they began to walk slowly back towards the castle she said, untruthfully, "I don't know. I've never really thought about it."

The older woman laughed. "Exactly," she said. "That's why you're so good at it. It comes naturally and that shows."

Caroline frowned, suddenly aware of the world's very limiting expectations of her and of her future.

In the seventh month of the Queen's second pregnancy Colonel Blackrock took the day off. "Funeral," he explained gruffly to his colleagues. When the King asked sympathetically if the deceased was kith or kin Blackrock looked solemn and said that the dead man had been at school with him. Also that he had been a member of the same club. To his wife he said, "Dusty Fanshawe's funeral today. You don't feel like coming, I suppose?"

Lady Blackrock, who had as far as she could recollect never met Colonel Fanshawe, said "No dear" and then, feeling that this demanded some qualification, added "I'd forgotten it was today. Will you be home? Or will you stay in town?"

Blackrock told her he would stay at the club. There was no need, but it was nice to take advantage of the excuse. As he sat, stiffly, in the pew at the back of the church waiting for Dusty Fanshawe's coffin, he allowed himself a tiny twinge of guilt about playing truant from Dorothy. The twinge did not last long.

The church was small. Saxon, Blackrock guessed, with a heavy Victorian gloss. The congregation was respectable, and, he judged, mainly drawn from the area. Dusty had been a justice of the peace and, some years before, master of the local hunt. Very few of them, he supposed, would have known much about

Fanshawe's true career. It had been easy enough for him to dismiss his job—"Oh Ministry of Defense wallah, y'know. Just shuffling bumf about the place." Blackrock had heard him say this once or twice, self-deprecatingly, implying that his career had finished when he left the regular army, that the high spot of his life had been his command of the Lancers. Dusty Fanshawe had been blessed by providence with a bland, round, fool's face, and he had managed to link this to a bland, round, fool's manner. It made him an obvious candidate for Intelligence and he had, in his supposed bumf-shuffling days at the Ministry, risen high. Very high. But that fatuous manner and appearance had fooled his own people too. It was very late in the day that Dusty's sexual proclivities had come to light. Then there had been an unsatisfactory revelation about one or two of the friendships, and the growing suspicion that Dusty was mixed up with the Czechs. Blackrock had sat in on the interrogations. Fanshawe had given nothing away, but he was retired all the same. Properly this time. Everyone agreed he should be allowed to finish his days in peace provided he kept his nose clean. And he'd managed that, until the writer fellow had started nosing around. The writer was astute and indefatigable. He had rumbled. Hence the car crash. Pity.

Blackrock looked at the printed service sheet. Even as he absorbed the words of the processional first hymn, he heard the organ change from a muted sepulchral strum to a musical throat clearing as the organist played, very loudly, the first few bars of "Immortal, Invisible God Only Wise." The congregation stood, coughing and shuffling and rustling its service sheets as Dusty Fanshawe's coffin entered on the shoulders of the undertaker's men, the paleness of their faces accentuated by the black serge suits. Blackrock watched; he liked order, symmetry, stories with beginnings and ends. The justice and the finality of the moment appealed to him.

He was reflecting thus, on the order of things, when a man in a heavy overcoat with an astrakhan collar eased into the pew alongside. Blackrock half turned, took in the puffy expensive features of his friend and colleague Henry Cathcart, smiled fleetingly, and turned back to the coffin, which was now proceeding jerkily up the aisle to its resting place before the altar. Out of the corner of his eye he noticed Cathcart crossing himself. Henry had always inclined to High Church. In fact, dimly, Blackrock had an idea that he had gone over to Rome at some point. That was not Blackrock's style. He enjoyed pomp and ceremony but not what he regarded as the effeminacy of Catholicism. He liked his Christianity muscular.

The singing ceased. The pallbearers lowered Dusty onto his table. The congregation stood, uncertain of its next move, then descended to its knees.

"Useful turn out," said Cathcart, sotto voce.

Blackrock inclined his head almost imperceptibly. He did not like talking in church, especially at solemn moments. And this was unquestionably a solemn moment. An impartial observer, knowing of the part which these two had played in the dead man's death, would have thought them inexpressibly cynical and hypocritical. Yet Blackrock felt neither. Fanshawe had stepped knowingly out of line and he had paid the price. True, Blackrock had approved his execution, but he felt no more guilt about that than any hanging judge passing sentence.

"Man that is born of woman," the priest intoned, "hath but a short time to live and is full of misery."

Quite, thought Blackrock. He was a fatalist. If God had meant Dusty Fanshawe to live longer, then he would have ordered things differently. One could say, in fact, that in the matter of Dusty's death, Blackrock and Fanshawe had been acting on the behalf of the order of things. Perhaps that was stretching the point. After all, it was not they who had adjusted the brake linings of Fanshawe's Allegro. Fanshawe had always been a reckless driver, but seventy was far too fast for the bend. He would probably have slid off the road into those oaks even if the brakes *had* worked. Blackrock supposed their people must have fixed the accelerator as well as the brakes. Just as well. One could never be too sure.

The congregation stood again. Psalm time. This was a very old-fashioned funeral. "Yea though I walk through the valley of the shadow of death, I will fear no evil for thou art with me; thy rod and thy staff comfort me." Yes. Well. Blackrock joined in the singing, his voice still firm as it had been since he was a young man. He enjoyed singing. Most Harrovians did. Alongside him Cathcart sang too, his voice fuller and plummier. "But thy loving-kindness and mercy shall follow me all the days of my life: and I will dwell in the house of the Lord for ever."

Later when they moved out of the church to bury the coffin in the family plot, just past the end of the avenue of yews, Blackrock and Cathcart stayed some distance away watching the last rites through narrowed eyes. Blackrock poked at the gravel with the ferrule of his umbrella. Cathcart, who had no umbrella, kept his hands deep in his pockets.

"Shame really," said Blackrock.

"Shame?" Cathcart's voice gave no suggestion of feeling.

Blackrock nodded towards the graveside where the coffin was even now being lowered into place. The cleric's robes fluttered lightly. He looked like a magpie, ruffled.

"I wouldn't say so. It comes equally to us all, and makes us all equal when it comes!"

Blackrock shrugged. "Nevertheless," he said, "any man's death diminishes me, because I am involved in Mankind; and therefore never send to know for whom the bell tolls; It tolls for thee."

"Dusty was on borrowed time," Cathcart said. "He knew that as well as anyone. He betrayed us—you, me, the country, the system, everything. He was lucky to hang on as long as he did. We both know that. So did he."

Blackrock stabbed viciously at a molehill by the side of the path. "Yes," he said, "But even so—"

"Oh come on." Cathcart took him by the elbow. "You need a drink. I've got a car waiting. I take it you came by train. I'll give you a lift back. Are you dining?"

In the car, an elderly ministerial Rover driven by a chauffeuse in austere olive green uniform, Cathcart produced a flask of cognac.

"All well at Buck House?" he asked solicitously.

"Can't complain," said Blackrock, drinking gratefully from the stainless steel thimble of brandy. "All seems set fair for the time being."

Cathcart leaned back and sipped from his own cup as the car moved easily towards the eastbound lanes of the M4 motorway. "I often wonder if we were right," he said forcefully.

"About Dusty?"

Cathcart laughed shortly. "I'm afraid there are more pressing things to worry about than Dusty. No, I was thinking of the abdication and all that."

"Bit late to have second thoughts of that." Blackrock stared moodily out at the Wiltshire Downs disappearing into the dusk and thought of the King's parents, exiled and virtually incommunicado in New Zealand. The Palace Putsch, all his own work. "It was necessary at the time," he said, "and it's worked out very well."

"Do you ever hear anything?" Cathcart asked.

"No. We keep very strictly to that part of the deal." Blackrock's voice was icy. "The only way we could persuade the left to call off their hounds was by promising no links between the last lot and the boy. He had to be left alone; otherwise we'd have had the Republic before you could say knife."

"But there's nothing . . ." Cathcart seemed worried. "Nothing unofficial? No friends acting as courier or anything?"

"Nothing," Blackrock said, "except what New Zealand tells us. They're very comfortable. It's a splendid estate I'm told. The fishing's excellent, there are horses." He smiled. "They can listen to the World Service—what's left of it. I understand they subscribe to *Country Life.*"

Cathcart laughed and poured another measure of cognac. The heavy glass panel between passengers and driver was secure, the intercom off.

"And the King?" he asked. "Doesn't he miss them? Isn't he lonely? He worries me. We have a lot riding on him."

"It's not mentioned," Blackrock said. "It's as if they had never been. He's an orphan as far as we're concerned."

"Hmmm," Cathcart said.

They drove on in silence. It had been, they both realized, a desperate throw. Circumstances had combined horribly. The amount of money in the Swiss accounts had amazed everyone. For days there was a real danger of bloody revolution. Luckily the Prime Minister had been a pragmatist. The last of the Labor moderates. He hadn't really wanted the monarchy out altogether, and he had been prepared to compromise. Hence the sacrifice. It was Blackrock himself who had presented the terms: immediate exile, a week to pack, keep a hell of a lot of money, take whoever wants to come with you, leave the boy, don't come back. It had been a close run thing but the boy was liked. People were prepared to give him a chance. His hands were clean. But there had been moments . . . Blackrock winced at the memory.

"The feeling in Cabinet," Cathcart said, "is that the marriage has paid off. Our private soundings suggest that even the left are a bit fazed by it."

"I hope you're right," Blackrock said. "She's certainly done well so far, but I can't help feeling a little apprehensive. She can't spend the whole of the rest of her life being pregnant."

"I suppose not," Cathcart sighed. "You did say you'd dine?"

"I'm staying at the club," said Blackrock, "so if you don't mind eating there?"

"Admirable," said Cathcart, "We'll try a bottle of that Lynch Bages I was telling you about."

Behind them in the darkness of a country churchyard, the body of Dusty Fanshawe lay unconsidered, six feet underground.

CHAPTER

*I*T WAS a boy.

For the tenth time that morning Maurice Henderson repeated the details. "Seven pounds four ounces. Yes, doing very well. Yes, the King was present throughout the labor. No, I'm sorry I'm not going to answer that, you know perfectly well I'm not, in fact it's damn silly of you to ask in the first place. Quite easy as these things go. No, no epidural; the Queen is a believer in natural childbirth. No, nothing has been said about education. Yes, I know Eton like people to be put down at birth. No. No. That's very good of you. Thank you. Good-bye."

He turned off the switch on the archaic wooden amplifier on his desk. They must have been among the first of their kind, and though still adequate, they always gave him the feeling that he was on the bridge of a destroyer in World War II, summoning the crew to battle stations. They had been put in, he thought, in the time of Commander Colville, most autocratic and haughty of palace press officers. *He* would never have stooped to answering such intimate questions about a royal birth. A crisp notice pinned to the palace railings was as far as he was prepared to go. Times had changed. Not necessarily, thought

Henderson sourly, for the better.

Not that he didn't like the job. In fact he liked it almost too much. The palace was a comfortable billet. His two assistants were hardworking and competent, his secretaries likewise. His colleagues were sometimes absurd but always polite and sometimes even congenial. He enjoyed the traveling, though not when the King insisted on piloting the helicopter, still less when he took the controls of one of the antiquated piston-engined Andovers of the King's Flight. They should have been mothballed years ago, but they gave an impression of comparative penury which the Royals liked to cultivate. More than his journeys on official tour, when protocol required him to dress for dinner on the royal yacht and ingratiate himself to foreign dignitaries, Henderson liked the advance trips he made on his own, preparing the ground for state visits. The rule was that a British monarch could only make one state visit to a country during his reign. By the end of the previous reign the Queen was running out of eligible countries, but her successor started out with carte blanche to go where he wanted. Henderson had enjoyed a memorable week in France planning that visit, and another in Norway. He was due, shortly, in Mexico and then Nigeria. There was talk of Zimbabwe too.

All this was fun, but though it was difficult to be precise about it Henderson sensed storms in the offing. On the surface things were bright enough. The polls showed the Royal Family on a continuing upward curve. In the House of Commons a review of the Civil List had passed off with little trouble. Blackrock had appeared before a Select Committee and pointed out that with inflation now running over thirty percent the King just couldn't manage without more money. Scarcely a hair was turned. Republicanism was not fashionable and the more left-wing MPs had had the sense to keep quiet. The press was friendly to the point of being boring, and there hadn't been an anti-monarchy demonstration of any consequence for years. The birth of Princess Elizabeth had been a marginal anticlimax, since the nation in its predictably chauvinist way had clearly wanted a prince, but the royal couple could hardly be blamed for that. A second child, and this one a boy, so soon after the first was almost miraculous.

"She may not be British," remarked Henderson's former editor over lunch at the Etoile, "but she breeds well."

Henderson had concurred, and now that the infant prince was safely delivered he recognized the justice of the remark still more, even though he would have preferred it to be less crudely expressed. It was a judgment with depressing undertones. The main function of royal consorts was procreative. The Queen had now done all that was required of her in this line. She would probably be expected to produce one or two more little princes just to make the succession doubly sure, but the pressure was now off. And being a royal mother was not like being an ordinary mother. No sooner had the Princess Elizabeth been born than she acquired a whole household of her own. *Two* nannies, no less—boot-faced Scottish ladies laden with qualifications, from Norland; housemaids to look after the nannies; a nursery footman to fetch and carry; a nursery detective to follow the royal perambulator at a discreet distance. Not much place in this scheme of things for a mere mother. The Queen had been told that she could spend an hour or so with the infant in the morning and another hour, perhaps two, in the evening when the child was being bathed. She had objected that she was going to breast-feed the baby. Mrs. Macpherson had pursed her lips and said nothing.

Not that the King regarded his wife simply as a brood mare. At least if he did he was too much of an English gentleman to admit it. Still, Henderson thought he detected a definite cooling of the King's ardor. He seemed, in public, to be courteous, attentive and loving, but he was also very busy. Every evening there were the boxes to be done. Being conscientious, he read everything that came over from the Cabinet Office before he signed it. He was a slow reader. Increasingly often he ate at his desk. Henderson noticed that the spontaneous excursions to the theater or to Annabels or to one of a half dozen discreetly expensive West End restaurants had ceased. They had been frequent during the royal courtship . . .

The phone rang again. It was Fred Crombie, an old friend from Fleet Street, asking the same questions about the new prince. Henderson repeated the information dully. He had it by heart.

"Do you think they'll stop now?" the journalist asked, eventually.

"What?" Henderson was caught off guard.

"Are they going to have a neat nuclear family, or go batting on like Victoria and Albert?"

"God," Henderson said, "I don't know."

"Well perhaps you could find out." The journalist laughed. "You PR men are all the same. Poachers turned gamekeepers are the worst of the lot."

"Sorry, it's not the sort of thing I ask about."

"Well you should." Crombie laughed. "You know we love the Royals but we're all tits and ass now. If your majestic employers go on being quite so bloody respectable and middle class we aren't going to have anything to write about the bastards."

Crombie was an Australian. Henderson knew he was uncouth. In his experience, Australian journalists—certainly those on popular newspapers—were rarely anything else; but this one was shrewd, too. Very shrewd.

"I'm not with you," Henderson said. "I thought you loved us."

"Oh we do, we do, Maurice. It's just that I'm not finding you that easy to write about."

"You're going to write pages about the new prince."

The Australian laughed. "Nine day wonder. We'll have forgotten the little fellow in a week or two. We need something to get our teeth into. I was brought up on Princess Margaret. Great copy. Townsend. Tony Snowdon. Roddy Llewellyn. Remember him? Christ, whatever happened to Roddy Llewellyn?"

"You surely aren't asking me to give you another Margaret?" Henderson sounded appalled.

"Could do worse. Like I say, she was great copy."

"But not exactly wonderful for the royal image."

"On the contrary old sport. Always useful to have a black

sheep knocking around the ranch. The more ghastly Aunt Margaret seemed, the more we all loved the Queen. Question of contrast."

"Oh." Henderson was inclined to agree but wasn't going to. Certainly not over the open telephone in his Buckingham Palace office. "Look," he said, suddenly, 'I'd better go. Everyone wants to know what color the future sovereign's eyes are."

His friend chuckled. "Right you are Maurice, old son, I'm on your side you know, but not everyone is. I hear the appalling Payola has surfaced again. On the other side of the Atlantic. They say he's made a sale."

"Christ!" Henderson sat up very straight in his chair. "Who to?"

"Don't know. Just picked it up from Follett on the Foreign Desk. He'd been talking to Scott in New York. I'll let you know if I hear any more. See you. 'Bye."

He hung up and Henderson sat, thinking. The "appalling Payola" was an Italian, real name Panini, who had once had a vacation romance with a young American college girl called Caroline Knight. He had surfaced soon after the royal wedding bearing photographs, more or less innocuous, but still marginally embarrassing, and had begun with an attempt at what the palace had construed as blackmail. On being rebuffed by Henderson, he had hawked his wares up and down Fleet Street but found no takers. Henderson had had a word with the editors, convinced them that there was no muck to rake, that the affair had been an *affaire*, no more no less, that it had taken place before Queen Caroline met her husband, and that it was nobody else's business. More to the point, there was no story. Caroline had dated a number of men in the past, one of whom was running for Congress. Fleet Street made up their minds that they were more interesting, and the papers seemed content with their fulsome if innocuous remarks about Caroline's essential "niceness," "intelligence" and "good humour." Panini wanted the world to know that she was good in bed, but the world it seemed had not wanted to listen and he had returned to Como, chastened. Henderson had hoped he wouldn't hear of him again.

He drummed his fingers on the leather surface of his desk. It was an unwelcome sign that Crombie had thought it worth warning him. Henderson wasn't fooled by the apparent casualness with which he had told him. That was Crombie's style, and it meant the situation was potentially dangerous. If Panini sold some story, true or not, to an American scandal sheet, then there was a chance the British press would pick it up. That way, they could plead innocence; they would simply be reporting what was news elsewhere. "As Queen Caroline of England gave birth to an heir to Britain's throne a thirty-two-year-old Italian told of his week of passion with the Vermont-born beauty." Et cetera, et cetera. "THE QUEEN'S PAST: EXCLUSIVE." Oh God.

He depressed the switch and asked his secretary to get him the Foreign Office—not that he was too confident of their intelligence capability, at least not in situations like this. And so it turned out. The man he spoke to said he'd heard nothing. Certainly nothing had been published, but that was hardly the point. He needed to have advance warning. Publication would be too late. He looked at his watch—11:00 A.M. Six in the morning New York time. Too early to phone.

A call came in from the *Daily Mail*'s medical correspondent wanting to know which doctors had been present. He answered the man's questions automatically, thinking all the time of what Crombie had told him and trying to decide whether or not to confide in Blackrock. If he was lucky, nothing would happen and Blackrock need never know there had been a flap. But if it did happen, Blackrock should learn from him, not from some other source. He needed to retain Blackrock's approval, whether he wanted it or not.

When he had finished with the *Daily Mail* he went straight across to Blackrock's office. Sir Evelyn was writing on a foolscap pad. The *Times* crossword lay on one corner of his desk, completed as usual.

"I thought I ought to warn you," Henderson said, "Panini's back."

Blackrock regarded him frostily. "The seducer of our sovereign lady?"

"Yes."

"I thought we got rid of him?" Blackrock sounded testy, as if he had more important matters to attend to.

"We did get rid of him. He's back."

"Too bad." Blackrock did not look very concerned. "No one listened to him last time. Why should they listen to him now?"

"Because he's gone to the States."

"Ah." This time Blackrock looked a little shaken. "I take your point. Americans will listen to anything. What's he hawking?"

"Don't know for sure. Nights of passion under the southern sun. Barbara Cartland, only sexy."

"It's not funny." The colonel was decidedly put out. "We're doing a damn fine job putting the monarchy back on its feet, I don't want it loused up by some oversexed Italiano."

"No. I agree."

Blackrock glowered at him. "Well, stop him."

"I'll try, naturally," Henderson said, "but our writ doesn't run in the States, the way it does here. They're not amenable to pressure in quite the same way."

"Hmmm." Blackrock tapped at his teeth with the end of his gold mechanical pencil. "I'm more concerned with the future than the past, Maurice. I don't give a stuff if the Queen screwed around before she came here, but I most certainly care what she gets up to over the next few years. That's between us two for now, and we'll talk more later. But I have a nasty feeling we're going to have more to worry about than this Panini fellow."

"Nevertheless . . ." Henderson wanted to stay with the matter at hand. "If the story does get around—"

"Deny everything," Blackrock barked. "Most of it will be lies anyway. And it's our word against his. We'll just say it's all lies and tell him to bugger off. Now you push off and milk this son and heir story for all it's worth. It may be the last chance for a while to produce some really *positive* publicity."

"I don't entirely catch your drift," Henderson said, wondering why his composure had been so suddenly disturbed twice in half an hour and for no easily discernible reason.

Blackrock smiled. "There ariseth a little cloud out of the sea, like a man's hand," he said softly, then stopped. "Just a hunch," he said. "Bit of a premonition, that's all. Probably nothing in it."

"Bullshit," said the small bald man in the wide striped blazer. He pushed his spoon fiercely into his bowl of chili and leaned across the table toward his two companions. "I say it's bullshit." He abandoned the spoon and picked up his glass of beer. "And even if it wasn't . . . who cares? I mean who *cares* if this broad got herself laid? It's a long time ago. Everybody gets themselves laid when they're that age. Don't matter who they get to be later. I'll bet Mamie Eisenhower got herself laid when she was a kid."

Hermann Schnabel grinned without much evidence of humor.

"You care, Fred, baby. Which is why we're sitting around this table having this interesting discussion." He too leaned forward so that he and his companion were almost literally eyeball to eyeball. "Now do you buy or do Sandro and I take it across the street to someone who'll appreciate it?"

"You take it across the street," Fred said, through a mouthful of wine and chili. "You take it anywhere you want. They'll say it's bullshit, same as I do. She's just had a kid, dammit, she's a respectable family lady. You think people are going to want to buy this crap? You think *I* want to buy this crap?"

"Yes," said Schnabel, "I do. You're already bargaining with me."

By the time the editor had finished his chili, he had bought. It would be ghostwritten by his best man and it would be as spicy as what he had just eaten. Hot stuff. Too bad the photographs were so tame.

"Hell," he said, "if we could get nude shots of Jackie then surely to God it's possible to get nude shots of Caroline."

But Panini and Schnabel said no, not yet anyway. And Fred had accordingly pushed their price down another twenty percent. Not that Schnabel minded that, despite the fuss he made. He wasn't in it for the money.

News of the buy did not take long to reach London, and Henderson had an early tip-off from Crombie. Actually it was more than a tip, it was the first attempt at getting a story out of it.

"Your people surely won't buy it?" Henderson said.

"No need, old son. Once this rag in the States comes out with the stuff it's fair game. We don't have to buy anything. We just repeat the story with appropriate comments."

"Yes," Henderson said, "of course." Henderson could visualize only too well the dramatic front page story: "American scandalmonger tells story of Queen and Italian playboy," while the editorial columns would produce pious platitudes about the bad taste of the revelations, particularly "at a time like this."

"What do you want?" Henderson asked.

"I don't want anything," Crombie said. "Just tell me what you're doing about it and give me the official line."

"Who else knows about this?"

"My source is good. I guess it'll be all round New York by lunch tomorrow. Fred Kandinski will make a big PR pitch as soon as he's ready."

"Is there any way he could be stopped?"

"Not without making an even bigger stink than there's going to be anyway."

"But it's all in the past."

"So's any scandal you care to mention. All the best stories have happened. That's what news is about."

"When are you going to run it?"

"New York are interviewing Kandinski and lover boy. I'm doing the London end. We'll run it tomorrow."

Henderson sighed. "And there's no way we can stop you?"

" 'Fraid not, old son."

"You've got to hold off till tomorrow."

"No way. The others will have caught up by then. We want an exclusive. It'll be like the old days."

"Even the *Express* hasn't had a scoop since the R-101 went up," Henderson said drily, "not unless you count Martin Bormann." A few years back the *Express* had revealed exclusively that Martin Bormann the Nazi leader was alive and well in South America. The story fell apart and the paper had been left with egg on its face. They had not forgotten.

"I know it's not that great a story, but it's ours and it'll get read," Crombie said, "call me back when you know what to say."

"Not much more than 'no comment' I'm afraid," Henderson said, "but I'll call you by four this afternoon." He hung up. "Oh bloody hell!" he exclaimed, then swept up some papers from his desk and went out to confer with Blackrock.

"You've done very well," Sir Evelyn said, before he could unburden himself. "His Majesty is extremely pleased."

"Oh." Henderson was embarrassed. "It was nothing. It wrote itself, as we say in the trade."

"No need to be modest." Blackrock smiled, "we've had enough bad publicity in this place to know how difficult it is to get a good press."

There was some truth in this. Even the Communist *Morning Star* had reported the birth of the prince with less than its usual unpleasantness, and the rest of the newspapers had been fulsome. They had managed to convey somehow that the birth was the result of some extraordinarily brilliant performance on the part of the royal couple.

"I think the country needed cheering up," said Henderson. "Everything else is so bloody awful. It's taken people's minds off petrol rationing."

Blackrock laughed. "Now we'll have to come up with something to take their mind off food rationing," he said. "What do you have to tell me?"

Henderson adopted his most serious, purposeful look.

"You remember I warned you that we might be in for trouble over Panini and the Queen's, er, premarital entanglements."

Blackrock put down his pen and frowned, concentrating for the first time.

"I thought I told you to shut the little bugger up."

"It was too late, sir. And as I think I explained, he's surfaced on the other side of the pond. I can't do much in the States except stir up more interest."

"Did you talk to Cathcart?"

"No." Henderson was surprised. This hardly seemed a case for a Cabinet minister, even for one as silkily influential as Henry Cathcart.

"Better talk to him now then . . ."

"I don't see," began Henderson, but Blackrock cut him off. Henderson was perplexed by his change of attitude. When he had first mentioned Panini and the Queen he had seemed quite cool about it, but now he was almost displaying signs of panic.

"First of all," Blackrock said, picking up his pen again and beginning to make notes, "tell me what's happened."

Henderson spelled it out and Blackrock wrote hurriedly, not interrupting except to ask about Fred Kandinski and his magazine. Henderson knew comparatively little, nor was he able to answer Blackrock's questions about Panini's agent. Blackrock seemed to think it unlikely that Panini had sold the story on his own. It didn't strike Henderson as important.

Blackrock dialed Cathcart's private number himself. It was classified, and he kept it in his head, not divulging it to his secretary or colleagues. Cathcart must have answered at once because Blackrock immediately launched into a resumé of the tale, then listened patiently saying little more than "yes," "no" and once "Well, try it out on your CIA friends anyway," and then again, "I suppose a White House contact *is* overkill, and as you say it would only make it worse. That damn-fool President can't even manage her own news."

When he put the phone down he said to Henderson, "You're right. Not much to do." They sat in silence. Outside the guard was being changed. Through the lace curtains came the muffled sound of shouted commands and a fife and drum band playing "Lilliburlero." Finally Blackrock said "Better talk to Simpson and the Queen and put a statement together. Then clear it with His Majesty. No, on second thought I'd better talk to him first. You stay here and listen in. Always assuming we can raise him on secure voice."

The King was in the North Sea visiting oil rigs, Britain's only chance of fending off bankruptcy even though most of the oil was already mortgaged or sold off to international oil companies. The King knew he was well advised to identify with the "oilies," out there in the autumn gales saving his country's bacon.

"You know," Blackrock said, as they waited for the call to come through, "if this government doesn't pull through, there's going to be one hell of a crisis."

"There's one hell of a crisis already, don't you think?"

"Nothing compared to what may happen. There'll be a real constitutional crisis. Those chaps aren't going to keep the monarchy on this time. Not if the country swings as far left as it could over something like this. It'll be a republic."

"But they couldn't do that."

"It's been done elsewhere. We've had two close shaves ourselves." Outside the band was playing "The Thin Red Line," an essay in imperial nostalgia. The drums rattled defiantly as if daring any mere Socialist to threaten a monarchy which had reigned more than a thousand years.

"The country would never stand for it," Henderson said. "They're too popular."

"At the moment they are," replied Sir Evelyn, "but public opinion's damned fickle. You of all people should know that. It was the only sensible thing Harold Wilson said when he was Prime Minister. A week in politics *is* a long time. And the one fact of political life which changes more quickly than anything is popularity. Look what happened to Churchill in 1945. There was hardly a man in the entire country who believed the Labor Party could defeat Churchill. Everyone thought he was there for life, and look what happened. Out on his ear. That can happen to the Royal Family now. And if that happens it's curtains."

"You really think so?" asked Henderson. He thought his superior was being melodramatic but he was still too new a recruit to court circles to risk saying so.

"It could. I'm going to make damn sure it doesn't, but it could.

And if it does get too close for comfort, I'll make sure he goes to the country."

A couple of years ago Henderson would have been aghast. Now he was merely surprised. "Appeal over the head of Parliament?" he asked.

"Quite. If Edward VIII had tried it in 1936 it could have worked, and he was a rotten apple. This one's all right."

The secure phone rang, and the secretary depressed the switch.

"Good morning sir," he said, when the King came on the line. "I'm sorry to drag you away from the drilling, but I'm afraid we have a little domestic crisis." He outlined the news succinctly.

When he had done so there was a pause, then the King's voice entered the room on air thick with static. It sounded so like an old broadcast that Henderson had to remind himself that the king was not in fact talking to the nation but to him and Evelyn Blackrock alone.

"What do your propose?" he was asking.

"We have to prepare some sort of statement," Blackrock said. "Maurice Henderson's here with me now. He'll knock something up and we'll release it as soon as possible."

"Wouldn't it be better to say nothing?" The King sounded harassed and ill at ease. Apart from his detective and valet and the paraphernalia of royal progress he had comparatively little support on this outing—only an equerry, young Somerset, who was inexperienced and none too bright, and the Energy Minister—a poor member of a mediocre Cabinet.

"With respect, sir, I think we have to say something. If the Queen agrees, I have it in mind to deny the whole story as a pack of lies."

"I doubt she'll do that." The King's voice had risen an octave. "She was fond of Panini and I don't think she'd be happy about lending her name to any deception." A pause. "Nor, of course, would I. When do you have to do it?"

Blackrock glanced at Henderson and motioned to him to speak.

"By this afternoon I think, sir,' he said. "The press are on to the story already and they need a comment by then."

"Better talk to the Queen. It's her past, not mine—" There was a tone as the scrambler dropped synchronization. The circuit went dead, though there was no telling whether the King had terminated the conversation himself or if it was the result of some storm at sea.

It was odd that the Queen's private secretary should have been called Simpson, the same name as the woman, Wallis Simpson, who had all but wrecked the monarchy half a century before. He was not the Queen's choice, and she tolerated him with ill-concealed misgivings. Like so many at court he had been educated at Eton. His parents had been killed when he was in his first year at Oxford and a well-connected godfather had found him employment first at the College of Arms, home of Britain's heralds, and later, when a vacancy occurred, in the palace itself. He was in his mid-forties, unmarried, with a slight stoop and an air of dandruff and old cats.

"I really don't think the Queen is well enough to see anyone yet," he said, fussily, when Henderson entered his office after a brusque, barely polite knock.

"Oh surely," Henderson said. "It's ten days since the child was born."

"Prince Arthur is eleven days old." Simpson ran his finger around the inside of his starched white collar and twitched. "In the National Health Service I'm told they don't allow mothers out of hospital for a fortnight."

Henderson lowered himself into the leather armchair in front of Simpson's desk and looked at the Fragonard behind him. The royal picture collection was one of the best in the world. There was so much of it that many fine works were stored in the vaults, a few of the best were on loan to museums around the world or on show in the little gallery by the mews. A great many extraordinarily valuable and beautiful paintings were hung in the offices of men who didn't know the difference between a Fragonard and a Norman Rockwell.

"She didn't do it on the National Health, and this isn't hospital. Blackrock and I have to see her within the next hour or so and I am asking you to arrange a convenient moment."

"She isn't seeing anyone," Simpson said. "Not even Sir Evelyn. I'm sorry. Doctor's orders." He grinned queasily. He was one of those people who live to ninety yet appear permanently unwell.

"Doctors don't know beans," said a voice in the doorway. "Not one of those doctors ever gave birth. I am up and around and I am available for appointments, so what's the problem?"

Henderson liked the Queen. He stood quickly and turned to greet her. She was wearing a lilac kaftan high on the neck and flowing to the ground. He guessed idly that she was not wearing shoes. She was smoking.

"Good morning Ma'am," he said, and heard Simpson echo the line faintly in the background.

"Hi," she said, teeth gleaming. "So what's up?" She crossed to the leather-topped fender which surrounded Simpson's fireplace and perched on it, crossing her legs. "Ashtray, Eric?" she said to Simpson, adding immediately, "oh, I forgot. You don't, do you. Just like my husband." She tapped ash into the grate and sighed. "Never mind. Tell me all. What's happened?"

"Henderson's the one with the problem, Ma'am," Simpson said, "but I don't think there's any need to bother you. I'm sure we can sort it out."

"I'll decide that," she said. "Up until now I've decided I've not been bothered enough. I'd prefer it if you boys let *me* help you sort it out. I don't like to be coddled. It's not my style."

Henderson took a deep breath. Of all the courtiers he had been most informal in his dealings with the Queen, but dealings so far had been infrequent. She had been almost permanently pregnant and the barrier presented by Simpson, the nannies and indeed the King himself had been all too effective.

"The problem," he began, "is that Signor Panini, whom I believe you once knew, has sold some memoirs to an American publication of some kind."

To Henderson's amazement, the Queen took the news with

icy calm. "From your tone," she said, "you're not talking about the *Christian Science Monitor.*"

"Something called *Gossip Magazine,* Ma'am," he said.

She smiled. "Sounds delightful. Do they pay much? Oh, and do stop calling me 'Ma'am.' Part of my new postnatal resolution is to have fewer people call me Ma'am." She threw Simpson a mocking smile. "You especially, Eric, okay?" Simpson looked pained.

"It's a sort of glossy scandal sheet as far as I can see," Henderson went on. "I imagine they pay well enough if they think it's worth it."

"I'd hate to see Sandro being short-changed by some funky little Manhattan hustler," she said, lighting another Marlboro. "So what's the problem?"

Simpson coughed in a manner which seemed, somehow, ingratiating but at the same time patronizing. "The problem, Ma'am, is . . ." he hesitated, looking at Henderson, "that these memoirs of Mr. Panini are likely to be less than discreet and may cause embarrassment."

"You mean he'll say he slept with me." She said it witheringly, with contempt in every syllable.

"Well . . ." Simpson was clearly shocked. "In a manner of speaking, yes."

"And you're afraid he'll say I was a good lay, is that it?"

Simpson bowed his head and subjected the top of his desk to intense scrutiny.

"The trouble," said Henderson, "is that our press will pick it up. In the past when Panini tried to sell direct to them they wouldn't buy, but now that the story is going to be in print they won't feel inhibited. That's what journalistic ethics are all about."

"So?"

"Well." Now Henderson was embarrassed. "The fact of the matter is . . . Well . . . Not to put too fine a point on it, you are the Queen—"

"That's right," she snapped, "and I don't intend to forget it.

Say what you like about the story, but you must not imply that I was a virgin bride. I want no lies. Little lies lead to bigger ones. And Simpson, I want to do the diary for the next three months and I want to review all the patronages and I want to go through all the Royal Warrant Holders. I'll be in my room in fifteen minutes."

She smiled at them, flung her cigarette nonchalantly into the grate and walked out leaving behind two surprised and discomfited royal employees.

Why in hell is Panini doing this? I don't get it. We had good times together. The idea of his heavily ghosted and much "improved" reminiscences being drooled over by every pervert in town is quite upsetting. It's not that I'm ashamed of anything, only that some things are just, well, private. Is that very prudish? I don't feel like it is. All the same I will not tell a lie. Just because I prefer a little privacy and respect doesn't mean that I have to deny that I had a premarital affaire *with a very handsome Italian man.*
(I think his being Italian has a lot to do with Blackrock's objections. His ideas about Italians are based on whatever happened at Benghazi in World War II.)
So I'm just going to have to tough it out. Trouble is it's going to make it that much more difficult to start reorganizing my life. No problems with that little creep Simpson, but the others are different. Blackrock is so sexless it hurts but he's hostile and he's dangerous.
Still, I'm Queen, and he's a glorified flunkey. And I've given Bunny an heir.
Thank God for my tiny perfect prince!

Hermann Schnabel was pleased with life. Not only had he sold Panini's story but he was doing well in his efforts to infiltrate New York society—or at least that tiny part of New York society to which Caroline Knight had once belonged. The bed in which he was lying this morning belonged to an attractive brunette whom he had first picked up at the Frankfurt Book Fair the previous year. She lay beside him, still asleep, exhausted by the pleasures of the night. Schnabel was a demanding and unorthodox lover, but as always, his motives were more complex than most men's. The girl, Barbara, was one of the youngest vice-presidents in U.S. publishing and a fringe member of the same set as Caroline Knight and Joanne Hollis. She was also a committed single with a healthy appetite for sex. Her career didn't give her time to satisfy the demands of a continuing relationship and in social terms she was easily bored by men. She liked going to bed with them, however, and kept a large stable of regular casuals, most of them from out of town.

This much Schnabel had discovered before going to Frankfurt, where he had presented himself as a self-employed literary agent and scout. There was an element of truth in this, and in any case there were enough hustlers and freelancers in the entrepreneurial world of book buying and selling for no one to suspect or even inquire too deeply. Besides, Barbara had made it clear from the first that she wasn't interested in his mind.

She stirred lightly and moved closer to him, nuzzled his chest with her lips and put her hand between his legs. Schnabel wondered idly why the English disliked mixing business with pleasure and responded with mounting enthusiasm. Twenty minutes later they rolled apart and lay side by side staring silently at the ceiling.

"Do you really want to come to this party?" the girl asked.

"Yes. I'd like to meet your friends."

"I'm not sure I want my friends to meet you."

"Why not?" asked Schnabel trying hard to keep irritation out of his voice. "Are you ashamed of me?"

"I don't like my friends to know who I screw."

"They needn't know. I can just be a business associate."

"They'll know," she said. "One look at you and they'll get the picture. 'Barbie always did like hairy little men,' they'll say."

"Not so little."

She laughed. "Maybe not where it matters but once you're in a dark suit you are."

"Does that matter?"

"Oh, hell," she said. "No, I guess it doesn't matter."

She went to shower while he lay back with hands clasped behind his head, staring up at the mirror, appraising his reflection.

"It'll be very boring," she called through the curtain. "All book biz. You'll be bored."

He listened to the water cascading on to the tiles.

"Aren't your friends interesting?"

"No. As a matter of fact they're quite dull."

She came back into the room wrapped in a towel.

"Do you want to meet here or at the hotel?" he asked, looking at her legs.

"Come by here about six." She ran her tongue between her teeth. "We don't have to leave till after seven, so we'll have time for a little . . ."

Schnabel lay back and watched her drying her back.

"Sexy lady," he said, though more as a matter of fact than a compliment.

When she had left the house he went and ran himself a bath. The party *would* be boring, an informal launch for a new cookbook of brunch recipes, written and illustrated by two of Barbara's old college friends. He knew that they were also friends of Caroline Knight and that they still kept up with Joanne Hollis. Tonight he should be able to establish real contact. If his instincts were right it was time to put his plans into operation.

There was comparatively little for him to do before the evening. He had just the one engagement, a lunch-hour meeting in the park. Before that he dressed in a sober dark two-piece suit and took a cab to his hotel, where he checked back in, using the name Harry Smith under which he was registered and by which he was generally known in New York. He had found it more convenient to almost totally abandon the name Schnabel in recent months, and he invariably travelled on a British passport. His hotel, on Lexington and Fifty-first, was full of Smiths, most of them on package tours and staying less than a week. It was adequate for his needs and, more important, the staff had no time to recognize a name or a face. When he left no one would remember him.

He made a couple of phone calls from his room, one to check his flight home the following evening, the other to Kandinski to say good-bye and to make sure that the story was in hand. Then, pausing to buy a *Times* and a pack of Camels in the foyer, he walked to Fifth Avenue and sat for twenty minutes in St. Patrick's Cathedral. Although he had long since renounced any formal belief (he had been brought up a Lutheran) he found churches comforting and cool. They were ideal for settling the pulse and for getting thoughts in order.

In St. Patrick's the organist was practicing Bach fugues while a trickle of worshippers moved in and out, giving the church an air of business which Anglican churches invariably lack. Schnabel sat in a pew and thought about God. He had an uneasy feeling that there might be a God. If so he was not on His side, at least not on the side of the God of Fifth Avenue. This was a right wing Republican God, God of Money, God of the Bourgeoisie, God of the Haves and not the Have-nots. He was part of a whole system which Schnabel wanted overthrown. There was no logic to it, just as there was no logic to monarchy and the absurd social order which sustained it. Schnabel was no theorist, but his emotional commitment to the politics of the socialist bloc was complete. Most of those who espoused left wing ideals in the West were still critical of the Kremlin's real-politik, of the crude bully-boy philosophies of the Soviets. Not Schnabel. He knew only too well that power came from the gun barrel, and he was not impressed by what passed for radicals over here. They were spoiled brats playing games. He wanted a people's republic in Britain which would be an off-shore satellite of the Soviet empire. From it Western Europe could be squeezed and squeezed until communism stretched from John O'Groats to Vladivostok.

An old woman, grey-haired with gold in her teeth, entered his pew, knelt and crossed herself. Schnabel watched as she muttered her prayers, head bent and covered by an old black shawl. Italian, he guessed. The organist stopped, and Schnabel glanced at his watch. He had just time to saunter up Fifth Avenue and past the horse-drawn carriages into the park. Guttman was meeting him at twelve.

Outside the sun was shining and he stood for a moment readjusting to the brightness. More from force of habit than any real concern he looked around to make sure that he was not being followed.

The horses were by the Plaza as usual, on the far side of the street near the park, their sad plumes jerking as they ate moodily from their feedbags. Their drivers stood fat and lethargic, halfheartedly accosting likely looking tourists as they wandered by, not seeming to care overmuch whether they sold a ride or not. Guttman was standing between the first and second carriages, wearing a snappy lightweight suit in two-tone brown seersucker and carrying a black attaché case. Neither item, Schnabel noted, had been bought in Berlin.

He waited for the light to change, then crossed to the rank and, casually, asked Guttman the time. "Good morning, Hermann," Guttman said. "We are quite safe. I came up on the shuttle from Washington during the rush hour. It is almost impossible to follow anyone on that. Anyway, the Americans are much more interested in making life difficult for the Bulgarians at the moment. The Bulgarians are so, so obvious. Poison darts, capsules in the tips of umbrellas, exploding fountain pens." He shrugged and wrinkled his nose fastidiously. "They watch too many old Bond films in Sofia."

"You've put on weight," Schnabel said.

Guttman glanced meaningfully at his friend's stomach. "The pot is calling the kettle black," he declared playfully. "Shall we eat then and become fatter still?"

"If you like."

Guttman took him by the elbow. "Lüchow's," he said. "No one goes there unless they are from out of town. We won't see anyone. And the pilsener is good."

They took a cab downtown and began to talk. They had known each other many years now, ever since Guttman had been an inexperienced diplomat at the East German Embassy in

London. Schnabel had been in his first post-graduate year at the London School of Economics and Political Science then, and his zealousness had led him naturally toward the *echte Orthodoxie* of Walter Ulbricht's German Democratic Republic. East Germany stank in the nostrils of Western liberals, but for the young Düsseldorf marxist it was Utopian. Guttman had taken him up, not certain how the zeal could best be harnessed or even controlled, but recognizing that there was a talent and a dedication which could one day be useful.

"It is beginning," said Schnabel. The traffic in Manhattan was as bad as London. They were being passed by a stream of joggers.

"Ah," Guttman smiled, "you are going to overthrow the King."

"You may laugh," Schnabel said, "but it's possible. In fact I know it can be done."

"So you have told me. I applaud your optimism. But the English have had kings and queens a long time now."

"Too long."

Guttman inclined his head. "What you say is true, but if my memory of English history is correct, regicide has been a singularly unprofitable calling. And even when one king is disposed of they invariably find another."

"Times change."

"Agreed."

"The monarchy is not stable."

"Arguably."

"It is the most important obstacle to socialism."

Guttman frowned. "The British say it is also the most important obstacle to fascism."

"What about the Japanese and Hirohito? Or Mussolini and Victor Emmanuel? Emperors and kings always support fascism. Look at Edward VIII, the Duke of Windsor. He was a fascist."

"But the English got rid of him."

They arrived at the restaurant. Guttman paid the driver, tipping lavishly.

"When I was in London," he said, smiling, "the English had

74

a saying which they were very fond of. They used to say 'It couldn't happen here.' Do they still say that?"

"Oh yes," Schnabel said. "They believe it, too." He laughed, and his friend laughed with him. They went on chuckling until their chilled lager beer arrived with two plates of cherrystone clams and a pile of brown bread and butter. Then they tucked their napkins into their necks and fell silent, concentrating on food and drink, for all the world like any pair of German businessmen from out of town.

CHAPTER

4

$\mathscr{E}$RIC SIMPSON was in a panic. He was so upset that he had stayed at home for two days, feigning sickness. Not that he was really malingering. Even though his illness was entirely psychosomatic and had no physical cause, he felt feverish and unwell. He tried reading, but was unable to concentrate. He had the radio on but realized that he was not taking it in either. There was no television in his apartment so he could not lull his mind with that. Phonograph records were not working, nor patience. He even slept badly, despite the sleeping pills, and he had taken his phone off the hook.

On the afternoon of the third day, around tea time, he heard a taxi. Looking out from behind the net curtains he saw that it was Henderson. He swore. The only way out was in the lift. There was only one lift. Besides he was not dressed. There was no way he could make a bolt for it. He toyed with the idea of refusing to answer the bell but recognized, even in his depressed and confused state, that this would only make matters worse. He had, after all, told his secretary that he was unwell and not to be disturbed. He was within his rights. Henderson had no business pursuing him like this.

By the time Henderson rang the doorbell Simpson was in his dressing gown—a heavy woollen number from Marks and Spencer. Although he knew it was Henderson he still made a show of opening the door furtively on its chain and peering through the crack.

"Oh," he said, when he had done so, "it's you." He half closed the door, released the chain and opened the door again to admit his visitor, shutting it the instant he was inside.

"Hello," Henderson said, anxious to appear affable, though he was in fact profoundly irritated. "What's up? You all right?" He smelled stale cat.

"Some sort of virus," Simpson said. "I should be all right in a day or two." He led the way down the corridor to the drawing room, neat but cluttered. It was a large room but fussy.

"We were concerned," Henderson said. "Your phone was permanently busy. Then the post office said it was out of order but they couldn't put a repair man on to it for about six weeks. They're short staffed."

"You needn't have worried," Simpson said. "I was going to come in tomorrow anyway. Do sit down. Would you like a cup of tea? The kettle's on."

"Thank you, yes," Henderson said. "Milk, no sugar."

Simpson excused himself, leaving Henderson to peruse the photographs which cluttered every available surface. They were mainly portraits, many signed, some royal. Somehow none of them had the look of relations or even close friends. The smiles were too fixed, the poses too formal. All gave the impression of being handouts, the sort of pictures that TV personalities send to their fans. They confirmed Henderson's image of a life lived almost entirely at secondhand.

"What does the doctor say?" he asked when his host came back with the tea things.

Simpson flushed. "I haven't seen him," he said. "He's away, that is, and I don't trust the locum."

"Oh." Henderson took the cup and sipped at the rather weak Earl Grey. "Well, that's your business of course." He paused. "I'm glad to find you so much better, because the fact of the matter is that we've been rather concerned about your mistress over the last few days. We were looking to you for a certain amount of assistance, not to say clarification."

It was Simpson's turn to say "Oh," and he did so with the air of a man who has no idea what is being implied. Henderson was not deceived but he did not call the bluff.

"When we both talked to her the other day she asked you to go back in fifteen minutes and discuss her diary and the patronages."

"Yes."

"And did you?"

"Yes."

"And?"

Simpson pursed his lips. "I was going to tell you in due course."

"I'd like you to tell me now," Henderson said, "before I have any more shocks."

"Such as?"

This time Henderson allowed his irritation to come through. "That evening," he said, "about two hours after you left for your sickbed, she drove down to Glastonbury Castle to stay with the Cokers where, I may say, she has remained ever since, strictly incommunicado. Lady Coker says she won't come to the phone and that's all there is to it. I can't talk to her about the Panini business. Not that there's anything she can say that will improve that tasteless little episode. But I want to talk to her about all the other nonsenses."

"Like what?" Simpson looked pained.

"I had a call from the girl who's running the Woman of the Year luncheon. We agreed ages ago that the Queen would turn that down. They asked her to make the main speech. Now, they tell me, she's changed her mind. I've been called by two of the oldest and most distinguished warrant holders who say they have been informed by the Queen that she no longer requires their flowers or their confectionery. And the Girl Guides say she has resigned as their patron." He glared at Simpson. "So what the hell's going on? While the King is still flying around the North Sea and remote parts of the Highlands and Islands, you and the Queen both go to ground. And all hell's broken loose." He drained his tea and accepted the offer of a refill, then stood and paced over to the window which looked out on to a communal garden. The trees were almost bare now, the dry brown leaves swept up into piles by the gardener. "So just what is going on? That's what I want to know."

Simpson was very pale.

"She promised she'd do nothing until the King got back," he said, weakly. "But she was in a very strange mood. You saw her. I've never seen her like that before. She wouldn't listen."

"How do you mean?" Henderson was impatient.

"She said she wanted to take on some more interesting engagements. She was bored with flower shows and hospital visits, she needed some challenges. And she said she was fed up with having to get her clothes from Hartnell and her cheese from Paxton and Whitfield. She said she wanted to start from scratch. We argued about it, as much as I dared, and we agreed that we should discuss it again when the King returned and she had the chance to talk it over with him."

"Like hell," Henderson said. "Why didn't you tell me all this?"

Simpson looked truly ill now. "I didn't think it was urgent. I thought it was just, you know, postnatal oppression or whatever they call it. I thought she'd forget the whole business in the morning."

"Evidently she didn't," Henderson said. "And so we have a whole series of problems. How do you suppose I'm going to explain all this to the media?"

Simpson buried his head in his hands. "Oh God," he said, abjectly. Then after a long pause he said, "You know, I think she smokes pot."

"She *what?*"

"You know. Pot. Marijuana. You roll it yourself, like an ordinary cigarette—"

"I know what one *does* with it," Henderson said, though he

was a drinking, not a smoking man. "But what do you mean, she smokes it? How do you know?"

"The other night," Simpson said, "she seemed a bit strange. She had a blank look in her eyes and she kept giggling. I confess I put it down to reaction after the birth until I noticed that she was smoking, but she *wasn't* smoking those great long Marlboro's. This was a little shrivelled thing. It smelt like bonfires or those herbal cigarettes you used to buy at Culpepers."

"Did you say anything?"

"What could one say?"

Henderson saw the justice of this.

"Was this the first time? You hadn't noticed anything like it before?"

"No. At least I don't think so. She can sometimes seem a little peculiar. But then we're very different people. We don't really understand one another."

"It's called the generation gap," Henderson said. Dimly, he was beginning to wonder if it wasn't more than a generation gap. It had seemed to him that Queen Caroline had adjusted magnificently. She had been modern graciousness personified. She had rarely spoken out of turn. She had seemed born to be Queen. But now . . .

"I'd better get back. Will you be in your office tomorrow?" His voice took on a tone halfway between threat and supplication. "I think you should."

"I see that," Simpson agreed. "I know you think I'm not pulling my weight, but I really am feeling pretty seedy. I'll try."

"I should try exceedingly hard if I were you," Henderson said. "The King is scheduled to get in late tonight, which I think means the Queen will come back from Glastonbury. And we're all going to have to settle down to some serious talking." He stood and put his cup on the tray. "I'll see myself out."

It was a mistake to come down here with Isobel Coker. I
had the idea she might turn into another Joanne, someone I
could really trust and confide in; but somehow it isn't
working out that way. It's not that she isn't well meaning,

81

*just that we aren't on the same wavelength. I don't believe
I had realized what an All American girl I am until I
penetrated English society. As an Ambassador's daughter I
thought I was prepared for Buckingham Palace to be
different, but I really had not expected to feel so at sea
with ordinary Britishers. Sometimes I feel as if I come
from Venus, not Vermont. Even Simpson, who is supposed
to be my own personal chief of staff, appears to have
divided loyalties. He was obviously aghast when I told him
I was canceling the warrants, and I thought he was going
to have some sort of an attack when I said I was going
ahead with the Woman of the Year lunch speech. The girl
organizing it sounded sort of surprised when I spoke to her
too. I just wish I had an ally, a real ally who could
understand what I'm all about. People seem to regard me
as a threat, which is ludicrous. I just don't want to be a
cipher. It's such a waste.*

In Lüchow's the two German expatriates lingered over coffee,
cognac and short fat genuine Havanas that Guttman had
managed to slip through U.S. Customs.

"It's very unorthodox," Guttman said.

"Is that so bad?"

"Not at all. I like it."

"So you'll underwrite the exercise?"

"No problem. How much do you need?"

Schnabel pretended to think, though he had actually worked
it out months ago. "Ten thousand down. Five thousand a month
with the possibility of extra injections to meet necessary capital
expenditures."

"Pounds?"

"Yes."

Guttman raised his eyebrows. "You're playing for high
stakes. Will that be enough?"

"It should be," said Schnabel. "The potential is there, but the
outlay is not great. It calls for ingenuity but not too much
money. Besides," he laughed, "I took twenty percent of Panini's
fee."

"Very well," said Guttman, "I will make the necessary arrangements."

Schnabel raised his glass. "Prosit," he said and tapped it lightly against Guttman's. "Success."

"Prosit," said Guttman.

It was raining in central London. In the forty acres of garden behind Buckingham Palace it was damp and cold. The flamingoes on the lake looked bedraggled and desolate as the wind whipped through King James's mulberry garden and the Indian chestnuts which shielded the sanctuary from the gaze of London's taller buildings. Blackrock and Henderson stood under umbrellas in front of the Bow Room Terrace and peered wetly up at the cloud. Blackrock glanced at his watch.

"He's going to have to stop doing this," he said angrily. "He's too old, and it's too dangerous."

"And too bloody uncomfortable for those that stand and wait," Henderson growled. He was reasonably dry above knee level but his lower trouser legs were becoming quite sodden.

"He's five minutes late already." Blackrock rubbed his toe along the grass and watched it turn to mud. The lawn was bathed in spotlight as if there was about to be an evening rugby game.

"That sounds like him," Henderson said, straining for the sound of an engine in the sky.

"I can only hear traffic," Blackrock retorted. "At least the Queen has the sense to come by car."

The Queen had arrived back from Glastonbury half an hour ago. She had brought Lady Coker, who was in Blackrock's estimation "perfectly sound" and probably the nearest the Queen had to a real friend at court. Henderson had not thought of it before, but he was beginning to realize how cut off and isolated the Queen must have felt these last two years. The King was her only real friend and they worked him too hard.

"It *is* him," he said. From the clouds above came a dull popping roar, moving at first, then stationary. Seconds later the scarlet bulk of the King's twin-engined Coronation-class helicopter dropped through the drifting clouds and descended toward the flat lawn of grass and camomile. From the roof the royal standard fluttered bravely in the wind which was making the aircraft yaw violently from side to side.

"Inherently unsafe," Blackrock muttered. "Friend of mine was killed in a chopper in Aden. Dropped like a stone. He's too old to go on flying it. If he were a professional he'd have been phased out years ago. I shall get Cathcart to make the PM raise it at the Tuesday meeting."

The helicopter landed with Blackrock still grumbling. As the engines slowed, subsided and ceased altogether the rotor blades wilted like dying petals until they drooped, inert and pendulous. The main door opened outward producing three metal steps, and seconds later the familiar figure of the King, stocky in an old sheepskin flying jacket, came down the stairs and began to walk jauntily towards them. Blackrock and Henderson walked to greet him, Henderson a few paces behind. The King did not pause as they met, but continued to walk briskly towards the terrace steps. His two servants fell in alongside.

"Evening Evelyn, evening Maurice. Bloody awful flight. Foul night. Let's go and get ourselves a drink."

"Good evening sir; yes sir," the murmured deferential agreements of courtiers. The King ascended the terrace steps two at a time. "The Queen home? I spoke to her in Somerset this morning. She said she'd be back."

"She arrived home just under an hour ago," Blackrock said.

They paused by the lift. Footmen hovered.

"How did she seem? I hope this Panini affair hasn't upset her too much."

The two courtiers shuffled their feet. "I haven't had a chance to talk to her yet," Blackrock said. "She went straight to her apartments and said she wasn't to be disturbed."

"Oh." The lift moved slowly. It was very old. "Those oil rig men have a hell of a life," the King said.

The lift shuddered to a halt. The gate opened. Another footman hovered. In the distance a door slammed.

"You chaps don't realize what a soft option you have," the

King continued. "No drink out there, no women, bloody awful weather."

"Good money," Blackrock said.

The King frowned. "Money isn't everything."

They went into the King's study, as cluttered in its way as Eric Simpson's drawing room, but more virile. Over the fireplace was a Matabele assegai between two stags' heads, both shot in the deer forests near Balmoral. On the coffee table was a group of Inuit carvings in soapstone. There were one or two undistinguished watercolors, mainly landscapes; a number of books, mostly large and glossy; and a salmon, stuffed. The King went to the bottles on a wheeled trolley in one corner.

"Scotch, you two? Ice? Water?" He dispensed whisky for all three, diluted them with Malvern water from a bottle, handed them to Blackrock and Henderson, then sat in a comfortable but frayed armchair.

"Well," he said, and looked at Blackrock. He appeared tired, and the fatigue was aging him. The lines around his face and eyes were deeper than usual; his hair, windblown, was more obviously sparse.

"The Panini memoirs appear to have been less damaging than we might have expected," Blackrock said. He held his whisky in both hands, letting his fingertips rock the heavy glass so that the amber liquid lapped up and down gently. "The postbag is running three to one in favor of the Queen and it's not unduly heavy. Maurice has done his usual exemplary job with Fleet Street so they haven't been too sensational in their coverage. The editorials are unanimously in our favor."

"So I should bloody well hope," the King said.

"They could have been extremely hostile. At times in the past they would have been. We would be ill advised to be complacent."

Henderson thought the King was about to demur, but he said nothing, only took a long draught of Scotch which he swilled round his mouth thoughtfully.

"As I made clear," Blackrock continued, "our line has been to issue a formal refusal to comment and couple this with off-the-record briefings to editors and proprietors and a few special contacts. I think I'm right in saying that everyone was broadly sympathetic to our position." He looked at Henderson inquiringly.

"Yes," Henderson nodded. "In general the papers felt they had to tell people about the story because it had been published in the States. On the other hand they agreed that what the Queen did in private before she met you, sir, has nothing to do with either the press or the public."

"Very decent of them I'm sure." The King smiled. "I'm curious as to why the press and public are so often thought of as being the same. I never seem to have any trouble with the public."

Neither Blackrock nor Henderson spoke. Then the King said, "So the Panini episode is closed."

"In a manner of speaking, sir, though it is surprising how these affairs continue to haunt us. Remember Chappaquidick? It was that which finally forced Kennedy out of public life. It was a skeleton which was never removed from the closet."

"Hardly comparable," the King said.

"Comparable in one unfortunate respect sir," said Blackrock. "It is now on the record. Our enemies, the Queen's enemies, the enemies of the realm may use it in future to fuel their criticisms and their attacks."

"I take your point," the King said. "But I don't think any fair-minded person would expect the Queen to have behaved differently, especially when at that stage the idea of becoming Queen had never even entered her head." He was sounding petulant. He must have realized, Henderson thought, that any criticism was quite as much criticism of him for making a bad choice as it was criticism of the Queen herself.

Blackrock changed the subject. "Simpson tells us that the Queen is revising her patronages and warrant holders and making some quite significant changes in her schedule."

"Such as?"

Blackrock told him.

The King frowned. "Have you discussed this with her?"

"No sir. She's been at Glastonbury since Tuesday, and she hasn't been taking any calls."

The King went to the trolley and poured himself a second Scotch. "You chaps help yourselves," he said, though neither of the others was more than half way through his drink. "Damn," he said when he'd filled his glass. There was a prolonged silence during which everyone tried hard to avoid everyone else's eyes. Finally the King said, "Why didn't Simpson explain the situation to her?"

"I think he tried," Henderson said, "but he didn't get very far."

The King seemed not to hear. "You can't just go changing everything without consulting people," he said, "I've always made it clear that this is a team effort. One for all and all for one, and if that isn't done then the whole bloody shooting match goes up in a cloud of smoke."

"Perhaps," Blackrock said, "if you could have a word with Her Majesty you could persuade her to change her mind."

"From what you say, the harm's been done."

"Oh," Blackrock said, smiling silkily, "if we can persuade her that she's made a mistake then I think we can find ways and means of minimizing the damage. After all it is only a few days since her confinement. It would be very unusual if she weren't suffering some form of nervous reaction."

"I'll talk to her," the King said. "It's probably my fault. As you must realize by now I'm rather good at taking people for granted. Especially those I need most." He stood. "Goodnight, gentlemen," he said, "and thank you."

Outside in the interminable corridor with its thick vermilion carpet, Blackrock put a hand on Henderson's shoulder. "Fasten your seat belt," he said, "I think we're in for a bumpy ride."

In New York, Hermann Schnabel knotted his tie and then turned at Barbara's request to hook up her dress at the back.

"You look good," Herman said, as she shook out her hair and turned to face him.

"You look short, fat and hairy," she said, smiling, then kissed him on the nose. "But you're very good at it."

If Hermann Schnabel had been a cat he would have purred. "I'd much rather stay in tonight," she said.

"But you can't. You have social obligations to your friends.

"Oh come on," she said, "fix us a drink. We have time."

He went into the kitchen and poured two jiggers of Scotch over ice. He hoped tonight was going to be a success. It would be very boring if Joanne Hollis didn't show up—even more boring if he wasn't able to ingratiate himself. He worried that she would not be so susceptible to short fat hairies, so he would have to be at his most svelte and interesting. He would also have to work fast. It might be his only chance. He took the drinks back into the drawing room and they knocked them back quickly, then walked out to the elevator and went down to the parking lot.

Barbara drove her aquamarine Porsche so flamboyantly that it took scarcely any time to reach the apartment building in the Village where the party was being held. Drinks were served on the roof among ferns and potted bay trees. On the turntable of the elaborate quadrophonic sound system, Bob Marley and the Wailers were revolving at a gentle thirty-three and a third.

"Isn't reggae just magic?" said an angular blonde in shocking pink pajamas.

"Just magic," said an anemic Woody Allen look-alike.

Barbara greeted them both perfunctorily but made no effort to introduce Schnabel. A waiter in a white jacket and bow tie was circulating with a tray of drinks. Barbara took a tequila sunrise, Schnabel a martini. A stout, florid man whom Schnabel recognized as a minor talk show host came across and kissed Barbara noisily on both cheeks. She tolerated this frigidly and introduced Schnabel, then took Schnabel by the arm and led him to the edge of the roof. "Boring and crude," she said. A few blocks to the north a siren wailed, came closer, passed underneath and faded toward Wall Street. Around them the city was glowing in the dusk. There was no way to persuade Manhattan that the world faced an energy crisis.

"They're not *all* boring," Schnabel said. "*You're* not boring.

How can you have boring friends?"

"Easy."

"But, some of them must be interesting. Caroline Knight for instance."

"Yeah, she was sort of interesting until she went to England and married that King of hers."

"That doesn't make her dull."

"It makes her distant," Barbara said. "Can you get me another drink?"

He walked across to the bar and picked up two more drinks. Passing through the throng he was faintly depressed. There was no sign of Joanne Hollis, and most of the guests exuded the self-conscious outrageousness of aging youth. When he returned, Barbara was talking almost animatedly to a conventionally smart looking couple in their mid-thirties. He wore a grey two-piece suit, polka dot tie, white shirt and heavy spectacles. She was in a black dress and pearls. Barbara introduced them as Simon and Annie Waterman. He was a partner in a law practice. She restored porcelain and gave little dinner parties for twenty-four. They were telling Barbara how they hadn't seen her in years. Then Schnabel pricked up his ears as they began to talk about Caroline Knight. They had evidently been to stay with her a few months ago at Sandringham. Annie Waterman pronounced it Sandring-HAM with all the accent on the final syllable.

"How was she?" Barbara asked.

"Oh, sort of so-so," Annie said. "He's kind of . . . well, I guess you could say 'preoccupied.' Cute in a British way but, oh I don't know."

"Apart from her family, she was saying that we were the first people she'd even dared to ask over. She said everyone else was too far out of touch. The British seemed incredibly conventional." Simon Waterman smiled condescendingly.

"Not *all* the British," Schnabel interjected.

"Maybe not," Annie said, "but you should have seen some of the fossils that came out of the woodwork at Sandringham. Guys in wigs, would you believe. And you should have been at afternoon tea. God knows why they aren't more obese, you've never seen so many damn cucumber sandwiches and handmade cookies."

"Sounds marvelous," Barbara said. "What's in the handmade cookies?"

"Chocolate," Simon said. "So much chocolate you've never seen in your life. Very dark and just a little cookie wafer, crunchy in the middle."

"By courtesy of the royal biscuit-maker," added Annie in a passable Oxford accent, "and most frightfully good, don't you know."

"You putting down my British friends?" asked a new voice, sardonically. Schnabel looked up and felt a tremor of anticipation. There, leaning against a piece of white trellis-work, was the girl he recognized immediately as the Queen of England's matron of honor. She looked mildly amused, slightly drunk and about ten pounds heavier than when he had watched the wedding on television.

Annie Waterman blushed. "I was telling them about Sandringham. We stayed with Caroline at the palace there."

"House," Joanne Hollis said, "Sandringham House. Sandringham is merely a house. Balmoral is a castle. Windsor is a castle. Buckingham is a palace. Caroline wrote. I understand you didn't enjoy the charades."

Annie Waterman blushed again. "We thought it was a little, well a little *jejune.*"

"My," said Joanne, making saucer eyes, "there's a fancy word I haven't heard in ages. Hi, Simon," she said, and "Hi, Barbara" and as Barbara introduced Schnabel she murmured "Nice meeting you" while giving Barbara a simmering look which made it perfectly plain that she knew exactly what it was that brought the two of them together.

"Did Caroline tell you about the charades we played at Windsor?" she asked.

"No," Annie said, rather too quickly, "I didn't know you'd been to stay. Caroline said she hadn't seen anyone from this side of the Atlantic. Not for years."

"That's right," Joanne said, "I was the last. I'm quite surprised she felt confident enough to ask anyone else—even such a right straight couple as you two."

"So tell me," said Barbara, "what happened?"

"Oh," Joanne said. The waiter with the tray arrived as if drawn by some obscure process of telepathy. The group helped itself to second and third glasses. On the roof, fairy lights began to twinkle and the music turned to Bach's Brandenburgs. A 747 en route to Kennedy appeared between rather than above two office blocks. Sirens whooped, the spooky, almost human sound that invariably woke Schnabel in the New York night and gave him pause for fear. Although he lived most of his time in England, where such visitations were supposed never to occur, Schnabel was in terror of the dawn raid, the sudden footsteps, the forced doors, the men with the wide shoulders and expressionless faces—theirs or ours, he would imagine himself wondering in the London night. He felt his stomach tighten and sipped gratefully at his drink, then turned back to the conversation.

"The British Royals have always had this mania for charades," Joanne was saying. She brushed a stray strand of hair out of her eyes and smiled a little lopsidedly, unquestionably a little the worse for wear. "It wasn't much of a weekend," said Joanne. "It was pretty awful. I'd met the King before and I'd been to the wedding, and he seemed charming and bright and fun to be with, but he'd changed. Maybe it was me and Caroline. He'd gotten stuffy and uptight. He was always out shooting birds or riding after foxes in a red coat and a hard hat. And if he wasn't doing that he was closeted with some minister or one of his palace flunkies. Caroline was strange, too. She was newly pregnant with the first child and still on cloud nine. I don't think she realized what was happening to her. On the surface she was cossetted and pampered and had every whim indulged. She wanted a sauna bath, the King ordered in the royal sauna bath manufacturer. She wanted tennis lessons, the King hired the coach of the British Davis Cup Team. Champagne, she gets champagne; caviar, caviar. But some ordinary freedom, a walk in the park, a ride on a bus, a trip to the theater. Forget it." She paused and sipped her drink. In the party light-illuminated gloom Hermann Schnabel's eyes gleamed like a ferret's. He had hoped for something like this, but never so quickly and easily. It was wonderful to have one's intuitions confirmed so exactly. Joanne continued her story. "I'd only been in the palace an hour or two when I realized what was happening. I wanted to go riding like we used to in London before she was married. They have a track in Hyde Park called Rotten Row. 'Say Caroline' I said, 'what do you say we go riding in the park? We can call down for your grooms to saddle up a couple of horses. It won't take long, and it's a gorgeous day.' She just looked at me for a while. Then she said, 'Are you crazy or something? I can't just do that.' I remember she was knitting something for the baby —a little sweater or something, as if she couldn't have ordered all the damn woolens in the world from Harrods whenever she wanted. So I said, 'Why *not*, Caroline? You're the Queen of England. You ought to be able to do whatever you want, within reason.' And she looked at me a long time and then she said, 'Is that what you think? Is that what you really think?' I didn't answer. There was nothing I could say. She was a prisoner in that mausoleum at the end of the Mall. She used to tell me she could make a great job of it. Job, that's laughable."

Her little audience was spellbound now. Around them other small groups were talking and laughing quietly, as if in time to the Bach. It was a discreet, decorous gathering. Inside the room a pile of the new brunch cookbooks lay undisturbed.

"So what happened? What did you do in the charades?" Annie Waterman asked.

Joanne seemed to suddenly realize the extent of her indiscretion. For a moment Schnabel was afraid she would falter, but instead she took another gulp of her drink and went on.

"For a few days I just watched what was going on," she said. "I guess I was trying to figure out how far she had been indoctrinated by all those fops and blue-rinse ladies-in-waiting. She was very uptight the whole time, and she kept allowing herself to be bullied by her own secretary, a tight-assed little cipher named Simpson. He was writing all her letters for her until I pointed that out and she began to get a grip again. That weekend we went down to Windsor. It sounds fascinating, but it wasn't. The King was playing polo both days at some place called Smith's Lawn just outside the castle, and he had some meetings, and on Saturday the Archbishop of Canterbury was coming to dinner. What a disappointment he was. And his wife! You should have seen her. She was like a bull elephant in drag, and a brain to match. We had to hear the Archbishop preach in St. George's Chapel, which at least was pretty. The only moment of spontaneity in the whole weekend was the charades after dinner Sunday. There were about a dozen of us all told, and I had an idea of how we could make it a little more entertaining. I was expecting Caroline to sit it out, but she'd had a couple of drinks when I suggested it and she agreed."

She stopped talking and looked around at the little group. "Could someone fix me another drink," she asked. "All this talking is making me dry."

Schnabel moved easily to the drinks tray and brought her another cocktail. She smiled at him slightly curiously, then drank.

"We did a slice of life," she went on, "a piece of not so distant British history: the seduction of King Edward VIII by Wallis Simpson. We made it pretty raunchy too, a touch of burlesque, to put it mildly."

"Edward VIII and Mrs. Simpson raunchy?" Waterman was quietly disbelieving. "That's about as easy as trying to make *Gone with the Wind* into a skin flick."

Joanne laughed. "We managed," she said. "We'd had a few, so it was a little rough around the edges, but we made the point."

"Which was?" Waterman again.

"That the British can be cold, patronizing, arrogant schmucks and that not all Americans are loud, vulgar country boys and girls with straw in their hair."

"How did that go down," Schnabel asked, "as if I didn't know."

"Like a lead balloon." She giggled. "They just sat there like the stuffed stags in the billiard room. No one said a word until it was over."

"And then?"

"The British do these things so well," she said, imitating upper-class English accents. "They ignored it. They made polite conversation and pretended nothing had happened. But the party broke up a little earlier than expected. The King didn't say anything until bed. He was like ice, Caroline said. She said it was like being beaten up only he never laid a finger on her. Matter of fact I think she rather enjoyed it." She turned to one side to take a sip from her glass. "Anyway, he forgave her. Sort of. Hell, they love each other, I guess, but it isn't easy for them. You can't change peoples' upbringing and background overnight. I was on the first plane home, and that, ladies and gentlemen, is the story of my life with the British Royal Family. Maybe I should sell it to someone, like that jerk Panini. Funny thing is though I heard from Caroline yesterday. First time in ages. First time since the charade visit, in fact."

"What did she say?" Barbara asked.

"Nothing much. You know, kiss and be friends, how she'd missed hearing from me. How now that she'd had the kids she was going to be her own woman again, whatever that means. I think it was some sort of an olive branch."

Schnabel felt the adrenalin pumping. It was moving too smoothly, everything fitting too perfectly. It mustn't be rushed.

The publicity director from the publishers barged in on their little group. He said, "There's some wonderful food nobody's touching over here. Come on in out of the cold and meet the authors. They're just going to say a few words."

Schnabel had forgotten the public occasion of the party, and so, he guessed, had most of the other guests. The book's editor introduced the two writers, who prattled agreeably but not, mercifully, for long. After that the guests went after the food. Schnabel stayed near Joanne Hollis, sitting next to her at the corner of a table as they munched through an assortment of brunch concoctions. He ingratiated himself carefully and with some effect, made sure that Joanne's glass was kept replenished with chablis, and waited for his moment. Finally, while coffee was being served, Barbara went to freshen up. Schnabel had been talking about the anti-nuclear movement and its comparative lack of support in Britain.

"You see," he said, "that's the kind of thing your friend Caroline ought to be involving herself with. It's too easy for her to be the colonel of one or two regiments, or to go to Wimbledon or the Chelsea Flower Show. It's a waste of herself and a waste of her position. I hear she was a real live wire in the anti-nuclear movement when she was in college."

"She sure was," Joanne said.

"She could do so much," Schnabel persisted. "There's no need for the monarchy in Britain to be so reactionary. They may have let themselves become the prisoners of the Conservative Party, of the Church of England, of the Establishment, but there is no necessity for it. The King should represent *all* his people and speak out when he feels strongly about something."

"I know." Joanne seemed interested. Schnabel hoped she was not too drunk. At least the coffee was strong.

"If Queen Caroline gave her support to those of us who are genuinely concerned about the way things are going, who really feel we have to be more careful about . . . not just nuclear power but about the way we exploit the world . . . about the seal hunt, the indiscriminate mining for uranium, the deforestation program in Brazil. There is so much to do and I understand that before she became Queen she was really quite interested in doing it. I think that's been stifled."

"She was quite a little eco-freak in her way. But those courtiers have gotten hold of her, they really have."

"Well." Schnabel shrugged. He didn't have much time. "Now is probably the time for her to take a little initiative on her own. You said that you had heard from her. It sounds as if perhaps she might be persuaded to branch out a little."

He hoped he wasn't going too fast. He wanted her sober enough to take in what he was saying but not so sober she was suspicious. Out of the corner of his eye he saw Barbara come back into the room.

"Listen," he said, "I'd like to talk some more about this." He gave her one of his cards in the name of Harry Smith. "May I call you tomorrow? I have an idea."

She took the card and put it in her handbag, then smiled at him. "You can reach me at work any time after ten," she said, "at Bambergers. Extension 508." He glanced nervously toward the doorway and saw that Barbara had been waylaid. She was deep in conversation and not looking in their direction. Joanne followed his gaze. "Nice girl," she said, "you known her long?"

CHAPTER

*Back home late, but Bunny still away. Home—don't I
wish. The palace has about as much charm as the Kremlin.
It's like getting back to the office on Monday morning.
Thought of waiting up for Bunny but decided not to. I
don't want to have a fight in the middle of the night, and
I can't help feeling there's one coming. He doesn't mind
some hypocrisy, in fact he enjoys it; so I doubt he'll
understand why I don't want to go on endorsing a bunch
of outmoded grocers. And he won't approve my going down
to the Cokers without telling him. I'm surprised he doesn't
buy me a goddamn chastity belt. I don't understand why
he acts like this. Sometimes he's unrecognizable. Then I get
a glimpse of the old Bunny and it's tantalizing. Looked in
on the nursery. Kids both asleep but I gave them a quick
kiss. They looked adorable.*

*I*T WAS unofficial policy for the Royal Family's letters not
to be opened if they were from close personal friends. The
mail was carefully screened for letters from cranks, eccentrics,
sometimes even psychopaths, and only those which had the

sender's name and address clearly written on them were allowed through unopened—if the writers belonged to a short and very confidential list. Joanne Hollis's name remained on that list, but with some special reservations. A personal letter from her to the Queen was under no circumstances to be opened by anyone else, but its arrival was to be quietly notified first to Simpson and then, by him, to Blackrock.

The Queen opened the envelope from Joanne with a silver knife sent in to her on the breakfast tray with the pot of Earl Grey tea, the brown egg lightly boiled, the toasted wholemeal bread, the *Times* and the *Daily Mail*. She and her husband had separate bedrooms by convention rather than choice. Kings and queens had *always* had separate rooms and this, like other traditions they scrupulously maintained, was something of a charade; for during their courtship, and indeed during the early months of their marriage, they had shared both bedroom and bed. Recently they had been sleeping apart more often than not. Pregnancy and pressure of work were the principal excuses for this though not always the reasons.

The letter was written in ballpoint pen on a flimsy blue air-mail form, about how good it was to hear from her after all this time, how Joanne hoped their friendship could now be renewed, how pleased she was about the children. Routine words. The sting was in the tail:

"Met a guy the other night (at a party for Betsy Robart's and Jackie Donovan's brunchbook) who tried to enlist my aid in getting you to back his conservation group over there. His name is Harry Smith and the organization is run by someone called Julian Locke. Smith is one of Barbara's men (!) but he seemed perfectly okay and was very well informed. I said there was no harm in Locke at least writing to you. The group is called 'The Friends of Man,' by the way."

The Queen read the letter a second time, frowning slightly. Dear Joanne. The charade incident had been a real faux pas, of course, but when you thought about it, it was a trivial enough mistake. A lapse of taste, but forgiveable. She herself had been forgiven—sort of—almost at once. Maybe it was time for her to let Joanne off the hook, too. Even if her husband was not prepared to let bygones be bygones, she had regretted having abandoned her oldest friendship so whimsically. She pushed the breakfast tray away from her and got out of bed, walking to a Regency escritoire in the corner under a small Turner watercolor of a Thameside sunset. Taking a thick creamy sheet of palace writing paper with its simple crest and the maroon "Buckingham Palace" legend, she wrote, "My dear Joanne, Great to hear from you . . ." Her writing sloped forward, looping, forceful; it flowed easily, covering the page with an effusion of apology and self-criticism, invitation, recrimination and promises of change to come. "I like the sound of the environment group," she wrote on the second page. "I had gotten myself into something of a straitjacket. Everyone here is fixated on conventions. They're terrified of offending anyone. As a result they don't really please anyone. So I'm making a promise to myself that I won't waste any more of my opportunities. This could be a position of real influence, Joanne, it really could. So if Mr. Locke writes in with a sensible suggestion I may just involve myself. I know the conservation field and it's a nice apolitical entree back into affairs. Perfect for a queen!"

She sealed the letter into an envelope, licking the gummed flap herself. She went into her adjoining dressing room, ignored the safe calf-length skirt and cashmere sweater and found instead a pair of jeans—expensive, tailored jeans, but jeans all the same. She pulled them on and found to her irritation that she was unable to button them at the waist. Considering how soon it was since her confinement her figure had snapped back remarkably, but it was still not trim enough for the jeans. Reluctantly she put on the skirt. Instead of the sweater, however, she dug out a white silk shirt and left two more buttons undone than recently. It was a tiny protest, but a protest nonetheless. Her breasts had always been good. Right now they were larger than usual but in perfect shape. She stood in front of the mirror and breathed in, wishing that her stomach was flatter. She would work on it.

At her desk she buzzed for Simpson. He came in almost at

once clutching the usual sheaf of papers, She flashed him a devastating smile.

"How are you Eric?"

Simpson's smile was wan.

"A little under the weather, ma'am."

"I'm sorry," she said unconvincingly. "I thought you'd be better by now. You should have stayed at home."

"It's quite all right, ma'am. Probably something I ate. I'm fine, really."

"Good." She lit a cigarette, not because she wanted one but because she knew that Simpson disapproved. "While you were off sick I unscrambled a few things," she said. "I decided to do the Women of the Year lunch. And some of those warrant holders haven't made a thing for me since the wedding. So I thought it time we cancelled the contract." She fixed him with a stern and meaningful stare. "If you see what I mean."

"Yes, ma'am." Simpson had not sat down. He had not been invited to. He shifted his weight and made as if to consult the papers clipped to a stiff piece of board. "Mr. Henderson mentioned it to me. He said there had been some difficulty—"

"Difficulty?" She smiled more glacially this time, and there was an edge to her voice that he did not remember hearing before.

"Mr. Henderson seemed to think—"

She cut him short. "I'll speak to Maurice. What's all that?" She nodded at his papers.

"Oh," he said, "this and that. One or two requests for you to deal with. The menu for tomorrow's lunch. The wardrobe for the President of Finland's visit. Nothing to speak of."

"Have you had a letter from someone named Locke?"

"Locke?" He frowned. He had no recollection of the name. He had no idea what she was getting at. He did not like her tone. "I don't think so, ma'am."

"He runs an outfit that's part of the conservation lobby, and they're looking for a sponsor. He's going to write. When he does I'd like you to make sure the letter comes straight through to me."

"Yes, of course, ma'am."

Behind him the door opened without a knock. From the Queen's reaction of self-conscious coolness and some apprehension Simpson realized it was her husband. He turned to go.

"Just a minute Simpson," she said, almost angrily. "It's important that I see that letter as soon as it comes in. Do you read me?"

"I'll make absolutely sure." He walked out past the King, bowing slightly as he went. The King did not acknowledge him, and seemed, indeed, not to have seen him at all.

As soon as the door closed the King smiled and walked quickly to the desk, where he kissed his wife on both cheeks. "I didn't wake you last night," he said. "I was late and I heard you'd had a long day."

"Not so long," she said. "I took a day or two off from the kids. Stayed with the Cokers in Somerset."

"You never mentioned it," he said, gently chiding.

"Do I have to check with you before I go to the country for two days?"

"Don't be silly. You're a free agent. You can come and go as you please."

"Ha." She got up and strode to the window, where she lit another cigarette and remained staring out at the gardens below. It was raining and the water beat against the glass in a regular rhythm, soft, repetitive, a sort of torture if one listened hard enough.

"What do you mean 'ha'? Aren't you happy here?"

"Not particularly, no." She turned back to face him. "Does that surprise you?"

He said nothing, seemingly perplexed, then sat down heavily in one of the armchairs. "What's wrong?" he asked. "You have two perfect children, all the money you could possibly want, houses, servants. You don't even have to work for it. So what are you on about? What more do you want?"

"Some freedom," she said bitterly.

He looked at her with a condescending smile. Watching it from where she stood by the window it seemed to her that it was the smile of a man who could despise her. She had seen it before. It was the smile men smiled when confronted by a woman. Kings especially. She saw that now, and it was horrible. Why had he changed so?

On an inlaid Pembroke table at her side was a Nymphenburg porcelain model of a nymph and shepherd by Franz Bustelli, eighteenth century, exquisitely made, in perfect condition, valuable though not priceless. Queen Caroline picked it up and hurled it at her husband, who swayed easily out of its path so that it shattered against a wall behind him. For a moment he gazed at her, his face quite blank, then without saying anything at all, he simply got up and left. In her study the Queen stood and listened to the rain. A moment later she tasted salt and, putting a hand to her cheek, realized that she was crying.

"Relax," Schnabel said, "you only sent the letter three days ago. The mail is terrible. She has to write a reply. What do you expect?"

Julian Locke ran his hand through lank hair and sighed. "I just don't like it," he said, "living with this pretense. I don't care about conservation. I don't care if all the whales in the oceans are turned into soap. I don't care if tigers in Bengal are made into rugs. I care about politics. I want a revolution, not all this crap." He waved his hand in the general direction of the walls. They were covered in maps, photographs, charts, diagrams. All were concerned with aspects of conservation. Cuddly seals stared prettily from Arctic ice, rhinoceroses looked belligerent and defiant. A nuclear reactor squatted obtrusively in a picturesque mountain landscape with a fluorescent red "No" across it. In a corner sat Sam, typing lethargically, just as she had done in the old days of the People's Revolutionary Crusade. These offices were more lavishly appointed than their revolutionary predecessors' and so were its occupants. Julian had had his hair cut and wore a dark suit with white shirt and plain businessman's tie. Sam looked groomed and lipsticked in a shirt and skirt and stockings with seams. There was a carpet on the floor, drinks in the cupboard. Conservation had to be up-market, high profile, if you were looking for royal patronage.

"You were only playing before," Schnabel said. "Now the game is over. You have grown up and come of age. You may really achieve something."

"Oh put a sock in it, Hermann," Sam said. "I don't know what makes you think the Queen will have anything to do with us. If she wants to save whales there are plenty of other ways to do it. She's not going to support some two-bit organization like this."

"Ah," Schnabel tapped his nose. "You forget two things, Samantha dear. One, I have intuition, and two, I have laid plans. I have sown seeds. She'll come through, you'll see."

"You foreigners don't have the first idea about how royalty works," she said. "They don't just take things on because they think it's a good idea. They only support the *right* causes. *Safe* causes. We're not safe, we're left-wing, anti-industry, anti-progress—"

"This Queen *is* foreign, as you put it. So perhaps I understand her better than you British. And you are no longer lefties, you are conservationists. Politically you are neutral, perhaps even moderate. For God's sake let us remember that, or we may be lost. And please do not forget that before she was married, Her Majesty was as ardent a conservationist as we are now."

"Let's face it," Julian said, "the only way to deal with royalty is to knock it off. We should do what the Bolsheviks did at Ekaterinburg. The IRA had it right when they blew up Mountbatten."

"And what did that achieve?" Schnabel coldly asked. "There was probably more sympathy for the royals after that piece of silliness than at any time since the war. It took years to offset the effect that stunt had on public opinion. Kill them after you've won, but until you have your victory you have to turn them to your advantage. The Russians waited until the revolution before they eliminated their royal family," said Schnabel. "We still have to achieve our revolution. Then we can indulge ourselves..." He smiled. "So. How is our list of vice-presidents? How many have accepted?"

"The list's here," Julian said sulkily. He handed over a piece of letterhead notepaper on which he had scrawled about twenty names. Some had been crossed out, others checked. Schnabel read it carefully with an amused grin. "Pity about Sir Bernard," he said. "He would have added a note of real seriousness. Dame Diana is all very well in her way but we don't want that much showbiz. Lord Yetminster sounds like a catch. Who's he?"

"I just found him in *Who's Who*," Sam said. "He had bird-watching down as a recreation so he seemed likely."

Schnabel's grin widened as he read further. "Rear Admiral Fawcett will join anything if he thinks it's to his advantage. Do we have a Labor MP as well?"

"Stuart Holland turned us down," Julian said. "I'm going to have a try for Giles Radice. My cousin was at school with him."

"Fine," said Schnabel. "It's a question of balance. It would be ironic if we were labeled too right-wing because of Admiral Fawcett."

Fawcett was the Conservative Member of Parliament for Sheen Central, a garrulous blatherer who attracted far more publicity than he deserved while abler politicians got on with their work. The other honorary vice-presidents completed the ragbag of personalities, conservationists and joiners who were traditionally featured on the letterheads of organizations such as the Friends of Man.

"Do you want to send a follow-up letter to the Queen now? It might help to show her the list." Julian smiled. "She may find it persuasive."

"We can't seem that eager," Schnabel said. "We are certain to have an inquiry from some royal bureaucrat before too long. The list will come in then. Just hold on to it."

"We'll see." Locke went to the filing cabinet and placed it carefully in the folder marked with a "Q" for Queen. He wished he felt more optimistic.

Eric Simpson had made a point of lurking near the Queen's study after his sudden dismissal. He had seen that the King was in an unusually agitated state of mind and was perplexed by her references to a Julian Locke and to conservation. It was then that the crash of the porcelain ornament against the wall followed by the King's footsteps broke into his deliberations. He made himself scarce and retreated swiftly to the sanctuary of his own office, where in a few minutes he located the letter from Locke. It was sitting in the tray marked "Pending" which was reserved for nonurgent requests awaiting the answer "no."

He read it twice. It was a standard request; he dealt with hundreds like it every year. Three paragraphs long, it was typed on an electric machine with a large typeface. The paper was thick and expensive, the heading professionally designed, the address, in Marylebone, respectable without being ostentatious. The appeal was couched in moderate, civilized English, explaining that the organization was dedicated to the achievement of a ten-point program by the beginning of the next century. The points were not spelled out but seemed a bit woolly. Mr. Locke said he appreciated the Queen's full and demanding schedule but hoped that she might nevertheless be prepared to lend her name to the one organization in the field which had definite plans and aspirations and a date by which they wished to achieve them.

Normally Simpson would have sent a two line turndown, but this time, he realized, he would have to pass it on to the Queen. He would do it later. Meanwhile he picked up the phone and dialled a friend of his who worked at the Royal Society for the Prevention of Cruelty to Animals.

"What do you know about a group called the Friends of Man?" he asked, coming straight to the point.

"Not much," his contact admitted. "They're new and they seem aboveboard. I've seen their literature. It's glossy, well documented, perfectly sound. But honestly they don't have anything very new to offer which isn't already covered off by organizations such as ours."

"Do you know anything about someone called Julian Locke?"

"Only that he's their secretary. I've met him a couple of times —a World Wildlife Fund cocktail party and the sea mammal conference. A bit wet behind the ears but committed and agreeable enough. Why do you ask?'

"I don't want this to get out but they've asked the Queen to be their patron."

"And you'll say no, I presume."

"Should I?"

"I should have thought so. There are quite enough conservation bodies already without adding to the confusion. Nothing wrong with this lot, but they'd be much better advised to devote their energies to helping the chaps who are already in the business and know what they're about."

"I'm inclined to agree," Simpson said. After a few half-hearted pleasantries, he thanked his friend and hung up. Simpson sighed. He supposed it wouldn't much matter if the Queen was involved with the Friends of Man. It was important to steer clear of controversy, but conservation and ecology had always been defined in the palace rulebook as noncontroversial, and the Royals had been lending their name to various eco-nut bodies since the fifties. So long as it didn't get in the way of their hunting, shooting and fishing no one minded. He looked again at the letter and decided to call Locke directly and see if he could defuse the situation. He was going to have to brief Sir Evelyn eventually and Sir Evelyn was eagle-eyed when it came to loopholes and impatient of slack staff work.

"Mr. Locke, please," he said when Sam answered. Her voice sounded well educated and civil. Simpson noted the fact and tentatively awarded the Friends of Man some plus marks.

"Ah, Mr. Locke," he said, when Julian came on the phone. "Eric Simpson here, at Buckingham Palace. I was just phoning to say that we had received your letter, which of course will be dealt with in the normal way. There were just a few routine questions I'd like an answer to if you have a moment. Good. Thank you."

Twenty minutes later Simpson was reassured, if not wholly at ease. Locke had been blandly polite. He was impressed by the vice-presidency of Lord Yetminster and Rear Admiral Fawcett, M.P. The group's aims seemed unspectacular, in tune with the received wisdom of the times. Some of the conservation groups had used their aspirations as a tool to bash capitalism, but Locke spoke calmly and intelligently of the need to cooperate with industry over the problems of industrial waste, the economical recycling of glass and plastic. He emphasized the commercial as well as environmental advantages of developing alternatives to the internal combustion engine and oil-based energy. And so on. Boring, thought Simpson. If she wanted to do it, why not?

At the end of it he decided to take the letter through to the Queen straightaway, as she had instructed, and as he paced back along the corridors to the Queen's study he looked a happy courtier.

"The letter from Mr. Locke, ma'am," he said when he had been readmitted. "I thought you'd want to see it as soon as it arrived." He noted as he spoke that the Queen's eyes were pink-rimmed, presumably from tears, but that she seemed to have regained her composure. She was smoking once again, though this time it was not a gesture. Her nerves really did seem to need steadying.

"It arrived just now?"

Simpson let the irony—if it was irony—pass unremarked, and just handed it over the desk. She read it quickly, then leaned back and looked inquiringly at her secretary. "You'd prefer me not to do it?"

"I'd prefer you not to do it," Simpson echoed.

"Why?"

"Well, ma'am, there are already half a dozen groups like this which enjoy royal patronage. My view is that this just duplicates what others are trying to do."

"And my view is that the other groups achieve very little. This one's new, so give it a chance."

Simpson looked at the carpet. "That's a point of view, of course, but with respect—"

"I really wish you wouldn't say that," she said abruptly. "It means exactly the opposite of what it sounds like. You weren't going to say anything with respect, you were going to say it with contempt." She paused. "I'm sorry, Eric," she went on, making a conscious effort to relax. "Bad day, I guess. I didn't mean that.

But I am taking the job on. Patron of the Friends of Man, okay? And when you let them know, make it clear that I'm not going to be a figurehead. Do you follow?"

"Are you sure you don't want time to consider, ma'am? It is customary to make certain inquiries to establish the bona fides of a new organization. To make sure that you aren't compromised."

"If I give you time to make all the usual inquiries you have in mind, then the opportunity will have gone. I've made up my mind."

"Very well, ma'am." He bowed and turned to leave.

"And I want to see the letter before it goes out."

"Yes, of course."

As he retraced his steps to his own office he was surprised to meet his own secretary halfway along a corridor. She seemed flustered.

"I came to find you," she said, "Sir Evelyn wants you. He came round himself. He's in one of his moods."

Simpson changed course. Like most of the palace staff he was frightened of Blackrock's moods, which were legendary. He had better find him as quickly as possible. Any procrastination would make him angrier still. There would be charges of incompetence. He wondered what was wrong. Blackrock couldn't have known about the Friends of Man already, even with his hypersensitive antennae.

As Simpson entered the private secretary's office, he reflected that an outsider would not have known what a vile temper Colonel Sir Evelyn Blackrock was in. He seemed detached, cool, devoid of all apparent emotion. This in itself was ominous. The angrier he was the less angry he appeared. Simpson knew this and, seeing the little man sitting grey and immobile behind his desk, he was afraid. He was also alarmed to see Maurice Henderson already in the room. These two seemed to him to be cementing an unhealthy alliance.

Henderson smiled at him. He was, had Simpson known it, quite sympathetic to Simpson's plight. There but for the grace of God, he knew, stood he.

"She had a letter from the Hollis woman this morning," Blackrock said without looking up. "Why wasn't I told?"

"You *were* told," said Simpson. "You're telling me something I didn't know myself. I'm the one who wasn't told—"

"Don't be impertinent."

A long silence. Simpson was still standing. Blackrock had not yet looked up. He was staring at his hands, which rested palm down on the blotter in front of him. They were as motionless as his face.

"His Majesty is concerned. This morning the Queen became extremely overwrought. She began talking about freedom, said she was unhappy. This is strictly between the three of us, but at the end of the meeting she threw some damned figurine at him. His Majesty and I are of the opinion that she is in need of an immediate holiday, possibly of medical attention, and that she should cancel all her engagements forthwith. Do either of you have any reason why this should not be done?"

"She won't wear it," said Simpson. "She is in a very forceful mood."

"She'll have to do as she's told."

"She won't," Simpson said. "I don't think that's the way to handle her. Not at the moment."

"She's obviously been handled bloody awfully up until now," Blackrock snapped.

"Do we know what was in the letter from the Hollis woman?" Henderson asked. "It looks pretty obvious that there was something in it which upset her. Hollis has always stirred things up. She's a bad influence. We know that."

"The King mentioned another letter," Blackrock said, "something the Queen was expecting. A letter you had to let her see as soon as it arrived. Now what was that?"

"She told me that Joanne Hollis had met someone connected with a conservation group called the Friends of Man. They wanted the Queen to become their patron and were going to write. She said she wanted to see the letter as soon as it came in."

"And has it?"

"Yes."

"And?"

"I showed it to her."

"Damnation." Sir Evelyn said this evenly, almost flatly, but there was no mistaking his irritation.

"I really didn't have any alternative . . ." Simpson said.

Henderson came to his aid. "I see that," he said. "What do we know about these people? I've never heard of them."

"They're new," Simpson said. "I spoke to a friend of mine at the RSPCA. He knows his way round the conservation circuit. He seemed to think they were all right, superfluous to requirement but nothing known against them. Then I rang Locke."

"Locke?"

"The one who wrote the letter. Julian Locke."

Sir Evelyn scribbled the name on his pad, tore the sheet of paper off and folded it carefully in four. "Go on," he said.

"He was very plausible and polite and he gave me the names of some of their vice-presidents. Lord Yetminster for instance. And Rear Admiral Fawcett, the Member for Sheen."

"They'd do anything for a cream bun," said Blackrock. "Are the others the same?"

Simpson ran swiftly through more names while Blackrock's expression grew grimmer.

"Rentasponsor," Henderson said when Simpson had finished.

"Why is the Queen so keen to take this on?" asked Blackrock, tapping his teeth with his gold mechanical pencil. "She used to be mixed up with the conservation circus. We've always known that. But I was under the impression she'd grown out of it. She hasn't done much for those other groups of which she's already a patron. Her liking for mink borders on the vulgar." He paused, not really seeming to expect a response to this, and glanced sharply at Simpson. "Could you get us the Hollis letter?"

"It's personal," Simpson said, "she'll reply to it in longhand. It won't go into the filing system."

"Where would she keep it?"

"I don't know."

"Then find out. And I want to see her reply before it leaves the palace."

Simpson was shocked but he said nothing. Henderson was less surprised but he also kept quiet. He believed the Queen could take the Friends of Man job and make a success out of it. It might even be good for her. But now was hardly the time to say so.

Blackrock stood up sharply, bristling, his grizzled moustache making him look like a small predatory animal. "I want this nonsense nipped in the bud," he said menacingly, "before it ends in tears."

Upstairs the Queen crumpled another attempted letter into a ball and threw it into the waste basket. The ashtray was full. Her physician had been in to see her and had expressed displeasure. So had nanny who had come in briefly with the new royal prince. The Princess Royal, now two, had been ushered in for a ritual five minutes' play and had wrinkled her nose and said "smoke," lisping over the "s" but making her disgust quite plain. The Queen hoped she would like her daughter more when she was a little older, but she was very much afraid she would grow up into a prig.

She picked up Julian Locke's letter, thought for a moment and looked out of the window. It was grey and sullen, though not actually raining. "The hell with it," she said out loud, and smiled.

Five minutes later she had on sturdy walking shoes, a masculine-looking, belted gaberdine mackintosh and a silk headscarf. The coat buttoned high at the neck, covering the lower half of her chin. The scarf covered her hair and the top of her forehead. It was not a disguise but it was the next best thing. On a day like today there would be hundreds of similarly dressed women in the West End of London. She would excite very little attention, and even those who thought they recognized her face would know from the clothes that they had made a mistake. Normally, of course, she did all her travelling by car with a lady-in-waiting in tow as well as an armed detective. Even the free wheeling

Scandinavian royals travelled about with some sort of attendant. It was unheard of for a British Royal to venture out alone like this. Fine, she was an American. Americans understood about democracy . . .

It occurred to her that she was breaking every rule in the book, but because of that she sensed she would get away with it and no one would know or care. She was in prison but only because she let it be done. If she went out of the side entrance by the royal mews she could pretend she was going to talk to the Crown Equerry, old Crawshaw. On her way downstairs she ran through the story in her mind. She would pretend to be consulting him about her new charger, the one she would ride at next year's Trooping the Color. As it happened, however, no one asked her where she was going. If she had thought harder she would have realized that no one but her husband and Blackrock would have dared ask. She was, after all, the Queen. No one ever asked the Queen where she was going because usually, of course, somebody else knew.

The uniformed police on the gate were concerned only with preventing unwelcome or unauthorized visitors. They were not interested in departures. As she passed through they hardly gave her a glance, concerned as they were in the interrogation of two men in the uniform grey of middle-ranking civil servants. The ceremonial sentries gazed straight ahead looking neither to left nor right.

Outside, on the pavement stained dark grey with rain she turned right into Lower Grosvenor Place. This route took her away from the crowds of tourists who, even out of season and in this inclement weather, still crowded the front gates of the palace in the hope of seeing a royal person getting in or out in one of the unmarked Rolls-Royces. By walking this way she was quickly absorbed into an anonymous London where few people even thought about the fact that the high brick wall which towered above her was all that separated the public from the secluded royal gardens. People would have been surprised enough to find the Queen walking by herself down the Mall. Here it would have been inconceivable.

To her surprise she realized that her mouth was dry. Fear? Excitement? Neither made sense to her. It had been so easy, so routine.

And why not? she asked herself. What could be more usual than for a woman to put on a coat and go out for a walk without telling her husband or the servants. Millions of women did it every day.

The ease of the operation was, in a way, reassuring. She had begun to think that the guards were there to keep her in rather than keep intruders out. Now she was not so sure. Perhaps it was all in her mind. Perhaps she *was* free to come and go as she pleased. Maybe she could be her own woman after all, if she was careful.

At Grosvenor Place she crossed the road and walked north to Hyde Park Corner, where she took the underground walkway into Hyde Park itself. The wind was blowing directly into her face now, catching piles of dark brown leaves and lifting them in miniature tornados. There were very few people around. She passed a woman, dressed much like herself, exercising a bedraggled Afghan. The woman did not even glance at her. A tramp lay on a park bench, his rotten boots stuffed with newspaper to keep out the wet. Along the south of the park two horsemen cantered down Rotten Row. The Queen hunched her shoulders and strode on purposefully, relishing this fleeting freedom as if she were a truant from school.

There was another underground walkway at Marble Arch and she ducked into it, realizing as she passed a supplicant violinist sprawled against the wall that she had no money with her. Normally Lady Coker or another lady-in-waiting would have carried the cash. Without Lady Coker she was temporarily destitute.

She was nearing her goal now. Two or three minutes more of brisk walking and she was in Bryanston Square, elegantly porticoed, its aristocratic terraces now converted into apartments, office suites and a private nursing home. Halfway along the left she stopped and consulted the row of brass address plates, reading past one indicating a public relations agency, another a documentary filmmaker and third on the list, "The Friends of Man." She braced herself, then entered the hallway and pressed the button for the elevator.

There was no attendant and no other passenger. She examined herself freely in the mirror. She looked windblown and damp, but as she shook her hair free from the restricting scarf she became immediately recognizable and unequivocally beautiful. The elevator stopped, the door slid open and she stepped out into a small but expensively appointed reception area. A svelte blonde receptionist hired by Julian Locke less than a month before sat behind an oversized white plastic desk talking in a languid intimate tone which made it clear that she was on a personal call. She looked up and put the phone down in midsentence.

"Can I help?" she asked, evidently disbelieving.

"I've come to see Mr. Locke," she said, fazed by the receptionist's confusion, "Julian Locke."

"Hang on." The girl stood, revealing long well-shaped legs in tight green trousers. "Who shall I say . . . ?"

For a moment the two stared at each other, embarrassed by each other's embarrassment. Then Caroline smiled and the girl smiled back, relaxing a little.

"Just tell Mr. Locke," said the Queen, "that it's his new patron."

After the Cabinet meeting Henry Cathcart stayed behind. It had been a stormy session, hardly surprising in the light of the catastrophic by-election result which had come through from Trowbridge and Melksham in the small hours. A thirty-two percent swing against the government was unprecedented. Even half that in a general election and the Conservatives would be annihilated. In Cabinet the doves had argued feverishly for another compromise with the unions. It seemed to them that a national strike was inevitable if the government did not abandon its policy to withhold welfare payments from strikers' families. The hawks on the other hand maintained that the country would respect them for taking the unpopular view, sticking to their guns and standing up to the unions. The Cabinet, like the country, was dangerously divided, and Prime Minister Potter seemed paralyzed. His inertia and indecision could not be passed off as statesmanlike pragmatism much longer.

"Not good," Potter said lugubriously as they sat alone in the Cabinet office.

Cathcart thought how much older the PM had become over the last few weeks. He was not yet sixty but looked nearer seventy. "Just thank God we have at least a year before a general election," Cathcart said.

"I don't know why we should wait that long," Potter said. "I don't see the remotest chance of things getting better before then. Have you seen the Central Policy Review Staff forecasts on the economy?"

"Yes," Cathcart said.

"Well if that gets out, we've had it." Potter's expression was grim.

"It's not exactly our fault. Dock strike, miners' strike, rail strike, not to mention the international situation." Cathcart heard himself whistling in the dark. He sounded shrill. "Seems to me," he said, "that we have to appeal to people's patriotism. Can't they be made to see that most of the unrest is politically motivated? It's subversion, no more, no less."

"We've got precious few options," Potter said. "We need every bit of help we can get. How are your friends at the palace? Can we count on them?"

Cathcart made a face. "It depends if the left are going to ask for the abolition of the monarchy, as they did before the abdication, or whether they go for something more modest this time. At the moment it looks as if they'll stick to demands for cutting the monarchy down to size."

"I don't want any stepping out of line," Potter said, with feeling. "Is there a problem?"

"I'm not sure yet." Cathcart did not want to alarm the old boy until it became really necessary. But he did want to prepare him. "I had a curious call from Evelyn Blackrock asking me to have someone checked out."

"Oh?" Potter did not seem unduly concerned. "Not another mole?" he said, "I don't think I can take some bloody equerry turning out to be a KGB man."

"I don't think so," Cathcart said. "Evelyn wasn't forthcoming. The man isn't significant." He paused. "Though there *is* a file."

"There is?" Potter's voice took on a note of concern. "Who is he?"

"No one in particular." Cathcart began to wish he hadn't raised the subject. "I'm more concerned about the Queen, as a matter of fact."

Potter looked surprised. "Surely she's the ace in the deck?" he said. "Top of all the polls. Son and heir. Most dramatic injection of new blood since the Battenbergs. And much to be preferred . . ."

"Well," Cathcart said, "she's displaying some disturbing signs *of* the Battenbergs'. I understand she's cancelled some of the royal warrants under her name. Also overruled a refusal to make a speech to the Women of the Year lunch."

"Did Blackrock tell you about this?" Potter was alert now, sensing danger.

"No." Cathcart sighed. "We're lunching shortly. Naturally we'll discuss it then. This came from independent sources."

"I hope they're reliable."

"Oh yes." Cathcart shrugged. "There may be nothing in it. But I want to be sure. We don't want trouble."

"We've got enough trouble as it is," Potter said mournfully. He fixed his colleague with a grim stare. "It must be understood that there is to be no stepping out of line at the palace," he said. "The public won't stand for it. The King must understand that. And I can't guarantee the government's support if they willfully court popular disapproval. Do I make myself clear?"

"Perfectly."

"Then make sure it's clear to Queen Caroline too. She and her husband have to do as they're told or they're out, as they would do well to remember. They'll be lucky to get off with an affluent exile in New Zealand like his parents. If the left get their way it could mean a real upheaval, and I fancy regicide may enjoy a return to fashion. You can make that clear to Her Majesty too."

Cathcart nodded and said nothing. He wondered if the Prime Minister was exaggerating the danger. On balance he thought not. But it would not be easy to make their majesties recognize it. They tended to believe their own publicity, and as yet the publicity was still good.

CHAPTER

$\mathcal{I}$ T WAS more than an hour before anyone discovered that
the Queen was missing. Various people had wanted her,
but each of them had assumed she was with someone else. There
were plenty of places she might be: in the nursery with nanny
and children, pacing the camomile lawns, swimming in the
palace pool. She might, God knows, have been in bed with her
husband. The one thing that never occurred to anyone was that
she might have gone absent without leave.

At half past twelve the King, who had been abstractedly
working on Cabinet papers and other documents, decided that
she had had enough time to cool off and that the moment was
ripe for reconciliation. He called Simpson.

"She wasn't in her room when I looked half an hour ago sir."

"Find her for me, would you?"

And so Simpson, who had had a busy, worried morning, set
off on a search. Twenty minutes later the King phoned through
a second time. This time he sounded crotchety. Simpson said he
was about to try the gardens. He was beginning to worry. Five
minutes later, after a lightning search around the grounds and
a swift interrogation of the gardeners and a couple of footmen,

he discovered that the Queen had been seen heading toward the mews. Simpson hurried across to the Crown Equerry's office, where he found Brigadier Crawshaw, relaxing rheumy-eyed over a stiff gin. He said he hadn't seen the Queen for days. This time Simpson sprinted back to the main palace building and arrived in his office, panting, to find the King waiting for him there, angry and impatient.

"What's going on?" he asked.

Simpson gulped. "I . . . can't find her," he said.

"Since when?"

"Just over an hour ago, sir. She was seen walking towards the mews and I assumed she'd gone to see the equerry. He says he hasn't seen her all day."

"The gates. Have you checked the gates?"

"No sir."

"Then check the gates and report back to me at once. If I'm not in my room I'll be with Blackrock." He thrust his hands deep into the pockets of his deep, waisted tweed jacket and pursed his lips, then shook his head in exasperation and bewilderment. "I don't know," he said, "I really don't."

The police on the back gate were not helpful. They sounded busy and preoccupied and in no mood to appreciate the urgency of Simpson's questioning. Under pressure one of them conceded that it was possible that a woman of roughly the Queen's build and appearance might have left through the gate an hour or so ago, but they could hardly be sure. They were short-staffed, they couldn't cope with people leaving the bloody grounds, it was as much as they could do to check all the bleeders coming in. The policeman was obviously prepared to grumble on for hours. Simpson cut in with uncharacteristic brusqueness.

"Was it her?"

"Could have been. Can't say."

"Thank you for nothing."

He slammed the receiver back onto its cradle and ran out of the room in the direction of the King's study. The door to it was open. Inside the King sat at his desk. With him were Blackrock,

Henderson and Chief Inspector Macpherson. Macpherson, known to the world as "Tartan," was on permanent assignment from the Metropolitan Police as head of royal security. He had the barrel build of a linebacker and, normally, an expression of almost serene self-assurance. As Simpson came in, however, he was looking quite edgy.

"He canna stay with her all the time, sir," he was saying. "You know that. There's no call for it. The second Her Majesty is off out of the building, then he'll be there just as I am with you. But it's not the same indoors. You know that, sir."

The King looked as if he knew nothing of the kind.

"Well?" he snapped at Simpson.

"They say she might have left the gates about an hour ago?"

"What do you mean 'might'?"

"Exactly that I'm afraid. They say they can't be sure. There's no checkout, just a checkin."

The King grimaced. "Are you trying to tell me that the Queen walked through those gates and the police just didn't notice?"

"Yes, sir."

The King passed calloused fingers through thinning hair. "Bloody hell," he said, then glanced at Macpherson. "Is that possible, Tartan?"

The big policeman smiled uneasily. "I suppose it's . . . possible, sir. Like Mr. Simpson says there's no real checkout procedure. It's awful difficult to get into the palace if you've no authority, but I suppose it's awful easy to get out."

"We have to accept the fact that Her Majesty has left the building?" This from Blackrock, not aimed at anyone in particular. No one answered, so he continued. "That being the case where has she gone?"

"She may just have gone walkabout," Henderson said.

"Don't be facetious," Blackrock said.

"I'm not," he said. "If she's . . . disturbed . . . then she may just have gone out for no reason other than that she just had to get out and be on her own for a few minutes. Maybe everything's got on top of her. If she's feeling claustrophobic, she may have no more idea of where she's going than we do."

"She probably has no money," Simpson said, "she can't go far. She has no car."

"Are we sure of that?" Blackrock asked.

Tartan Macpherson nodded. "There's no way anyone can take a car from the pool without an authority. The mews would know."

"What about a private car? That car park round the side is full of them," Simpson said.

"You're not seriously suggesting that Queen Caroline would go out to the car park and pinch the first car she found," the King said.

Simpson flushed. "No sir . . . of course not."

"Seems plain to me," said the King, "that she's walking and that she probably left the palace an hour ago, maybe an hour and a half. In which case she couldn't have gone more than . . ." His face fell as he began to feel the full embarrassment of his situation. "I suppose we have to accept that if she really did leave the palace then, she could have walked three or four more miles or so."

The thought of scouring the city for a radius of three or more miles around Buckingham Palace was deeply depressing.

"Where do these conservationist chappies hang out?" Blackrock asked morosely. "If she has gone anywhere specific that seems as likely as anywhere."

"Bryanston Square," Simpson said.

"Half an hour on foot," Henderson said, "up Birdcage Walk and along Park Lane and you're almost there. No problem."

"Worth a try," said Macpherson, getting to his feet. "Shall I go round?"

"No," Blackrock said. "If she is there, the last thing we want to do is let them know she's playing truant or that we disapprove of her patronizing them."

"Does that matter?" the King asked.

"The press," Henderson replied. "They'd have a field day."

"They'd never know."

"I think we have to consider that our friend Locke might be on to the press straightaway," Blackrock said. "It's what your former colleagues would describe as "a good story," eh, Henderson?"

Henderson nodded.

"My view," Blackrock continued, "is that we have to sweat it out. If we do that, then I'd say there's a better than even chance that we'll have her back within the hour, without there being any fuss."

"I can't agree." Macpherson seemed anxious to redeem himself for the disaster. "We'll sort the publicity out later. For the moment we have to find the Queen. If she's out on her own, she's also a target for any loony who happens across her path. It could be dangerous and it's bound to be disagreeable. I want to go up to this place in Bryanston Square straightaway."

"And then what?" Blackrock asked gently. "Bring her back by force? Really."

"She'll come of her own free will," the policeman muttered.

"She *went* of her own free will," Blackrock reminded him, "I don't honestly think we have any alternative but to sit tight. If something happens to her we'll know soon enough. And if not then she'll be home before too long."

"And meanwhile we do nothing?" The King was clearly impatient for action. "We can't just sit here while the Queen of England is missing, God knows where. Anything could happen to her. I feel morally bound to look for her. It's negligent enough of us to let her escape—" He was startled to have used the word, yet he went on, "but it's damn near criminal to accept it and sit here twiddling our thumbs."

"She couldn't have been kidnapped?" Simpson asked tremulously. He had noticed that no one had suggested the possibility; now he realized why raising it had been left to him. Like Macpherson, he clearly felt himself officially responsible for what had happened. If heads were going to roll, his would be one of the first.

"Kidnapping seems unlikely," Blackrock said, biting back the irritation he felt. He hated old women like Simpson. There had been too many in his regiment in North Africa. They got in the way with their dithering and dickering and finer sensibilities.

On the other hand the continual impatience, this mania for "doing something"—no matter what—which was one of the King's principal failings, was just as dangerous. "I propose," he continued, "that we give it until . . ." He consulted his pocket watch. "Three o'clock."

"And if she's not back by then?" Macpherson was obviously not happy. If he had his way the whole city would be at red alert, every policeman would have his leave cancelled, the world and his wife would know there was trouble up at palace. "We think again," said Blackrock. "But I doubt we'll need to."

"Agreed," the King said. "We meet again at three, unless you hear to the contrary." He pursed his lips and stuck his chin out in his familiar, defiant fashion. He was angry, he was worried, but most of all he was hurt. This was an attack on his authority, on his manhood even, and a public one at that. The insult stung. In another age he would have put his wife across his knee and spanked her bottom. He had half a mind to do just that. He smiled ruefully at the thought of it. The Victorians had a healthier attitude. Woman's place in the home, speaking when spoken to and all that. Then he remembered why the nineteenth century was called the Victorian age. Unlikely, he supposed, that Prince Albert would ever have put the great Queen Victoria over his knee. Come to think of it there was an unhealthy tradition of dominant women in the British royal house. He must make sure that, without resorting to anything crude, he asserted himself properly. He was, after all, the King of England.

As her husband reflected, the Queen was, as Blackrock had predicted, heading for home. Her spirits, as she cut across Hyde Park, sensible heels squelching into the sodden turf, were higher than they had been for months. If anyone had bothered to look closely at her face through the thin, misty drizzle, they would have seen that she was smiling ecstatically, almost laughing, and that her eyes, which had recently seemed almost leaden, now sparkled with excitement.

Her conversation with Julian Locke had gone far better than she could have hoped. For the first time in ages she had not felt patronized or unnaturally revered. Her life for two years had been divided between those like her husband, Blackrock, the royal dukes and most of the British aristocracy, who treated her —consciously or not—as an ingenue from an alien and inferior world; and the rest, who were so awestruck by the resonance and antiquity of her titles that they were virtually tongue-tied. Yes ma'am, no ma'am. Three bags full, ma'am. A curtsey here, a bow here. God, how she hated it. But Locke had been different.

She tramped across the thick mud of Rotten Row, wishing she had worn boots. Locke reminded her of the past. Not so much of Panini, who had been exotic and fairly mindless, but of the average young man in her life. Julian was educated, fluent and mildly sardonic, well dressed but not ostentatiously so. He had made her feel human again, normal. Somehow being Queen had nothing to do with normality. Even her babies were taken away from her and brought up by somebody else. She was a constant focus of the public on the one hand and of the royal bureaucracy on the other, but there had been a time when she was privileged but freer, an individual in her own right, appreciated for the strength of her mind and her body and not, God help her, for her damned title.

The palace was not far away now. At Hyde Park Corner she hesitated. To her right Knightsbridge led, invitingly, toward Harrods and Sloane Street. She remembered meals at the Basil Street Hotel, thought wistfully of cocktails at the Berkeley. For a moment she wondered whether she might treat herself to one of the Berkeley's dry martinis or a whisky sour. She had no money, but surely when they realized who she was there would be no problem arranging credit. It occurred to her that she had not personally signed a check in two years.

She turned left into the labyrinthine walkways and toward Constitution Hill. She might not have the confidence for a drink in the Berkeley or a tour of Harrods, but she did at least have the guts to walk back through her own front door. Just because she sneaked *out* by the side way didn't mean she had to sneak back through on the way in. It was her house. It might belong to the nation but it was hers for life—or at least for the King's life. When he died, she'd be shunted off down the road to Clarence House or St. James's or Kensington Palace . . .

There was a small crowd at the palace gates. Caroline ignored them and took no notice of the two elderly ladies in transparent plastic raincoats who nudged each other and whispered "It's her" with goggle eyes. She did, however, smile ravishingly at the policemen in their sentry box. They in turn were sufficiently well trained to smile back and say coolly "Good afternoon, your Majesty." As soon as she was halfway across the forecourt, one of them picked up the telephone and called Sir Evelyn's office as directed. "She's back sir," he said. "Just walked through the gates." Only when he put the phone down did he say to his companion: "Bloody hell. What's going on?"

Inside the building Queen Caroline handed her soaked coat to a footman. Her shoes were uncomfortable, damp and too tight. Instead of enduring the discomfort of wearing them upstairs until she could remove them discreetly and privately, she bent down and eased them off.

"My feet are killing me." She smiled at the servant, whose expressionless expression never faltered. "Have these sent up when they've been cleaned. They'll have to go back."

"Yes ma'am." He bowed stiffly and then picked the shoes adroitly from the carpet.

"Thank you," she said, then removed her scarf, shook her head to let her hair loose and marched down the corridor in her stockinged feet. She felt better than she had done for months, and when she got to her apartment she rang down and ordered a hamburger with fries and ketchup. Bunny so disapproved of what he considered her unseemly transatlantic taste for junk food that she had virtually given it up, though she was just as disparaging about his fondness for stale cheese and warm beer. She lit a Marlboro and exhaled. A moment later there was a gentle knock on her door.

"Come," she said. It was her husband. He glanced at her cigarette, smiled a shade sheepishly and said nothing. He was carrying a bottle of champagne.

"Do you have any glasses?" he asked.

She stared at him, unblinking. "I may have," she said finally. But she did not get up or offer him the slightest promise of a welcome. He continued to smile, but without much confidence.

"Let's see," he said, putting the bottle down on a coffee table alongside a copy of *Country Life*, "if I remember rightly you keep your glasses . . ." He walked slowly along the cupboard doors set into the paneling along one wall and stopped at the extreme right. "Here," he said, and opened the door with a flourish. "Right first time." He took out two tulip-shaped wine glasses, opened the champagne expertly so that none spilled and the cork made only a cordial pop, and poured. Caroline sat back in her chair and watched, languidly smoking her cigarette.

"By the way," he said, "I ordered some smoked salmon sandwiches."

"Good. I ordered a burger. With fries and ketchup."

"Oh." He frowned, but lightly as if perplexed, not angry. "So you ordered salmon."

"I thought you might like some. You like smoked salmon."

"You didn't cancel the burger."

"No, I didn't cancel the burger, as you put it."

Now she smiled, tentatively. "Well that's good news," she said. She reached across the desk for the glass which he had given her and held it up so that she could watch the bubbles rising through the pale golden liquid.

"Well," he said, and raised his glass in a muted salute.

"Well," she replied, the smile just a shade more pronounced than it had been. She raised her glass in response, and they both drank.

"I—"

"I . . ." They both began the sentence simultaneously, then stopped together. Their confusion was covered by a knock on the door. It was the smoked salmon on a silver tray. Behind it another servant carried another tray with an enormous silver-plated dome on it. It looked large enough to conceal a baron of beef, let alone a humble hamburger. The King and Queen kept silence while the two trays were put down and did not start to speak again until the servants had bowed and reversed out of the

127

door. This time the King got in first.

"I thought we should have a talk." She inclined her head and looked up at him from beneath lowered lashes, but she said nothing. She felt herself weakening but was damned if she was going to show it, let alone make this any easier for him.

"I've been thinking," he said.

She took the cover off the hamburger. The bun was charred at the edges. She lifted the top half of the bun and saw that the burger itself was overdone and shrivelled. She replaced bun and dome.

"I guess I'll have some smoked salmon."

He proffered the plate and she took two of the delicate, crustless triangles. They were cut so thin they melted the second they were in her mouth.

"I thought you and I should have a little talk," he said.

"I guess we should,' she said. "Last time we had a little talk I threw something at you. Or had you forgotten?"

"You missed."

"I always was a lousy shot," she said, taking another sandwich. "What do you want to talk about?"

"You, and freedom."

"Uh-oh," she muttered, mouth full of brown bread and fish. She swallowed. "That's where we were at when I threw the nymph and shepherd. I didn't think you had a particularly clear idea of what I was talking about."

"Perhaps not."

"You have now though?"

"I've been doing some thinking, yes."

Christ, she thought to herself, he's pussyfooting. He's worried.

"You mean you've been talking to Blackrock."

He didn't answer. Instead he said, "You disappeared. I was worried, Caroline. Very worried."

"You said I could come and go as I pleased—"

"That's not the point, you know it isn't. We aren't like other people, you and I. I didn't know where you'd gone. Something might have happened."

"I'm a big girl."

"You're the Queen. That makes you vulnerable. You know that."

"Yes. I know that."

A maid had lit the fire in her absence. It was fuelled with some form of smokeless coal that seemed to smoke nonetheless. It gave out neither heat nor light.

"It's a question of security. It's dangerous to go out without one of Tartan's people."

"If you say so."

"You know it is."

"Yes. I know it is." She paused, then held out her glass for a refill. "Have you ever thought what it's been like for *me* these past two years?"

He gazed at her, trying to read her mind, desperate to know how he should respond. "I don't know," he said, eventually, defeated.

"I've lost my . . ." she groped for the word. "I don't know. My individuality. My privacy. My self-respect. I don't feel I'm me any longer. It's as if I'd been taken over by outsiders. I don't just mean you, I mean Blackrock and Simpson and the government and the people. Everything. I can't even walk out of my own house without the whole gang of you being thrown into a tizzy. My children are taken care of by strangers. My clothes are dictated by outsiders. I'm . . . a convenience. I'm being used. Yes, even by you. I'm just . . ."

"A bird in a gilded cage."

"That's a cliché, but yes, exactly that."

He pursed his lips. "It has to be like that," he said, on more familiar ground now.

"It does *not* have to be like that." She had raised her voice and regretted it. "Not like it has been, I mean." She qualified the remark. "I can be myself without disgracing you all. I wish you'd understand that. You do things, you take initiatives, you *lead.*" She got up and walked to the fireplace, ran her fingers through her long hair and stared with distaste at the smoking lumps of coalite. "I wish you could understand that I can be more use as a human being than a puppet. I'm not made like the Lady Cokers of this world who went to one of your English public schools. I'm different. I'm me. I wish you'd see that."

"What do you want?' he asked weakly. "You're talking in abstracts. You know I want what's best for you, but there are other things to be considered too."

"I want you to trust me, Bunny," she said softly. "Is that so very difficult? I'm your wife."

Now he too got to his feet and walked to the window, where he stood gazing out at the gardens. Oddly, she had never thought of him as being vulnerable, but now as she watched him apparently rapt in deliberation she sensed his weakness.

"What is this organization, Caroline?" he asked. "Did you go and see them this morning?"

"The Friends of Man? They're an environmentalist group. I like their ideas, I like their style and I want to help them."

"What's wrong with the RSPCA or Friends of the Earth or any of the others? There are hundreds of conservation groups and they've all got a pedigree. They're decent, respectable, honest—"

"And fundamentally useless," she butted in. "The world's in a mess. We're using up our resources all the time. We poison the atmosphere, we're crueller to animals than we've ever been. I think these people might be able to do something about it. Unlike all your perfectly respectable and perfectly ineffectual organizations."

He sighed. "Darling," he said, moving towards her, "you know we're on a knife edge here. We can't just give our names to anyone who asks. We can't be too controversial."

She flushed. "Bunny," she said, "I love you, but this is not some rinky-dink gang of radicals. They're all right. And I'm not going to be too controversial. I'm just going to do what I think's right. You have to allow for that."

She looked into his eyes until he avoided her stare.

"Yes," he said slowly. "But please, for all our sakes, be careful."

Now at last she felt it was safe to kiss him.

"A new leaf," she said, disengaging, "based on mutual trust. It'll work, you'll see." She refilled their glasses and touched hers lightly against her husband's. "To the family firm," she said. "And no rocking of the boat." She went back to the chair behind her desk. "I mentioned," she said, "that I was reviewing all my appointments. It's inappropriate to list people who never supply me with anything. I've done a new one." She held out a sheet of paper. "They're all 'decent, respectable and honest,' but you'd better check it through. Oh and darling, I wonder if, very tactfully, you could make it clear to nanny that from now on I'm in charge. She insists on putting Arthur into a nightdress."

The King grinned wanly. It hurt him to see her looking so happy. "Of course," he answered. "Just remember though: *mutual* trust. There has to be give and take."

The King did not tell his secretary about this conversation until the following morning after breakfast. By then he was feeling relaxed and fairly confident of his wife's good intentions. They had spent a happy, loving night together and, contrary to usual practice, both royal infants had been invited up to their father's bed for a kiss, cuddle and morning feeding. Instead of going for a solitary jog around the grounds, the King had swum a lazy ten lengths of the palace pool while his wife swam some of the way alongside. Normally she was a stronger swimmer than he but she was not completely back in shape after childbirth and retired after two lengths.

It was customary for King and secretary to meet for half an hour every morning and run through the day's schedule and any other matters of moment. This morning it was obvious what was uppermost in both men's minds, but they avoided any mention of it.

"The new French Ambassador is coming to present his credentials at twelve," said Blackrock, riffling papers. "I've allowed him half an hour, sir."

"Sherry?"

"We usually offer the froggoes spirits. And I understand His Excellency is a drinking man."

"He's an aristocrat I see." The King was looking at the papers on his desk. "Have I met him?"

"Not that I can establish. He's a racing man though. It's conceivable."

"Anything else to know?"

"Not really. Middle-of-the-road Quai d'Orsay chap. Late fifties. Overweight. Mistress in a smart apartment somewhere. Wife wheeled out for official functions."

"Is the mistress coming to London?" The King laughed.

"I think she's staying in Paris. Available for weekends I imagine."

"Sounds all right. Why am I lunching at the Confederation of British Industry?"

"Their request," Blackrock said. "I think they aim to get in some discreet lobbying about your China trip."

"But that's not for six months."

"That's not long in terms of export drives."

"Do I need a detailed brief?"

Blackrock deliberated for a second. "No," he said, "it's a listening exercise. Whatever they want—if it's definite enough— they'll follow up in writing. All you have to do is look sympathetic and intelligent."

The King grinned. "I *am* sympathetic and intelligent." Both men laughed. Nervously. They respected each other, worked well together, but there was never real friendship between them. The King was wary of Blackrock's inflexible adherence to the rules and sensed, correctly, that in party political terms Sir Evelyn was significantly to the right of himself. Conversely Blackrock felt that for all his monarch's dedication and virility he was a bit soft at the center.

"Otherwise straightforward," the King said.

"There's the concert at the Festival Hall. In aid of the Save the Children Fund."

"That's straightforward enough. Except for the Stockhausen. I can't think who the hell put that in. I shall listen to the Berlioz and sleep through the Stockhausen. Caroline will enjoy it, though."

Colonel Blackrock had barely heard of Stockhausen. His favorite composer was Elgar, although had Sousa not had the misfortune to have been foreign he would have run a close second. Nevertheless the remark gave him the lead for which he had been waiting. He coughed. "Her Majesty will be accompanying you?" He gave the question the very slightest suspicion of surprise.

The King fielded the question with a judicious straight answer. "Of course. Was there any reason why she shouldn't?"

"Well sir," Blackrock judged it best to be at his most formal, if not obsequious—he was never *quite* obsequious—"I had rather thought that in the light of yesterday's, ah, disappearance, we might be revising our plans for Her Majesty. Allow for what the union negotiators call 'a cooling-off period.' Is she seeing a doctor?"

"I have had a talk with Her Majesty." The King shifted in his seat. This was going to be difficult for him. He disliked unpleasantness even when it was as polite as he knew this was going to be. "And in the light of what she says I've decided to pursue a rather different attitude."

"How do you mean sir?"

"Well." The King began to doodle on his blotter. "I don't think my wife's entirely happy with her role."

Blackrock's voice had become very soft and he spoke slowly. "I'm sorry to hear that sir."

"And it seemed to me that perhaps we were all being, how shall I put it, unnecessarily constricting."

He stopped. Blackrock raised an eyebrow a bare millimeter. "Go on sir."

"She's a young, energetic, intelligent woman and she feels she's not being given enough to do. And on mature consideration I must say I'm bound to agree." The King said it firmly.

"With respect sir," Blackrock's voice betrayed a hint of weariness, "she's had two children in as many years. I'd hardly call that a life of leisure."

"She's had the children. I don't think there's any call for further pregnancies. Not for the time being."

"I don't wish to seem indelicate sir," Blackrock hesitated

briefly, "but you do still have only the one male heir. Should anything happen—"

The King cut him short. "I'm not saying there won't be more children in time. I'm simply pointing out that as far as breeding goes we've done our job for the time being." He had spoken crudely on purpose. They sat silently for a moment, before the King continued in a more muted tone. "Listen Blackrock," he said, "you know me well enough to understand that I'm not an advocate of women's lib, but the point is that when we've had queens in this country their husbands have carved out really quite important roles for themselves. They have been significant people in their own right, complementing their wives without ever attempting to usurp them. Wouldn't you agree?'

"You're thinking of Prince Albert and Prince Philip?"

"Yes," the King was quite animated now. "Just because Queen Caroline is a woman doesn't mean that she can't be like one of them. Otherwise I'm afraid she may end up like the other Queen Caroline."

"You're losing me sir," said Blackrock, fingering his moustache. "You mean George IV's wife?"

"Precisely."

"I don't understand why your wife, sir, should *not* comport herself in the same manner as George VI's queen, or his father's."

The King sighed and dropped the ballpoint with which he had been scribbling a caricature of Blackrock. It was a good one, making the courtier resemble a fox terrier, teeth bared, hackles up. "Because she's different for one thing. And because times have changed for another."

Blackrock shook his head. "Forgive me sir, but on the one hand you tell me you're afraid the Queen will turn out like the Queen Caroline who died a hundred and fifty years ago, and on the other you tell me times have changed. I don't understand."

The King put his hand to his head and passed his palm across his forehead and down his cheek as if he were wiping off the sweat from a hard chukka at polo. "If you can't beat them, join them," he said.

"What?" Blackrock asked.

"Oh nothing." He repeated the gesture, then braced himself, sitting more upright in the high-backed leather chair. "That walk yesterday," he said. "As we guessed, she went off to see these Friends of Man people and I'm afraid that she agreed to become their patron."

"That's unfortunate of course," Blackrock said, "but hardly irrevocable."

"Irrevocable is exactly what it is."

It was Blackrock's turn to put a hand to his head. He fingered his neck. During the North African campaign he had been hit there. Shell fragments. There was shrapnel still lodged in the flesh. He noticed it most in moments of stress.

"How so sir?"

"I mean that I have accepted the fact. Given her my consent."

"Is that wise sir?" The private secretary was dangerously still.

"Possibly not, but I had no alternative."

"I would have advised against it."

To himself the King wondered how Blackrock handled relations with his own wife. Lady Blackrock was a good inch taller than her husband, almost as broad as she was tall and much given to hats. He suspected that for all the little colonel's iron execution of his official duties he was less than forceful in the privacy of his own home.

"For once I would have had to reject your advice," he said, a little pompously. "Listen," he said, more gently, "you know what she's like. She's feeling frustrated and down in the mouth and she wants to get on and *do* something. I'm sure these people are perfectly harmless and she'll probably get bored of it all after a while. But if I don't let her have her head now and then we're going to be in trouble. You know what it's like. After all," and he allowed himself a mischievous twinkle, "you're a married man. Don't tell me you've never given a little ground when it's suited you."

Blackrock was not amused. "I hope you're right," he replied stiffly.

"I know you're worried about the future." The King eased

back into his chair. He sensed he was going to win this time, even though he knew the victory could be short-lived. "I think we've all been guilty of expecting the Queen to conform to our idea of how things should be done without really considering *her* ideas. New blood can be good for the dynasty. Look at the Mountbattens and the Saxe-Coburgs. I'm going to let the Queen have a much greater say in running her own affairs."

Blackrock fingered the scar on his neck and said nothing.

"We're a family firm," the King said, "or we're nothing."

"Quite," said Blackrock, and his disapproval hung in the air, like a guillotine. He particularly disliked that adage about the family firm. It made the Royal Family sound like tradesmen. For a moment the two of them stared at each other on the verge of a dangerous exchange, a real test of strength. But the moment passed. Blackrock shuffled his papers into a neat pile, returned them to his file and snapped it shut. Then he stood, smoothing his creaseless trousers. "Well," he said, and made a show of examining his watch, "time waits for no man." And he left, walking very stiffly, as unbending as one of the guardsmen beyond the palace railings.

CHAPTER

7

*P*ART OF Henderson's job was keeping in touch. The King and Queen were necessarily isolated from their people. They met them under stilted, unnatural circumstances. They never travelled on public transportation, they never went around the corner to buy an evening newspaper or dropped into the local pub for a pint and some gossip. They couldn't, even if they wanted to. Blackrock and the other courtiers were, by upbringing and temperament, just as aloof, preferring the cloistered environs of their clubs, the company of their own kind. They were in no way men of the people. In a formal sense the palace knew what was going on in the world, but Henderson was practically the only person there who knew at first hand.

Of all his contacts in Fleet Street he found Fred Crombie, the reporter who had tipped him off over the Panini pictures, the most reliable and the most perceptive. He lunched with him occasionally, usually in Rules', the plush Edwardian restaurant in Maiden Lane, long a favorite with palace press men. And equally often he met him for an early morning swim at the Royal Automobile Club in Pall Mall.

It was pure coincidence, as far as Henderson could tell, that shortly after the Queen's brief escape Crombie happened to remark:

"Queen all right, is she?"

"Fine. Why do you ask?"

"I dunno. Just wondered. Had a feeling she might be a bit, well, restless, you could say. My missus was peculiar after our second. Now that Her Maj has produced a son and heir, she may have a nasty sense of being redundant."

"I doubt it. There's plenty for her to do."

The Australian looked doubtful. "She's a real asset, you know. More than the King, if I'm any judge. She's too good to waste."

Privately Henderson agreed with Crombie's concern, and he was, not for the first time, impressed by his shrewdness. But all he said out loud was, "We won't waste her, don't worry."

Bunny warned me that little Colonel Blackrock had done a number when he told him about our patching things up. You'd think Blackrock would be pleased to see us so harmonious, but forget it. The fact is, he knows that he'd be the first head to roll in a revolution. He may have been a hero when he served under Montgomery at El Alamein, but he's running scared now for all that he cloaks it under a bogus concern for what he calls the national interest. Sure enough he asked to see me on what he, in his persnickety, affected style, described as a matter of some urgency, and then treated me to a long spiel about the "delicacy of our situation." I got the whole history of the second abdication at the grade school level. He seems to think that because the election results are running against the government we should be the ones concerned. The way he talks you'd think that the Conservative Party and we were the same. I told him I'd always been a Democrat and a liberal one at that, and he said they didn't want any of that nonsense here. Evidently he has a hot line to the Cabinet office, or so he would like me to think. He says that the abdication only happened because Bunny's parents wouldn't listen to the politicians. The politicians told them they would have to cut down on spending money so

*obviously and so frivolously and they just went on
spending until it became a scandal.
He doesn't seem to realize that the situation is completely
changed now. There is no suggestion that Bunny or I are
in any way corrupt, thank God. And we're not big
spenders. We're just trying to do a difficult job the best we
can. And in my book that means doing what I believe.
Blackrock didn't like that. "Oh," he said, all
self-importance, "so you think you know better than the
elected government of this country, do you? That's what
your mother and father-in-law thought." They thought
that because they'd been around so long and had such a
success with jubilees and all that crap they could do what
they liked. That's the gospel according to Blackrock, from
which he infers that I'm about to go the same route. After
a while he realized he just wasn't going to budge me and,
for once, I have Bunny's support, grudging and tentative
though it may be. So he finally went away with his tail
between his legs, muttering about subversives and militants
and reminding me that I had been warned. Quelle
nonsense!*

Blackrock had been at work in his ground floor office since the
unusually early hour of 6:00 A.M. He had not found it easy to
sleep, indeed he seldom did these days, and the King's pusillani-
mous attitude towards his wife had not made it any easier.

At 7:30 he called Cathcart. "Henry," he said. It was an open
line, unlike the one between him and the Cabinet office which
was scrambled. "Can you lunch?"

Cathcart, sitting up in bed with his morning's letters and a
heavy breakfast cup of strong French coffee, did not for a moment imagine that the invitation was social.

He reached over to the pad on the bedside table. "Can do," he
said after a moment's hesitation. "Cabinet meeting will be over
by half past twelve. I'd like to be in the House for question time.
We could have a quick bite at the club. That's if you want to
eat."

"I don't think either of us are too busy for an eating lunch."

Blackrock laughed drily. "I'll book for one o'clock."

"Anything you want prepared?" asked Cathcart.

Blackrock considered. He was a stickler for correct security precautions, but the only people likely to be listening into this conversation were the Security Services. He didn't believe either he or Henry had anything to fear from them. Rather the reverse. "Locke." he said. "You might bone up on the file."

"Will do," said Henry Cathcart.

"As your Majesty wishes." Eric Simpson was in the Queen's study, a foolscap pad on his knees. He was uncomfortable. "No, your Majesty. Of course, your Majesty." God knows what had come over her since the dramatic escape to the Friends of Man. Henderson had remarked to him that she was like someone on speed, but he hadn't known what this meant and was reluctant to ask for fear of being thought naive.

"Absolutely, your Majesty," he agreed, scribbling frantically, "I'll see to it at once." For two years he had served a quiet, seemingly introspective monarch and now he was suddenly confronted with this harridan. He was afraid he would not be able to stand the strain.

"And now," said Caroline, enjoying the effect she was having on Simpson, "the Women of the Year lunch. You recall that I cancelled the refusal?"

Simpson inclined his head.

"It's next week."

"Oh yes, ma'am. Maurice Henderson and I took the liberty of penning a few thoughts. I don't imagine you'll want to make a long speech." He rummaged in a box file at his feet and came up after a few seconds with some sheets of typed paper stapled together. With a flourish he handed it across the desk top. "Maurice says he'd like your OK as soon as possible so that he can have it Xeroxed for distribution."

"For what?" Queen Caroline glowered at him.

"He wants to distribute it to the press," he said, nervously. "They need copies so that they can report it."

"Don't they have shorthand?"

"Not much."

"Well it's not possible." Her mouth was set firm. Simpson wasn't sure how to handle this. Henderson, he sensed, would do a better job. On the other hand he had to try.

"With respect ma'am, we feel it helps to avoid any danger of misrepresentation."

"That's too bad," she said with a flash of anger. "They'll have to do the best they can. I don't approve of handing out advance copies. Anyway it's not going to work because I won't be speaking from a prepared text."

Simpson gaped.

"I've never used a text before and I don't intend starting now," she said.

"But you haven't made a televised speech before."

"Not since I've been Queen. But we had a debating society in college—"

"It's hardly the same thing."

Caroline reached across the desk for her cigarettes. "Listen," she said, acidly, "in the two years that I have been here as your Queen I have been allowed—and I mean *allowed*—to open my mouth in public on approximately three occasions. I was permitted to 'name this ship *Ark Royal*,' and it was considered in order for me to say 'I declare the Ideal Home Exhibition open.' I have been allowed to smile and say 'thank you' when presented with bouquets of flowers. And that is all, dammit." She lit up and Simpson noticed her hand was shaking. "I prefer to deliver my own speeches," she said, "and I like to speak from my own notes. So it's impossible for a final draft to be circulated to anyone, even if I approved of the idea. Which I don't."

Eric Simpson sat and looked at her and sighed.

"Oh dear," he said, "I don't think it's going to be awfully popular among the press."

The Queen laughed humorlessly. "Why not?" she inquired.

Simpson looked at his feet. "Well . . ." he ventured finally.

"I'll tell you why not," she interrupted. "You want to see what I'm going to say because you don't trust me. You haven't trusted me for one moment. Not one of you. Well, if you won't trust me, how in hell am I supposed to trust you? If I let you vet what I'm going to say you'll just trample over it with your damn platitudes until it's . . . pure popcorn."

"With respect, ma'am—"

"The hell with your respect. I don't want your respect. I'm not interested in your respect. I'm interested in your loyalty to me. I'm interested in your doing a job of work for me. Me, do you understand? Not the King, not Sir Evelyn Blackrock, not Maurice Henderson, but me. Are you man enough for that?"

Simpson didn't look man enough for anything. "It hadn't occurred to me that we weren't all working together," he said, lamely. "It's always been a family business here."

"Yes, of course," the Queen said, meaningfully. She looked at Simpson with weary distaste. "The deal is that I'll go along with this," she waved the speech written for her by Simpson and Henderson, "and because we're such a warm and fuzzy family business as everyone keeps reminding me," she smiled mirthlessly, "I'll be delighted to hear any suggestions from my loyal staff and colleagues. But I will not be writing out a formal speech for you to duplicate and circulate to the press or anybody else. And so, just for once, neither you nor anyone will know what I'm going to say. It will be a lovely surprise."

"I see," Simpson said wanly.

"I hope so," said Queen Caroline.

The club of which Sir Evelyn Blackrock and Henry Cathcart were members was always busy at lunch. The social life of its members had changed over the years. Gentlemen had once taken the evening meal in their clubs and had lunch elsewhere. Now it was the reverse. Worse still, many members charged their membership subscription to expenses or at least deducted it at tax time. And they brought in business acquaintances. Of all this Blackrock and Cathcart disapproved, no less because they recognized that the club's changing style was a reflection of the changes that had taken place in the country as a whole. Jack was now as good as his master, Cathcart would say, and what's more shared the same club. It was all a matter of profound regret. At the last annual meeting one of the younger members, a peer of the realm who should have known better, had brought up the idea of admitting lady members. Blackrock and Cathcart had scotched that one.

"Dorothy well?" Cathcart inquired, a confirmed bachelor and something of a misogynist.

"Yes, thank you."

"In the country?"

"Yes."

Cathcart had not exchanged more than the most banal civilities with Lady Blackrock for as long as he could remember, and he was wholly indifferent to her wellbeing. Nevertheless the two men always began their conversations like this. Not until they had gone through these beginnings and ordered their meal could they talk seriously. The wine was ordered with ritual care by Cathcart, who prided himself on his knowledge of claret. It arrived, was decanted, Cathcart raised his glass, inspected the contents, lowered it, sniffed, took a little in his mouth, swallowed, paused with an expression of intense concentration on his faintly porcine face, and then nodded at the wine steward. Blackrock had found these charades by turns amusing, then irritating, and now merely accepted it with reluctant boredom.

"Well, Evelyn," Cathcart said, wiping his lips with his napkin, "what's your problem exactly?"

"It's Apple Pie." Blackrock said.

His friend tore a roll in half and began to butter it.

"Apple Pie," he said, "dear, oh dear. I was afraid there might be trouble with her."

"She shows signs," Blackrock said, sipping his wine, "of doing what used to be called 'her own thing.'"

Cathcart smiled. "Well, your man Locke. I assume that's connected with Apple Pie?"

"Afraid so." Blackrock sipped at his consommé. "Is it bad?"

"Not especially." Cathcart frowned. "He was a bit of a hothead at university. President of the Marxist Society. Fined for throwing things at the South African Ambassador's car. More enthusiasm than intellect."

"That's when the file started?"

"Quite so."

"And postgraduate?"

"He did a doctorate somewhere or other. On Marcuse, naturally enough. At least he started a doctorate. He doesn't seem to have finished it."

"What then?"

"Left wing politics. He became secretary of the People's Revolutionary Crusade."

"I don't recall it."

"No reason why you should. Supremely silly organization. They put up a couple of parliamentary candidates—not Locke, he minded the office—and lost. That's about the size of it."

"Is that all there is?" Blackrock asked.

"Not exactly, no. The PRC suddenly closed up shop and reopened as an environmental group called the Friends of Man."

"I'm afraid we have heard from them," Blackrock said, "but I don't know enough yet. What's in the file?"

"Nothing much. Security boys lost interest. They've got other fish to fry. There are enough real troublemakers without worrying about the Julian Lockes of this world. But you haven't told me where Apple Pie fits into all this."

Blackrock told him as succinctly as possible. By the time he had finished they were on pudding, steamed treacle sponge, a club specialty from the chef who had learned it as a young man in the kitchens at Stratfield Saye in the pay of the Duke of Wellington.

"Hmmm," Cathcart said. "Interesting. Depressing."

"Do you think so?"

"It could be. Don't you think? There's scope for trouble all right."

"My feelings exactly," Blackrock agreed. He pushed the sponge, half-finished, to one side. "We could be lucky, but the whole ecology thing is so damned amorphous there's no telling where they'll crop up next. The way they interpret their brief they can produce a statement on anything they like."

"And Locke's stance is likely to be anti-Establishment," said Cathcart.

"With his track record I should have thought so."

"Oh dear." Cathcart finished his pudding, scraping treacle absent-mindedly from the surface of the plate.

They took their coffee in the smoking room, each accompanying it with a small cigar. Although it was unlikely anyone would be too interested in their conversation they chose a corner well away from their fellow members in a bay window overlooking St. James's.

"What would you suggest we do?" Blackrock asked.

"Tell her to put a stop to it."

"Not possible. Golden Eagle's feeling bad about her treatment. Thinks we've been too hard on her. He suggests that she'll respond to a lighter rein."

"Could he be right?"

The two men considered the question for awhile.

"I think not," Blackrock said, "though it's possible. I tried talking sense to her. Hopeless. There's no particular malice in her but she simply doesn't know the form. Why in God's name he couldn't marry a Percy or a Cavendish I shall never know."

"It's worrisome." Cathcart took a pull on his cigar and looked thoughtfully at his old friend. "Evelyn, there's something you ought to know. The Prime Minister's a little anxious about your charges over in Buck House." He paused. He did very much hope Evelyn's nerve would hold. If there was to be a choice between crown and country he knew where *his* loyalties lay; he could never be entirely sure about Blackrock.

"As well he might be."

"If there's an election in the next few weeks we're finished. And you know what that means."

"There isn't going to be an election in the next few weeks."

Cathcart pursed his lips and looked knowing. "If things get much worse we could be forced into it. They very nearly had to put the troops in two days ago in Glasgow."

"I hadn't heard." Blackrock frowned.

"It was kept out of the press. The local Scots Nat MP

managed to defuse the situation. But only for a while. There are people up there damn near starving. It's very volatile. If we aren't careful the whole shooting match is liable to blow up in our faces."

Blackrock knew it was true. The country, battered by a never ceasing round of inflation, strikes, unemployment, shortages of all kinds was in lately a sullen and unpredictable mood. For an increasing percentage of the people there was no logic left in life.

"Which is why," said Cathcart, "it is absolutely vital that you people keep your house in order."

"Quite," said Blackrock.

"In the meantime, do you want me to put someone on to the Friends of Man?"

"If it can be done discreetly."

"Will do," said Cathcart briskly. He looked at his watch. "I'd better be off. I'd be grateful if you kept me posted."

Blackrock left soon afterwards, chastened. He bore no malice to anyone, or so he had convinced himself. He would enjoy, he thought, a quiet retirement: a hunting, shooting, fishing sort of retirement, a time to cultivate his roses and read Trollope. But to do that there would have to be an England untainted by Marxism and Republicanism and all the other damned "isms" which corroded modern life.

He was afraid for the future. So many of his countrymen had become unrecognizable. There had been a time, in the war, when he would have sworn that the British working man was the finest product of God's creation. He remembered his sergeant-major, his batman, his driver, all the troopers under his command. They had been the salt of the earth. But what had happened to them? Worse still, what had happened to their children? He would never have guessed that the spirit of victory would have turned so sour in half a lifetime. He remembered a time when men had trusted one another, when chaps had obeyed orders unquestioningly because they had respect and trust, and they believed that those who were entitled to give orders did so for the greater good of the community as a whole.

Call it feudalism if you like, Blackrock thought as he stamped angrily across the park on his way back to the palace, call it paternalism or even, as some ignorant fools did, "fascism," it had made the world a better place. . . .

Like all royal private secretaries, Blackrock knew when to keep quiet and when to speak up. This time he decided to speak up, but softly.

"I thought you ought to know sir," he said, at his afternoon meeting with the King, "that Intelligence have a file on Julian Locke."

"Locke?" The King sounded preoccupied.

Blackrock reminded him.

"Is it bad?" the King asked.

"It's difficult to say."

"Try me." The King leaned back and crossed his legs, anticipating a long and complex report, but Blackrock's outline took no more than two minutes. "As I see it," he said, in conclusion, "the worst reading of the situation is that Locke is an unreformed revolutionary who has abandoned his revolutionary 'crusade' in order to use this environmental group as a cover. In other words, he's intent on making trouble and he'll disguise that by pleading high moral intentions, using the Queen to boost his respectability."

"So that we'd be lending our name to a disguised revolution."

"In a nutshell."

The King winced. "What's the *best* reading?" he asked.

"That Locke is a reformed character running a perfectly respectable, quite harmless 'Keep Britain Tidy' group."

"Harmless?"

"Quite."

"And susceptible to some pressure?"

Blackrock raised his eyebrows. "Sorry sir," he said, "not with you . . ."

"I mean," the King said, "that if my wife, as patron, tried to push him in certain directions, then he'd be pushable."

"I suppose so." Blackrock looked and sounded unconvinced.

"It depends on whether or not he's undergone a conversion."

"Yes," the King sighed. "Awkward."

"Very."

"All right." The King unfolded his legs and leaned forward so that he was in a writing position, bent over the desk. "What do you want me to do?"

"In an ideal world," Blackrock said, "I'd like you to persuade Her Majesty to abandon the idea altogether."

"It's not an ideal world," the King said with feeling.

"No." Sir Evelyn smiled with what was intended as sympathy but which came out looking more censorious, "I think the best thing would be to have a friendly talk to her and point out that there's a file on Locke and that naturally we're concerned about it."

"It's a bit lame."

"Yes sir."

"I'll talk to her."

"Good." Sir Evelyn rose to leave and then, as if it were a sudden and unimportant afterthought said, "Oh and by the way sir, Simpson and Henderson tell me that Queen Caroline is to speak at the Women of the Year luncheon after all."

The King said nothing but nodded at Blackrock to continue.

"I have no particular worry about that, sir, except that I understand that she says she won't speak from a text. She'll use only her own notes."

"Oh God," the King said involuntarily, and then as Blackrock looked at the ceiling in an elaborately stagey attempt to pretend he hadn't heard, he said softly, "I'll talk to her."

When he had gone the King pencilled fiercely on his memo pad: "Caroline: Locke. Women of Year." If that was the agenda for a single day of his wife's emancipation he was not looking forward to the rest of life. And now he had his weekly audience with the Prime Minister, a session for which he felt disturbingly ill-briefed. People often asked him if he wouldn't have preferred a more normal career; if he wouldn't have liked being a manufacturer, or a brain surgeon, or, more probably, a naval officer. He could never answer convincingly because he had never lived with the possibility of choice. There had never been options for him as there were for others, but at times like this he could reflect on the peculiarity of his existence. There wasn't another job like this anywhere, and he was consigned to it by the accident of birth. At the moment he almost regretted it.

He had no chance to talk to his wife until bedtime. That evening there was a movie screening in support of a children's charity, followed by dinner. The new film was a Hollywood musical, very bad. Afterwards the royal couple were obliged to smile and listen politely to their hosts and hostesses, picking at the bland caterers' food until departing as early as decently possible. It all meant that their conversation had to wait until after midnight.

"So," he said, tentatively, as she sat at her dressing table. "I hear you have had quite a time on your first day as a liberated Queen."

She turned to see if he were serious or simply teasing.

"Meaning?"

"The Women of the Year lunch. I've had Blackrock on my back over that."

"Oh for heaven's sakes." She stood and tossed her head angrily. "Who's in charge around here, us or the servants? It's just crazy."

"That's one of our cruellest paradoxes, my love. I've told you that. We are the servants *and* the served."

She sighed. "Listen. I have been asked to make a speech. I have accepted. Our staff here presents me with a speech they would like me to make. I decline to do that, but agree to read it and incorporate anything that I like. They then say they have to have an advance copy of what I have to say so that it can be circulated. I tell them that I don't speak from a written draft, just notes, so there's nothing to circulate. So there we are."

"Oh, Caroline." He looked very tired, beginning to show age and strain despite his fitness. Sometimes she wished he could take his job a little less seriously.

"Bunny," she said softly, "you've got to trust me."

He shrugged. "I don't understand what you want to say to this gathering that you don't want to tell us. I can only assume it's something we won't like."

"It's not that at all. It's a point of principle. I just don't see why everything I say should be vetted by some goddam committee—of men, by the way—before it's allowed through my lips."

They faced each other, breathing rather heavily. "Just promise me," he said, "you won't say anything . . . silly."

She smiled back. "I promise I won't say anything silly. I shall talk simple common sense."

"About what?"

"Oh Bunny," she shook her head, "I'm not sure I even know yet. You have to trust me."

"I want to," he said, "only it may not be as easy as it should. Security have a file on your friend Julian Locke."

She gasped, and put a hand to her head, instantly wary of a frameup. "What kind of file?"

"It's classified," the King said, "I'm not sure what's in it, exactly."

She frowned. "What do you mean, not sure? They must have told you?"

"Not in so many words, no."

She sat down heavily. "Let's get this straight," she said, "Blackrock tells you that the British Intelligence Services have a file on Julian, but he won't tell you what's in it."

"I didn't ask, Caroline. The details aren't important, it's quite enough to know that there's a file. He's a suspicious character, a potential enemy, not to be casually trusted as you seem ready to do."

"I don't even know what he's *supposed* to be guilty of, let alone whether he is. You can't condemn a man on hearsay."

"It's not hearsay," her husband said evenly, "our intelligence people know what they're doing. They wouldn't have a file on someone unless they had a jolly good reason for it."

"How do I know?"

He looked at her grimly. "You're just going to have to take my word for it."

*It's not going to work. It's not. Oh hell. Intelligence has a
file on Julian. What does that mean? And I guess British
Intelligence is no less reactionary than the CIA. I suppose
he smoked at a party or doesn't vote Conservative. What's
in their file on me?*
*That's not the point though. I like the guy and I believe in
what he's trying to do. I can trust him until there's reason
not to, if I'm careful.*
*And I feel I'm right about my speech, too. I want men and
women who are on the breadline in the slums of Glasgow
and Manchester to realize that we're on their side too. We
represent all the citizens of this country. I realize that I
can't push that one too far too soon, but I know I'm right
to insist that this speech is my business and mine alone.*

The Panini story had died. For this Maurice Henderson was
duly grateful. He had been apprehensive, but his own hard
work plus the buoyant popularity of the Queen and the rest of
the Royal Family had meant the most perfunctory coverage in
the British press. Even the Americans, apart from *Gossip Magazine* itself, had given the story a wide berth. Henry Knight could
easily enough have put some pressure on the U.S. papers, or
asked the President's press secretary to do it. Now as Henderson
lurked in the wings at the Women of the Year luncheon at the
Savoy Hotel, he reflected nervously on his good fortune.

It was, as far as his perception of women's liberation was
concerned, a dispiriting occasion. It seemed to him a hen party
from which men were rigorously excluded. Hence his own
lunch in a small private room wired for sound. From the River
Room, overlooking the Thames, there came a high-pitched babble in which no single voice could be distinguished. Henderson
liked women and thought his attitudes toward them were as
enlightened and egalitarian as anyone's, but he disliked then en
masse in situations like this, just as he disliked similar all-male
functions. That, however, was not the only reason for his
unease. He was worried about the Queen's speech.

As he toyed with his solitary lunch Henderson reflected that
in anyone else her independence of spirit would have been ad-

mirable. Indeed, in objective moments, he did admire it. Every day he or Blackrock or Simpson or the King himself had used a mixture of bluster, cajolery, threat and pleading to persuade her to do as they asked. She refused. On the way to the Savoy Henderson had tried once more. All she said was "You're as bad as my husband, Maurice," and then flashing that impossible smile, she added coquettishly, "and I had hoped that you, of all people, would understand."

Henderson pushed his baked Alaska to one side and consulted his watch. Time to go downstairs. He had agreed with the organizers that he could enter unobtrusively when the speeches began, and stand at the end of the room by the doorway. The speeches were being recorded but he wanted to see as well as hear, and he also wanted to be able to fend off any supplementaries or deal with any aftermath. Whatever happened he wanted Queen Caroline out of the place fast before she could ad lib. He bundled up his files and papers and began to walk to the River Room.

The woman in charge of the presentations was a television personality by the name of Anthea Waters, hostess of an opinionated and controversial weekly half hour entitled "Anthea Waters Says . . ." When Henderson took up his position by the door he saw that she and Caroline were engaged in an animated if somewhat one-sided conversation, Anthea Waters talking and the Queen listening. On the other side of the Queen, a Cabinet minister known to be fond of the bottle stared vacantly into space as the novelist on her right tried desperately to capture her interest.

Henderson's amused observations were interrupted by the banging of a gavel by the only other male present, the toastperson.

"Your Majesty, Your Excellencies, Madam Mayoress, Ladies, pray silence for your chairwoman, Ms. Anthea Waters." The television personality rose to her feet and adjusted the microphone. There was a sudden electronic whine which provoked a ripple of laughter and then she was into her stride, introducing herself and then the guests. This was a protracted ritual since there were many guests to be identified and each one was expected to say a few words. Finally Ms. Waters arrived at the moment for which all had been waiting.

"We are uniquely privileged," she said, "to have with us today a woman who has done more for the Royal Family than anyone since Willy Hamilton." This reference to a long-retired Labor MP who had made a life's work of criticizing the Royal Family brought a round of laughter and applause. "Not only is Her Majesty Queen Caroline the most queenly looking Queen you could hope to see—" Anthea Waters smiled down at her guest of honor, "she is also the most queenly human being." Henderson winced. "But one thing about her that makes her really fabulous in my book is that she's like the rest of us. No toffee-nosed royal mystique for her. As we all know from a certain Italian gentleman," Henderson's mouth dropped open, "this lady is what they used to call a woman of the world—whether she's Queen Caroline or plain Ms. Knight. We have one red-blooded lady in the palace who has sown her wild oats, and let me be the first to say "Good for you, your Majesty." She raised her glass with one hand and with her other urged the assembly to its feet. Accordingly the women of the year stood and drank to the Queen. It was difficult for Henderson to make out whether the prolonged cheers were enthusiastic or merely sympathetic, but they were certainly heartfelt. He could not see the Queen through the colorful mass of bobbing hats and waving hands.

It was some moments before the applause subsided. Then the toastmaster portentously introduced the Queen. She looked, thought Henderson, ravishing. She wore a two-piece suit in some expensive tweed, and she was hatless so that her exquisite blonde hair could be seen in all its beauty. Sean, who as the result of her patronage was considered the smartest hairdresser in London since Vidal Sassoon was a boy, had been to the palace that morning and had been clever enough to make it seem entirely natural and uncoiffed. Even Henderson was astute enough to realize that such naturalness came very expensive. The toastmaster adjusted the microphone fussily. The Queen was at least six inches taller than Waters. She pushed a nonexistent hair from her forehead and smiled with less than her usual radiance. Henderson felt a twinge of sympathy and realized that he was at least as nervous as she.

"Madam Chairman," she began, in her clear, slightly drawling New England accent, "fellow . . ." she paused as if searching for a suitable word, glanced knowingly at Ms. Waters and said hesitantly, "ladies," as if that was emphatically not the word she had in mind. The audience laughed, unsure of itself, and then, seeing the Queen's grin, recognized that this was an intended joke and laughed more, then burst into a round of applause while she stood there waiting, cool as a mint julep. "I may say," she continued, evidently encouraged by the applause, "that while I am moderately accustomed to public speaking I am not at all accustomed to being introduced as a red-blooded lady who's sown her wild oats. It's not that I'd necessarily quarrel with the accuracy of the description, it's just that I'm not entirely sure how my husband will take it." This time the laughter was entirely spontaneous. Henderson winced.

Unlike most of those present he was thinking in terms of tomorrow's newspaper headlines. Of his interview with Sir Evelyn Blackrock. Worse still with the King. He bit his lip and prayed there was no worse to come.

"Seriously," the Queen said, when the laughter had died down, "I appreciate your asking me here today and I'm glad to be here in such distinguished company. I'm also humbled to be among so many people who qualify as Women of the Year because of their own efforts, because of their own achievements and their own hard work, rather than because they happen to have married into the right family." There was some laughter here, coupled with that polite throat clearing noise that well-fed gatherings produce when they feel they are required to register dissent.

"I am mindful that I am a foreigner in this country," she said, and this time there were several cries of "shame, shame" and "no, no." She paused, smiled and said, "That wasn't meant as an appeal for sympathy. I'm very proud of being born an American, just as I am proud of being accepted into this great country and accepted here today." This produced stupendous round of applause. Maurice Henderson, praying for no more gaffes, had to concede that she might have been born to it. "But foreigner or not," she continued, "I was very impressed by Ms. Waters's references to our womanhood. After all, what does it matter that you're born British and I'm born American, that I'm a queen and that you, according to the constitution, are my subjects? What matters is that we're all women. Now I'm not going to make too much of those memoii which were just mentioned, except to admit that yes, I was a little hurt, that someone I was once fond of should have exploited a friendship for commercial gain." This provoked nervous applause and some cries of "hear, hear." Henderson's fingers remained crossed. "And I would like to agree that in this final quarter of the twentieth century, it's surely to goodness an absurd hypocrisy to pretend that young men and women don't engage in premarital relations. And I have to tell you that even if I had known when I was going out with Mr. Panini that I was one day going to be your Queen, I can't honestly say that I would have conducted myself otherwise against that wonderful day. And I challenge any of you to have done differently." More applause, cheers and some table thumping. Henderson did not join in.

Now the Queen, aware that she was winning, flashed that famous smile, beamed it on the four corners of the River Room so that it encompassed every listener, and said, "I did not prepare a detailed address today because I wanted my words to have spontaneity and meaning. I didn't intend to impose on you by saying simply the first thing that came into my head, but neither did I mean to subject you to platitudes which had been vetted by a committee and circulated to the newspapers before I'd even delivered my message to you." Henderson swallowed hard during this round of applause. He was very apprehensive. "So what I have to say is this." She paused and surveyed the audience to see that they were all with her. She need not have bothered; they were agog. "I am not, nor ever have been, a militant member of the feminist movement. But I do believe that women like you

and me, whatever our position in society, are morally bound—
morally bound—to demonstrate our equality and independence.
I for myself am aware that during the last two years, when I
have to admit I have been busy producing two children and
learning about the job, I've probably seemed a little docile. Well,
from now on I'm going to try to make queenship a little more
personal, and a little more meaningful. I'm going to do my best
to offer leadership to the women of this country, not in any
trival or purely dramatic way but by taking on assignments and
saying things and doing things which are not just part of the
ritual but are part of me. And I hope, therefore, that next time
you invite me here as your guest I'll be here not just because of
who I married but because of who I am. Thank you all very
much."

She sat down to the sort of standing ovation normally reserved for pop stars and political party leaders on the eve of
victory. It was an acclamation made more dazzling by the popping of flashguns. Photographers, all but one male, had been
allowed in as soon as the Queen's speech was over, and now they
clustered around the top table, elbowing each other out of the
way, pushing and jostling waiters and even guests. Henderson,
shaken by the speeches, took a moment to see what was going
on, but then hurried forward and tried to impose some disci-
pline. "Come on you chaps, let them breathe," he shouted angrily. "Stand back." The toastmaster was banging with his
gavel. Anthea Waters was on her feet calling for attention.
Guests, spurred on by the unruly example of the photographers,
surged forward in a wedge of scented silks and furs. Henderson
fought his way around to the toastmaster and headwaiter, who
were gesticulating, gavelling and flapping ineffectually. "For
God's sake take a grip and help me get her out of here," he
shouted above the babble. Then he bent down to the Queen's
level and said, "Come on. Time to go home." He was half-afraid
that she would refuse but she nodded quite happily, and somehow managed to push her chair back and stand. "You can't go,
I haven't thanked you," wailed Anthea Waters, the perspiration
under her caked makeup dotting her face in leaky bubbles.

"Consider me thanked," Caroline said, cupping her hands in a megaphone shape and then, surprisingly, giving the personality a quick kiss on the cheek. She allowed Maurice to take her by the elbow and propel her toward the exit while the toastmaster and two waiters cleared a path, and the paparazzi walked backwards, fighting every inch of the way, firing their cameras as if they were machine pistols and treading hard on any guest foolish enough to impede them. They didn't let up until they were down the stairs, across the foyer and into the waiting Rolls. Even then the more agile among the photographers ran alongside, shooting wildly. Henderson sat back hard while Caroline waved graciously. Only when they had turned into the Strand did she relax. "Oh damn," she said, "We left Isobel Coker behind."

"I'm sorry," Henderson said, "I wanted you out of there fast. There simply wasn't time to pick up Lady Coker."

"Poor Isobel." The Queen giggled. "She'll have to come on by bus."

"I'm sure she'll manage," Henderson said drily.

"Oh Maurice, don't be so stuffy." She grinned at him. "How was I?"

Henderson closed his eyes. "Well," he said, "don't expect to be popular at home."

"What do you mean, Maurice?" She looked at him, worried now, the euphoria erased completely, "I thought I was okay. Did I do something wrong?"

Ahead of them at the end of the Mall loomed Buckingham Palace, the Royal Standard hanging limp from the flagpole. The memorial to Queen Victoria seemed like a reproach, a symbol of nineteenth-century correctness admonishing this libertine successor to the great white queen. "A red-blooded lady who's sown her wild oats," said Henderson reprovingly, and very wearily.

"But Maurice!" The Queen glared at the press secretary. "*She* said that. Not me."

"Oh, be your age!" Henderson stared out at the park, bleak in its winter colors. He was very angry. "Can't you understand?

You're not a TV personality like Anthea Waters. If you were I grant it would have been a quite impressive debut. You made yourself sound like a tart, not the Queen of England."

The queen sat in stunned silence.

"If I were a tart," she said quietly, "I'd hardly be the first of your goddam English queens who was."

The car swung in through the gates and purred across the gravel through the central arch and into the courtyard. A footman opened the door and bowed. Caroline alighted, head high, nostrils dilated, looking straight ahead. She marched to the glass doors which were opened from within to admit her. Henderson watched her disappear with a mixture of admiration, grief and fury. Then he walked slowly to his office, bracing himself for the ordeal that was most surely to come. He wished he wasn't so fond of her. It made the impending witch hunt an extraordinarily gloomy prospect.

CHAPTER

$\mathscr{C}$AROLINE REALIZED, when she got to her room, that she was trembling. She had been enjoying herself until that boor Maurice Henderson had been so unnecessarily deflating. It had seemed to her that she had managed to mix candor and discretion with exemplary diplomacy. Her audience had been impressed, in fact they'd been better than impressed, but now Maurice Henderson had done his best to spoil it. Damn him. She kicked off her shoes, lit a cigarette and buzzed for Simpson.

"Well?" she asked brusquely, when he crept in apprehensively, appearing to hide his impotence behind a sheaf of papers.

"Well, ma'am?"

"Well? Have you had complaints from our miserable press secretary?"

"No ma'am." Simpson shifted his feet and looked at his papers.

"For God's sake don't 'ma'am' me," she snapped. "It was a success. A great success. Whatever anyone else may say, it was a triumph. I don't care what anyone else says, and neither must you."

"Quite," Simpson said, looking perplexed.

"Just remember," Caroline said, "I expect absolute loyalty. And Simpson?"

"Yes."

"Call Mr. Locke at the Friends of Man and tell him that it will be quite in order for him to release the news about my association with his organization. Tell him that he can link it with my speech this afternoon."

Simpson looked still more puzzled. "Your Majesty?" he asked.

"I told them I'd be a little less docile," she said, "and that in future I could be expected to pull my weight and take some initiatives. Have you got the picture, Simpson?"

"Yes, your Majesty."

He sidled out and as he shut the door Caroline said, sotto voce, "Little nurd. He'll have to go."

She wasn't sure whether to feel elated or depressed. She would never have mentioned sex if it had not been for the Waters woman. Now she had put it on the line, along with her promise to be her own woman. She would have to live up to that, and the world would be watching. Because it was a public promise witnessed by Britain's most prominent women, covered by the press, radio and TV, it would be impossible for the palace to place obvious restrictions on her. She had won, she began to recognize, a tactical victory, and it was that which had upset Henderson and would upset the others. They would accuse her of pulling a fast one whereas, in reality, she had said the first thing that had come into her head. The irony was that she hadn't really meant it. It put her and the palace guard into what were known, in the vernacular, as "adversary positions." She didn't want that. Not really. And she certainly didn't want to be in an adversary position as far as Bunny was concerned. "Oh God," she said, and lit another cigarette. She felt a long way from home and a long way from friends and on an impulse she picked up the phone and asked the switchboard operator to get her New York.

"Joanne," she said after the succession of transatlantic bleeps and clicks, "It's me. Caro."

A disbelieving silence and then a shriek of pleasure. "Caro. My gosh! How *are* you?"

"I'm fine. At least I think I'm fine."

"You don't sound fine," said Joanne, "have you been drinking?"

"I had some wine at lunch," she answered absentmindedly, "But come on, I didn't call you to talk about my drinking. Joanne can you come stay with us?"

"Are you insane? You know I can't do that."

Caroline sighed. "I'm asking you to stay."

"But you can't do that."

"Sure I can. I can ask who I like."

"Your husband hates me. He won't go for it. You know he won't."

"Listen Joanne. I'm serious . . . this line is awful. I can fix things at my end. Can you just make it over here? Even if it's only for a few days. Stay for a weekend."

"Caro," Joanne said, and the disbelief in her voice carried across the Atlantic, disembodied though it was, and struck chill in the mind of her listening friend, the Queen. "Caro, don't you know what's been happening here since I got on the Windsor shitlist? Don't you have any idea?"

"Joanne . . ." Caroline had no idea what she was talking about.

"Caro, I've been followed. My phone has been tapped, I think. The other day my passport expired and I got the runaround trying to get it renewed. Eliot Carnegie wanted to ask me to a White House dinner and their chief of protocol just flat out told him I was persona non grata. I'm telling you Caro, your people have put the word out. Lucky I have some real friends, but as far as one whole section of the community goes I've become a nonperson."

Caroline felt faint. "Why didn't you tell me?"

"Because that would only have made it worse. For both of us. I wanted you to have the chance to fit into your new . . . role . . . without my screwing it up."

"But you wrote . . . I mean when you replied to my letter . . . you could have said . . ." The Queen put a hand to her temple. "Joanne, this is unreal."

"Listen," Joanne spoke quickly. "I'm sure this call is tapped too. I'm only telling you this to make you realize how out of the question it is for me to try to come stay with you. I was pleased and frankly a little surprised to discover that we're going to be allowed to carry on a correspondence, even if it's censored. I don't expect any more than that."

The Queen bit her lip. Presumably it was Blackrock. Blackrock and his cronies. In their world a single request to the right man at the Grosvenor Square Embassy would fix it, no questions asked. And she was the Queen, for God's sake.

"Listen, Joanne, I had no idea this had been going on, and I'm not putting up with it. Everyone seems to have forgotten who I am. I make my own rules."

There was silence from New York.

"Joanne, do you understand? I am asking you for one weekend. And I'm telling you that the Queen of England has the right to ask whomever she wants to spend the weekend with her. So what do you say?"

Another pause. Then. "I hear you, honey, but I think you're wrong. I mean, I think you're taking an unnecessary risk. I think you may have forgotten what it's like out here in the cold real world."

Caroline wanted to throttle Blackrock. "Joanne, don't be ridiculous. I know what I'm doing." She was shouting now, her voice on the edge of breakdown. "Will you just get over here?"

"Oh Jesus, Caro. I have to stay with people in Saratoga Saturday . . . I—"

"Then cancel. Joanne, I *need* you."

A longer pause as the Queen's friend considered. Then, "All right, Caro. I'll take a Friday night flight out of Kennedy so I'll be there first thing Saturday. But I have to be back by lunchtime Monday."

"You're a pal, Joanne. We'll be at Windsor. I'll send a car."

"Oh God," Joanne said, "Windsor. Don't remind me. I prom-

ise I'll curb my natural exuberance and be as dull and respectable as those tight-assed Watermans."

"I don't want you to, Joanne. Just get here on Saturday. I'll
see you then."

She put the phone down. Maybe the palace switchboard listened in on her calls, and Bunny's for that matter, and reported
them to Blackrock. She had sometimes thought she was paranoid about Blackrock and the others, but there had been too
many occasions lately when his omniscience could only be explained by that sort of eavesdropping. Unless he was psychic
. . .

At the Friends of Man office Julian Locke put down the receiver of his telephone and went out to the reception area.

"You hear that, Sam?"

Samantha nodded. She had a mouth full of peanut brittle but
she had listened in on Simpson's call as usual.

"Funny," Julian said, "the press release is ready to go out
anyway, but what did he mean about linking it with her
speech?"

Samantha swallowed the peanut brittle. "He sounded as if he
was reading from a prepared statement. I doubt whether he
knew himself.'

"Is the *News-Standard* in yet?" He glanced at the pile of unopened papers and folders on Sam's desk.

"It came in five minutes ago." She pulled it out from a pile of
other journals. "Hang on," she said, and started to peruse it.
"Ah. Look, there's a picture of Her Maj, arriving at the Savoy.
'Queen Caroline and the Women of the Year,' it says. Nothing
much. Just a preliminary. It's too early for a report of the
speech."

Julian looked up at the clock. "Almost time for the news," he
said. "Let's see." Together they went back into the office and
Julian turned on his radio just in time for the four o'clock time
signal. The first item was a plane crash in the Channel Islands.
No hope of survivors. But the Queen came second. "In a frank
speech at the Women of the Year luncheon, Queen Caroline

163

referred to press reports of premarital sex between herself and another man. Queen Caroline, who recently gave birth to a second child, told guests at London's Savoy Hotel that it was 'an absurd hypocrisy to pretend that young men and women don't engage in premarital relations.' The Queen also said that she expected to be taking on a number of new and more personal assignments in the future. Later a Buckingham Palace spokesman declined to speculate on what these might be, though he agreed that further announcements could be expected in due course. Football, and Manchester United's two million pound signing from New York—" Locke snapped off the sound and whistled. "I think Hermann Schnabel's a prophet," he said. "Let's put that release out to the Press Association. Now."

That afternoon was the worst Maurice Henderson had experienced since joining royal service. As soon as he got into his office, Deborah brought him coffee and bad news. Sir Evelyn wanted him. "Instanter," Deborah said. "He seemed rather cross." There were messages to phone half a dozen friends and contacts in the media, and, she told him, the two assistant press secretaries were paralyzed by uncertainty and ignorance of the facts. They had no idea what was going on and were being bullied by a succession of journalists asking questions about the Queen's sex life.

"Silly woman," Henderson said to no one in particular. "How perfectly bloody to be so well intentioned."

First he summoned his two assistants, one a Nigerian diplomat on assignment from Lagos, the other a woman with a long record of service at court, an immaculate knowledge of protocol but a marked distaste for contemporary journalism and journalists.

"I'm afraid the Queen's speech wasn't quite as discreetly phrased as it might have been," he told them. "Don't attempt to deny it but don't try to put any gloss or explanation on it, either on or off the record. In fact, be as silent and noncommital as you can manage. And don't let them trap you into any indiscretions."

"What exactly did she say?" the Nigerian asked.

"I've asked for a transcript," Henderson said, "and you'll both have copies as soon as possible. What happened was that that terrible Anthea Waters brought up the Panini story and the Queen referred to it. She didn't actually say she slept with him but she made it quite clear that she had and she also managed to commit herself to the proposition that young people generally slept together before marriage. Then she gave a whole lot of guff about not being part of the ritual and wanting to give more of a lead."

"What does that mean?"

"God knows. If you must speculate, do it where no one can hear you. And if the press ask, then you'll just have to say 'no comment.' I know it's corny but for the moment I can't think of anything better. Sorry. Now I've got to see Colonel Blackrock. I'll be back in half an hour and until then I'm afraid you'll just have to do the best you can."

They left, visibly discomfited, while Henderson collected his thoughts for Blackrock.

The little colonel was ominously controlled. As usual he looked impossibly neat, his Gieves flannel suiting creased in knife edges, his hair newly cut by Trumpers, regimental tie immaculately knotted. Nothing out of place. Not a speck of dirt on the highly polished black brogues, not a suspicion of lint on the lapels. When Henderson entered he was sitting at his desk fingering the scar on his neck and reading a handwritten report marked "Confidential."

"Not good," he said without looking up, "not good at all."

"You heard?"

"I heard."

Henderson had no idea how the news had got to Blackrock so fast. Lady Coker perhaps. Telephone operators reporting incoming press calls. Contacts among the Women of the Year guests. Probably all three. He had long since ceased to be surprised by Blackrock's intelligence capability.

"Response?" Blackrock snapped.

"Noncommittal," said Henderson. "Say nothing and hope it'll go away."

"Not good enough."

"Do you have a better idea?"

Colonel Blackrock drew in his cheeks in a grimace, a gesture of supreme irritation. Henderson decided to take the offensive.

"When all's said and done," he ventured, "she was only saying what everyone knows. People sleep together. No one who thought about it would ever have believed she was a virgin bride."

"Don't be ridiculous. That's not the point, you know damn well it isn't."

"It is part of the point," Henderson persisted. "A lot of people will agree with her and be thoroughly sympathetic. They liked it at the Savoy."

"I don't give a damn whether the people at the Savoy liked it. Do you think the bishops will like it? Or the Purity Brigade? It may go down with a lot of trendy lefties but they're not our constituency. The whole object of this exercise is to consolidate our support among our own people. The minute you start propagating free love and immorality you lose the basis of your support. It's exactly what people couldn't take about Edward VIII. All those damn tarts at Fort Belvedere. The one thing this monarchy won't be able to survive is a nymphomaniac Queen shooting her mouth off all over the place about the joy of sex."

"That's a gross exaggeration—"

"It's how half the country'll see it. You wait. Not everyone at the Savoy thought it was so bloody marvelous."

Henderson thought of the hard-drinking Cabinet minister; she was a notorious killjoy and hard-liner who was inclined to advocate castration for sex offenders of all kinds. He would hazard a small bet that she was one of the first of Sir Evelyn's angry callers.

"It will be interesting to see what tomorrow's papers say," he said.

"I'm glad you think so."

"The mail over the Panini memoirs was heavily in our favor."

"That was before she started telling the whole world about it herself. Now the lid, which we so carefully lowered onto that can of worms, is off for good."

"Oh really!" Henderson, who had been the first to acknowledge the folly of the speech, was becoming increasingly exasperated by the intemperance of Blackrock's reaction. "What's done is done. It's still true that anything we say will only make it worse. We have to suffer in silence."

Blackrock snorted but he did not disagree. Instead, after appearing to give the matter a few moments of his most concentrated thought, he said, "And then there's all this ineffable nonsense about a more meaningful and personal role which is not just part of a ritual." He shot Henderson a balefully hostile glance. "I'm not exaggerating that part of her little talk am I?"

"No."

"Well what in hell is it supposed to mean?"

"Your guess is about as good as mine. I can see what she appears to be getting at but it wouldn't surprise me to find that she's not altogether clear herself."

"That *is* encouraging," Blackrock said with heavy sarcasm.

"Well what do *you* think?" Henderson challenged him.

"It sounds to me like an ultimatum. A declaration of war. I think she's decided that the whole shebang is too stuffy for her taste and she's going to put some life into it. I'm being charitable."

Henderson nodded uncomfortably. "She was doing so well," he said.

"Granted," Blackrock agreed, "and we've got to make sure she continues to do well. We have to bring her to heel."

"That's not going to be easy. It's rather out in the open after today."

"Hmm." Blackrock scratched his neck. The buzzer on his desk went off. He flicked the switch savagely. "I said I wasn't to be disturbed."

"I'm sorry Sir Evelyn . . . it's the Press Office for Mr. Henderson. They said it was most important."

Blackrock glanced across at Henderson and cocked an eyebrow. Henderson nodded. "Okay," he said, "put them on." The two men waited impatiently but silently as Henderson's number two told them that the Press Association had just telephoned. They wanted to check the story that the Queen was to be the new patron of the Friends of Man, the first of the series of new assignments referred to in this afternoon's speech at the Savoy Hotel.

"Thank you," said Henderson evenly. "I'll deal. Don't worry about it. And if anyone else wants to know, refer them to me."

Blackrock turned off the machine and clicked his tongue. "Dear me," he said, "awkward."

"Yes," Henderson said. "I'd better get back to my post and pour some oil on these troubled waters."

"Quite," Blackrock said. "A stalling operation. Only thing possible. But one thing you ought to do is run a rule over Master Locke. Explain to him that he can *not* go putting out stories to the press without checking with us first. Not protocol. No chance of doing that today, I suppose?"

"I have to handle the inquiries about the speech. I think that's the main priority."

"Right. But have a look at Locke. I'd value your opinion. Besides, if HMQ is going into business with him we'd better try and play ball. To start with at least."

Certain stories catch the national consciousness. They become universal talking points so that for a day or two no one seems to be thinking of anything else. The next morning the newspapers were full of the words of Queen Caroline:

"The Queen and Sex."

"I challenge you to have done differently"—Queen.

"Red-blooded lady who has sown her wild oats" admits Queen.

Even the more serious papers carried lengthy reports, though they affected to be responsible. The *Times*, *Guardian* and *Telegraph* concentrated on her comments on the role of Queen in particular and women in general. In the popular papers there were cartoons, none very imaginative. Opinions were divided.

The more sensational papers were, predictably, the most shrill, either hysterically enthusiastic about "the Queen who speaks her mind" or hostile toward "washing the dirty royal linen in public." Serious, informed comment was equivocal. "The Queen: a curious speech" was the headline on the *Times*'s editorial. "Members of the Royal Family," said the Thunderer, "are of course in a position of peculiar sensitivity, and their speeches, while properly exhortatory, must necessarily eschew the controversial. The Queen's reaction to the publication of Mr. Panini's reminiscences must excite sympathy by its candour. But the forthright expression of such views will also arouse apprehension among the monarchy's supporters. On occasion the crown's advisors have been properly criticised for urging a passive role which neglects the very real potential for leadership that still resides in the person of the monarch. Such a policy is mistaken. But that is not to say that the public interest would be best served by a wholesale rejection of such advice."

"Bullshit," said the Queen, reading it over breakfast.

Blackrock, on the other hand, allowed himself the first smile of real pleasure since he had originally heard of the speech. It was useful to belong to the same club as the editor of the *Times* even if it was not necessarily agreeable.

Everywhere the Queen was a subject of gossip. Comedians joked about her in pubs and in the first of the winter pantomimes. Professors of sociology defended her on radio talk shows, guardians of popular morality wrote hostile letters and took part in radio phone-ins. The Buckingham Palace telephone number, democratically listed in the A to D volume of the London telephone directory, was tied up around the clock, and extra staff had to be brought in to deal with the mail, much of it anonymous and some of it obscene. Mr. Panini was besieged in a friend's villa near Catanzaro, Calabria, but the British press wilted before the carrot-and-stick diplomacy of Maurice Henderson and once again made no financial offers. Still, for almost a week there was scarcely another topic of conversation in the country, from the most elegant Mayfair salon to the most insalubrious Glaswegian tenement. The nation was split into two camps: the disgusted and the good-for-hers.

In the palace itself, the mood was edgy and sullen. Blackrock remonstrated with the King and the King talked to the Queen. The Queen nodded and smiled and said that she had not brought up the matter of sex herself and would not have alluded to it but for Anthea Waters. Her words had been light and bantering and in keeping with the character of the occasion. No one in their right mind could possibly be offended by what she had actually said. It was true that she had been misrepresented but that was not her fault. Blame the press and study the transcript. As for what she had to say about women's liberation and her own role, that was unexceptionable and she stuck to it. She personally couldn't see what the fuss was about.

"That's the trouble," said Blackrock when the King reported to him. "If she did understand what the fuss was about I'd feel confident of her not putting her foot in it again. But she really doesn't understand how the British will react to things. That, with respect, sir, is what Henderson and I and the others are here to advise you on. The *Times* had a point."

The King, who knew of Blackrock's association with the editor of the *Times* was not much impressed by this. But he nodded sadly and asked his secretary to understand that he would continue to talk to his wife and to channel her ambitions and frustrations in such a way that they would be a positive benefit to everyone.

Privately he was not optimistic. Henderson continued to urge a middle way but even he was not sure whether there was one or whether he was being incorrigibly romantic and muddle-headed. Simpson sulked ineffectually. Lady Coker, who had been very put out at being abandoned after lunch in the Savoy, was correct but glacial. Tartan Macpherson informally asked all his subordinates to pay particular attention to the Queen and her movements and quietly set about augmenting the palace guard detail.

After a flurry of interest in the Friends of Man and their new patron, Julian Locke was alarmed to see the attention of the press focussing on the spicier debate about the Queen and sex.

Perhaps he had worked too hard and effectively to make his organization respectable. To the media it sounded like any other tweedy, well-intentioned environmental group and rated no more than a footnote.

Hermann Schnabel seemed delighted by this development. He had ceased his visits to the office after, on his way there one day, he had noticed an anonymous looking Ford Cortina illegally parked on a double yellow line not more than twenty yards from the front door. Walking straight past he returned half an hour later to find the car still there. The driver was at the wheel. That evening he telephoned Locke at home but was careful not to mention his name, simply to arrange an immediate meeting at a nearby pub.

"I may be wrong," he said when they met up in the saloon bar, "but I think their suspicions are aroused. For the time being at least, I do not want any connection made between the two of us. From now on we meet here, same time each week. Never telephone me from the office. Call box to call box, and only then if it's urgent. Here's the number and contact schedule. Understand?"

Julian was skeptical. "What makes you think they'll worry about us?" he asked. "Seems to me she's doing a far better job of getting herself into hot water than we could ever do. We're redundant if you ask me."

"I'm not asking you. It's imperative that you don't go too fast. You have to make her trust you. We can't depend on her continuing to make a fool of herself of her own accord. We have to push her. But we can't push her until she's ready. We have to win her confidence. Do you understand?"

"Alright, Hermann."

The little German leaned forward and took another swig of warm beer. "Now listen. This is what you do . . ."

CHAPTER

I had not expected anything like this overreaction to what
I said. You would think there were no real issues to discuss.
I know that the British press has an insane appetite for
trivia but this has gone far beyond the yellow press.
I do know that I am now irrevocably committed. I can't
go back. On the one hand that's very daunting and on the
other it's a great release. I'm torn between hope and fear,
but it's too late to go back. The paradox is that if I were
to say something profound no one would pay any
attention, whereas a trivial comment about sex sets the
world on its ears. I simply can not see that an episode like
this is going to put "our whole future at risk," which is
apparently the official line.
It should encourage people that the real left papers and
magazines like the Morning Star and the New
Statesman and even The Militant have played it down.
It's the right wingers, the Express and the Telegraph,
who are making an issue of it.
Joanne arrives tomorrow. I haven't felt so excited in years.
It's like the end of the semester. It seems ages since I saw

her. So much water under the bridge. Please God let it be a success.

JOANNE HOLLIS ground the cigarette into the ashtray in the arm of her seat and took off the headset on which she had been listening to the rock channel. The seat belt sign had just come on and the stewardesses were still scrambling to clear breakfast. The favorable winds had put them twenty minutes ahead of schedule.

From the window she saw the Thames winding through the center of London as they turned into their final descent. She rubbed her eyes, sore from lack of sleep. She didn't like flying and seldom slept on planes. In fact she really would have preferred the weekend in Saratoga Springs escorted by her man of the moment, but her friendship with Caroline went back a long way and though she was, she liked to think, almost wholly lacking in sentiment, it was a friendship she treasured. Caroline had sounded lonely and desperate, and when Joanne read the news reports she understood why. It was a damnfool speech to have made, but typical of her friend. She herself would only have made it in order to stir things up, stick a pin in the butt of the British Establishment. Caroline, she was afraid, probably said what she said because she believed it.

The pilot's voice came over the cabin announcing system reporting that the ground temperature at Heathrow was four degrees Celsius and that it was bright and sunny, with a fine day expected. Joanne did not associate London with fine sunny weather and she did not connect Windsor Castle with happiness or fun. Apart from seeing her old friend, it was likely to be one hell of a weekend.

She had just checked through passport control when a ground hostess in the red, white and blue of British Airways came over and asked her if she was Joanne Hollis. Joanne never knew how this sort of thing was arranged but she supposed that if you were Queen of England you could set up almost anything you wanted.

"If you'd care to come this way, madam," the girl said. "Your baggage is being taken care of, so there's no need to worry about customs." Joanne followed her as if in a trance. She felt as if she had just had dinner because there was still the taste of brandy in her mouth. She wondered if she should ask where they were going since they were walking miles along slow-moving escalators. Everyone else seemed to be walking in the opposite direction.

Finally, after an age of walking and after negotiating several doors marked "Private," they emerged into a quiet corner of the airport where a plain black limousine with no license plates was standing in front of a building which looked like a World War II Quonset hut. A chauffeur in grey livery was loading Joanne's suitcase into the trunk of the car, and as she approached he shut it quite gently and then held the back door open for her, bowing as he did. Joanne, not used to such obsequiousness, suppressed the urge to giggle and then saw there was someone else already in the car.

"Hey Caro," she exclaimed as she climbed in and fell into the fragrant dark leather upholstery. They embraced awkwardly then sat back and looked at one another. Both found that they were blinking back tears.

"It was a nice day," the Queen said, "so I thought I'd come myself. Bunny's away."

"God, Caro. Do you realize it's been more than two years?"

Caroline nodded and smiled very tightly. She didn't say anything for fear of sounding distraught. Instead she reached out and held Joanne's hand in hers.

"Gee it's good to see you," she said when she'd regained some composure. "I have so much to tell you. You've got to see the kids. They're adorable."

"I was so glad to hear about your son. I would have sent something, only . . ."

Caroline smiled, blinking. "That's all right. I understand. Everything's changed."

The big black car turned almost noiselessly onto the highway and swung across into the outside fast lane. Joanne felt a slight kick in the back as the driver pushed it quickly up to the legal maximum of seventy and beyond.

"Shouldn't you have some security?" Joanne asked. "There's not even a car with us, let alone a motorcycle or something."

"No one knows where I am," the Queen said. "I only told them this morning, half an hour before we left. Anyway we don't go in for security the way the President does. It's not British style. But that guy up in front with the driver isn't just there to open doors and carry bags around. He's one of Tartan's men and I know he's armed."

"Oh." Joanne leaned back. "Mind if I smoke? It's still about four in the morning by my clock."

"Sure go ahead. I'll join you."

They lit their cigarettes and looked at the bright early morning speeding past.

"You say your husband's away?"

"Yes."

"Not on my account, I hope."

The Queen laughed. "He said 'I may have to have her in the house but I don't have to see her.'"

"You didn't have to fight over me?"

The Queen crossed her legs. She was wearing slacks, camel brown, beautifully cut. On top she had a rust-colored yachting smock with a hood over a cowl neck sweater.

"Not much. Bunny's in a state of shock. He doesn't know how to handle the new me. He doesn't even know whether he likes it or not."

"And what is the new me?"

Caroline wrinkled her nose and thought for a moment. The castle loomed ahead, its round grey towers like a child's fort. Joanne shuddered involuntarily. The central heating was terrible and she found it impossible to erase the memories of the debacle of her last visit.

"The old me. Premarital me."

"I read about the speech."

Caroline grimaced. "Not popular," she said. "I'd do the same again though. It was fair and honest and quite charming and perfectly innocuous."

"Modesty was never a problem for you," Joanne said. She laughed. "By the way, I bought some piña colada mix. When did you last have a piña colada?"

"Oh, Trinidad or Tobago or someplace, way back in the seventies. God knows."

They were climbing the hill now, though the car still made no more noise than advertised. The clock *was* noisier than the engine . . .

"Where has he gone?" Joanne asked. She wasn't altogether pleased about this development. Not that she relished spending a weekend in the King's company, but she was none too happy about his sudden absence. She certainly didn't want to be instrumental in any marital breakup.

"Gone hunting," Caroline said, "way down in Devon. He's staying with friends. Be back tomorrow, after lunch."

"Just in time to see me," Joanne said, "I have to leave pretty soon after four."

The car passed through gateposts and into the private quarter of the castle, away from the milling crowds who passed through the state apartments and St. George's Chapel, rubbernecking at royalty and its surroundings. "He'll be pleased about that. I think he honestly was trying to avoid you. Still I dare say the two of you can manage to be civil to each other for an hour or so."

"I dare say," Joanne echoed as they drew up at the private entrance. "You sound like the Queen of England alright."

"Give me a break," the Queen said. "Let's go eat some breakfast. I'm starving. You've no idea how great it is to see you."

It was a good day. The King was not the only person absent. The staff, including Blackrock and Henderson, normally stayed in London unless there was urgent business to discuss. And nanny had been given the weekend off to see an ailing sister near Edinburgh. Her deputy was more easily dominated, so that the little princess sat and scribbled with crayons while the two old friends caught up on two years of gossip. All morning the two just sat and talked, recapturing their old intimacy at once. Just before lunch they invaded the kitchen and commandeered the blender to mash up ice and rum and piña colada mix. Cook and kitchen maids pretended to be shocked but were actually reluctantly impressed.

"How about riding after lunch?" Caroline asked as they sipped the freezing drink.

"I don't have any gear."

"Easy to fix. Would you like to? It's no problem."

"Sure."

They had always ridden together, all over the world. They had ridden to hounds in New Hampshire and Vermont, though they had both been quickly put off by the snobbery of the riders and the killing of the foxes. They had ridden camels in Morocco, unsuccessfully, and donkeys in Spain, and once, by incredible good fortune, they had managed a turn on two of the famous Lippizaner stallions at the Spanish Riding School in Vienna. Both were experienced and skillful. It would be a nice way to spend the afternoon.

"Then there are some people coming to supper." Caroline grinned at her friend's obvious displeasure at this. She had clearly been hoping the two of them would sit up together and recreate their adolescence. "It's okay," she said, "nothing formal. You won't have to change. That guy you recommended, Julian Locke, the eco-freak. Remember?"

"Yeah."

"He rang and said they were committed to putting out a statement on something or other at some meeting and it was important to meet because he didn't feel he should go out on a limb without my say-so."

Joanne nodded. "Sounds responsible."

"Oh, how I wish you'd say that to our friend Blackrock and to Bunny. They act as if Julian were a paid-up member of the Communist Party. In fact they've told me that our intelligence services have a file on him because he was once some sort of revolutionary. Ever since that ludicrous affair in seventy-nine when they discovered that old faggot who took care of the royal pictures was working for the Soviets, they've been pathological about that kind of thing."

"They think Locke's working for the Soviets?"

The Queen ruffled her daughter's hair as she cuddled up to her and stuck a thumb in her mouth. "Not in so many words. But . . . Oh I don't know. Seems to me the Queen isn't supposed to consort with anyone unless they were educated at Eton or Roedean and ride to hounds and have at least three thousand acres and a title which goes back to William the Conqueror and before. Not only are they boring, they're unbelievably unpatriotic. The only reason they're not working for the Soviets is it's not in their interests. Half of them have fortunes stashed in the vaults of Swiss banks. And they'd sure as hell give the White House and the Pentagon every goddam secret they could lay their hands on if they had a left-wing government here. Most of them are a bunch of jerks, they really are. These people Bunny's staying with this weekend for instance. *He* has no chin whatever, and *she* has a voice you could cut diamonds with."

"You can't blame them for that."

"Well maybe not, but their attitudes are just . . . medieval. Joanne, they don't just employ people down there, they *own* them. And they've done it for centuries. You may think the feudal system's dead, but I assure you it's not."

"I don't remember you being so radical," Joanne said with mild surprise.

"That's because I'm not back home," Caroline said angrily.

"You made your bed, kiddo," Joanne said with bleak resignation, "and I guess you're just going to have to lie in it."

"Thanks Joanne, thanks a bunch." She went to the table and picked up the jug of piña colada, emptied it into their glasses. "You know, you're right. It's my bed and I'll lie in it, but I'm damned if I'll lie back and think of England. I'm taking an active part in proceedings from now on in. From now on it's a whole new ballgame."

"I'll drink to that," Joanne said, "I just hope you know what you're doing."

For a moment Caroline looked deathly solemn. "I hope so too, Joanne," she said. Then after reflecting and still looking unusually serious, she said: "You know I keep a diary now?"

Joanne shook her head.

"If anything happens to me, Joanne, I want you to have that diary. I'm going to tell Maurice Henderson where it is because I think he's honest and trustworthy. So if anything ever happens he'll have it and he'll know to give it to you. You understand?"

"What do you mean, 'if anything happens to you.' What are you worried about?"

The Queen didn't answer. Instead she drew her little girl closer to her and kissed her hair. "Come on," she said. "It's one o'clock. Let's eat."

Julian Locke drove an old MG, one of the last made in Britain. It rattled and let in the rain, but it was noisy and raffish and had a certain style, and on a dry night like this one it brought back the fun of driving. He was wearing a heavy leather jacket, a woollen scarf and a tweed cap, and on his feet he had a pair of old RAF surplus flying boots. These were essential. At his side, Sam was equally swathed in leather and wool.

"Are you sure she asked me too?" Sam said for the tenth time that day.

"I've told you," Julian answered. "I want you to be there. I want it witnessed. I want Hermann to know that I've done what he asked. Because if it misfires we've blown it."

"Seems odd to me that she agreed." Sam sank her hands deeper into the pocket of her capacious greatcoat. She hated Julian's car and her nose was cold. It was a frivolous bourgeois car, typical of young men she used to know who went to hunt balls and Young Conservative conferences.

"I don't like this business," she complained. "I mean, we may not have been getting anywhere at the PRC but at least it was honest. This is a charade."

Julian pressed hard on the accelerator and flashed his lights at a squat, well-filled station wagon in front. It pulled over to the left and the MG throbbed past noisily.

"The end justifies the means," he said. Privately he was un-happy with the turn that things had taken, though for a marginally different reason. He had an uneasy feeling that it was getting too heavy.

"I think means matter too," Sam said, "I actually quite value integrity. Unlike you and Hermann." She had been a pupil of Schnabel's once and he had tried to seduce her. So for that matter had Julian. Both had been rebuffed. She found both of them sexually unattractive. For that matter she found most men sexually rather disgusting and the act itself much overrated. Sex, she had observed, tended to warp the judgment. Which was why she indulged in it as little as possible. And certainly not with anyone with whom she was professionally involved.

"I'm not looking forward to this," she said. "She's our enemy, silly bitch, and I don't think, to coin a phrase, that we should break bread with her."

"From what I saw of her," Julian said, raising his voice over the engine's rattling roar, "I don't think she is a silly bitch. In fact if she hadn't had the misfortune to fall in love with the King I think she'd be all right."

"Don't be soft," Sam said.

They relapsed into silence. Revolutionary they might be, dismissive of titles and inherited wealth, scornful about history and castles, but like anybody born and bred in England they could not avoid a certain sense of awe at confronting royalty in the flesh. It was a gut reaction and one which they would both have denied and yet it was nonetheless real for that.

"We made good time," Julian said as they drove up the street that circles the castle walls and leaves the royal borough of Windsor on its right. At the main gate they stopped and told the policeman who they were. He checked their names on a list, then radioed through to a colleague somewhere else. Finally he waved them on. Julian parked where he had been told in a small courtyard about a quarter of a mile inside the gates. As they got out, a door opened as if by remote control and a footman in royal livery stood waiting under a single bulb lamp.

"Uncanny," Julian said. "Do you ever feel you're being watched?"

"We're expected, that's all."

Inside, the footman took their coats and led them along a corridor to a paneled drawing room hung with French tapestries. A fire was burning but there was no one there. The footman retreated, closing the door behind him. A minute or so later a door on the far side of the room opened and Caroline and Joanne entered.

"Hi," the Queen said, moving swiftly across to shake hands with Julian. She introduced Joanne. He introduced Sam. Everyone shook hands. A nervous silence followed. Then Joanne said: "I met your friend Harry Smith at a party back home. In fact you could say that he and I brought you together."

For an alarming second Julian found himself groping, then he remembered Schnabel's American alias. "Of course," he said, "Harry mentioned it. I'm glad he spoke highly of us."

A footman eased into the room and took their orders for drinks. Sam and Julian both asked for sherry because they felt it was the proper drink. The Queen sensed this. "I bet you'd both hate sherry," she said. "Have some gin. Joanne and I are both going to have martinis. Isn't that right, Joanne?"

Joanne agreed, grinning. Joanne found her more like the old Caroline all the time.

"It's just the four of us," Caroline said. "The King's away till tomorrow. And since we have business to discuss it seemed silly to invite anyone else. I hope you don't mind."

The two guests said they didn't mind. Sam was angry to find herself so docile and overawed, yet she found it impossible to be otherwise. She had a terror of appearing uncouth.

It was not until they moved into a small private dining room full of family photographs and English land- and seascapes that the Queen raised the subject that was on all their minds.

"Julian, you indicated you had some sort of a problem you wanted to discuss."

"Er, yes." He finished his mouthful, using the pause to compose the crucial first sentence, "The thing is," he said, "that we're about to come under pressure to declare ourselves on a subject which may embarrass you. And I wanted to say that if it really was going to embarrass you very much then we would quite understand if you felt you wanted to resign."

"Are you asking me to resign, Julian?"

"Good heavens no." He managed to look genuinely scandalized at the very suggestion. "It's just that you could be placed in an awkward situation."

The Queen wiped her mouth with the damask napkin. "I never expected this to be a ritual appointment," she said. "If unpopular things have to be said then I'm not afraid of saying them. What exactly is it that I'm likely to find embarrassing?"

Julian took a deep breath. "As you know, we support the abolition of certain practices—whaling and tiger hunting for example. Well now the joint coordinating committee want us to widen the campaign."

"What's the problem? Seems sound to me."

Julian put down his knife and fork. "One of the problems is fox hunting," he said. "They want to know whether or not we support fox hunting. Which is why it's potentially embarrassing."

"I'll say," Joanne said. "Do you two know where His Majesty is today?"

Julian and Sam shook their heads. Joanne turned to her friend. "Better tell them, Caro."

The Queen took a gulp of wine. "He's dining with the Master of the Tavistock Foxhounds," she said, "after a day's hunting."

"Well," Sam broke into the uneasy silence that followed this revelation, "that wraps that up."

"Wraps what up?" The Queen looked surprised.

"You'll have to resign. Pity." Sam said it with a shade too much sarcasm, as if she had known all along that the Queen was simply playing games and had no stomach for a serious dedication to their cause.

Caroline colored. "Like hell," she said, "I don't agree with fox hunting. Not since that day with Mr. Stewart's Cheshire. Do you remember, Joanne?"

Joanne nodded, grimacing slightly. The hounds had killed on open ground within sight and earshot of the riders. The fox had broken from a coppice and run almost headlong into a couple of straggling hounds which had become separated from the van. Hunting's supporters always said that death at the end of the hunt was swift and merciful. To Joanne and Caroline this particular death had seemed slow and painful. Caroline still remembered the baying of the hounds and their savage competition for the quarry.

"I don't approve of fox hunting," Caroline repeated, "and if I'm going to give you my support I'll have to make that plain and public. I know my husband hunts. I disagree with that and he knows I do. Okay, so our disagreement has been private up until now, but that's going to change. We're all adult."

"Oh Caro, are you sure?" It seemed to Joanne that the Queen was jeopardizing her position for a trivial cause. She didn't like killing foxes for the hell of it but she wasn't going to the wall for it.

"I'm not happy about it," Julian said slowly, "for a number of reasons. First it's throwing you in at the deep end. If we had established your patronage of the Friends of Man as serious and knowledgeable and informed then we could afford to risk a stand on something as controversial among certain circles as this. But it's too early. It looks like a cheap publicity gimmick. More than that, I think it *is* something of a gimmick. If you're talking about whales and tigers, then that is significant. They're threatened with extinction. But that's just not true of foxes. No one suggests they're endangered. If people go on hunting them it's not going to upset any ecological balance or threaten any species. I don't think it says much for the moral makeup of the people who hunt, but that's not our business."

"Which is?" Joanne asked innocently.

"To stop man fucking up his environment. Sorry. But you know what I mean. Ever since man started to become industrialized he's been making the world a dirtier, more brutalized place. We build million-ton supertankers that devastate thousands of square miles of ocean when they run aground. We invest in nuclear power plants that contaminate the landscape and the people in it. We disfigure the countryside with strip mining, we kill and exploit the innocent and the poor so that we can lead comfortable lives. Now I'm not condoning fox hunting. I'm just saying that it comes low on my list of priorities. There are more important things for us to worry about. And if we seem to make it too important we diffuse our energies."

"And open up some quite nasty wounds," Sam put in.

"That's true," Julian agreed.

"So what do you propose doing?" Caroline asked. "I'm not resigning less than a month after I joined. And I don't care whether you condemn hunting, *I* condemn hunting." She pushed her plate away leaving half the food uneaten.

"I'm going to propose that even if we agree to try to stop fox hunting, we make it plain that it's low on our list," Julian said. "I'm not going to waste our resources fooling around the countryside laying aniseed trails for the dogs and all that rubbish. I shall suggest that we sign a general statement saying that we deplore the killing of animals under all circumstances, whether for sport or commercial gain, but that naturally we will concentrate our energies on those species which are genuinely at risk."

"Sounds okay," Caroline said. She felt under the table for the bell push and depressed it with her foot. Servants arrived almost at once and cleared the table. "You must understand I'm on your side, Julian," Caroline said, "and I'm prepared to be controversial if it's a cause I believe in."

"Well that's good to know," Julian said, "because we can't rule out controversy in the future. But I'm going to try to play this one down. I'll keep you posted. And please remember that if it does seem to be becoming embarrassing, we'll quite understand if you want out.'

"Right," Caroline said, favoring him with a soft and grateful smile, "I appreciate your concern, though I assure you it's quite unnecessary."

"He's a nice boy," Caroline said after Julian and Sam had gone, and they were sitting up in nightgowns. "I wish there were more people who bothered to consult and ask instead of pushing and shoving and always assuming the worst."

"Maybe," Joanne said, "but I'd watch him if I were you. There's something a little too plausible about him. And the girl's a hard little number."

"You may be right about her," Caroline said, "but he's okay. He could even be my type."

"Oh Caroline," Joanne said, pretending to be shocked.

"Two year itch. Even royalty can be tempted into a little fantasy now and again."

"Don't be facetious." Joanne stared at her friend, forcing her to meet her gaze. "Things are all right, aren't they?" she asked gravely. "Between you two?"

The Queen held her eyes locked on Joanne's, then let them fall to the carpet. "Things are all right," she said.

Outside in the MG it was bitterly cold. A freezing fog, fueled by the Thames, lay low over the highway and kept their speed to a steady thirty. The heater was not working and there were so many cracks and holes in the bodywork that it would have taken a wood-burning stove to make real inroads on the cold.

"Worked like a charm," Julian said. "You have to hand it to Hermann. He reads her like a book."

"I suppose so," Sam said, lighting them a pair of strong French cigarettes. "Not so sure about the girlfriend though. She didn't like me."

"Remember the phrase she used?" Julian smiled. "I'm prepared to be controversial if it's a cause I believe in! Now that's quite a promise. If we can get her to keep to that, we're home free."

"Hermann always said she'd do most of the work for us," Sam said, putting her feet up on the dashboard and watching the overhead lamps loom slowly out of the fog. "Looks as if he could be right. How *are* you going to handle the fox-hunting issue?"

"Oh, I made all that up. But the Queen came through her little test with flying colors. Now we have other plans for her." They drove in silence for a while. "Pity in a way. I rather like her, don't you?"

"Not specially," Sam said.

At ten-thirty the next morning, the Queen and Joanne attended matins in St. George's Chapel. Apart from the congregation there was a small crowd of tourists. Caroline smiled at them and as she said "Hello" and "Good morning" and "Have a good day" to them all, Joanne realized that she made a terrific Queen, if being one meant looking ravishing and being charming to the people. Inside the church they were conducted to the royal pew by the Dean himself, who led the service, preaching to them from the text at the beginning of the thirteenth chapter of Corinthians, "Though I speak with the tongues of men and of angels and have not charity, I am become as sounding brass or a tinkling cymbal."

After the service a slightly larger crowd applauded the two women. One or two offered hands to be shaken. One mother held up a baby to be kissed.

"Doesn't it feel strange?" Joanne asked as they retreated to the safety of the private quarters.

"You get used to it," Caroline said. "But it's strange all right. I worry about the kids. Bunny's had to put up with it all his life. It must warp you a little. We're going to have to send them away to school just to make sure they're not pestered."

"Sounds pretty gloomy," Joanne said.

"Sure. But what's the alternative? I could always abdicate I suppose, but that's a bad word round here." She laughed.

The King came back after lunch, limping. He had taken a fall on the hill above Exford, nothing serious, he said, the quack had checked him over and it was just bruising, right as rain in a couple of days and no one was to worry about it. He greeted Joanne courteously, kissed his wife, hugged his daughter and inspected his son, who was sleeping in the nursery. After these ceremonies he sat in front of the fire and talked amusingly about his weekend, describing the party, the weather, the country over which they had ridden. When Caroline described their weekend, Joanne added a few asides. He listened with little more than a grunt of abstracted interest until they got to the previous night's dinner.

"What?" he exclaimed with a fiercely disapproving expression. "You had him to supper *here?*"

"Yes."

"You know we don't do business on the weekends."

"You go hunting on the weekends. As a matter of fact it was about hunting that he wanted to talk."

"Oh?"

Joanne walked to a bookcase and pretended to study the collected works of Thackeray.

"As a matter of fact he wanted to warn me that there was a move to condemn fox hunting."

"Oh for God's sake."

"And he said he would understand perfectly if I wanted to resign rather than join in their condemnation."

"Very civil of him." The King spoke with irony. He was still angry but looked as if he might be prepared to be mollified. "So you've resigned?" he said.

"Of course I haven't resigned."

"Why ever not?" No hint of being mollified now.

"Because as you very well know I do not approve of fox hunting by you or anybody else and it would be hypocritical to pretend otherwise. I think you should give it up."

"Don't be absurd."

"It's no more absurd than expecting me to give up being patron of the Friends of Man."

"I've been hunting most of my life." He spoke quietly now. "My family have been hunting for the best part of a thousand years. And I'll not stop now because my wife doesn't hold with it."

"You said you'd stop if public opinion was against it."

"Public opinion, not my wife's opinion."

She sighed. "Let's not argue. It's been a good day so far."

"Until I got back you mean."

"No that's not what I mean. If it's any consolation, Julian has agreed to do everything he can to tone it down so that no nasty controversial fuss is made over your hobby. So you don't have to worry. We'll continue to concentrate on the threat to tigers and whales and not interfere with your 'sport.' I take it you don't approve of the wholesale extermination of whales and tigers?"

"Of course not. The trouble with people like Locke is that they simply don't understand about the balance of nature. Foxes are predators, they're ruthless killers themselves. Have you ever seen poultry after the fox has been among them? They don't kill to eat you know. They do it for fun."

"No reason for you to do the same."

"Now that is ridiculous. The killing is irrelevant."

"Then why do it?"

"Oh God!" he snapped. "I don't know what's the matter with you." He got up and walked out, slamming the door.

"Caroline," Joanne said, closing the copy of *Vanity Fair* which she had been pretending to read. "I don't think you handled that awfully well."

"No. I guess not. Oh Joanne. Am I doing the wrong thing?" Caroline slumped into a chair. "I'm trying to do what's best," she said, "I have a fantastic opportunity here for accomplishing something and yet they all seem to want me to behave like some kind of vegetable."

Joanne came and sat on the side of the chair and put her arm round her. "Don't go so fast. You're in too much of a hurry. Remember that time near Kitzbühel when you broke your leg? You tried to be hot stuff, taking a turn at God knows what speed, and all you got was a trip in the meatwagon and your leg in a cast. Same here. You'll get what you want, but not if you hurry it. For two years you've been the epitome of uxorial humility and obedience, and now suddenly you're telling the world about your sex life at society lunches in the West End and going after your husband's recreations in public. It's not surprising if he feels aggrieved."

"I suppose not." She pushed her hand through the long blonde hair. "You'll come over again, won't you? And we'll talk sometimes on the phone. It's been really good having you here again."

"Sure I will."

Joanne had to be at the airport in an hour, so she went up to pack, forgetting that it would have been done for her by one of the chambermaids. She was just wondering how much to tip when there was a knock on the door. It was the King. He was looking curiously vulnerable in baggy grey flannel trousers and an old V-neck sweater with a paisley ascot at the neck.

"Do you mind if I come in?" he asked.

"Sure." She continued to sit at the dressing table, brushing her hair even though it scarcely needed it.

"I'm sorry about just now."

"No need to be. I do know other married couples. Just because you're who you are doesn't stop the occasional blowup."

He sat down on the bed. "I wish it were just the occasional blowup as you put it, but I'm afraid it's more fundamental than that."

"Oh?" Joanne wasn't going to help him any more than she had to. She was Caroline's friend. The King was another matter.

"You've known her longer than I have. You probably know her better than I do. I wanted your advice."

"That's one hell of a thing for a husband to say about his wife."

"What?"

"That you think I know her better than you do."

He coughed, embarrassed. Poor guy, Joanne thought. Not really used to women for all that premarital publicity he used to enjoy.

"Do you love her?" she asked.

"Of course." He sounded confounded by the question.

"Really?"

"Yes, really." He said it as if it were a duty with which he faithfully complied rather than something spontaneous and inexplicable. He wasn't cold, she decided, just lacking in imagination.

"Well, try to understand her. Try to be sympathetic. She doesn't mean to make trouble."

The King made a despairing clicking noise through his teeth. "Couldn't you talk to her?"

"What would you want me to say?" She got up from the table

and put her hairbrushes into one of the pockets of her case.

"Just tell her not to be so . . . so headstrong."

"You'll never stop that. That's just Caroline. The best you can do is to get her to go a little more slowly and think of other people."

"Have you told her that?"

"The only person who can do that is you. I'll talk to her and I'll listen to her and I'll try to help her because she's my best and oldest friend. And I'm afraid that she needs all the help that she can get. But the least you as a loving husband can do is to offer her some understanding."

"Yes," the King said. He tugged unhappily at the bottom of his pullover. "Thank you," he said, "Caroline's very lucky to have you. I'm sorry I didn't realize before."

Joanne was touched by this uncharacteristic admission. "Forget it," she said, "just take care of her. And remember you're lucky to have her, crown or no crown."

This time she was driven to the airport alone in the back of the huge limousine. The Royal Family came to the door to see her off, King and Queen standing very close together. He held their daughter in his arms, waving her hand in the direction of the departing car. Caroline held the Prince. They looked, in the gathering dusk, like a model of the conventional nuclear family. Joanne waved out of the back window, then lit a cigarette and leaned back into the leather. "I warned her," she muttered to herself, "Jesus, we all warned her. And brother, were we ever right."

> *I feel drained and alone. It was absolutely wonderful having Joanne with me. It reminded me of a long time ago. There's so much between us that doesn't have to be said; we share so many assumptions, so much experience, we don't have to explain. There's no one else in the world like that. Not even Bunny. Sometimes Bunny least of all.*

The Andover stopped at the end of the runway, turned, and waited for takeoff clearance. Maurice Henderson tightened his seat belt and glanced across at Blackrock on the other side of the aisle. The private secretary was reading *Country Life*, though Henderson guessed it was not much more than a pretense. Blackrock disliked flying as much as he did, especially with the King at the controls. Air Commodore "Tiny" Follet would be sitting alongside in the copilot's seat, but from what Henderson had seen of him he would be as terrifying a pilot as His Majesty. And no help in a crisis. Tartan Macpherson had gone up the night before on the train. Sensible chap.

The plane's antiquated engines revved until the fuselage shook. People said that this contraption was intrinsically safer than a DC–10 but Henderson had his doubts. He shut his eyes and gripped the armrest as the Andover bucked along the runway and then rose heavily into the air. The Oxfordshire fields fell away beneath them, then the plane banked sharply to the left and climbed. Henderson's file slid off the seat beside him and fell to the floor.

"Damn" he said,

Blackrock looked up and grinned. "Cheer up" he said, "it's not that bad."

Henderson wasn't so sure. Superficially Blackrock was right. The flak over the Queen's speech had died down and she herself was proceeding on a happily even keel. She had managed to issue a few new royal warrants and cancel some old ones without giving undue offense. Her few public engagements had either been joint ones with the King or so mundane that a child of five could have managed them without mishap. But two peculiar happenings had dented Henderson's confidence. The first was his vetting of Julian Locke. Locke came to the palace, though he wasn't sure that was a wise move. He would have liked the opportunity to snoop around. The interview had passed off amicably enough. Locke was positively ingratiating. He said that he had approached the Queen quite out of the blue because she seemed a sympathetic person and because with a new organization he needed all the support he could get. He said he had been surprised that she accepted and very surprised indeed when she turned up at the office unexpectedly, but she seemed genuinely enthusiastic and anxious to help. He was very grateful to her. Henderson pointed out that the Royals were in a delicate and vulnerable position and he asked for Locke's assurance that he would not do anything to compromise her. Locke was immensely understanding, said that he had in fact raised the matter of fox hunting because he thought it was a potential problem. He had, he told Henderson, asked the Queen if she'd liked to reconsider her position and resign. But, he said, she wouldn't hear of it. Henderson did not know about this incident, though the Queen later confirmed it. No, there was nothing in what Locke said that gave cause for alarm. It was something about the man's style that worried him. A smoothness, an unctuousness, an excessive desire to please. To Henderson, who prided himself on an intuitive ability to read character at a glance, he seemed too good to be true: a natural con man.

The Andover levelled off a little above cloud level. Blackrock unbuckled his belt, stood up and stretched, smiled at Henderson and went forward to the flight deck, leaving him to his thoughts.

The second black spot had been a strange meeting the day before. The Queen had called him in to discuss a speech she was to make at a gala tea party to benefit the Albert Hall appeal. Henderson promised to get together some research notes on the Hall's history. She, for her part, promised to stick to them. "Roughly at least," she said. "Everyone tells me I mustn't rush my fences, so I'm being very sedate for a while. Not as sedate as before but still sedate."

He was about to take her leave when she became quite suspiciously portentous. "Maurice" she said, "I've told you before that I think of you as the most normal person in this place."

He was about to come back with some piece of badinage when he realized that that would be wrong. He was meant to shut up and listen. "I've also told you" she continued, "that I keep a diary. It's here." She walked to a small Joshua Reynolds portrait of a lady and lifted it from the wall. Underneath was a safe. "One or another of my predecessors was obviously security conscious. Old Queen Mary I expect. The key's here." She had gone back to her desk and opened a small drawer on the right hand side. "In fact I have two." She slipped one off the ring and handed it to Henderson. "You have one" she said, "then I'll feel happier. Now if anything happens to me I want you to pass the diary on to Joanne. Okay?"

"What do you mean? 'If anything happens'?" he asked.

"No questions, Maurice. Just promise."

"I promise."

"Fine" she said. "Now don't worry about it. It may never happen. But whatever you do, don't tell a soul."

He hadn't told anyone; nor would he, but it was a perplexing and worrying episode.

He smiled up at Blackrock as he came down the aisle from the flight deck.

"His nibs is in fine fettle" Blackrock said. "I'd put a stop to this flying nonsense except that it's almost the only time I see him really enjoying himself. We have to allow him that, don't you agree?"

"Absolutely."

"How are things?" Blackrock sounded casual, but Henderson knew Blackrock was never that. He knew too that Blackrock wanted to talk to him because he had insisted he come on this frankly routine trip to the regimental HQ of the Royal Regiment of Wales in Brecon. There was a Cardiff Rugby Club reception in the evening and a late afternoon walkabout, but nothing which couldn't have been handled perfectly adequately by one of his deputies or the very competent press officer from the Welsh Office.

"Fine."

Blackrock sat down. The only other passengers, the equerry and a valet were further back, out of earshot. Blackrock leaned across the aisle.

"Have you heard about last weekend?" he asked.

"What about last weekend?"

"Joanne Hollis was over. And Her Majesty asked Locke and his assistant to dinner on Saturday night. HM was off hunting."

"Oh." Henderson hadn't heard. He wondered if it was significant.

"What did you *really* make of Locke?" Blackrock asked. The two men had conferred after Henderson's informal vetting but Henderson had been fairly laconic. There was no point in voicing half-formed intuitions to Blackrock. Blackrock was far too demandingly incisive for that.

"I told you."

"No" Blackrock said, "that's just it. You didn't tell me. You were holding back. You didn't care for him but you haven't told me because you can't say why you don't like him."

"I admit," Henderson said, choosing his words carefully, "that he wasn't my type. But you can't hold that against him."

"*I* can," Blackrock said. "And what do you make of this secret meeting?"

"What do you mean secret?"

"No one was told. The Locke invitation was only issued after HM had left the country and after I'd left the building."

"How do you know?"

"Never mind that" Blackrock rasped irritably. "So you haven't heard anything?"

"No."

"I see." Blackrock grimaced. "Odd, wouldn't you say?"

"In what way?"

"She chooses a weekend when she knows HM is going to be away; then she invites her old friend Joanne over, and we know all about what happened with her on her last visit. And then she asks Locke and his sidekick over for a meal. I find that sinister."

"It may not look altogether straightforward. And it may not be what we'd prefer. But I think it's a bit strong to call it sinister."

"I don't like it."

"Maybe not. But I don't see what we can do."

"Leave it to me." Blackrock said, and returned to his *Country Life*.

Henderson did not think about the conversation again until they arrived at regimental HQ. There, brooding over the routine but still demanding business of dealing with the requests of Harlech Television, the South Wales *Echo*, and innumerable other newspapers of which he had never heard, he noticed Blackrock sidling up to the commanding officer. There was a muffled conversation, as the result of which Blackrock was led away. He reappeared ten minutes later looking pleased with himself. Henderson even thought he saw him wink.

That evening Caroline was on her own. Husband out again. Nanny back. Some people must think she has a glamorous life and yet here she was abandoned and alone, eating a solitary hamburger and watching a repeat of a very old Kojak on TV. She decided to write up her diary, which, recently, she had been neglecting.

Hell, I wish I knew why I feel like I do. I guess it's the result of being cut off from everyone and everything I'm used to, and seeing that just the merest, tiniest effort to be normal is treated with such an extraordinary mixture of hysteria and hostility and God knows what else. Here I sit on my own in front of the television in this echoing mausoleum of a palace and everywhere else in the world I feel there are people having fun. I'm even scared to go down to the nursery to watch the kids sleeping because I'll have to run the gauntlet of that damned nanny. Now I know that must seem ridiculous but it will at least give an idea of my state of mind.
The truth is I feel threatened—threatened by the gloomy buildings I have to call my home, threatened by the loveless life I lead, above all threatened by the palace zombies, Blackrock and his merry men. They seem dedicated to making me a zombie too. God knows, I don't mind a fight but these days I feel physically afraid of what the future holds for me.
Maybe I can make something out of Julian's Friends of Man. I'll try but it's not enough. Oh I know, I have the kids but I don't feel I have kids like other people have kids. I feel I have a little prince and a little princess, not a little son and a little daughter. Just like I feel I have a king for a husband not a human being. I don't mean that unkindly.

He's a sweet, kind, funny, lovable guy and I wish he were in magazines or banking.

I have to stop being self pitying. But I feel so desperately alone . . .

CHAPTER

"*I* TOLD you not to call me unless there was an emergency."
Hermann Schnabel spoke viciously. He wished he did not
have to delegate. And he was beginning to doubt Locke's effec-
tiveness. He was going soft. Losing his nerve. Maybe it had been
a mistake to turn him into a pseudorespectable conservationist.
It was affecting his brain and his morale.

"It *is* an emergency, Hermann." Julian was very flustered.
His pale complexion was beaded with sweat. He stirred the cup
of expresso coffee frenetically and kept peering through the
grimy glass of the coffee bar as if he thought he had been followed. "We've been burgled."

"Oh" Schnabel kept his voice down and did not allow it to
betray the slightest surprise or concern. "So why is that an
emergency?"

"Because they weren't looking for money."

"How do you know that?"

"They'd gone through the filing cabinets and the desk draw-
ers. There were five hundred pounds in the safe. They didn't
touch it."

"Sounds careless." Schnabel's mind was grappling with the

problem of the carelessness. It suggested amateurs. If so who? No amateur would want to look at the papers of an environmental action group.

"They were disturbed. Night watchman." Julian fingered his teaspoon.

"Have you called the police?"

"Not yet. I thought I'd better clear it with you first."

"Oh, you must certainly call the police," Hermann said. "It would seem most peculiar not to."

"But they haven't taken anything."

"As far as you can see. But that's not significant. You've got to report it. It's expected."

"Right." Julian seemed relieved.

"And" Schnabel said, "it would be correct to inform Mr. Henderson at Buckingham Palace."

"Oh?" Julian had been very wary of Henderson. He had seemed to him to have a dogged persistence which was alarming.

"He asked you not to do anything to compromise the Queen. He asked to be kept informed. I think he should be told about a burglary, particularly," Schnabel grinned meaningfully, "if they were after papers."

"I'm not with you."

"Listen. The only people who would expect to find anything interesting in your files are the palace and their allies. Your so-called burglary must have been organized by them. I think we should let them know that *we* know. And at the same time I think you should have a word with your patron. She wouldn't be very happy to think that her husband or her servants are acting like common thieves."

"That's mixing it, isn't it?" Julian rubbed at the plate glass which was misting up badly.

"Relax" Schnabel said. "And when you talk to your new friend try to sound hurt. This is a fine chance to seem aggrieved. It puts the ball in their court, don't you think? And now you'd better go before someone traces you here. Don't be afraid to start fighting back a little. She may be ready for it."

After Locke had gone, Hermann Schnabel sat in the little cafe pondering. It seemed to him that things were going nicely. This bungled burglary could prove a godsend. He had to conduct a seminar at 11:30 but on his way there he would call on a friend who had a friend on the magazine *Private Eye*. Despite its aging staff, the *Eye* continued with its traditions of speculative exposé. The magazine did not allow awkward gaps in evidence to interfere with its innuendoes. In this case the most they would do would be to check with Julian that there had been a burglary. Whatever inference they chose to draw from that was their own affair. Schnabel finished his coffee and paid his bill.

Their Majesties were visiting Buckinghamshire that day. Routine trip: general pressing of flesh, baring of gums, chance to meet the people, nothing to get excited about. That was the official, though more succinctly and politely expressed, view of the exercise, except that Tartan Macpherson was apprehensive.

"I canna put my finger on it precisely, Sir Evelyn" the policeman said, shortly before their scheduled time of departure, "but I'm not happy."

Blackrock pursed his lips. "Definite increase in the number of abusive letters and phone calls" he said, "but that's a very unsatisfactory barometer. Do you have any specific worries? Anything we should be looking out for?"

"There's a deal of local unemployment" said Macpherson, "racial disturbances too. I fancy we may be seeing a few demonstrations. But it's not that exactly, it's more by way of being a feeling. If you know what I mean."

Unfortunately Blackrock did know. Macpherson was a good police officer, hired by Blackrock himself. And, as Blackrock realized, he got most of his results through intuition. He had a superlative nose for trouble.

At first all went smoothly enough. The cavalcade drove easily through the hodgepodge of commuter towns twenty miles west of London and attracted nothing worse than a single badly aimed egg which spattered against the window of the limousine in which Blackrock and Tartan Macpherson were following their King and Queen. On the whole people seemed to love them. They wanted to touch, as they always had.

Things turned nasty after lunch, in a new town just outside High Wycombe. This was the scene of yet another walkabout, and the glass and concrete shopping district was jammed with crowds. They seemed loyal enough; there was a sea of Union Jacks, and a huge cheer erupted as the Royal Rolls-Royce drew up and King and Queen alighted. Behind them Blackrock and Macpherson glanced around, sniffing the atmosphere like gundogs.

"Something's wrong," Macpherson said suddenly.

Blackrock raised an eyebrow.

"They're all white," Macpherson said. "This place is sixty percent Sikh and not a turban in sight." He hurried off in search of authority and information while Blackrock moved swiftly to the fringe of the royal party, where he clung like a limpet. Even before Macpherson returned he knew that the Scot's sixth sense had not let him down. Above the happy noise of greeting which enveloped them he could hear another sound, the harsher frightening hubbub of a mob getting out of hand. Seconds later Macpherson returned.

"Bloody chaos" he announced sotto voce to the Private Secretary, "couple of thousand of them, totally inadequate barricades and a handful of inexperienced bobbies. They'll be all over us in a few minutes. We've got to get everyone into the cars."

On occasions like this there was an established drill: Act swiftly, ask questions later. It was Tartan Macpherson's job to protect the Royal Family and it was a condition of his employment that they cooperate with him. As soon as he and Blackrock gave the alarm, the royal party turned around and headed back to the cars at a brisk pace.

Except for the Queen.

She was talking to a group of schoolchildren, enjoying herself. "Hello. What's your name . . . Where do you come from . . . How nice . . . No, I left my crown at the palace . . ." When Henderson asked her to come back to the cars she shrugged him away. When he persisted she turned on him. "Leave me alone Maurice," she said crisply, "it's the most important day of their lives for these kids. You're spoiling it."

"It's an emergency, ma'am. There's a riot going on over there. The police can't control it. Orders." He took her by the elbow but she shook him off. Then, to his horror, she began to walk rapidly in the direction of the disturbances. The noise was now much greater and much more threatening. There was a crash of broken glass. Henderson hesitated, turned, and saw that everyone else was halfway back to the cars, also that the friendly patriotic crowd around them was beginning to dissolve.

What happened next was confused, although all newspapers carried reports and photographs of the incident the next day. As they turned the corner, the mob was on the point of breaking through the all too thin cordon of police, behind which a senior officer was yelling through a megaphone in a futile attempt to keep order. Caroline, whether from obstinacy, concern or a misguided sense of duty, approached the officer, took the megaphone from him and began to address the crowd herself. For a moment there was a stunned silence. Her voice seemed to hypnotize her audience, as she appealed for quiet and conciliation and a spirit of mutual understanding. But seconds later someone threw a rock through a store window. There was a roar of applause as the glass splintered, and the massed Sikhs surged forward chanting slogans in Urdu.

The thin blue line stretched, buckled and finally broke. A handful of police formed a circle around Henderson and the Queen and began to beat a passage back to the car. Mercifully the rioters were more interested in smashing storefronts and looting than they were in attacking the Queen, though there were moments when Henderson was afraid they would turn on them. It took twenty minutes for them to regain the relative safety of the cars, cordoned off by more lines of truncheon-wielding police, and then as suddenly as it had started the incident was over.

The cars and the police motorcycles swirled away into the Buckinghamshire countryside, deceptive in its peaceful verdure, and in the privacy of the leading Rolls the King turned to his wife, both of them grey-faced with anger and fright. "What the hell did you do that for?" he asked viciously.

*I just wanted to talk them down. If there have to be kings'
queens then it's got to be our job to listen to people's
complaints and try to do something about them. Bunny
doesn't see it like that. He keeps telling me about the
tightrope we walk. I've let the side down again, everyone is
angry—not one person concedes that I did the correct thing
and that running away was shirking their responsibility.
They aren't concerned for me as a person at all, they just
seem worried by the effect it's all going to have on "the
institution" and on "morale." Two policemen were badly
hurt, and a dozen or so Sikhs—though no one gives a
damn about them—and I think Macpherson blames me for
it. I wish my family and my friends understood that I'm
trying to do what's best.*

Henderson's friend, Crombie, was depressing.

"Our reader-reactions are three to one against," he told him.
"That dangerous. You've got to keep her under control. She's
losing all the goodwill she's built up in the last couple of years,
and it's so unnecessary."

Henderson nodded and wished he knew what to do.

"She may have been wrong," he said that evening as he entertained Blackrock with a stiff Scotch and soda in his modest
apartments in St. James's Palace, "but you can't help admiring
her. She was rather impressive."

"She flagrantly disobeyed Tartan and yourself," Blackrock
said testily. "Suppose she'd been hurt. What then, eh? I'm sorry
but rules are rules and they've got to be obeyed. I wish we could
persuade HM to get her into line."

"He's tried, hasn't he?"

"To what effect?" Blackrock asked rhetorically. "I'm afraid,
between you and me, that I'm beginning to question who wears
the pajamas in that particular household. Can't *you* have a word
with her? She seems to like you."

"I've tried in an oblique sort of way. I think you're more likely
to have some effect."

"She doesn't like me," Blackrock said with feeling. "Never

has. I've got a strong feeling that she regards me as an out and out enemy."

"Oh surely not." Henderson knew it was true but he was not going to admit it to Blackrock. Besides, there was something else he wanted to try out on the older man.

"The other half?" he asked. Blackrock consulted his watch. He had missed his usual train. There was time for another gin before the next one. "Don't mind if I do."

"By the way," Henderson said, fiddling with the ice bucket to disguise the seriousness of his remark. "I had a call from Locke after we got back from our trip. He was in rather a state. It appears they've been burgled."

"Who?" Blackrock did not seem in the least interested or concerned. Henderson began to revise his suspicions.

"The Friends of Man. Their office. People broke in last night and went through all the files. Funny."

"Why funny?" Blackrock took a silver cigarette case from an inside pocket and offered Henderson one. "Turkish," he said. "Only smoke after work." Henderson accepted one of the oval Abdullas.

"Just seems a funny place to work over. I can't see why anyone should want to know what's in the Friends of Man files."

"I shouldn't imagine it's very significant" Blackrock said, drawing on the pungent cigarette. "Probably just some amateur who didn't know where to look for the cash. If they have any cash."

Henderson frowned. "The police thought it was a professional job. They'd got in without damaging any locks, they'd left no prints. But they did leave £500 in the safe."

Blackrock raised his eyebrows. "Why did Locke call the police if nothing was taken?"

"He didn't," Henderson said. "The night watchman did."

"Very interesting" Blackrock said. "Do you have a theory? Or Locke?"

"Locke seems to be completely in the dark" Henderson said, "I don't know what he thinks. I just wondered, in view of what you said about Intelligence having a file on Locke, whether it could have been done by them. It just seemed a possibility . . ."

Blackrock considered quickly and made his mind up at once. In a conspiracy, especially one which goes wrong, however marginally, the fewer people involved the better. He was not going to tell Henderson anything about Cathcart ordering a search. But he knew Henderson suspected something and he realized that by not confirming those suspicions he might, paradoxically, reinforce them. He was not sure enough of the press secretary and so he simply drained his glass and said blandly, "I should have a word with Tartan. He's the security wallah. But I'd hardly think they'd make such a balls of a simple job. Must rush if I'm going to get that train." He allowed Henderson to help him on with his coat, picked up his briefcase and umbrella and walked to the door. "You must dine with us soon," he said, "I'll talk to my wife."

"I'd like that," Henderson said, letting him out.

It was a regular ritual, this intention to invite him to dinner. There was no real likelihood of Blackrock's putting the invitation into effect any more than there was a chance of Henderson's accepting, as both men well knew.

Henderson shut the door and wondered how many other little deceptions they were both practicing.

"I thought you'd better come over straightaway." Cathcart was not as composed as usual. He was pacing up and down his office rubbing the palms of his hands together. "I'm afraid our men were less than successful," he said.

Blackrock sat in the chair in front of the desk, watching his old friend moving restlessly from one side of the room to the other.

"They what?" he asked, deliberately. He was not accustomed to failure. When he had used the secure line at the Royal Regiment of Wales HQ in Brecon to set this escapade in motion he had not anticipated any mistakes. "It was a perfectly straightforward commission," he said icily, "are you telling me something went wrong?"

"Night watchman interrupted them," Cathcart said uncomfortably, "when they were half-finished."

"Oh, for God's sake." Blackrock fingered the war wound at his neck. "Did they get away? They surely didn't allow themselves to be caught?"

"Oh they got away, all right. But they didn't find a thing. Nothing. I'm afraid we may have been barking up the wrong tree."

"And because they neglected to take any of the money we now have the makings of a little Watergate." Blackrock bristled. It sounded like incompetence. Its potential repercussions alarmed him.

"They can't pin it on us, Evelyn." But Cathcart did not sound convinced.

"Have you told Potter?"

Cathcart sat down at the desk and tugged at his cuffs. He liked to display a half inch or so of starched white at each wrist. Blackrock was always surprised by his vanity. "No. Not yet." He glanced at his watch. "He'll see us in ten minutes. He wants to talk about this incident with the Sikhs."

Blackrock frowned.

"And," Cathcart continued, "there are one or two other things. Straws in the wind possibly, but unnerving all the same."

"Such as?"

"Police picked up a couple of Trots carrying bomb-making equipment in Doncaster two days ago. They found this." He passed over a grubby, Xeroxed paper, stapled together in one corner, badly typed. At the top of the first page the legend "Smash the System" was stenciled crudely. Underneath was the usual semiliterate call to arms of the revolutionary left. "I've circled the relevant paragraph," he said, and Blackrock skimmed the page until he got to the section ringed in emphatic, thick blue pencil.

"Rid the people of Fascist Royalty," it said in large letters. "Ever since the second abdication the British people have been duped by the capitalist propaganda machine into believing that the King and Queen are their friends. Crap! There is no change in the palace. The so-called King of England and his American whore are just the last in a line of tyrannical parasites who have bled this country white for thousands of years. They must be eliminated. Brothers and sisters on the left must campaign to have final abolition of the monarchy written into Labor's Manifesto for the next election. But if the bourgeois politicians won't do it, then the people must. Vermin must be exterminated."

Blackrock passed the paper back. "Do you take that sort of thing seriously?"

Cathcart grimaced. "No alternative. They had enough explosive in their little bomb factory to reduce Buck House to rubble. Not that I believe they'll do that, but—" He picked up another paper from his desk and passed it to the King's secretary, "take a gander at that. *If* Labor win next time round, this man will be in the Cabinet. And he's not the only one to think like that."

Blackrock glanced at the heading. It was a copy of a weekend speech made by the opposition spokesman on education, a leading member of the parliamentary left.

"Second page" Cathcart said, "I've circled that, too." Blackrock read, frowning with both concentration and anger. It was, in effect, a rerun of the revolutionary pamphlet, more moderately phrased: "Hereditary monarchy has no place in a socialist Britain. And so in the words of that great republican Oliver Cromwell I say to that anachronistic creature who sits on our anachronistic throne: 'You have sat too long here for any good you have been doing. Depart, I say, and let us have done with you. In the name of God, go!' "

"Ironic" said Blackrock, "that Cromwell should have used those words to democratically elected members of Parliament. If those bastards ever get rid of the monarchy we'll have a bloody dictatorship. And I mean bloody."

"I couldn't agree more, Evelyn." Cathcart smiled weakly, "But you see what I mean. There's a real danger of Labor going in to the election with a republican program. And they'll use any ammunition they can. Which is one reason the PM is worried." He looked at his watch again. "We'd better go and see him now," he said. "Doesn't do to keep the great man waiting."

The following Saturday, the Queen attended her first executive council meeting of the Friends of Man. She had told Julian that she wanted to be more than a figurehead, so he had agreed that in addition to their regular phone conversations she should sit in on the quarterly council meetings. These were largely formal. They were intended to evaluate progress and to agree on a rough program for the following three months. The Queen drove herself with only a detective for company.

The council was not well attended. Rear Admiral Fawcett, the Member of Sheen Central was there; and Lord Yetminster. The admiral was a backbench Tory MP of a kind widely believed extinct—all character and no brain. Lord Yetminster was his equivalent in the House of Lords, a rubicund backwoodsman with no malice in him whatever and no intelligence to speak of. There was also a severe looking woman, a don from Oxford; an intense young Labor MP; and a tweedy professor who was introduced to her as the country's leading expert on water. She sighed inwardly and told herself that even this was preferable to hunting and state occasions.

Julian began by reading the apologies for absence, a list longer than the list of those present. Sam, in tight jeans and boots with a tweed jacket and a 1950s Campaign for Nuclear Disarmament badge in the lapel, took the minutes.

After absences, Julian read a somewhat technical and inconclusive report of the previous three months. Caroline found her attention wandering until she heard him announcing her recruitment by the "Friends" as their patron. This he described as one of the most significant achievements of the society's brief life, not least because, he suggested, attempting a joke, "One of our principal aims is to preserve endangered species, so it seems only right that we should have a representative from one of the rarest and most endangered species left on earth, namely the hereditary monarchy." Caroline led the half-hearted laughter.

Eventually, the report, including a dry summary of the attempted break-in, was accepted and they moved to plans for the next quarter. "Now that our membership has topped ten thousand," Julian said, "it seems to me that it's time we began to use them more effectively. If we could mobilize even a tenth, we'd have a useful team for, say, picketing the Soviet Embassy." A discussion ensued about the desirability or otherwise of picketing and it was finally agreed that the term was misleading. Nothing violent would be done, and nothing which violated the law. Caroline breathed a sigh of relief. Despite her good resolutions, she had been shaken badly by recent events and she had no wish to get on the wrong side of the law too.

"The seal hunt" said one of the Eton-cropped women from Oxford. "What about the seal hunt?"

"What *about* the seal hunt, Dame Mary?" asked Julian.

"I propose that we do something about it. I mean, are we against killing wild animals or aren't we?"

Julian consulted his papers. "We've been through this before," he said, "and last time we agreed to support the call for a moratorium on the hunt which all the anti-seal hunt groups have been asking for since the mid-seventies. Do we want to go further than that?"

"I'd like to propose, one, that we send volunteers to try to stop the hunt if it takes place next year; and two, that we ask our new patron to intercede with the Canadian Prime Minister on his visit her in January."

"Is the Canadian Prime Minister coming in January?" Julian asked.

Caroline nodded. "I'd be happy to talk to him about it. I'll need a good briefing beforehand."

"We can arrange that" Julian said. He nodded at Sam to make sure that she noted it in the minutes.

The meeting adjourned at 6:30 and it was obviously expected that she would leave first. The thought of Buckingham Palace with nobody in it but servants and sleeping children filled her with gloom. "Saturday night and nowhere to go" she thought to herself. Aloud she said. "I'd like a word with Julian on his own if that's all right, so feel free to just go on home. I'd much rather we had as little protocol here as possible. As far as I'm concerned on this council we're all equal." People murmured approvingly and began to shuffle out. Sam said "Do you mind if I knock off too? I have a date."

Julian looked inquiringly at Caroline, who shook her head.

"I won't need a witness" she said, smiling.

After Sam had left, Caroline went to the window and looked out into the street below. Her car, an unremarkable Triumph Stag sportscar, was still parked across the street with the detective at the wheel. When she turned around, Julian was sitting down, looking expectant.

"Well?" he said, "Don't tell me you don't want to resign over the stag-hunting issue?"

"No" she said, shaking her head, "I just wondered if you were doing anything tonight?"

He swallowed hard and said nothing. The question had obviously surprised him.

"Oh, I'm sorry" Caroline said. She realized, self-pityingly, that it must be alarming for a young man to be asked out by the Queen of England. Worse, Julian was probably her junior, if only by a couple of years.

"I'm sorry" she said. "It was just a thought. You see my husband is away until tomorrow and I particularly wanted to go and see *Confederates*. It's on at the Plaza. I could go on my own, but I'm not awfully keen on going without company." She paused. "I could ask the detective to come and see it, but I'm not sure we have that much in common." She smiled sympathetically at Julian's astonishment.

"Oh well, just a thought" she said, wanly. She picked up her handbag. "We'll be in touch then."

At last Julian managed to get words out. "No, no . . ." he said. "Hang on. Of course . . . I'd be delighted. I haven't seen it and I haven't got anything on but . . . I mean . . . should you? I mean are you allowed to go walking into cinemas just like that?"

"Movies are easy" she said, brightening. "People have been slipping out of Buckingham Palace to take in a movie since the first talkies." She laughed. "If you really want to do it you'll have to get the tickets—I'll pay you later—and then I'll meet you in the foyer just before the lights go out. You'd better get three tickets. The detective will have to come but he's very discreet. He'll sit a few rows away and pretend he's with someone else."

She looked at his expression and laughed. "Don't look so scandalized. I won't be recognized in the dark. I'll wear a head-scarf and glasses if you insist. And we're just going to a movie, not a speakeasy. Do you want to do it?"

"Of course I do. I'd be delighted. Really."

"Great. I'll see you in the foyer of the Plaza just two minutes before the show starts. Okay?"

"Okay."

And before he could reconsider she was out of the door and tripping downstairs feeling deliciously, though quite innocently, bad.

It was an enjoyable film, only loosely based on the book of the same name about Stonewall Jackson's campaign in the American Civil War. The detective, a sound, naturally taciturn Londoner named Angell, did not betray the slightest surprise at the outing. One of the palace drivers took the Stag to the theater. The Queen and Angell went into the foyer where Julian waited with the tickets. Angell took his and melted into the background until the picture was finished. Caroline and Julian hardly had time to exchange words. She made him buy her popcorn as they went in, though she insisted on paying for the tickets. Afterward she said, "Julian, that was terrific. Thanks a million. I'd offer you dinner but I guess if I did that I'd be pushing my luck. I'll call you soon." And with a breezy wave, she was out of the door, down the steps into the car and away up the Haymarket, leaving him more nearly in love with her than he had been before.

It was approaching Christmas. One night late in November, Caroline switched on the traditional lights in Regent Street. She took little Lizzie and, as a concession to the Christmas spirit, included nanny on the trip. None of them saw the police hustling away the anti-royalist demonstrators, and there were loyalists enough to make enthusiastic audience. There was a special cheer for the little princess.

She shopped at Harrods and Hamleys and made a lightning dash to New York to raid Bloomingdale's and F.A.O. Schwarz's. She made plans for the festivities at Sandringham, supervised the ordering of crystallized fruits and peaches in cognac from Fortnums, signed Christmas cards, attended an ecumenical carol service at Westminster Cathedral along with the Anglican Archbishop and the Catholic Cardinal and the Greek Orthodox Patriarch. From time to time she talked to Julian on the telephone but there were no more excursions to the movies because the King had not been away. In fact he canceled one weekend trip and, briefly, Caroline wondered if Detective Constable Angell had spilled the beans.

Her husband was loving and solicitous as he always was when she was good. And, faute de mieux, she was very good indeed through Advent. There seemed no temptation to be otherwise. For a time it was almost as if she had expunged the desire to shake off her traces and assert herself. In fact she was so good she almost believed it herself. Even Blackrock favored her with the ghost of a smile.

The best news of all was that her parents were coming to Sandringham for the festivities. She had neglected them shamefully during the last few months. They had flown over briefly for the christening, but during the months of postnatal crisis through which she had been passing she had almost ignored them. Occasionally she spoke to her mother on the telephone but she never hinted that anything was other than "Just fine, mom, just fine. Lizzie's teething, and Arthur's put on another five ounces and he has ears just like Bunny's. And Bunny sends his love. Yes, he's fine mom, just fine."

Joanne would not be coming for Christmas but there were plans for the New Year and possibly a summer trip when Bunny went salmon fishing in Iceland. The King would probably never forgive Joanne for the unspeakable lapse of taste after dinner during charades, but he had been favorably impressed by her last brief weekend, despite the supper meeting with Julian and Sam. He thought Joanne had a good effect on his wife. She had cheered her up, at least.

"She needs a friend" he said to Blackrock one day in an unusual moment of near-intimacy. The little colonel had shrugged and made a noncommittal humming sound and the King had left it at that. Blackrock had his value, indeed he was indispensable, but he was not exactly a marriage counselor.

The coming of Christmas did not lull Blackrock, and although he was passably satisfied with the Queen there was one small blot which upset him. Just as he was getting over the bungled burglary at the Friends of Man, a paragraph appeared in *Private Eye* magazine. Blackrock did not take *Private Eye* on principle: it was scurrilous, mischievous and inimical to all he held most dear. Cathcart read it avidly and it was Cathcart who showed him the offending paragraph. It was quite short and reported simply that a person or persons unknown had broken into the offices of the Friends of Man (secretary: "former revolutionary Julian Locke") and gone through the files leaving behind a "sum not unadjacent to £500. It is an open secret" continued the *Eye* "that diminutive palace mastermind Sir Evelyn Blackrock was not amused when the First Lady agreed to patronize Julian's eco-freaks. Like other palace bureaucrats the gnomelike colonel is believed to have contacts not a million miles from Military Intelligence. But he is not helping police with their enquiries. For further news of life in Buck House, watch this space."

"Very unfortunate" Cathcart said, as they sat in their usual corner at the club. "Very."

"But no one believes anything they read in *that* magazine." Sir Evelyn looked down on the traffic in St. James's as if he could summon up twelve good men and true who would vouch for the truth of this immediately.

"I wish I could agree. Look what happened to Goldsmith."

"That's quite different. We're talking about the Royal Family."

Cathcart frowned. "Apple Pie is exactly the sort of person the

Eye would like to start a campaign over. And once they get hold of an idea they don't let go of it. If they believe there is a rift at court they'll latch onto it like terriers."

"It seems incredible your people didn't find anything at that office," Blackrock said accusingly. "Couldn't they go back and have another try?"

"They'd turned the place upside down" Cathcart replied, whispering, "and found nothing. It would be criminal folly to send them back."

"What about Locke's flat?"

"You must be joking. It was a shrewd move of Locke's, tipping off the *Eye* like that. It means you have to go carefully."

"I always go carefully" Blackrock said testily. He was not accustomed to receive advice. His business was giving it.

"That may not be enough this time." Cathcart's voice became ingratiatingly silky, and Blackrock's heart sank. He knew that tone of old. It meant bad news. "PM had a visit from the Leader of the Opposition. Courtesy call, in the main. They get on surprisingly well together despite what you read in the press. Entrenous, he's responding quite well to old Potter's continuing appeal to his patriotism. He doesn't want an election when the economy and everything else is in such a bloody awful mess. If he's brought in with a big majority he'll be forced into God knows what kind of left wing nonsense. The tail will be wagging the dog. He knows that."

I've always thought him extraordinarily wet" Blackrock said with feeling.

Cathcart glanced at him sharply. "Yes. Well" he said. "Just now he's being remarkably cooperative. But . . ." he lowered his voice, "He says he may not be able to hold out against the party over the monarchy. He personally is perfectly happy to keep your people on provided they stick to the terms of our arrangement. Which on the whole is happening. But his rank and file evidently think otherwise. He says they may have to go republican."

"I doubt that would be wise of them," Blackrock said. "The latest polls are still enthusiastic."

"Not as good as they were." Cathcart poured another cup of coffee. "You can't expect people to like the look of the King and Queen when there's fuel rationing and scarcely enough to eat. I agree there are probably more people "for" than "agin," but an election campaign which zones in hard on inherited wealth, privilege and all the rest is going to be pretty persuasive in the context of the austerity we're enduring at the moment. And there's no sign of our turning any corners in that respect. Rather the reverse."

"And what would Potter do?"

"He'll fight it of course" Cathcart said. "He's certainly not going to abandon them. King and country is what the Conservatives are all about. But I don't think people regard them as indivisible like they used to. You can love your country without loving your King. If you follow me?"

"Perfectly."

"So." Cathcart sounded rather lame, "if they're going to be an election issue they must do as we say. And if there's any question of their losing us the election, well," he smiled diffidently, "who can tell? The PM is anxious to win. So are we all, aren't we?" He smiled again, more menacing this time . . . .

Henry and Rose Knight came to Sandringham by train after staying a couple of days at the Connaught in London to catch up on old friends and acquaintances. These had, inevitably, multiplied since their daughter became Queen, but several were longstanding friends—influential men of substance and connection. Henry valued their views and appreciated their advice. One of the world's great listeners, he remembered what he heard and he knew how to act on it.

Caroline came to the little Norfolk station to greet them herself. Arthur was at the house with nanny but she had Lizzie in the back of the Land Rover. Another Rover followed with a driver and detective, ostensibly to carry her parents' bags but actually a concession to an urgent prime ministerial plea for greater security. The Irish Republicans had carried out a series of daring raids and murders, and there had been, quite unexpectedly, a return to the half-forgotten practice of aircraft hijacking. Authorities everywhere had grown lax, and now had to tighten up. As always in this season of goodwill there was an increase in the number of threats. Every newspaper office, television station, government department and foreign embassy was burdened with them, and the palace was no exception. It was a full-time job to know which were the work of cranks and which were to be taken seriously, and Tartan and his men were concerned about some of the phone calls and letters. One or two, anonymous as usual, accused the Queen of being a "niggerlover" and threatened violence. Hence the escorts, and armed police on motorcycles positioned in unobtrusive turnoffs along the route of every royal drive, even one as short and routine as this.

The train was ten minutes late. Queen and daughter waited for it in the stationmaster's office. The stationmaster provided tea and a glass of Coca-Cola for the child and reminisced about the old days. He came from thereabouts and had beaten for pheasant on the Sandringham Estate in King George VI's day. He remembered the king giving him a half crown for his trouble. "'Twere a terrible shock," he said, "the day he died." He sat on the plain wooden chair staring into his tea, remembering. It was what Caroline liked about Sandringham and Balmoral. The relationship with people was more personal than in London and Windsor; here in Norfolk the family was part of the land and the natives spoke of Edward VII, who had first bought the estate, and all his descendants, as if being the local squire was more important than being King of England. Here the stationmaster and the postmistress and the parson all treated her and Bunny with respect, but they treated them as if they were human too.

"That'll be her now," said the stationmaster as the whistle of a train sounded from outside. "Come along and say hello to your grandparents." He took Lizzie by the hand and led her out onto the platform, where the posters advertising holidays in Yarmouth and Lowestoft were the only reminders that winter was not a permanent condition.

"You look well," her mother said, sizing her up as she sat alongside her on the drive back to the house.

"Thanks, mom," she said, "you too."

"And Lizzie's getting to be a big girl now, aren't you, honey?"

Princess Elizabeth, in the back seat with her grandfather, squirmed with embarrassment.

"We're going to be very quiet this Christmas," Caroline said, "just family. Local friends for the Boxing Day shoot. I hope you won't be bored."

Henry Knight smoothed his silver hair and chuckled. "Your mother and I won't be bored," he said. "A good quiet family Christmas is just about all the excitement we old folk can stand. Isn't that right, Rose?"

His wife smiled indulgently. "Ever since your elder statesman father turned sixty he's been pretending to be an old man," she said. "But ever since you asked us for Christmas, he's been talking about how much he's looking forward to shooting those famous Sandringham pheasants of yours."

"Terrific," Caroline said. "Bunny will be pleased."

She said it with no malice, and yet had she not been concentrating on the road ahead she would have seen her mother turn and look at her father with a knowing expression which suggested that they had some suspicions.

On Christmas Eve, Caroline and the King stood in the great hall greeting the tenants and workers and handing out the Christmas boxes. Later the four adults attended midnight service at the little church. Next morning they were back for matins, Lizzie in a new scarlet coat with a fur-lined hood, making a happy picture for the solitary agency photographer forced out to record the royal Christmas churchgoing for the nation's breakfast tables.

There was snow on the ground. Back at the big house they watched the King's Christmas broadcast to the nation. Against a gloomy background of violence and industrial disputes, with the future of the monarchy itself under threat, he somehow managed to tell his people that their lot need not be so very bad, that there were some things in life which could not be measured in the crude currency of the times. " 'Whatsoever things are true' " he quoted, " 'whatsoever things are honest, whatsoever things are just, whatsoever things are pure, whatsoever things are lovely, whatsoever things are of good report, if there be any virtue and if there be any praise, think on these things.' " For a few seconds the cameras froze on that sensitive, doubt-wracked sovereign's face, and there was silence. Then the face dissolved into a fluttering royal standard and the national anthem boomed out. By the fire, Oliver, the Queen's Labrador, stirred briefly. Caroline looked around her at the ugly Edwardian sumptuousness of the room, the heavy velvet drapes, the walnut and mahogany escritoires and sofa tables, the handful of Postimpressionist paintings and sketches; the little Henry Moore bronze; the family portraits by the leading Royal Academicians of the century.

"It's easy for *us* to talk like that," she said, bitterly. "We don't have to worry about the roof over our heads, or where the next meal is coming from, or whether some bureaucrat is going to close down our children's school." No one answered. Then her husband said, softly, "Let's not quarrel. Not on Christmas Day." And the subject was dropped.

Next day, however, it was taken up by her mother. They had gone out to the blinds with their menfolk, the King typically English in elderly plus fours and eider-stuffed jacket, armed with his grandfather's Purdey twelve-gauges. It was a clean crisp day with a pale blue cloudless sky. The shooting was so good that the barrels of the guns became too hot to touch and even Henry Knight, an indifferent shot, was bringing birds down as fast as the dogs could bring them in.

After an hour or two Mrs. Knight and her daughter wandered away from the guns toward the woods which ran to the north of the park. Despite the sun the ground was very hard underfoot. Occasionally they would crunch across a frozen puddle, their boots breaking the ice with a harsh snapping sound. From time to time Caroline would pick up a stick for Oliver, who loped along beside them, saliva dribbling from his mouth as he anticipated each throw.

"Everything *is* all right, dear?" her mother asked when the silence had lasted a little too long. Caroline knew she was screwing herself up for something special and had—perversely perhaps—no intention of making it easy for her.

"How do you mean 'everything'?"

"You know, dear, everything. You and the King. Being Queen. Life. Everything." Mrs. Knight bent down and picked her own stick for the dog. "Some of the things in the papers have been, well, disturbing. Your speech at the Savoy . . . this environmental organization . . . the business with the Pakistanis the other day—"

"Sikhs," said Caroline.

"Okay, Sikhs."

They were consciously not looking at each other. In the distance the guns thumped away; otherwise it was very quiet, just their voices and the sound of their boots on the iron-hard ground. A long way off a car could be heard on the public road, beyond the estate boundary.

"Everything's fine, mom." She was annoyed to hear her voice sounding so tremulous and unsure.

"Wouldn't it help to talk about it?" asked Mrs. Knight, "it's what family are for."

Caroline scuffed at the ground with the toe of her boot. "No kidding, mom, there's nothing to talk about."

"Yesterday," her mother persisted, "you were so needlessly unreasonable about his broadcast. He wanted your reassurance, Caroline—very badly. He's not a very self-assured person, deep down; he needs your support."

"Look mother," she snapped angrily, "who's side are you on?"

The guns were very distant now. Oliver began to bark for a stick to be thrown to him, but he was ignored. The two women had stopped walking.

"I hadn't realized it was a question of sides," Mrs. Knight said at last.

Caroline blinked back the tears that threatened.

"I didn't mean it to be, mom. Let's drop it, okay?" She threw a stick for Oliver and began to walk briskly back toward the house.

The next day it was her father's turn. She had gone into the library and Henry Knight followed her in.

"Hi, dad," she said, making a slightly too obvious performance of scanning the shelves.

"Hello, Caroline," he said, gravely. He was wearing his most sepulchral expression. "Can we sit down and have a talk."

"Well," she began, "I have to go and talk with cook, and I . . ." Then she took full note of her father's expression and manner and sat down in one of the frayed brown leather chairs. "Sure, dad," she said, "go ahead. Shoot."

Mr. Knight sat down in a chair opposite and took out the pipe he always used as a prop in moments of high drama and seriousness.

"Your mother and I are worried about you," he said, taking little pinches of tobacco from the tin and pressing them into the bowl of the pipe with his thumb. He did not look up from this operation.

"Yeah," Caroline said, feeling a prickling sensation run up her spine. "Mom and I talked yesterday."

"Your mother told me you didn't want to talk."

"That's not a hundred percent accurate," Caroline said. "What I actually said was that there was nothing to talk about."

Henry Knight finished packing the pipe, struck a match and sucked the flame noisily down into the bowl. In between puffs he said: "You and I . . . uh . . . know that's not . . . uh . . . true, Caroline."

The tingling in her spine was stronger, and she felt her face reddening—sensations she had experienced as a child when she was caught in a lie or even a trivial embarrassment like getting her multiplication table wrong or mis-conjugating simple French verbs. For Chrissake, she breathed to herself, get a grip on yourself.

"I had a call from Charles Miller about two weeks ago," her father said. "You remember Charles?"

She nodded. Charles Miller was a big wheel in the State Department. Had been Ambassador in London in the late seventies, and now virtually ran U.S. relations with Western Europe from his office in Washington. But London was his special baby. He and her father had been friends for years.

"Charles asked me to drop by next time I was in town, and it so happened I had the opportunity to do that on the way over."

She nodded again, waiting while he sucked at the awful pipe. More smoke billowed into the room.

"He wanted to talk about *you.*"

"Is that so?"

"Yes, that's so." Henry Knight leaned forward. Oh God, she thought, get it over with. Come to the point. This is excruciating.

"The fact is, you're a pretty important lady right now—"

"I'm married to the King of England if that's what you mean."

"Now, Caroline, don't be smart. Charles Miller called me in as an act of friendship, but he was deeply concerned. Deeply concerned."

"About what?"

"He'd been reading the reports from the Embassy very carefully, and he said they didn't make very healthy reading where you were concerned. Caroline, he said he was afraid you might be on the point of doing something pretty dumb. He felt that if I could help put matters in perspective for you . . ."

She shook her head, disbelieving. "Are you trying to tell me that the American Embassy here hasn't got better things to do than send back tittle tattle to the State Department and then haul you in to gossip about it."

"Be reasonable darling. You're the Queen of England. Don't you understand what that means today?"

"I'm beginning to," she said bitterly, "and number one is that it means that nobody cares a nickel about me as me. All they care about is me as Queen, as a goddamn symbol. Even you, my own father—"

"Caroline, that's ridiculous. Your mother and I love you more than anyone else in the world. You know we do. But that's not the point. The point is, sweetheart, that you can't be 'just you' any more. You can't go slipping off to some rendezvous with a protest organization whenever you feel like it. You can't go disregarding your security advisers, which your mother is worried sick about. And you can't make speeches off the cuff without telling people what you're going to do. I'm astonished that this isn't second nature to you, after the upbringing and the exposure you've had. Do you imagine the President's husband can do that? Do you think for a minute that he can say, I'm going to make a speech to the Washington Press Club and I'm not going to tell any one of you White House staffers what the hell I'm going to say. Do you imagine he could get away with that? The American people wouldn't stand for it."

She wanted to get up and walk out, but her legs wouldn't move. She couldn't agree with what he was saying, yet, because he was her father, and because she wanted more than anything to be able to rely on him and trust him, she could not argue with him, either. She put her hand to her face.

"Oh dad—" she said.

He waited, puffing at the pipe, for her to pull herself together. He would have liked nothing better than to walk across the room and comfort her with an arm around her shoulder, but that wasn't possible now.

"Let me spell it out for you," he said. "The administration regards Britain as central to the defense of Western Europe. They don't trust the French. They don't like the way the Germans have been facing east. So with Italy gone that leaves Britain."

"Dad, I don't want or need a lecture on the NATO alliance."

He stood up, jabbing the stem of the pipe at her. "Seems to me that's exactly what you need, young lady. Now, you'll hear me out."

She bit her lip and waited.

"Now," he continued, "right or wrong this administration values its relationship with Britain, and in particular with this present British government. They wouldn't be prepared to stand by and see anything happen here which would rock the boat. The world needs stability here, and from where Charles Miller sits in Washington there looks to be one institution which guarantees British stability more than anything else. You're a vital part of that institution. And you're an American, by God. Can't you understand that?"

Unable to speak, she nodded bleakly.

"Up until a few months ago we all agree you did a superb job. But recently you've been screwing up, Caro. The tide of public opinion is beginning to show signs of turning against you. You know how fragile the monarchy's position is over here. And the State Department's view is that if the monarchy goes down the tubes then this whole damn country goes with it. The left takes over. Britain opts out of NATO. Our bases here are closed down. And a thousand years of democratic freedom goes out the window. I don't want that to happen. There isn't one American citizen from the White House on down that wants that to happen. But one reason I don't want it is that I don't want the world to say that in the end it was my . . . my own daughter . . ."

His voice choked with the emotion of the moment. Henry Knight's problem, it was said in the corridors of power, was that he believed his own lines. It was never more true than now. Caroline too was overcome, but it was rage and disbelief that brought the tears to her eyes and caused the dry pain in her throat. How could he, of all people? Was she the only person in the world who was normal? What was this, conspiracy? What were they trying to do to her? How could anyone believe that her mostly trivial and pathetic attempts to reassert her individuality were some kind of dark threat to Western democracy.

"Father," she said very quietly, willing her voice to support her in this crisis, "you know that I have always tried to do what I believe to be right. It was you and mother who taught me that. You're much older than I am, you have more experience than I have, but you're also of a different generation and you must understand that sometimes there is a conflict between what you want and what your loved ones want. I know that I have a duty to you and to my family and my friends and both my countries, but in the end my duty is to my conscience. I promise you that I see no need for conflict in this. If there is a conflict, then it's not of my making. But whatever happens believe this: I owe something to a lot of other people, I owe something to myself, but more than anything I . . . I owe something to whatsoever things are true and whatsoever things are honest. And don't you forget it."

She stood and walked out of the library with a deportment that would have been a credit to any queen in history. Only when she had slammed the door on the father she loved, did she run upstairs and fling herself sobbing on her bed.

CHAPTER

*T*HE MATTER was not raised again. After Christmas, a few guests arrived for brief stays—the Cokers, the Duke and Duchess of Dorset, the Crombie-Clarks. A gaggle of Cabinet ministers came for a privy council meeting and stayed for tea. In their presence a scrupulous politeness was maintained, a politeness that extended into every area of the royal couple's life together, displacing the warmth and intimacy that had once existed between them. Their guests couldn't put their finger on it but it would have been an insensitive visitor who did not sense a brooding mistrust in the Sandringham air.

Back in London Caroline could at least take refuge in activity. Life at Sandringham with its languorous, formal pattern of family breakfast, lunch, tea and dinner gave way to the London routine of snatched meals at the desk and, by way of contrast, inordinately lengthy banquets. Blackrock, Simpson, Henderson and the rest of the palace secretariat were back at their desks after the Christmas break. There were royal visits to China and West Africa to look forward to; a Commonwealth prime ministers' conference to host; not to mention a threatened general election. But the first important royal occasion was the official visit of the Canadian Prime Minister's Hector Macfarlane, and the visit of Mr. Macfarlane filled Caroline with foreboding.

A week before his arrival, Julian Locke came in for a briefing.

"Rather a lot I'm afraid," he said, plonking a heavy folder on her desk. On the outside it had the historic photograph of a hunter with his heavy hakapik club raised high above a cowering baby seal.

"Ugh," she said, "it *is* revolting. To be frank I wouldn't object if they killed them cleanly with a gun or something humane, but this is just ghastly."

"Better not let our colleagues hear you saying things like that," Julian said. "Besides, it's meant to be revolting."

"I suppose so. Now what can I do for you?"

"First of all, you have to master this brief. Macfarlane is an old-fashioned Tammany Hall style politician, which means he's a bully who operates most effectively in smoke-filled rooms. He's not what you'd call sophisticated, but he knows his facts. You'll have to be on good form to get the better of him in argument, though from what I hear, your problem is going to be to get him to take you seriously enough to even have a serious argument. He likes women to know their place and he certainly doesn't believe in sexual equality."

"There's a lot of that around," Caroline said with feeling.

"You ought to know, by the way, that we're using his visit to flex our muscles. There may be some demonstrations. Noisy ones."

"Oh." She grimaced. "I suppose I'm going to be on the receiving end of some of it."

"We can't get near the palace, even if we wanted to. You know that."

"But the Canadians are giving this black tie affair at Claridges. I'll be there. Am I going to have things thrown at me just for turning up?"

Julian shrugged. "Maybe, though not by us. That's life."

"Hmmm. Sort of awkward, isn't it?"

"What?"

"Me being on both sides of the fence at once."

"You're not the only one. The Royal Society for the Prevention of Cruelty to Animals . . . where does that put your husband?"

"Nowhere much. They don't have 'Patron HM the King' on their letterhead. It's royal in name only."

"Well, taking us on was always going to pose a few problems. You were the first to see that, do you remember?"

She sighed. "I guess so." Outside the guard was being changed. The band was playing "Lillibullero" . . . "Lero, lero, Lillibullero" . . . the tune that signalled the BBC World Service News. She had heard it in her youth, everywhere from Moose Jaw to the Khyber and beyond. It had been a reminder of civilization, a remembrance of civilization. Now the tinny piping of the fifes and the rattle of drums sounded like a reproach. Was she really selling out? And if so, to whom?

"I've been under a little pressure," she said. "I'm afraid not everyone here sees eye to eye with our aspirations."

"You're not having second thoughts?"

"I'm having a lot of thoughts."

"You've no idea what it means to us having you as patron."

She laughed. "I think I can guess," she said. "Are we through? I have another appointment."

She pressed the bell under the desk with her foot.

"I enjoyed the movie we saw," he said as they reached the door.

"Good," she said, "I did too."

He hesitated. "If you're ever, you know, at a loose end . . ." he colored. "I mean, I feel a bit inhibited about asking, but if you were ever free and felt like seeing something else . . . we might even be able to find somewhere discreet enough for dinner afterwards."

She smiled. She felt like saying it was the first time anyone had asked her out in years, but thought better of it. It wouldn't have been true anyway. The Womens Royal Army Corps, the Friends of Covent Garden, the Sherborne Abbey Appeal Fund, the Not Forgotten Association, the Committee of the Hurlingham Club, the Lord Mayor of London and Lady Reddle, the

President and Fellows of Trinity College, Oxford . . . why, for heaven's sake, they had *all* asked her to dine with them in the last few weeks. But it was a long time since a young man had done so, even as diffidently as this. She couldn't help feeling flattered. But all she said was, "That's sweet of you, but . . ." and then, not wishing to close yet another door, she finished: "Maybe I'll call you."

"Our American friends tell me her father had very little joy with Apple Pie," said Cathcart, crumbling one of the club's crusty rolls in finely manicured fingers. "And now to help matters the Canadians are putting their oar in."

"The Canadians?" Blackrock pronounced the word with incredulity.

"Their wretched seals."

"Oh, that," Blackrock said, "that's a hardy annual. Surely they've learned to live with that."

"Their new government's inclined to be bullish. Very sensitive about insults to the glorious Maple Leaf. Macfarlane's a frightful four-letter man. My chaps tell me there's going to be quite a reception committee waiting for him—including Apple Pie's gang."

"Even she would think twice about going out on the streets with them," said Blackrock, examining his soup warily, "anyway it won't just be the Friends of Man. It'll be all the other tweedies and trendies. I'm not too fussed about this one."

"Well," Cathcart said, "I hope you're right. I heard another funny story about Apple Pie."

"Don't expect me to find it funny."

"Only rumor, of course, but one of my chaps came in with a story about a secret assignation one evening when Golden Eagle was out of town."

"The supper party at Windsor?" Blackrock said defensively. He was aware that Cathcart was poaching on his ground. "I know all about that."

"No." Cathcart's eyes gleamed. He sensed a small victory. "No, this was an assignation at a cinema. With a man."

"What?" Blackrock could not conceal his astonishment. "Is there any evidence?"

"Not admissible."

"I'd rule that one right out, then," Blackrock said with exaggerated confidence. He had noticed the visit to the theater, which was logged like any other. It hadn't disturbed him at the time. Everything was in order. The car had been checked in and out. She had taken a detective. No problem. But he had better have a word with the policeman. Things were bad enough as they were without sex too. With an unconvincing heartiness he said, "Sorry they dropped Botham, but he is getting a bit long in the tooth for it, wouldn't you say?"

Henry Cathcart smiled. Too obvious, he thought, Evelyn always was bad at pretending not to be hurt . . .

Just before they parted Cathcart said, "Seriously, Evelyn . . . suppose this was true about Apple Pie and a man?"

"If it were true," Blackrock said, very seriously, "we'd have to consider our options."

"Quite."

"But I don't believe it's possible."

There was a very long pause. Then Cathcart said, deliberately and very coldly, "There's always the Dusty Fanshawe option."

Cathcart gazed at him steadily, trying him out, searching for some complicity. Blackrock returned the look, perplexed, then after a while, incredulous.

"You're surely not suggesting . . ." he said, "what it seems to me you could be suggesting . . ."

Cathcart continued to watch him.

"No," the little colonel said, "It's too much. Not to be contemplated."

"Getting squeamish, Evelyn?" Cathcart murmured. He rubbed his chin thoughtfully. "Greater love" he quoted, "hath no man than this, that a man lay down his life for his friends. I don't think the Gospel was being deliberately sexist. Women can be martyrs too."

"You're not serious?"

"Never more so." Cathcart surveyed Blackrock's faltering expression and leaned forward, dropping his voice to a point only marginally above whispering pitch. "Listen," he said, "Potter's got to call an election soon. The way things are we'll be annihilated. If that happens it's curtains for the monarchy. We know that, don't we?"

"I suppose so, but—"

"We *know* it." Cathcart said fiercely. "I've seen the manifesto. They're pledged to hold presidential elections within two years. No messing about. They're hard men, Evelyn, and if we're beaten as badly as I think we're going to be, then they'll be our new masters. No two ways about it."

"But what you're proposing—"

"I propose, old friend, that Apple Pie may have to go the same way as poor old Dusty. Only this time it won't look like an accident. It'll be a cut and dried case of left wing atrocity. The backlash would be formidable."

Blackrock stared blankly, seemed about to speak, then shook his head vehemently. "Out of the question" he said. "Better a Marxist revolution than that. We did not have this conversation."

Cathcart grinned sardonically. "You think about it," he said. "You just think about it."

Half an hour later, after an unsatisfactory interview with Angell, Blackrock was little the wiser. Angell said that he had accompanied Her Majesty to the Plaza Cinema and had remained with her throughout the performance of the film *Confederates,* which he seemed to have greatly enjoyed. He escorted Her Majesty from the cinema and they drove straight back to the palace. When Blackrock asked if the Queen had met anyone at the cinema, Angell replied. "That I couldn't say, sir." However he phrased the question, Blackrock got the same answer. When Angell had gone he had a word with his superior, Tartan Macpherson, but the Scot said he couldn't help. Angell, he said ambiguously, was the soul of discretion. "Besides which," he said, "it would be asking a man to spy on his master and mistress, and that I canna do. I wouldna do it misself." Which left Blackrock not only none the wiser, but enraged.

The Canadian Prime Minister was a Canadian of the old school, Toronto Scot with a sentimental attachment to the "auld country." He was dour and puritanical, with a deep suspicion of the United States, the Province of Quebec and anybody who did not, at least in the first instance, hail from the United Kingdom—and preferably from Glasgow or Belfast. His only vice was whisky, and although he was not a popular, let alone a charismatic figure, he was a consummate fixer. He carried the whiff of corruption with him like the aroma of old cigars, but he had yet to be found out. His forthright opinions acknowledged few grey areas. Things were black or they were white, and the blackest thing in his book was "namby-pamby liberalism." The only thing that he shared with his best-known recent predecessor, Pierre Elliot Trudeau, was a supreme and widely professed hatred of bleeding hearts.

As the High Commission's steel-grey Cadillac swept him up to Claridge's Hotel in Mayfair he was, therefore, disgusted—though not daunted—to find himself the target of a mob of several hundred demonstrators carrying placards with such slogans as "Save Our Seals," "Macfarlane is a murderer" and "Go home seal slayer." He was tempted to do what Trudeau used to do and wave two fingers at them, but being a strong believer in the dignity of the Canadian premiership he paid not the slightest attention as he marched from the limousine to the front door of the hotel, running the gauntlet of jeers and abuse but protected from physical harm by a large force of metropolitan police, burly arms linked in a human chain.

Only inside the foyer did he turn to his High Commissioner, with a face like a Norman peasant, and say "We gonna have this all the way through, Pierre?"

And when the High Commissioner nodded gravely and said he was afraid so, the Prime Minister looked at him and said, with great vehemence, "Shit."

The High Commissioner, who had served as a senior minister in a former administration and for years sat as a political opponent of Macfarlane's in the Ottawa House of Commons, suppressed as smile and remarked: "Perhaps you had better remonstrate with Her Majesty. Her Majesty has assumed many of the characteristics of her adopted people. She is now one of Britain's leading animal lovers. In fact she is the patron of an environmental group named the Friends of Man. They are in the van of the protests about the seal cull."

"Huh." The lift stopped and they proceeded along the corridor in silence while the PM digested this piece of information. "I could use a drink," he said when they got inside. There was a catholic selection of unopened bottles on a reproduction Louis XV sideboard. The Prime Minister fixed himself a large rye on the rocks and motioned to the High Commissioner to help himself.

"Are you serious?" Macfarlane asked.

"Serious?"

"About the Queen?"

"Sure I'm serious."

"Then you'd better get her to call off her troops."

The High Commissioner cocked an eyebrow in an expression of total disbelief.

"Listen, Pierre. If we were in Moscow or even Washington, I might expect something like this. But this is the mother of the Commonwealth, the land from which most of us sprung, and the least I'm entitled to is some sort of respect. It's bad enough to have to put up with the rabble outside, but it's downright intolerable to have it backed up by the Queen of Canada herself. God bless her." He downed his whisky in a single gulp and poured himself another. "You get on to those guys at Buckingham Palace and you tell them to get off their butts. Explain to them that it's crazinesses like this which undermine the accords we expect to enjoy between our two countries."

The High Commissioner sighed. "I'll have a word with Sir Evelyn Blackrock" he said.

The Prime Minister smiled. "You do just that" he said. "Whoever *he* may be."

Unsurprisingly, the High Commissioner's delicate and diplomatic telephone overture to the palace was received with corresponding courtesy. Blackrock expressed his concern, quite understood that the attentions of the seal lovers were unwelcome and tiresome, but pointed out that whatever the views of the government and the monarchy, people were free to demonstrate in support of their legitimately held views. There was, he pointed, out considerable public feeling on the question of seals. When he had finished his formal reply, Blackrock said, "Look Pierre, I understand your problem. I'll do what I can, but I don't hold out a lot of hope."

There was a distinct pause at the other end of the line. Then the High Commissioner said, "I read you, Sir Evelyn. Unfortunately, our Prime Minister is something of what the Americans call a redneck. Sangfroid is not his strong point."

"Quite." Blackrock sighed. "We'll just have to keep our fingers crossed over the next three days," he said, and put the phone down. After a moment's pause, Sir Evelyn Blackrock swore.

The Queen had done her homework. The briefing binder had been full and complicated but she felt she had mastered it. Now, as she stood in the Music Room waiting for the formal procession into dinner, she found her mind overflowing with statistics on the mortality rates and surplus production of Northwest Atlantic harp seals . . . and flooded with horrific pictures of cuddly innocent whitecoat seals being clubbed to death, of pack ice stained red with their blood . . . She smiled, nodding sympathetically as the dowdy wife of the Canadian Prime Minister told an interminable anecdote about her infant grandson. But her mind was elsewhere.

Because this was a full State Banquet, gentlemen were in white tie and tails and ladies in full-length gowns. The Queen wore a tiara and the blue sash of the Order of the Garter across a shimmering, diamond-encrusted dress of white raw silk. Her hair, unusually, was piled high on her head, revealing a classic neck and looking far more formal than she ever did by day. It was, she had to admit, a stifling get-up for a pretty stifling occasion but she enjoyed looking good, and she knew that to-night she was at her regal best.

The procession was always a bore. As always on such occasions, a footman had toured the palace swinging a censer of lavender incense to freshen the air for distinguished visitors, and the corridors smelled of it. Along these lavender-smelling passages the royal party walked sedately until just before they arrived at the entrance to the Ball Room. There the Lord Chamberlain and the Lord Steward, elderly nobles grown grey in the service of the crown, turned on their heels and walked backward into the room. It was an absurd practice and Caroline had complained about it, albeit half-heartedly. "Done it since time began," the Lord Chamberlain told her. "No reason to stop now."

The Ball Room, more commonly used for investitures, was looking sumptuous. The best wines of Burgundy and Bordeaux had been decanted into golden flagons on the sideboards. Under the fifty-inch gold candelabra, commissioned by the Prince Regent at the beginning of the nineteenth century, a huge horseshoe table was laid for dinner. The china, hand-painted in apple green, was the Louis XV Sevres Grand Service. All around the room, footmen in scarlet jackets with gold braid, knee breeches, pink stockings and powdered wigs gave the scene a Ruritanian, fin de siècle atmosphere in which the Canadian PM and his wife seemed hopelessly at sea. What modern touches there were had been kept out of sight: At the head of the table, hidden in the enormous flower arrangements, were red and green lights operated by a steward standing behind the King and Queen. Thus all the waiters could be signalled to begin serving at the same time, a bizarre fusion of feudal tradition and twentieth-century technology.

"It's quite a show you put on here your Majesty" said the Canadian premier. He had had a good day. Lunch at Downing Street with his British counterpart, meetings with selected bankers and captains of industry, and leaders of the Canadian community in Britain, all helped along by a few drinks on the way. Caroline flinched from the smell of stale rye as she acknowledged the compliment.

"Thank you," she said. "It's the largest state apartment we

have. One hundred and twenty-three feet by sixty. Built for Queen Victoria in 1855."

"Is that so?" he said, smiling good naturedly. He had been whisked with such efficiency from one sequestered engagement to another that he had barely noticed the demonstrators. It was a cold damp day and there had been snow flurries. This diminished the pickets' enthusiasm and improved his temper no end. Like the Duke of Wellington, he enjoyed looking out from warmth and comfort and "seeing the damn people get wet."

"Are you enjoying your stay?" Caroline asked, with self-conscious grace. "I hope Claridges are looking after you?"

"Indeed they are, your Majesty. Indeed they are." Footmen were now serving lobster bisque and a dry Madeira. The Prime Minister eyed both with some misgivings.

"Is this your first visit here?" she asked.

"I haven't been here since I was stationed near Rickmansworth with the armed forces," he said, with pride. "Are you acquainted with Rickmansworth?"

Her Majesty was, sadly, unacquainted with Rickmansworth, but their conversation limped forward nonetheless, politely lurching up a series of trivial cul-de-sacs but steering well clear of anything interesting, let alone controversial. All around them distinguished and titled ladies and gentlemen did the same.

The Queen did not move into the attack until the palace waiters were distributing pudding, a glorified ice cream sundae in a meringue case, heavily impregnated with maple syrup in honour of their guest. She had by this stage done a fair job of captivating Macfarlane. He was not interested in women's minds but he had always had a healthy respect for their bodies, and whatever else he might suspect about Her Majesty he had to admit that she was some woman.

"Mr. Macfarlane—" she said, favoring him with a more than usually ravishing smile.

"Oh, call me Hector," he said. He had managed to get a waiter to fix him a rye and ginger, sparing himself the torture of having to drink the sugary white Bordeaux everyone else was having with the bombe.

She smiled again. "I wanted to have a word with you about the seal hunt."

A flinty look came into his eye. He reached for his drink.

"You may know that I'm the patron of a group called the Friends of Man," she continued.

"I *had* heard."

He was irritated now. Angry even. Caroline realized it as quickly as it had happened. He had the mean look of a fighting drunk. She hoped they would be still able to discuss this in a civilized fashion, and there was no way to pull out now. She had promised Julian and the others that she would take it up with Macfarlane and there would never be a better opportunity than this.

"We're very concerned about what's going to happen up there this year. I mean, all we ask is a moratorium and an impartial inquiry. After all, two hundred thousand seals are going to be killed."

"That's pure sentiment," Macfarlane said. "If those damn seals didn't look like teddy bears do you think anyone would care?"

"With respect, I'm not a particularly sentimental person, and I'll willingly concede that the hunt is an unfortunate necessity if an impartial inquiry says so; but I do think there is a case to be answered."

Macfarlane set his jaw in the obstinate pose long familiar to students of Canadian politics.

"I don't propose to continue this discussion," he said. "The seal cull is probably the most efficiently administered animal harvest in the history of man. Our government has bent over backwards to satisfy the snivelling demands of woolly minded liberals like your friends, and frankly we've got better things to worry about. So should you. What in hell are you and your friends doing about Ulster. Eh?"

"I'm sorry" said the Queen. "None of us are happy about Ulster, but I can't see that the seal hunt is a related issue." She was having a tough time keeping her temper.

"It's a question of what you think's important," said Macfarlane, "human beings or vermin."

Caroline was aware that people had noticed their tiff. No one stared, but all around her there was a noticeable shifting and embarrassment. Diplomacy dictated an immediate climbdown. The Prime Minister, uncouth or not, was a guest, an honored guest not just of hers personally but of the government and the country; she knew she should shut up. But she also knew that it had to be done in a way that would not leave her standing accused, in her own eyes above all, of cowardice and hypocrisy.

"It's because I care deeply about human beings," she said "that I want them to behave with humanity. Clubbing hundreds of thousands of seals to death seems to me on the face of it an inhumane way to carry on. I'd like to know how you justify it."

Hector Macfarlane fixed her with an angry stare. "You may be the Queen of England," he said, "but you are also a silly little fool." Whereupon he very deliberately turned his back and began to talk to the hitherto neglected guest on his right.

Caroline felt tears of frustration welling up. For all the embarrassed politeness which made fellow guests pretend that nothing was wrong, she knew that many of them must have heard, or at the very least realized that there had been an altercation in which she had been rudely snubbed. The situation had become impossible. She would have to leave. She turned her head and addressed the liveried footman standing behind her chair.

"Would you mind," she said, beginning to stand, "I feel a little faint." The footman quickly pulled back her chair and held out an arm for support if necessary. Although she did not—could not—look at the guests, she was aware of a sudden lull in the conversation, quickly filled in as people realized that something was wrong and, in the best British tradition, carried on as if nothing had happened. As she walked out of the Ball Room she was aware that everyone was watching while trying to appear utterly oblivious of her exit. Even the band of the Irish Guards who had played light music in the musicians' gallery through the meal faltered momentarily. For the Queen to leave the room in the middle of a state banquet was unprecedented.

But then for a guest, however distinguished, to publicly call Her Majesty a fool, was virtual treason. . . .

"I will not do it," she shouted. "I will not! How can you even ask? The man is disgusting. He's a drunk. And he was gratuitously insulting. He turned his back on me. He called me a fool. What kind of a husband are you to even think of asking me to apologize to that moron?"

The King was still in his white tie and tails; after the formal speeches at the dinner he had been closeted with Blackrock and Prime Minister Potter for over an hour. Both the private secretary and the Prime Minister could, regrettably, see only one way out. The Queen would have to apologize. The apology could be private, but it must be made or there would be a serious rift in Anglo-Canadian relations. That was, Potter said, exceedingly undesirable. The King listened morosely and agreed to ask his wife. The Prime Minister then spoke in more general terms. He said that he, personally, was concerned about the apparently independent behavior of the Queen in recent months. People were beginning to become restless. The Americans had expressed displeasure, through official and unofficial channels. With a general election looming, the opposition could be expected to make capital out of any trouble at the palace. It was no secret that they would prefer a republic. If they caught even a whiff of popular resentment about the Royal Family, they would draft a referendum on the monarchy as soon as they came to power. Potter did not wish to seem melodramatic, but he was nervous. He did not want the monarchy to be an issue in any election campaign, but if the Queen did not toe the line then the opposition might well try. And he personally could not be answerable for the consequences

"You'll have to apologize," the King told Caroline. "I know it's not easy, and I daresay he was offensive, but he's our guest. It's inexcusable to bend his ear about those bloody seals. Especially during a state banquet. You were his hostess."

"And what if I don't?" she said.

"You have no choice," he said. "You *must* apologize."

"Or what?"

He sighed. "Caroline," he said, "I don't want to threaten you. It's ridiculous, but you must see that what happened tonight was inexcusable. The Canadians are just about our oldest and most reliable allies. Macfarlane is our friend, one of the very few absolutely dependable friends Britain has in the world. We cannot insult him. I don't know how else to put it. We cannot."

"But the seal hunt," she said. "Surely to God one should be able to talk honestly to one's oldest and most reliable allies about something that one believes to be morally wrong."

He fingered the set of miniature medals on his chest. "I'm not discussing it," he said, "you don't have to see him again. We have agreed that you can have a diplomatic bout of flu for a day or two. But if he doesn't have a written apology by lunchtime tomorrow he's going to start being difficult. We do a lot of trade with Canada. He'll start making life difficult there. We use their western prairies as battle training grounds for our tanks and artillery. He'll be difficult about that. We need their support at the U.N., especially over Ulster, now that the Americans are getting sticky."

"All because I walked out on him after complaining about the seal hunt?"

"He's not a reasonable man. Very few politicians are. And a mild freeze in our relations with Canada will hurt us more than them."

"Will it hurt *us?*"

"Us?" The King looked surprised.

"You. Me. The children" she said, "I don't have such an all-embracing sense of 'us' as you seem to."

He ignored the gibe. "We need more money," he said. "At present we can rely on this government to make sure we get it. But it has to be voted through Parliament; you know that. If we don't do what this government wants then they'll plead national poverty as an excuse for not revising the Civil List to give us more."

"We can sell a picture or two."

"Don't be silly. They're not even ours, they belong to the

country." He moved toward her. "Listen," he said, a note of pleading in his voice, "it's a hostile world out there. We need all the friends we can find, and we can't afford to alienate them for no good reason. I don't want to end my days like King Farouk or the Shah or even the poor old Duke of Windsor, flitting from one clapped out seaside resort to another wondering when some lunatic is going to finish me off with a hunting rifle or a little piece of plastic explosive. We can't always do what we want to do. If we want to enjoy what really matters to us we have to compromise over the smaller things."

He was close enough to touch her now. She looked tired and miserable but very alluring in her nightgown of handworked batik. He put out a hand to caress her cheek. She let it rest there for a second, then turned away. "I'm very tired" she said, "I'd like to sleep on it. I'll let you know in the morning."

He let the hand fall to his side. "Goodnight" he said.

"Goodnight."

When he had left her, she took a sheet of plain Buckingham Palace stationery and scrawled on it. "Dear Mr. Macfarlane, please forgive me for my rudeness last night. I did not wish to offend you and I am most sorry if I have done so." She signed it in her tough, forward-sloping hand, "Caroline R." It seemed to be the least abject formula. She did not seal it. It would presumably have to be cleared by Bunny and by Blackrock.

She wondered if they realized what their victory had cost.

The Macfarlane flap was featured in the papers with precisely the sort of innuendo which did the most damage. There had been no journalists present at the banquet, but the *Daily Telegraph* had enterprisingly managed to get hold of the story for its final edition. Under the heading: "Mystery of Queen's Illness," their court correspondent wrote,

> I understand Queen Caroline was forced to leave last night's banquet for the Canadian Prime Minister, Mr Macfarlane, due to a mystery illness. The Queen was apparently taken ill towards the end of the meal and retired to her room before the speeches. Shortly before

she left the dinner, Queen Caroline was seen to be in animated conversation with Mr Macfarlane and there is some speculation that she may have raised the matter of Canada's annual seal cull which takes place off the coast of Newfoundland later this year. The Queen is patron of the Friends of Man, the ecology group, many of whose members have been demonstrating against the cull during Mr Macfarlane's visit. A Buckingham Palace spokesman said that the Queen was suffering from a mild viral infection and had cancelled all engagements for the next two days on medical advice. Mr Macfarlane returns to Ottawa the day after tomorrow.

"Bastards!" Maurice Henderson exclaimed as he took his morning coffee in the staff common room. He was speaking to Simpson, but a handful of assistants and equerries listened from the fringes of the room. "I've had the world and his wife on the phone as the result of that piece. No one believes she's ill. Everyone thinks she had a row with Macfarlane and now the Canadians are threatening to put out a statement."

"They can't do that." Simpson stirred his coffee feverishly. The trials of the last few months had diminished him still further. He had lost weight and hair, and seemed permanently furtive, constantly awaiting a final dire retribution from on high.

"They can do what they want. If Macfarlane isn't satisfied with her apology they're almost certain to put something out."

"And will he be satisfied?" Simpson asked timidly. "It *was* an apology, and after all he did say some very rude things. He ought to be satisfied."

"People like that are never satisfied" Henderson said dourly. He had met his share of bullies in Fleet Street. "Personally I'm not sure she should have apologized, but that's by the way. It's done now. If the Canadians choose to leak the note of apology then we're really in trouble. It wasn't my decision thank God. How is she?"

"Very quiet," Simpson said thoughtfully. He seemed to be

realizing it for the first time. "And calm." He looked over at Henderson.

"I don't like it either," he said. "Sounds ominous."

The Queen's note of apology, duly approved by Blackrock and the King, was sent over to Claridge's by special messenger. Macfarlane read it quickly and then handed it to his High Commissioner.

"What do you think?" he asked.

"I don't think we could expect more."

"Maybe. Maybe not." The Prime Minister smiled. "Big crowd downstairs?"

"So so."

"Demonstrators?"

"Yes."

"Press?"

"Yes."

The High Commissioner was worried. Doubly so when Macfarlane said, "Come on Pierre. You and I are going to take a stroll across to Macdonald House." Although Macdonald House, the less magnificent but larger of the two Canadian High Commission buildings in London, was only five minutes' walk from the hotel, the trip was usually made by car.

The two men took the elevator to the lobby. Outside in the street the crowd of demonstrators recognized Macfarlane and began to chant a chorus of abuse and imprecation. Flashbulbs popped, and someone threw a tomato which smashed with a messy thud against the glass of the swing doors. The High Commission chauffeur gunned the car's engine into life and a Claridge's doorman opened the door. But this time the High Commissioner did not take the car. Instead he sauntered over to the crowd in an arrogantly casual manner, hands in his pockets.

"You guys give me a pain in the ass" he drawled, loudly enough to be heard. "Why don't you just pack it in."

This was greeted with boos, hisses and general jeering noises.

"Any of you here from an outfit called the Friends of Man?"

In the middle of renewed booing and much shoving and push-ing between crowd and police, mostly of a genial nature, a small group was identified as being Friends of Man. The group in-cluded Samantha, aggressively vociferous and tomboyish in a tweed jacket and cap. "Bastard," she shouted shrilly, "mur-derer." She was enjoying herself more than she had for ages. This was like the old days.

"I had a friendly little discussion with your leader, Queen Caroline, last night" he called, directing his words straight at Sam. "You go talk to her about seals. She knows better now. Why, she even wrote me this morning to say how wrong and sorry she was."

"Crap," Samantha shrieked as the crowd booed and hissed Macfarlane.

"Oh no," he shouted back. He reached in his pocket and pulled out the Queen's letter. "Crap it isn't," he roared, waving it aloft as if it were a banner. Then he stuffed it back in his pocket and turned on his heel. "Come on Pierre" he said, "let's get away from this scum." And he set off down Brook Street pursued by the throng of police, demonstrators and newsmen with the little High Commissioner trotting dutifully at his heels.

"Merde" the High Commissioner swore. "You're crazy."

A journalist thrust himself at the Premier.

"Are you telling us that you and the Queen had a row at the palace banquet last night?"

"The Prime Minister isn't saying anything" shouted the High Commissioner."

"Would you show us that letter, Mr. Prime Minister?"

"What did the Queen say?"

"What did you say to the Queen?"

"Is she really ill?"

"Fuck off!"

"No comment."

"Move along there."

Finally they made it to Macdonald House, in through the sliding bullet-proof doors and to a quiet sanctuary.

"Jesus" said the High Commissioner, frigid with rage. "You really did it now."

"Yes" smirked Hector Macfarlane, "I did, didn't I?"

Henry Cathcart's office at the back of 10 Downing Street was small and unprepossessing. He reached it from the Cabinet Office entrance in Whitehall rather than through the Prime Minister's front door, so that few people outside realized that he was there, unobtrusively ensconced in the seat of power with easy access to the PM.

"I thought it better if we met here" he said to his old friend. "We're getting far too much publicity already."

"Quite" said Blackrock, easing himself into the uncomfortable upright arm chair provided by the Civil Service. He could never understand why Cathcart's office was so ostentatiously drab.

"This is getting beyond a joke." Catheart said. "You've seen the evening paper? He pushed the *News-Standard* under Blackrock's nose. There was a front page picture of Macfarlane with some demonstrators.

The headline read "Queen in row over seal hunt."

"Unfortunate" Blackrock conceded.

"You could say so." Cathcart drummed with his fingers. His face, always pink, was unhealthily blotchy. There were dark pouches under his eyes. Blackrock, who kept himself in exceptional shape for a man of his age, suspected that his old school-friend had been hitting the bottle. As well as he might. The government was in worse shape than ever. There were defections on the back benches. Tonight's vote of confidence in the House of Commons could be lost if there were enough abstentions among the government's supporters. The last thing they could afford was this sort of embarrassment. And Cathcart, as minister with special responsibility for the Royal Family, was the man who carried the ball. Today's Cabinet meeting must have been stormy.

"The apology misfired," Blackrock said. "Henderson's playing the 'no comment' game as well as he can. 'Private conversations between members of the Royal Family and their guests not a matter about which I can speculate . . . Purely private . . . Likewise any letter which may or may not have been written, purely personal and private capacity.' You know the form."

Cathcart looked unimpressed. "I know the form. What about the Canadians?"

"Lamontaine, their High Commissioner, is a decent sort of chap for a froggo," Blackrock said. "He'll play ball. At least when he's rid of that bugger Macfarlane."

"The PM was going to announce an election tomorrow." Cathcart smiled. "Though naturally that's been shelved now. Unless things go against us in the Commons. Between you and me, we expect to pull through that, though it'll be nip and tuck. But we can't go on with this lame duck administration any longer. Potter's in appalling shape. I don't know that he'll be able to take much more." He gazed at Blackrock. "Have you thought any more about our conversation?"

"No" Blackrock lied, a little too quickly for credibility.

"Hmm." Cathcart appeared to consider. Then he said, "I wish you would. It may turn out to be the only solution. Sacrifices, Evelyn, are sometimes necessary."

Blackrock said nothing, and after a moment Cathcart said, "For the time being, however, she'll have to be put on ice. No public engagements of any kind. You've already said she has a viral infection. Now it's pneumonia. And shut her up. Make it clear to her, and to him, that it's an order. There wasn't a single dissenting voice in Cabinet. To be frank, we're pretty fed up with her and her nonsense. The general feeling is that she's letting the side down."

"Quite. I'll tell her she's under house arrest."

"You won't have to bother. Potter is going to talk to His Majesty this evening. It'll look better coming from him. I just want to be sure you enforce it."

Blackrock nodded, more disturbed than he cared to admit. Against his inclination he found himself thinking gloomily of the late Dusty Fanshawe.

The latest polls on the Royal Family had shown a disturbing

downward swing in the monarchy's popularity. The benefits of
Prince Arthur's birth were wearing off sooner than he had
hoped. There was no question that something drastic had to be
considered.

"And after the election?"

Cathcart shrugged. "One thing at a time," he said. He stood.
"Can you keep the Queen under control?"

"Can do."

"Good man," Cathcart said, and showed him to the door.

"One thing at a time," Blackrock muttered as he strode down
Whitehall, "but what about after the election?"

That evening when the Canadians gave their own ceremonial
banquet Potter asked the King for half an hour immediately
afterwards. In a bleak twenty-minute interview, Potter vouch-
safed his belief that the Queen, left to her own devices, could
prove the straw that broke the Tory government's back and lost
the King his crown. He might, he conceded, be wrong, but it
was not a risk he wished to take. The King listened gravely and
said very little, but in the end he promised to do as he had been
asked. The Queen would be, as he put it, confined to barracks
until after the election.

He told her himself, the following morning over breakfast, a
meal made miserable by the newspapers which were full of the
story, and of hostile comments. "A Jane Fonda in the Palace,"
said one commentator. Another dragged up that forgotten
flower child of the seventies, Margaret Trudeau. They were
nearly unanimous in their criticism.

"The honeymoon sure is over," Caroline said dispiritedly as
she poured milk on her cereal.

"I'm afraid so," he said, "I had words with the Prime Minister
last night. He's told me that you're to cancel all your engagements."

"I already have" she said, "until that bastard's gone back to
his frozen boondocks."

"More than that. I mean until the election."

"The election?" she spluttered. She had been swimming earlier and her eyes were red-rimmed though whether from the

chlorine in the palace pool or from tears and sleeplessness it was impossible to tell. "When in God's name is that?"

"Too soon to say. They'll hang on as long as possible."

"It's out of the question." Without thinking she reached in the folds of her gown for her pack of Marlboros and lit a cigarette with trembling hands.

"I wish you wouldn't smoke in front of the child," he said waspishly.

"She doesn't mind. Do you, Lizzie?" The child was very quiet, then slipped off her chair and went to her mother, who cradled her briefly. "Run along to nanny" Caroline said "while mummy and daddy talk."

"It's an order" the King said tersely. "Potter insists."

"And suppose I say no?"

The atmosphere was thick with a sense of failure, of misunderstanding, of lost hopes and illusions. The King's voice was drained of all feeling when he replied. "This time you can't say no. You have no option."

Caroline stubbed out a cigarette half-smoked on a side plate, then lit another. "You mean you'd coerce me. Force me to stay here and not go out. You'd keep me a prisoner?"

"The only option you have is to obey voluntarily, or to be coerced as you put it. I'm sorry. You can't say you weren't warned." He hated saying it. But it was necessary and it was the truth.

"And after the election?"

"Then," her husband said, "we have to think again. With luck we can make a fresh start, get things straightened out." He bit his lip. "God, Caroline, don't think I'm enjoying this. I have no alternative. They can't trust you; daren't trust you. You have to be stopped. For your own good."

"If that's what you think," she muttered, "I don't know what you believe any more. I used to respect you, you know. I used to see you as someone who stood for values, who had integrity. Now you seem to me as much of an accommodater as anyone else. You're afraid to do anything that might upset the system or rock the boat. You're only interested in survival. You just

249

want to hang on to what you've got, no matter what the cost."

"From now until the election," he said, "you have to stay here. If you want to go to Windsor or Sandringham or Balmoral, we can discuss it when you're feeling more rational. And if you try to do anything silly we should be clear about one thing at least: It will be the end for us. And by 'us,' I mean you and me and the children."

"You mean" she said bitterly, "if I try to escape."

But he did not answer. He just walked out of the room and down to his office without so much as looking at her. For ten minutes after he had gone she sat staring at the breakfast table, not smoking, not eating, not drinking, and scarcely daring even to think.

CHAPTER

There's no one I can trust. No one who cares for me. No one who understands me. I'm a prisoner. Even my husband is my enemy. I am to be watched and guarded as if I were in an asylum. I honestly believe they expect me to slash my wrists or throw myself out a bedroom window. They could be right. With me out of the way everyone could get on with their life in tranquillity. Right now I worry that Joanne is being hounded by thugs from the CIA or the FBI. They've probably closed down the Friends of Man, put Julian away somewhere . . . Sometimes I think I may be going out of my mind. I've got to talk to someone. Maybe I should get religion. Or ask for a shrink. Even if I did, who could I trust? Can I ever trust anyone again?

𝓑ITTER DAYS. In a gloomy world ravaged by political and economic storms, battered by freak blizzards which killed hundreds in Western Europe and by unemployment so severe that half of Britain appeared to be out of work, the Queen's illness was a matter of comment and speculation and concern, but it was not central. Toward the end of January a prison warden was killed by a car bomb in West London and responsibility was claimed by a group calling itself the British Republican Army; and over the next few weeks the BRA staged a series of bombings, bank raids and kidnappings reminiscent of the Italian Red Brigades and the German Baader-Meinhof gang. They were apparently republicans but they were pledged to overthrow the whole capitalist system rather than just the monarchy. The monarchy, retreating into its shell, keeping the Queen under wraps, kept as low a profile as it could. The King inspected troops, toured various parts of the country and was much photographed. But he said very little and was seldom quoted.

The Queen herself wrote copiously in her diary. Henderson, who went out of his way to continue as if nothing had happened, saw her almost daily and knew how much she was writing. It worried him. She was becoming obsessive—so much so that he tried to tease her about it.

"Anyone would think you were writing for publication. You're like Gibbon," he said, "scribble, scribble, scribble, eh?"

"Don't make fun of me, Maurice" she said, very seriously. She had become a sad woman since her confinement, he thought. In fact the possibility that she really was ill was one which had occurred to him but not evidently to her or anyone else who mattered. What depressed him was that the spark had gone out of her. The vivacity had disappeared.

Soon after the incident with the Canadians she told Maurice she wanted to ask him a favor.

"You know what's going on, Maurice," she said. "They call it house arrest in South Africa."

Maurice made mild clucking noises of disagreement but she silenced him.

"I'm not asking for sympathy" she said, "I'm asking for practical help. I'm damn sure someone is reading all my letters even if it's only my husband. I don't ask for much privacy but I do want to think that I can exchange some letters uncensored."

Henderson said nothing, but he did not demur. He knew that she was almost certainly right.

"Would you mind acting as a courier for me?"

He frowned. He was putting his head on the block. If anyone found out that he was helping the Queen to avoid Blackrock's censorship he would be in fearful trouble.

"Please" she said, her eyes pleading with him. "Nothing indiscreet. I'll level with you. There are two people who my enemies here would not like me to correspond with. You know that Joanne Hollis is my oldest friend. I don't want anyone eavesdropping on what we have to say to each other, even if it's not very significant. And I want to keep in touch with Julian Locke over the Friends of Man. I know that would be, shall we say, 'frowned on.'"

"I don't know" Henderson said, "I don't like it."

"Look" she said, "I promise I'm not going to put anything in those letters that will represent the slightest risk. I daren't. You know that. God knows what would happen."

"All right," Henderson said reluctantly, and Caroline managed to preserve at least some sort of normal human contact during her confinement. Neither correspondence was especially intimate. That with Joanne was more so but she confined her most revealing outpourings to the diary. Indeed she deliberately tried to make her letters to Joanne as optimistic as possible. It was not in her interests to alarm her, for if Joanne realized how completely wrong everything was going, her concern was likely to make matters worse. The correspondence with Locke was at first briskly formal, concerned almost exclusively with Friends of Man business. But gradually their tone relaxed. Locke started to include little snippets of gossip about members of the committee, comments on films and plays he had been to see, exhibitions he had visited, books he had read. Before either of them realized what was happening their weekly letters became more an expression of friendship rather than of a business relationship. Each, unknown to the other, waited for them eagerly and was disappointed if they did not arrive, as they nearly always did, on schedule. Henderson brought Locke's weekly report with him on Monday mornings, for it invariably dropped through his letter box in the first post that day. On Thursdays he collected the Queen's reply and usually managed to slip it into the mailbox during the day so that it arrived at Locke's home on Friday morning or Saturday at the latest.

When he received his first royal missive, Julian mentioned it both to Sam and to Schnabel, but later he gave up doing so, and under questioning maintained that there was silence from the palace.

"I don't believe him," Sam said one evening to Schnabel. She had arranged a meeting specifically to express her worries.

"I can't prove anything," she said, "but I think Julian's holding out on us. He's been very odd recently, especially when I mention our great and good and lovely patron. If it wasn't so patently ludicrous, I'd say he'd got something going there."

Schnabel chuckled. "That's fine," he said. "Remain as vigilant as possible, but say nothing to Julian. If he is turning into a monarchist convert, we can make it work to our advantage."

It was not until one frozen day in what should have been spring that Prime Minister Potter went on television and announced that he was going to the people. He did so against a background of almost unalleviated despondency. The country, like its Queen, seemed drained of enthusiasm and vitality and yet it was difficult to see how the divided and rancorous socialist opposition would greatly improve matters. The choice facing the electorate was between depression in a democracy or depression under a proletarian dictatorship—or so Potter and the Tories portrayed the choice. The Socialists declared that the country's condition was the result of Tory misrule, and incompetent managment, capitalism, so-called free enterprise, and the anachronistic system of constitutional monarchy. Under socialist government inequalities would be swept away once and for all. There would be state ownership of land, of banking, of the building societies. Private medicine and private education would be done away with and there would be a series of widespread constitutional reforms designed to give power to the people. When the manifesto appeared it duly included the commitment to a republic under an elected president.

Under a heading "The Monarchy," it proclaimed: "This will

be abolished as a matter of urgency, though not without first submitting the matter to a full referendum of the British people. It is recognized that such an important matter should be submitted to a special vote but the Labour Party is confident of obtaining the necessary two-thirds majority for finally ending an institution which has greatly contributed to our present parlous position and helped to make us a laughing stock in the world community. The Royal Family's private income and possessions will be taxed in the normal way and its members will be given the opportunity to continue to live in Britain as ordinary citizens. It is also the policy of the Labour Party to abolish the House of Lords and all titles, whether hereditary or not."

"Referendum my arse," Cathcart opined as he and Sir Evelyn Blackrock stood side by side in the hall of the club. In front of them the ticker tape machine chattered restlessly, spewing out a report on the weekend's campaign speeches. "If they get in, they'll phrase the referendum so bloody one-sidedly that your lot won't have a chance. Don't say I didn't warn you." He was in a bitter mood. Even though he had a five thousand majority in his own constituency, he hadn't a hope of holding it—not with the polls showing a twenty percent lead for Labor. And increasing . . .

"Doesn't look very promising" Blackrock said.

"Promising? It's going to be a bloody massacre." He turned and led the way towards the dining room. "Unless we do something . . . decisive." He put a hand on Blackrock's shoulder. "I think," he murmured, "it's time you and I had another little chat about Apple Pie."

As the election campaign continued Queen Caroline found that she had become used to her virtual imprisonment. She played long and lovingly with her children; she read Hardy and Tolstoy, which made her gloomy, and Dickens and Jane Austen, which cheered her up; she listened to music; she watched old movies on her husband's video recorder. She followed the election campaign with detached interest on television and in the newspapers. At Sandringham she took Oliver for long walks

255

around the estate, accompanied by one of the keepers as a security measure—no hardship since he was an affable countryman who instructed her in the mysteries of the woods and parkland. He showed her the badgers' sett and the track of a stoat in the morning snow and talked for hours about the rearing of birds and the training of dogs, until she began to wonder whether she might not abandon any aspirations of being intelligent and concerned about worldly matters. She could, she decided, quite happily become a fifty-year-old county lady in sensible shoes and sensible tweeds, surrounded by dogs and knitting patterns and a loving family.

Above all, she wrote her diary.

> . . . *a sort of self-imposed lobotomy, and maybe that's what I need. I'd be like Mamie Eisenhower or Mrs. Prime Minister Potter. But dammit, I want to be Eleanor Roosevelt. At least. I wish they'd realize that I can be useful. If they'd wanted a puppet, they should have made sure Bunny married one of those godforsaken debutantes he was always trying to seduce. But come election day "I shall be released." Either that or we all go into exile in the footsteps of the King of Greece and the Shah and the rest of that pathetic caravanserai. Maybe that's the best way out. You have to face it: Hereditary monarchy is a holdover, a sham and a farce, even more so when it's the tool of a bureaucrat like Blackrock. Jesus I hate that man . . .*

Caroline and the King had grown still further apart in the last few weeks; both had retreated into themselves. It was not that there was anything as positive as hatred or even dislike between them. Far worse, they seemed politely indifferent. Even if divorce had been possible—and for a king of England, especially this one, it was inconceivable—it would have been difficult to show adequate grounds. They lived together in a state of studied civility. From time to time one or the other displayed melting signs of affection, but somehow these were never reciprocated. Each felt betrayed by the other.

Perhaps they still loved one another. It was hard to tell, but they told themselves it was probably no worse than other more ordinary marriages the world over: not as good as they had hoped, but not as bad, perhaps, as they had feared. For the King there was ample escape. He played hard. He hunted, shot, fished and practiced his polo. He worked hard too, spent longer poring over state papers and working on his "boxes." And it seemed to Caroline that he stayed away longer and more often, especially in the convivially all-male atmosphere of the officers' mess or the great dining halls of the City Guilds. He was turning into that archetypal British caricature, the clubbable man. His attitude to her was much like Blackrock's to Lady Blackrock. "He will hold thee," she quoted bitterly, "when his passion shall have spent its novel force, something better than his dog, a little dearer than his horse." Ah well, she thought: They warned me.

This is a crazy country. We're right in the middle of the most venomous election campaign you can imagine, a campaign which apparently is likely to mean the end of the whole democratic system in this country (and incidentally of us along the way) and we are all being wheeled out for Trooping the Color. Great display of national unity. The Brigade of Guards demonstrating their loyalty and affection. May be the last time the color is trooped, unless of course they decide to troop it for our successor, President Benn, which is always in the cards . . .
I am finally allowed out. Big deal. According to Bunny who was told by Blackrock who was told by Henry Cathcart, this is an official government decision, endorsed by the Cabinet. I have to look drawn and ill and regal and glamorous and affecting, and I'm to travel to the Horse Guards by coach, God help me. They seem to think it will win votes or something. Their machinations are beyond me. Blackrock told Bunny it's a reward for being good, which is such a fatuous idea I want to scream.

On a sharp bright morning the rickety old Irish State Coach was hauled across the palace forecourt by four Oldenburg bay horses from the royal mews. The Irish State Coach had been bought from a Dublin coach builder in 1852, and though it still looked pretty enough for a Cinderella, every revolution of its antique wheels was an adventure. Inside, the Queen prepared to wave and smile and radiate a benign happiness which was none the less convincing for being almost completely artificial.

The coach was escorted by a squadron of Household Cavalry, cuirasses gleaming, plumes dancing, every one of their massive, high-stepping chargers sleekly groomed so that they shone as brightly as their riders' armor. She waved at a tour group of Americans with Polaroids and plastic raincoats. It was tempting to lean out of the window and call breezily, "Hi! Where you from?," but she let it pass. She was out on parole.

The clatter of the cavalry had an oddly soporific effect, lulling her into daydreams. She thought wistfully of Joanne, and of a day when the two of them plus two beaux whose names she could not remember had gone to a country harness meet in upstate New York. It must have been the high clip-clopping of the horses that reminded her. She recalled their breath steaming in the cold, the flimsy rigs creaking like the state coach. They had drunk hot cider and eaten German sausage. She could see the glowing embers of charcoal in the braziers even now, and smell the charring of the roast pork. Oh for the simple life, she sighed, before she had met her King, her King who even now was riding out from his palace behind her, stiff-backed on his stallion, impossibly glamorous in the uniform of the colonel of the Coldstreams. She leaned back and closed her eyes as the coach swung right in the direction of Whitehall.

Then the bomb went off.

It was the first one she had ever heard outside the movies; she did not at first recognize it for what it was. The concussion was stunning, raw, not like fireworks on the Fourth of July but jagged-edged, undisciplined, and the force of the explosion seemed to stop the coach in its tracks and hurl her back into the heavy swansdown and leather of the upholstery.

"Oh my God," she exclaimed stupidly in the numb silence which followed the blast.

"What happened? What happened?"

Even as she asked there was the beginning of noise as if of people waking from sleep. People were screaming, horses were neighing. In the distance sirens started to wail. Seconds later a postilion, bleeding from a cut above one eye, threw the door open and helped her out.

"Are you all right," she asked, anxiously examining the blood.

He put his hand to the cut. "It's nothing, ma'am," he said. "Bit of glass. Not like those poor buggers." He gestured up the road. The bomb must have been detonated under the street somehow, just as the leading file of Household Cavalry passed over it; men and horses lay on the road dead, dying, injured. Some of the spectators had caught it too, though mercifully few since the police had kept the crowds back for security. The tail end of the squadron had escaped almost unscathed, and these men were now hurrying forward in an attempt to bring some succor to those who could use it. It was obvious that it was too late for many of them.

"Oh God!" the Queen said, "What's being done?"

The first of the ambulances screamed past and shuddered to a halt with a squealing of tires, its blue light winking. An officer in the full dress uniform of the Blues and Royals came running up as fast as his spurs, thigh-length boots and clanking sword would allow. He saluted. "Ma'am," he said briskly, "permission to escort you to your place."

She gazed at him, still stunned. He was very young, she thought, foolishly, not more than about twenty.

"I'm not sure," she said. "That is . . ."

Another car drew up alongside. One of the palace unmarkeds. Blackrock leaped out of the back, wearing a black bowler hat and carrying a rolled umbrella. "Thank you, lieutenant," he said, "I'll take Her Majesty on in the car. You'd better get back to your men."

The officer saluted again smartly and turned back toward the carnage. Stretcher bearers were covering the dead and moving the wounded to the waiting ambulances. An officer with a pistol was shooting the horses who writhed crippled on the ground, to prevent them from injuring the rescue workers. "I think we should carry on," Blackrock said. "Nothing practical we can do here. The one satisfaction we should deny these bastards is getting the parade held up."

"The show goes on, eh Blackrock?" she asked bitterly.

He flinched. "I'm afraid so, ma'am."

She nodded. "Of course," she said, and let him put her in the car. Moments later, after skirting the scene of the disaster where the acrid smell of explosives still hung in the air, she found herself ascending the stairs of Horse Guards, being guided to her seat, being given, at her request, a glass of water, and then watching stiff upper-lipped with the rest of the audience as the Brigade of Guards marched and wheeled in its formal annual tribute to the monarch. The bands beat out martial rhythms, the guardsmen stamped their feet and held their line steady, and her husband the King sat very still on his horse, his great black bearskin helping to make him seem bereft of any emotion.

Only afterwards, at the palace, when she learned that seventeen men had been killed in the outrage, did she break down and cry. And for once her husband comforted her, and took his own comfort in doing so.

That evening, about an hour before close of play, Sir Evelyn Blackrock and Henry Cathcart met by arrangement at Lord's Cricket Ground. They were both members of Marylebone Cricket Club. It had seemed preferable to meet on neutral ground and away from their respective offices.

"I see," Cathcart said, "that the BRA have claimed responsibility for this morning." He, like Blackrock, was staring at the game through a pair of ancient field glasses. The play was quiet, uneventful, timeless; two English counties, Middlesex and Hampshire, locked in languid combat.

"Yes." Blackrock lowered his glasses. They were seated in the very top tier of the eccentric Gothic pavilion at the west end of the ground. There was no one else near them; in fact there could not have been more than a couple of hundred people in a stadium that could accommodate twenty thousand. "Dreadful business. I suppose we were right to carry on." Blackrock glanced at his friend, seeking support.

"Of course," Cathcart said. "Steady under fire. You mustn't show them you're rattled."

"Even if one is rattled."

Below them on the dry, yellowing grass, one of the batsmen hit the ball square to the mid-wicket boundary. There was a faint splutter of applause from the drinkers outside the tavern.

"You're not rattled, Evelyn?" Cathcart's voice was grimly amused.

"A fortnight to election day and you're still a mile behind. Of course I'm rattled."

Cathcart scanned the grandstand with his binoculars. "Today's little massacre should win us back some lost ground. We *are* the party of law and order. If we catch the bastards we'll string them up. If the left catch them, they'll give them a so-called life sentence, which will be commuted to five years or so and served in a glorified holiday camp. Nothing like a little bloody anarchist terrorism to turn the great British public Conservative."

"Balls," Blackrock said. "Potter's past it. You have to face the fact that this government's made an unholy mess of things and that's what we're paying for now."

"Oh, good shot!" Cathcart put down the glasses and clapped, slowly, the lonely sound of his hands echoing along the empty benches like a lament. "I met a friend from Washington on the staff of their National Security Council who said his people had contingency plans to put in a 'force de frappe' if the left got out of control. There's now a second American aircraft carrier in the North Atlantic. That U.S. amphibious assault exercise group is still in Norway, three weeks after the rest of the NATO troop components packed up and went home. Disturbing, wouldn't you say?"

"We've all heard that kind of speculation," Blackrock said irritably. "I can't believe it. What did you want to talk about, anyway? I don't have very much time."

"Let's go for a walk," Cathcart said. "I want to talk to you about Apple Pie." He got up and led the way downstairs and out onto the tarmac behind the pavilion. They began to walk very slowly around the ground, deep in earnest conversation. An onlooker would have assumed they were discussing cricket.

"The fact is, old boy," Cathcart said putting a hand on Colonel Blackrock's shoulder, "that since you weren't inclined to be all that cooperative about a rerun of the Fanshawe accident . . . I decided to go ahead on my own. Not entirely successfully as you know. Someone made a mistake and pushed the button a few seconds early . . ."

Blackrock said nothing more until they entered the long dark tunnel under the grandstand. "You mean" he said, "it wasn't the BRA."

"I don't think I need to be *too* specific, Evelyn—"

"Jesus Christ, Henry, you killed seventeen men. *Our* men." The colonel's observation was hissed out angrily.

"Don't be so damned sentimental, Evelyn." Cathcart was on edge, acutely conscious of having failed again. "What's seventeen men when you're fighting to save civilized life in this damn country? I don't think you quite understand what's going to happen if the left take power. Afghanistan was a bloody picnic compared to what's going to happen here. I promise. I can't say more than that, but the signals are there."

"Even so" Blackrock said weakly, "it's not right."

"You weren't so damned squeamish when we were dealing with Fanshawe."

"Dusty betrayed us," Blackrock said. "There's a difference."

"It's too late for scruples." Cathcart kicked at an empty beer can and sent it clattering into the gutter, where it came to rest in a pile of orange peel and abandoned score cards. "I want her disposed of for two reasons. One, she's a dangerous liability. Two, she's the martyr we want. People won't vote for a party linked to the murder of an innocent young mother of two—and their Queen to boot."

The emerged into the open air again and swung right behind the cheap seats at the Nursery End.

"What exactly are you suggesting?"

Cathcart relaxed perceptibly. Evelyn was showing some interest. They were past first base.

"I'm suggesting that the marriage was a mistake. She's fundamentally unstable, and before long she'll destroy us all. At times like this her sort of frivolous willfulness just won't be tolerated. Even under a Conservative government it would be difficult to get away with; under a left-wing government it's inconceivable. So she has to go. And fast. Divorce is out of the question, as we all know. Besides, the King doesn't believe in it. So there's only the one answer."

"You can't kill her." Blackrock's voice was flat but unequivocal.

"I tell you it's the only thing that would win the election. Can you imagine the outrage?"

"But the Labor Party would condemn it along with everyone else. No one believes that even a left-wing Labor Government would condone the murder of the Queen."

Cathcart snorted. "I don't think there's any doubt that if Labor get in with as big a majority as looks likely, this country will be another Poland or Hungary. At least fifty percent of the new parliamentary labor party are Moscow men. You really are surprisingly sanguine, Evelyn. You'll be in the salt mines by Christmas."

They paused by the sight screens and watched the final over. The players seemed bored. There was no urgency in their movements. One or two of the fielders had their hands in their pockets.

"You can't kill her," Blackrock said, more dubiously this time. "It's just that . . ." He paused. "I see what you're suggesting. It would be very difficult to vote for a republican Marxist government after that sort of atrocity. It would produce quite an outburst of patriotism."

Cathcart smiled. "At least you accept the principle," he said. "But if you won't soil your hands, what exactly can you propose as an alternative?"

"I don't understand anything any more. There's been a volte-face. I've been pardoned; suddenly I am an asset.

*Blackrock says the cabinet has agreed that I can show my
face again. I'm supposed to keep my nose clean, but at the
same time they're telling me I'm going to be allowed to go
to see the Friends and Julian. I don't get it . . .*

Inasmuch as the aim of the bombing had been to damage the
monarchy it was supremely counterproductive. In that sense
Cathcart was clearly correct. Letters of support for the monarchy flooded the palace and filled the correspondence columns of
all newspapers. Schnabel, who had been purring with pleasure
over the obvious trouble in the palace and the Queen's way-
wardness, was livid with rage.

"Amateurs" he complained heatedly to Samantha at one of
their now regular conferences. "They've bungled it and set us
back months. Why can't they leave revolution to professionals?
Like everything else there is a right and a wrong way of doing
things."

"They killed some soldiers," Sam said lamely.

"Don't be a child," Schnabel said. "A soldier is only a class
enemy because of the orders he is made to carry out. Do you
think that common soldiers, even those in the Household Cavalry, come from the aristocracy? Do me a favor."

Samantha blushed. Much as she disliked him, she had respect
for Schnabel's revolutionary credentials and wanted to impress.

"The Queen's out of quarantine anyway" she said. "She's
coming to next week's executive meeting."

"Good news."

"What about her and Julian?"

"He's not saying much. But I suspect the worst."

"That's good," he said. "We must try to exploit it. Blackrock
and his cronies have been very flexible about Her Majesty's
misdemeanors so far; but if we could manage to mix in some
evidence of . . . sexual indiscretion, they might prove a little less
forgiving. Don't you think?"

Samantha shrugged. "You could be right. What do you want
to do?"

Schnabel leaned forward confidentially. "Every summer of

his life" he said, "His Gracious Majesty goes fishing in Iceland. My information is that he will be going there shortly, and that our friend and your patron will not be going with him—Very cold, Iceland," he chuckled. "Very spartan and inhospitable. Not a country to attract Her Majesty. So with a little gentle persuasion, while the cat is away, the mice will play."

Samantha returned his conspiratorial grin.

"Watch carefully," he said, "and encourage in every way possible. She is a lonely woman. She must start to seek a little solace. Julian may hang back. Make sure that he doesn't. Discreetly, you understand. He must suspect nothing."

"Okay," Sam said, "I'll do what I can. Poor Julian." And she laughed.

At the next executive meeting, the Queen was once more chaperoned by Detective Constable Angell who waited opposite the building scrutinizing the entrance. Since the BRA bomb had so narrowly missed the Irish State Coach, Angell and Macpherson's other officers were more heavily armed and equipped with an emergency radio set which could summon police assistance at a moment's notice. There had been some talk of more stringent security measures but everyone, Blackrock, King and Cabinet included, agreed that even the most armorplated protection could never guarantee safety against a determined enemy, and that for King and Queen to adopt the style of some banana republic dictator was unthinkable. They would not ride around in tanks with military escorts.

It was almost eight o'clock by the time the meeting broke up. The King was at a Royal Marine dinner and would not be back until almost midnight. As before, the Queen hovered. It was too late for a film, but she had no wish to return to the bleak solitude of the palace. All the others had left except for Julian, Samantha and the Labor MP.

"I feel like some curry" Samantha said, buttoning up her coat. "Anyone coming with me?"

"I'll join you," Smithers said. "I have to check in at campaign headquarters later, but I'm in no rush."

They glanced at Julian and the Queen, questioning, unsure. Julian looked at Caroline. This was the first time they had met since their enforced estrangement and the increasingly affectionate exchange of letters. Caroline thought for a moment. Bunny was out and she was not expected home for anything in particular. Angell was with her and could stand guard outside the restaurant. She would be with three others; there would be some security—and propriety—in their numbers.

"Sure," she said, "why not?"

Constable Angell was none too pleased about having to stay on duty for an extra two hours, but he scarcely showed it. He was not particularly happy about the security angle either, but his not to reason why, he decided. The Queen suggested he come in with them and sit at another table, but he didn't care for Indian food, so he stayed outside, listening to the radio in the car, and chain-smoking.

Inside, the four of them sat at a corner table screened off from the rest of the diners by a piece of trellising hung about with some slightly sad greenhouse plants. They ate tandoori chicken, kebabs and dhal, drank beer and talked about travel and films and theaters. Their conversation was apolitical, relaxed and friendly. Sam deftly hid her republican and egalitarian fervor. She found herself enjoying Caroline's company, though she had no problem in differentiating between her liking for the person and her hatred for the institution. She was pleased to see that Caroline and Julian were getting along better than their professional relationship demanded; also that they seemed to know a surprising amount about each other's tastes. They were on the verge of that instantly recognizable denominator of the close relationship: the private joke. Toward the end of their meal Sam steered the conversation to music. She herself admitted to a fondness for heavy rock. Caroline had been a jazz fan. The men were moderately tone deaf and neutral.

"They're putting on a three-day rock festival at Otley," Sam said casually, "a real nostalgia trip. Woodstock and all that. I think they're trying to get the Stones together for it."

"That's a joke," Julian said. "Geriatric rock."

"They're not *that* old," Sam protested.

"I've always wanted to go to one of those things," Charles said.

"We ought to get up a party," said Samantha.

The others murmured a halfhearted assent. It was the kind of idea that came to people after dinner. Usually it would be forgotten by morning.

I thought I was past the age for making new friends, but Julian really is a nice man. Actually I'd love to go to the rock concert, if there was a group of us. Safety in numbers. Would Bunny mind? But why should he—no one need ever know. Anyway, in a few weeks' time I have a feeling we're going to be out of a job and we'll be able to go to all the rock concerts we want. The opinion polls gave a little hiccup after the bomb but we're back to normal now. The Conservatives don't have a snowball's chance in hell.

"I've got to get going," Caroline said, "or they'll be sending out search parties." The others laughed. "But don't let me break up the party." She stood to go, and they stood with her.

"I'll see you to the chauffeur, at least," Julian said with a sudden rush of gallantry.

"All right," she said. "'Night, Charles, 'night Sam." Then Julian showed her across the restaurant to the door where the proprietor stood rubbing his hands and smiling ingratiatingly. Miraculously, no one had noticed her identity.

"Don't come out," she said, "it's freezing."

"That's okay," said Julian, "I'd better make sure you make it to your car."

Outside she saw that Angell had parked the Stag directly opposite in a yellow zone. She waved across the street at him and he stubbed out his cigarette, turned off the radio and started the engine.

"Thanks," Caroline said to Julian. "That was really great. I enjoyed it. I haven't had a curry in years." She leaned forward slightly, offering her cheek to be kissed. He, awkwardly, kissed it and then, as she turned her head and gave him the other, he kissed her with a little more assurance, allowing his hands to rest momentarily on her shoulders.

"Goodnight," he said. "Take care."

"And you," she said. "Bye for now."

From the car, Angell watched coldly. He didn't mean to spy, but he would have to file a report. If he didn't, and someone else found out what had been going on, they'd have his guts for garters.

CHAPTER

*A*LTHOUGH SHE suspected that censorship had been partially lifted, Caroline quietly maintained the link with Joanne through Maurice Henderson. She felt happier with it. Soon after the bombing Henderson left her a letter.

"Darling Caro," it began, "I was so relieved to hear you were all right. It must have been terrible. All three of the networks here ran long specials on it. I thought both of you were fantastic at the Trooping. You looked so calm and collected . . ." A couple of paragraphs later came some surprising news: "Caro, I'd just love to come over as soon as I get a chance but life has gotten sort of complicated just recently. Simon and Annie Waterman have split up and I have to tell you that Si has moved in to my place. I never would have seen it coming; in fact I started out not liking him all that much, but, well, you know how these things are. He and Annie have been drifting apart for years. Then he found her in bed with a professor of elocution from NYU and I was glad to see that he walked out immediately. I don't know what's happening right now, but Si and I have plans to take a vacation in Europe. Would it be okay if we stayed, or do your people still draw the line at divorcees? Si sends his love. . . ."

Caroline put the letter down on the desk top. She felt a little betrayed. Simon Waterman was a prig and not much of a lawyer; she didn't like him much, either. Still, if it made Joanne happy . . . She took her diary from the safe and began to write.

"So you think we may be over the worst?" Colonel Blackrock swung at a Keep Off the Grass sign with the ferrule of his tightly rolled umbrella. The sun shone on the flamingoes in the lake and sparkled on the turrets and pinnacles of Whitehall. Saint James's Park in summer was still, thank God, a confoundedly attractive part of the world.

"All I know," Maurice Henderson answered, hurrying to keep pace with the old soldier's brisk strides, "is that she seems quite sunny and serene and she's giving Simpson a very easy time. I think the bomb shook her up. At all events there's been nothing about heading up new societies or making unchecked speeches or anything. Isobel Coker says much the same. She seems quite sunny and contented."

"She seems transformed," Blackrock agreed as they turned left toward the Duke of York's steps. "My only concern is the Friends of Man. I'd like her to give them up now. Do you think that's possible?"

"I doubt it somehow." Henderson hoped Blackrock had not heard of the correspondence he had been ferrying between the Queen and Locke. The old man's intelligence system worked quietly. "But they were fairly shattered over the seal hunt business and Hector Macfarlane. My impression is that they'll quietly retreat into the woodwork."

"I hope you're right. That's one of the things I want to thrash out with you and Cathcart. Seems that fellow Angell, her detective, has got some well-placed friends in Special Branch. Apparently the other night, after a Friends of Man meeting, she and one or two of the others went out to an Indian restaurant in Marylebone High Street."

"With Angell in tow?"

"Oh, yes" Blackrock said, "she played it all by the book, nothing like that time she went on furlough. Angell sat outside in the car."

"Can't see anything wrong with that." They were out of the park now, nearing Cathcart's club. Henderson was still uneasy about the letters.

"Unfortunately that's not Cathcart's view."

"Why not?"

"Oh, he'll explain. It appears the others were Locke and his girl Samantha, and Charles Smithers, the member for Newcastle, St. James."

"He's some sort of crypto-Marxist isn't he?"

"So they say. I used to hunt with his father before the war. Nice enough chap. Cathcart feels she shouldn't be seen with that sort of person in public."

They arrived at the club's Regency portico. The steps were peopled with dark-suited members and their guests, scurrying lunchwards. Cathcart was in the bar on the first floor.

"You remember Maurice Henderson," Blackrock said in a sentence that was halfway between a question and a statement. They shook hands and did not talk business until they were seated in the dining room, twenty minutes and a stiff gin later.

"Maurice takes the view that Apple Pie's in good shape," Blackrock said.

"I see," Cathcart said. "You've not heard this latest report then?"

"Sir Evelyn just told me."

"I'd hardly call that being in good order."

"Surely you can't blame her for having a meal with people on one of her committees? We haven't stopped her being patron after all."

"You can blame her for kissing people on the pavement in a busy street," Cathcart said. He stirred his soup and frowned.

"I didn't know about that," Henderson said.

"No," Blackrock said, looking accusing.

"I didn't think it was something one should discuss over the phone," Cathcart said.

"Now you see why I'm not happy."

"There's hardly anything sinister in it," Henderson said, "if she's prepared to do it on the pavement of Marylebone High Street."

"Suppose she'd been spotted. What then?"

"Evidently she was spotted," Henderson said, "or we wouldn't be talking about it. I'm sorry, I just don't see anything damaging about kissing someone goodnight after dinner in a restaurant. I kiss all sorts of people but it doesn't mean I'm having a raging affair with them."

"You're rather more gullible than *Private Eye* would be."

Later that afternoon Cathcart telephoned Blackrock.

"You alone?"

"Yes," Blackrock said.

"I don't altogether trust that Henderson. Surprisingly wet behind the ears."

"I know what you mean," Blackrock said, "but he is well liked in certain quarters."

"Then let's use him when necessary, but let's not treat him to any confidences."

"No."

"Right you are then," Cathcart said breezily. "Regards to Dorothy."

"Rather." Sir Evelyn Blackrock carefully replaced the receiver in its cradle and fingered his neck. He did not care for conspiracy, unless it was one entirely of his own making.

She *was* quiet and subdued, though she was not sure why. It was not just the bomb outrage—upsetting as it was—that made her keep a low profile. Suddenly she didn't trust herself.

She and Bunny pursued an armed truce, treading warily, even tentatively enjoying each other in bed but with none of the unselfconscious passion that had characterized their earlier lovemaking. He seemed to need her twice a week; she took what pleasure she could from his gentle but mechanical attentions. Once or twice, when he was on one of his frequent trips, she and

Julian repeated their excursion to the movie theater, always with the watchful Angell in tow. There were no more kisses, and in the darkness of the theater they were scrupulously careful to avoid the slightest physical contact. Their meetings were outwardly chaste and innocent, and yet both of them, without confiding in the other, began to feel dangerously guilty.

Caroline liked Locke, but there was nothing sexual there. Or so she told herself. She felt neglected by her husband, and she needed a friend. It was as simple as that. There was no impropriety in it, though she had to concede that as her sense of abandonment became more acute she found herself relying more and more on Locke's companionship. He for his part liked her but was not yet ready to declare himself, nor even admit to himself that he wanted her.

Caroline was particularly unnerved by Samantha, who was always charming and friendly enough but who gave the impression that she was permanently watching for some indiscretion or lapse. Invariably she chatted away about music, using their conversation in the Indian restaurant as a starting point. She seemed genuinely eager to get a group together for the Otley Rock Festival, if only to convert Caroline to the charms of her kind of music.

"How long have you known Samantha?" Caroline asked one evening as they went down to the car.

"More or less forever," Julian said, with the sort of offhand finality which warned her not to pursue the matter.

"All ready to go," Henry Cathcart said. They were sitting in the park watching tourists feed ducks. The headline on Blackrock's *News Standard* said: "Labour Lead stretches to thirty percent. Pound at All Time Low."

"I heard," Blackrock said, "that our American cousins are putting combat troops into Ruislip and Heyford."

Cathcart looked at him sharply but said nothing.

"It's true then?"

Cathcart crossed his legs. "You're not supposed to know," he said. "No one knows. Even we don't know how many, exactly."

"But it *is* true?"

Cathcart did not reply and Blackrock took this for an affirmation.

"Dangerous game, Henry," he said.

"Not half as dangerous as the one we're playing," Cathcart answered. "If that goes wrong, we've had it."

"It's not going to though, is it?"

"*Hoffentlich,*" said Cathcart dubiously. "It's our last chance. Only two days before the election."

"It's the only time that I know she'll be at Windsor." Blackrock was defensive. "She may be there before then, but I don't know for certain."

"And you're sure she'll go out riding?"

"She always does."

"And on her own?"

Blackrock nodded.

"And the King's away for certain?" Cathcart persisted. "I want the whole thing wrapped up and tidy before he can get back."

"He says he always goes fishing at this time of year, and that if he cancels it will look panicky. He asked Potter, and Potter gave him the okay."

"Of course he did," Cathcart said smiling. "I do have some influence."

"Does Potter know?" Blackrock was not sure whether he *wanted* Potter to know. Prime ministerial approval would make him happier for reasons of his own, but the more people were involved in the conspiracy the more leaky it might prove.

"As much as he needs to know." Cathcart sighed. "I hope you aren't getting cold feet."

"I've told you before," Blackrock said, "I reserve the right to cancel if necessary."

"That's not in your power."

"Of course it is. I should simply tip her off. Warn her not to go riding."

"I hope you won't do that, Evelyn." There was no mistaking

the menace in Cathcart's voice, but Blackrock had been around too long for that, too.

"I don't frighten easily," he replied. "And do remember, we're on the same side."

"I do hope so, Evelyn," said his fellow Old Harrovian. "I really do hope so."

"What will you do when I'm in Iceland?" the King asked one night, after a more than usually successful session of lovemaking. Caroline lay with her head nuzzling his shoulder, feeling nostalgic about their early days together.

"Console myself with a lover," she said, softly mocking.

"Seriously." He moved sideways, sliding his arm under her back. "Why don't you go up to Balmoral?"

"I'm not that crazy about Balmorality," she said. "I'll commute between here and Windsor. It's all arranged."

"Won't you be bored?"

"I thought Joanne might come to stay. She has a man. She could bring him. You met him, Simon Waterman. He was married to Annie. They split up. You liked him."

"I remember." The King laughed. "I said he was quite civilized for an American."

"Huh," she snorted affectionately.

But he still hadn't answered her.

"Would that be all right?"

"Yes. I don't see why not. As long as she behaves."

"I'll make sure she does," she said. "We could take in some theater, a concert or two. Maybe go to Stratford."

"I wouldn't mind taking you to Stratford myself, actually."

"That would be nice. We haven't been to the theater for ages." She kissed his earlobe. "We were always at the theater in the old days."

"You make it sound like ancient history," he said reproachfully.

"Well?"

"We've only been married two and a half years."

"Almost three."

"That's not long," he said.

"Three years in marriage is a long time."

"Maybe."

He pulled his arm away and sat up. "I must go to bed," he said. "Heavy day tomorrow." He bent over and kissed her on the forehead. "Thank you, darling," he said.

"Don't mention it. Any time."

She said it lightly enough, but the thought kept her awake for another hour: She had not anticipated marriage to a man who wanted separate beds.

The King was as good as his word. Joanne's visit during his fortnight of fishing was confirmed. Joanne was all set to come, but Waterman could not leave his law practice until after the first week, so Caroline would have her friend to herself for a few days. She looked forward to it and spent days planning outings to theaters and concerts. Oddly, the palace authorities still seemed pleased with her.

When Cathcart heard about the impending visit of Joanne he was surprised and angry.

"Golden Eagle is adamant, Henry," Blackrock explained to him, "and she is her oldest friend. No one's going to make a fuss if they're seen together. She'll take her mind off Locke."

Cathcart did not sound impressed. . . .

A week before the King's trip, Caroline went to the Friends of Man for a committee meeting.

"Julian and I are definitely going to Otley," Samantha said afterward. "It would be super if you could come."

"When is it?" Caroline felt pressured.

"Ten days' time. The weekend of the seventeenth. I'd love you to hear the Fuzz."

"I'll think about it," Caroline said. "I've got my friend Joanne staying, and someone else, and my husband's away." She laughed shortly, "I'm not sure it's anything I should be seen at."

"No one need ever know. There'll be hundreds of thousands there."

"I don't think so," she said. "But I'll ask my friends."

"Well don't leave it too late. I've got half a dozen tickets, and they're like gold dust."

Later Sam phoned Schnabel. "She's beginning to bite," she said. "Can you bring some pressure to bear through Joanne Hollis? She's the one staying."

"I'll call a friend in New York," Schnabel said. "How's Julian?"

"Worrying," Sam said. "I don't know how much to tell him."

"What have you told him?"

"Nothing. But he must realize that there's a purpose in my banging on about Otley."

"Go on saying nothing. If your reading is right, and I think it is, then he'll be too excited about having a day out with our friend to worry about us."

I have no business being so excited. I try to excuse myself by saying it's something to do with the mood of the country. Jesus, everyone is jittery. There have been some more bombs, but nobody hurt much. The election is obviously no contest. Then we have a referendum to decide what happens to us. I think we could win that, but no one else seems to agree. Anyway I realize that's just an excuse for my excitement and I feel guilty because I know that the real reason is that Bunny is going away and Joanne is coming to stay and it's going to be like old times. We can maybe smoke some grass and talk and fool around. I hate myself because I adore Bunny but it will just be sensational to feel free and uninhibited and un-British for a change. I don't think I'll ever understand these people. They have to be the least spontaneous in the world. Even Julian, sweet as he is, is so uptight I can't believe it. I just want to cut loose, have a little fun for a change . . .

Joanne was to arrive at Heathrow half an hour after Bunny left. Caroline had brought nanny and the children to see their father off. He was in better spirits than at any time since the bomb, taking only an equerry, a valet and a single detective. By royal standards he was travelling light, though he had enough fishing tackle to equip a trawler.

"Be good, darlings," he said. He picked up Lizzie and kissed her on both cheeks. "Look after mummy," he said. He did the same to his son. "Bye-bye, Sunshine." Then he kissed the Queen.

"Bye, darling."

"Bye, darling."

"I'll bring you a salmon."

"Do that. Have a good time."

"I will. You too."

Finally he kissed nanny, then bounded up the steps of the plane. The little party watched as the plane taxied away, then Caroline shook hands with the Lord President of the Council, the Lord Lieutenant of Middlesex, and the airport manager who had been hovering in the background. There was no way you could escape the trappings of monarchy, at least not when the King was around. Now that he was airborne, the principal dignitaries felt free to leave, though the Queen and her little group were still protected by considerable if unobtrusive security. A senior management official also stayed with her. He would remain until she too was waved off the premises.

Joanne's flight was ten minutes early. This time she was brought off before any of the other passengers and Caroline waited by the Rolls on the tarmac at the bottom of the steps. The two friends embraced fondly and everyone piled into the car for Windsor. Almost the first thing Joanne said after the greetings were complete was "One thing I'm determined to do is get to the Otley Rock Festival. I hear it's going to be unbelievable. Can you get tickets?"

"It's possible," Caroline said cautiously, "but I'm told they're like gold dust."

The Otley Rock Festival filled her with foreboding. She knew that neither Blackrock nor Bunny would approve but that in itself did not concern her. Their objections were founded in snobbishness and prudery; at rock festivals people smoked marijuana and were careless about clothing. Tant pis. What worried her was that it was not her own idea. On the one hand Joanne and on the other Samantha and Julian kept pestering her for a decision.

The next morning as she and Joanne were riding alone in Windsor Great Park, they reined in and Caroline asked, "Jo, why are you so up for this Otley concert?"

Her friend shrugged. "Because it's going to be an event. First concert the Fuzz have given in over a year. Chance to see the Stones live. It'll be great. Aren't you up for it?"

Caroline looked perplexed. "I don't know. How did you hear about it?"

"There's been a lot of publicity in the music press, the *Times* ran a piece . . . and people talk. I know Barbie Mitchell was envying Si like crazy when he said he might be able to make it."

"Barbie?"

"Yeah."

Somewhere in Caroline's subconscious alarm bells rang. But she couldn't say why.

"Do you really want to go?"

"Hell yes. It'll be like old times."

Caroline looked at the enthusiasm in her friend's face and, for the first time since Joanne's arrival, she felt how much their friendship meant to her. "Okay," she said, "you're on." And she spurred her horse into a gallop, daring Joanne to race her across the springy parkland turf.

CHAPTER

$\mathscr{A}$S SOON as Hermann Schnabel heard the news from Samantha, he put in a call to *Gossip Magazine* in New York.

"Kandinski," he said, "Harry Smith here. The Panini diaries, remember?"

"Yeah, sure."

"Listen. I may have something for you. Can you recommend me a hot paparazzi-style photographer working out of London?"

"I got one or two kids over there who do good work for me. What's the story?"

"I can't tell you too much right now, but I want to propose a syndication deal. I'd handle British rights in the pictures myself. Is that okay by you?"

"Could be."

Kandinski gave him the names of three possible photographers. When Schnabel put the phone down he was almost purring with pleasure.

Julian Locke, revolutionary, had rich bourgeois parents who lived in a rich bourgeois house less than five miles from Otley Park, where the great rock festival was being held. They were fastidious, old-fashioned folk and they decided to move out for the weekend. The amplifiers on the sound stage were so loud that the rock music would be audible ten miles away, let alone five. They had friends in Gloucestershire, so they begged a weekend off them. Julian asked if he could borrow the house for the festival, and they agreed, still the worried but indulgent parents they had been since he was expelled from school.

The plan was that the party—Julian, Caroline, Simon Waterman and Joanne, Samantha and Charles Smithers—should pretend to be weekending chez Locke. The proper authorities would be told. Blackrock had taken advantage of his master's absence to spend the weekend at home, where he was hoping to work in his greenhouse. That meant that Simpson was in nominal charge, together with Macpherson.

They would indeed travel to the Locke's house, the Old Vicarage at Prenderville, but they would not stay long. Samantha and Joanne were both adamant that they should do the festival in style, taking sleeping bags and tents and spend the night. The campsite, they argued, would be as much fun as the concert itself. They promised Caroline she would never be recognized. "They won't be expecting you," Joanne said, "and most of them will be high as kites anyway. They won't be *capable* of recognizing you."

To make doubly sure, Caroline dug out her oldest jeans and shirt, and Samantha lent her her costermonger's cap. It wasn't much of a disguise, but it was more than enough. "Besides," Joanne said, "what does it matter. You're having a weekend out mixing with your people. What the hell's the harm in that? Seems about the same as your visiting a coal mine or attending a folk dance or something."

"You forget," Caroline said, "I've been burned."

"You're getting paranoid," Joanne said. "Where's your spunk? What was all that about wanting to be your own woman, do your own thing? Not getting trapped in the ritual? Good grief, if your husband can spend the weekend at horse trials at Badminton or polo in Cirencester, why in God's name can't you spend it at a rock festival in Otley Park?"

Caroline grinned. "You're good for me. You make me feel normal again."

But inwardly she was not so sure.

Something's weird. I can't put my finger on it, but I feel I'm not in control. That should be a good feeling but I have a sense of being carried along by the program. For once it's not Blackrock and the palace, but it's the same sense of being put under pressure—by Julian and Sam and even Joanne. They said there was a file on Julian; I wonder if that means anything? I guess there's a file on everybody now. Who cares . . .

They arrived at the Old Vicarage in the early evening, Detective Constable Angell driving, Simon Waterman in the front seat next to him and the girls in the back. The journey was tense and silent. No one felt like talking in front of Angell. The others were waiting for them by the garage. Julian's MG was not big enough, so Charles Smithers's anonymous Ford Cortina had been stacked with camping equipment. Angell stared at it, startled.

"It's okay, Angell," Caroline said. "We're spending a night under canvas. You can sleep in the car."

Angell looked more disturbed than she had ever seen him. "I understood we were spending the night at the Old Vicarage . . . I'm not sure about camping . . ."

"Oh, Angell." Caroline smiled sweetly. She was finally beginning to enter into the spirit of the enterprise. "The King is even now stretched out under the stars in remotest Iceland. I really don't see why his wife shouldn't do the same under a nice safe Home Counties sky."

Angell flushed. He did not take to being mocked, even by the Queen. Sullenly he climbed back into the car, and they set off once more, trailing the Cortina. Samantha had attached a Friends of Man banner to the radio aerial and tacked a Union Jack alongside it, so that it made a distinctive flag, an affirmation that this was the party of the British branch of the Friends of

Man. It would, she explained make it easy for them to regroup if they got lost. She did not explain that it had another purpose. Nor, twenty minutes later as they drove slowly into an already crowded parking lot in a hastily mown hayfield, did she draw anyone else's attention to the denim-suited couple on the big Harley Davidson who watched them drive past with studied interest, and then slipped into the line of cars behind them. She noticed that the girl already had a Leica with a telescopic lens slung around her neck, and that the paniers were stuffed with what was likely to be a professional's photographic gear. . . .

Night was beginning to draw in and everywhere there were camp fires. Although the concert did not start until ten the next day, there were easily several hundred thousand people gathered already. Temporary lavatories in green corrugated iron were the focal point of a small town of first aid stations, police field units, hot dog vans and a marquee-signposted "crash tent" where those who had not come with their own tents could crash out like anchovies in a can. Most of the cars were dilapidated bangers, their owners equally unkempt. Charles Smithers pulled in next to a rusty jalopy festooned with stickers and Angell, scowling, parked alongside.

As they got out he took Caroline to one side. "I don't like it," he whispered to her. "It's totally insecure."

"Don't be silly, Angell," she said, "we passed hundreds of your colleagues on the way in. If you're worried, go and tell them we're here. I'm sure they'll look after us."

"You're putting me in a very awkward position, ma'am."

Caroline smiled sympathetically. "I'm sorry," she said, "really. But it will be all right. And I'll stick up for you with Inspector Macpherson and the others." He grunted and turned away as the others began to load up their gear. When he was alone with the cars for a moment, he spoke into the police-frequency radio quietly, then replaced the handset and sat back in the carseat to think.

The campsite was next to the parking lot, adjoining some woods from which people were busy looting timber for their fires. Sam, clutching the makeshift flag now on the end of a bamboo cane, led the way to a corner spot which was still un-cluttered, and dropped her rucksack on the ground.

"Good a place as any" she called back, and everyone else agreed. It did not take them long to pitch the two small tents, unroll the sleeping bags and unpack their food. The men went off to find wood while the women laid things out. Behind them in the gathering gloom, a photographer took the special night sight from his assistant, fitted it to the Leica and began to shoot infrared film remorselessly. "Terrific," he muttered. "Incred-ible. Baby, we're going to make ourselves a ton of bread with these." In the distance, Detective Constable Angell watched and waited and bided his time.

It was a warm evening. All around the campsite the fires glowed, smoke mingling with the pungent herbal aroma of a fog of marijuana. The six of them cooked steaks and sausages, beans and tomatoes, drank Scotch and buckets of red jug wine, and relaxed. After they had eaten they huddled around the fire and Sam took out her guitar. She had a surprisingly deep, husky voice and she sang well, inviting the rest of them to join gently in the choruses. After a while Charles Smithers lit a joint of marijuana and passed it around the circle. They all took a drag and passed it on. Simon Waterman and Joanne huddled close together and occasionally exchanged soft sweet nothings; Charles Smithers lay down and put his head against Samantha's thigh as she sat cross-legged on the ground, singing softly. Caro-line felt muzzily content, her head full of alcohol and pot, and she did not move away when Julian pressed up against her. A little later when he found her hand and held it, she returned the pressure. And away in the darkness the photographer's assistant passed him another loaded camera and took away the other to empty and reload.

She didn't mean to make love to him, nor he to her, but gradually the drink and the drugs took a hold on them both, and when Joanne and Simon slipped away toward the woods, gig-gling erotically, it was not long before she allowed Julian to lead her away too. "Let's go for a walk," he said, tentative and embar-rassed to the last, and it was she who stopped him as soon as they had penetrated the woods and found a quiet and private place. All around them the night seemed charged with sex, and she felt no guilt whatever as she kissed him expertly and moved her hand inside his shirt. And behind them in the darkness a Leica clicked, its motor drive whirred and the photographer's heavy breathing matched their own.

But Detective Constable Angell still bided his time . . .

They woke early, cold and hung over, edgy and bad tempered, to march half a mile to the amphitheater where the concert was to be held. Caroline had only the most confused memories of the night. Her head ached. She had forgotten the penalties of drunkenness and her temper was not improved by the noise of the bands. All day as they sat, wedged into the enormous crowds, staring at the billowing canvas on the stage, their ears were assaulted by the deafening boom and shriek of a succession of groups. Caroline realized how far she had outgrown rock.

The photographer, who could afford to sit off at a distance courtesy of the telefoto lens, clicked merrily away. Huddled with her friends, the Queen would have been easily recognizable to anyone looking for her, but among these several hundred thousand she was simply another face in the crowd.

Angell, meanwhile, had not been idle. The arena was teeming with plainclothesmen in beards and jeans. They had all been tipped off. When the palace detective finally moved in, he would have plenty of support.

The concert did not end until almost midnight when the Fuzz finally gave their last, thunderous encore in a spectacular bonfire of laser beams and colored lights. "Thank God," Caroline thought, "that's over." They said taut good-byes in the parking lot, and Caroline allowed Julian to kiss her, but on the cheek only. She wanted to make clear—to him and perhaps to herself—that what had happened during the night was an aberration. A one-night stand. Not to be repeated. She hoped he was adult enough to get the message. She liked him after all, and as far as she could remember they had had a good time together.

Now she wanted to go back to being friends and colleagues. She lay in the back of the Stag as Angell drove furiously to Windsor and wondered why she felt so little guilt—and in its place the first stirrings of concern.

She had not observed the little scuffle that took place some two hours before the concert's end. She had not seen the photographer packing up his equipment, a thin smile of satisfaction on his face. As he had walked jauntily through the opening in the high corrugated iron perimeter wall, he had been surrounded by a dozen burly men who materialized suddenly out of the darkness. In a matter of seconds he was bundled into the back seat of a white police BMW along with his assistant. He did not need to ask why he was being arrested. Instead he slumped back in the seat and wondered what would happen now. There was no question of bluffing it out, he would tell them everything. He was frightened of the questioning, terrified of physical pain . . .

But he need not have worried. That was not Blackrock's style, or Cathcart's either. They would proceed softly. Efficiently, but without pain. Unless it finally became necessary to dispose of him. He might prove too much of a potential embarrassment to be allowed to live. The photographer did not think that far ahead as the BMW screamed toward London, lights ablaze, siren wailing.

Blackrock was pruning roses when the call came.

"The office, darling." His wife stood on the terrace, flanked by the Labradors, hands cupped in a megaphone shape at her mouth. "Office," she repeated. "It's urgent."

Grumbling, he went indoors where he listened at the phone, frowning and saying very little. Eventually he nodded and said: "Right you are. I'll be up in an hour and a half."

He had packed and changed in five minutes, accepted a cup of tea from Lady Blackrock, and was on the road within a quarter of an hour of the summons.

"Bloody woman," he kept muttering to himself as he drove fast but capably toward the rendezvous. "Bloody woman!"

His temper had subsided by the time he reached New Scotland Yard. He was like ice with the Commissioner and Cathcart, both of whom, like himself, had been pulled in from quiet, relaxing weekends.

"I thought it best to ask you to come in," the Commissioner said. "Not really our line of country, and I gather your chap Angell was keen that you should be involved."

"Quite right," Blackrock said, accepting milky coffee with distaste. "How long before they bring him in?"

"We don't know. I've left it to them to organize. I try to delegate."

"Quite," Blackrock said. He was not sure of the Commissioner. New to the job, he had come from the Devon constabulary where he was reputed to have done great things. But Devon was not London.

"The Commissioner has very kindly assigned us a room," Cathcart said. "We can have him to ourselves for a while at least. There may be a problem over criminal charges. Taking photographs *is* allowed . . ."

Blackrock did not reply. After a thoughtful sip of coffee however he asked the Commissioner if he would excuse them both. It was a delicate matter, as he was sure the Commissioner understood, and he would like a chance to have a private talk with his friend and colleague.

"Now," Blackrock hissed when they were alone in a comfortable functional interview room with a long table and chairs. "What the hell is all this?"

Cathcart shrugged and lit a Balkan Sobranie.

"Trouble," he said. "Big trouble."

Blackrock began to pace. "So she's gone to this rock festival or whatever it's called. That's bad. Now Angell says she's been spotted by some lensman. But only one. Otherwise no one's recognized her. That's bad all right, but it could be worse."

Cathcart grimaced. "It could be," he said, "and will, if there's another time. Do we know no one else has recognized her?"

"I suppose not." Blackrock sighed. "What are we going to do, Henry?"

"Angell thinks this photographer was tipped off," Cathcart said. "Or so I'm told. That implies she's been set up."

"Mmmm." Blackrock thought for a moment. "How long will it take to develop his film?"

"No time at all," Cathcart said. "They've got chaps in the lab here who can knock it off in a few minutes."

"And if it *is* a setup?" Blackrock felt nervous. "Have you heard anything? Any grounds for thinking there's a conspiracy on?"

"No more than usual," Cathcart said. "The only thing to do is wait and see what this photographer has to say for himself."

And so they waited. They talked around the subject for hours. Pots of tea were brought in. They dined, rather badly, with the Commissioner. It was a fraught, tense occasion in which terse exchanges of necessary politeness set all their nerves on edge. Blackrock had had the foresight to pack a volume of Gibbon, and after dinner he read halfheartedly while Cathcart and the Commissioner talked about shark fishing off the Cornish coast.

Just after ten the call came through.

The Commissioner listened intently for a few seconds, then replaced the receiver and turned to his guests.

"They're on their way," he said. "No problems." He smiled. "Brandy?" His guests declined. The Commissioner's worries were over; theirs were just beginning.

"Well."

Blackrock pressed his fingers together and gazed steadily at the man on the other side of the table. He was not impressed. Leather jackets seldom did impress him, especially accompanied by this sort of pansy good looks. He had encountered them all in the course of his employment at the palace. Some were decent enough in a servile sort of way, but the paparazzi type like this were the worst. Luckily, this one looked agreeably cowed. Blackrock wondered whether he had been beaten up or merely threatened. In fact, he guessed, neither—not necessary.

"Well," he said again. "Perhaps you'd like to tell us what you've been up to Mr., er . . . ?"

"Brown. Bill Brown."

"And you were taking photographs at the Otley, um . . . Rock Festival."

"No law against it," Brown said, with a smidgeon of emerging truculence.

Blackrock slapped it down. "We all know why we're here, and when we have your film printed up, which will be done in a few minutes, we'll have the proof, so there's really no point in pretending you were on a routine job. You're freelance, I take it? Self-employed?"

Brown nodded.

Cathcart spoke for the first time. "Someone told you Her Majesty the Queen would be attending the festival incognito." He was menacingly ingratiating. "I can quite see that photographs of her there would be very lucrative. I admire your enterprise and initiative. All we want to know is who tipped you off."

Silence.

"This is rather serious," Cathcart said, smiling. "In the present rather delicate political situation you must realize . . . that if pictures such as these were to be made public then certain people would be placed in a somewhat embarrassing position."

More silence. Brown, out of his depth, swallowed and cleared his throat.

"I don't want to seem melodramatic, Mr. Brown," Blackrock said, "but it may well be that there is a threat to national security involved here." The magic words. "I'm not at the moment suggesting that you have been *wittingly* involved in a plot to discredit the Royal Family, but it seems to me that you are most certainly an accessory to such a plot. We need to know who is behind it. I think I can safely say that your cooperation will not only help us, but—" and he paused for effect, "will help you too."

Brown found his voice. "Could I have a glass of water?"

Blackrock nodded, picked up the phone and passed on the request. Then he looked hard at their prisoner.

"Well?"

"His name was Schnabel," said Brown. "He came through *Gossip Magazine* in New York."

Blackrock glanced at Cathcart and scribbled. "Schnabel?" He spelled it out loud.

"Yes."

There was a knock on the door and a plainclothesman came in with a tray. On it was a jug of water, three glasses and a stack of prints.

"Most of these are contact prints, sir," he said. "We had one or two blown up, then we stopped, sir, and put the negatives in the vault for the moment . . ."

Blackrock thanked him, pushed the water toward the photographer and began to examine the prints. They were much as he would have expected. It was clearly the Queen. She was having a good time, though they were quite innocent, a young woman sitting about with friends. For a moment he wondered if they weren't exaggerating the significance of the business. Then he turned over a sheet of contacts and decided not. Despite himself he gasped. The print was grainy and a little blurred. For a moment he thought something had got fouled up, that some vice squad photographs had been mixed in with the others, but as the thought flashed through his mind he realized that the naked well-built blonde was the Queen of England.

There were a dozen of the pictures and they left nothing to the imagination. Two people were making love in the woods somewhere. The woman was clearly recognizable in at least half the shots. The man's face was obscured in all but the last two, because the photographer had been shooting from behind him, but in this final pair of prints the man was lying on his back with his face looking toward the camera. Blackrock recognized it from file photographs as the face of Julian Locke.

Silently, he passed them over to Cathcart.

After a moment or two Cathcart said, "We have to talk. Not here. My place."

Blackrock nodded, then glanced at Brown.

"And him?"

"We have to talk about him too."

"Right." Blackrock used the internal telephone again. He was shaken. This he had not anticipated. He knew she was willful, but he had not thought her venal. He no longer felt quite so compassionate.

Three quarters of an hour later, they were in the drawing room of Cathcart's flat. It was safer there. Neither man felt easy at Scotland Yard, where the police tended to play things by the book. In this case the book did not cover the rules. This was not an orthodox situation and there was no point in pretending it was.

"Are those the only photographs?" Blackrock asked, as much to himself as to Cathcart.

Cathcart nodded grimly. "We have to assume so," he said, "but there will be other opportunities. She's gone over the top this time. You must agree."

"I must agree." Blackrock hung his head and fingered the irritating shrapnel scar.

"She's an insupportable risk." Cathcart was pushing home his advantage. "Absolutely insupportable. She can't go on. We'll have to play our final card now. At once."

"Just a minute—"

"Our men are ready to go," Cathcart said. "The question is, what chance is there of her going for a ride in the park later today?"

"God knows," Blackrock said. "All we could do is to get the men in position and pray."

"Agreed," Cathcart said. "I was hoping you'd say that." He picked up the receiver and dialled a long series of numbers. "Green for Go," he said. "We can't wait for tomorrow, so get it done as soon as you can." He hung up and mopped his brow with a silk paisley handkerchief. "Have that drink now?" he asked. "I could sure use one." He poured two stiff brandies.

"What chance of picking up this Schnabel character?" Blackrock asked.

"About zero I should say," Cathcart said. "As soon as his photographer failed to show with the material, he'll have flown the coop. We'll get Master Locke though."

As it turned out, he was right on both counts. Schnabel had a keen instinct for danger, and when Brown failed to make the rendezvous he started to run and went to his fallbacks. He put in several calls to the photographer's flat from a series of phone booths on the Dover road, and when the last of these was answered by a flat cryptic voice, he recognized instantly that there had been a disaster.

All ports would, of course, have been alerted for a man named Schnabel, so he used his alias and backup passport. He was disappointed as he stood in the stern of the channel ferry and watched the Dover cliffs recede, but not completely disappointed. The extent of his defeat was not yet certain . . . nor even if, when all was decided, whether it would have to be a defeat at all . . .

CHAPTER

*M*INUTES AFTER Cathcart's phone call, an anonymous grey Rover with stolen license plates eased out of the Duke of York's barracks in the King's Road, Chelsea, and headed west, as he had carefully briefed them the week before. There were two occupants, both of them trained in clandestine and guerrila warfare, both ruthless and virtually without fear. And both of them had—unbeknownst to Cathcart—received a second, even more secret briefing by Sir Evelyn Blackrock.

In the trunk was enough high explosive to destroy a tank, also a two-way radio set and a pair of balaclava-style head masks of the type favored by terrorists the world over. Their careers had been so full of bizarre assassination, sabotage and destruction that they scarcely stopped to reflect that this was, by any standards, an eccentric mission. From a technical point of view it was straightforward. And the technical point of view was the one they understood.

Normally she went riding in the morning, but she had awakened late, feeling tired and hungover. By the time she had breakfasted, seen Joanne and Simon off to Paris, attended church, and played with the children, it was time for lunch. But it was a gorgeous day and she felt the need to get out into the fresh air. She was in good spirits.

Just before lunch she called to the stables and asked them to have her favorite mare ready for two-thirty. As usual, a stable girl would ride out to a remote part of the park and wait for her to make the rendezvous in one of the Range Rovers. It saved her having to hack all the way from the Castle and meant that she could ride for several miles and never see a soul. Although there was a public thoroughfare through the middle, and the public picnicked on the verges, the park was mostly private and security was lax to the point of being nonexistent. God knows why. Later, when questioned, Tartan Macpherson would put it down to precedent . . . Windsor was home turf, a Royal Borough no less, where members of the House of Sax-Coburg-Gotha, the House of Windsor and the House of Mountbatten tried to shake off at least some of the shackles and restraints of their official life.

So she always went to the meeting place alone.

The sun shone as she drove slowly down the long walk, and she felt elated and free. The breeze flicked at the collar of her shirt and cooled her face and neck and she sang softly to herself. She was meeting her horse and the girl by the old gnarled oak they called the Queen's Tree, and which, according to unlikely legend, had been planted in memory of Anne Boleyn. She drove slowly along the rough track and did not notice the anonymous grey car parked in the shade of a small copse. After a while the track petered out and she was crossing rough grass. The two horses were standing in the usual place, their groom between them. She stopped the car and got out. As she did, she saw to her surprise that the one holding the two horses was not a girl after all, and she was about to call out when she heard something behind her. She had time to half turn and catch a glimpse of a powerful figure just a foot away, his face hidden by a woolen mask with slits for mouth and eyes. She saw something in his hand and began to scream, but before she could make a sound his hand came over her mouth. She struggled for a second, felt her brain begin to numb, fought to stay conscious, then blacked out . . .

They heard the explosion as far away as Virginia Water. It must have been a very big bomb, they said. The largest piece of Range Rover anyone found was no bigger than a matchbook. She hadn't a hope, poor woman. There wasn't enough of her left to . . . well, it was horrible. All day the BBC played solemn music, the flags flew at half-mast, and a nation mourned.

Seldom had there been such an event. It was, for all its tragedy, immensely exciting. People were stunned and shocked, dismayed, heartbroken, horrified. Tears ran down the cheeks of grizzled newspaper vendors and of the BBC's veteran newscaster Angela Rippon as she gave the news. Parliament was adjourned at once, members standing in silent tribute and filing out without a word. Newspaper editors who had been sniping at the Queen for her indiscretions felt sudden shame and ordered up official photographs of Her Majesty in ceremonial costume, which they had set within a border of thick and mournful black, ready for a front page from which all else was banished.

A somber Sir Evelyn Blackrock tracked down the King on his remote river in Iceland and told him what had happened in tones of clipped and respectful commiseration. A VC–10 of the Royal Air Force was dispatched to Reykjavik to bring him home forthwith. Almost at once the messages of condolence began to pour in, from the Pope, from the President of the United States, from countries all over the world. That night, an ashen-faced Prime Minister appeared on television to announce that there was to be official mourning until after the funeral and that in consequence of the tragic assassination the general-election date would be postponed by two weeks. In a voice trembling with emotion he denounced the "violent and deluded men of the extremist British Republican Army who had cut down a young woman in the flower of her youth, a Queen yes, but also a mother of two small children, a woman, utterly defenseless, whose only crime in the eyes of her murderers was that . . . that *she was Our Queen.*"

The BRA, who admitted responsibility for the outrage in a

single untraceable phone call to the Press Association, were as elusive as ever. The police and the army were said to be making every possible attempt to bring the guilty men to justice. Road-blocks had been erected throughout the Home Counties. Special checkpoints were set up at Heathrow Airport. But no arrests were made. It was said that a second car, probably a Ford Cortina, had been blown up with the royal Range Rover, but this was not confirmed by the authorities, who were secretive, almost silent about the whole terrible business. One or two eye-witnesses claimed to have heard a helicopter shortly before the explosion, but this could not be confirmed.

"It seems to have worked," Blackrock said cautiously. They were in the communal gardens of the square in which Cathcart had his flat. A pair of trim middle-aged ladies in whites patted a tennis ball gingerly back and forth, and a Eurasian girl in a bikini lay on a towel sunning herself. An elderly gardener with brown canvas trousers secured at the waist by twine fiddled with a hose and sprinkler attachment. Otherwise the two conspirators were alone.

Cathcart smiled. "I do believe it has," he said, softly. Outside the garden traffic hummed, and although there was no chance of their being overheard, he kept his voice low. "The change in the opinion polls is quite remarkable." He fingered his thick black silk tie. Even in mourning, thought Blackrock, Henry Cathcart managed to appear smart and fashionable. "I think," he continued, "that we'll win, and with something to spare." He sighed. "Messy business. I'd have preferred something more straightforward."

Blackrock shook his head. "I'm glad we did it this way," he said, "more difficult, but, well, more British."

"You were getting soft in your old age," Cathcart said. "How's the King? Potter's concerned."

"He'll get over it," Blackrock said roughly. "Broken up, of course. Who wouldn't be? He was particularly unhappy about the body. Lack of body that is." He winced with embarrassment at his own joke. "We all told him there was nothing to see, but he needed a lot of convincing. Give him a few months and we'll find him a nice suitable boring duke's daughter."

"Which we should have done in the first place."

"Quite." Blackrock stretched out his legs, and hooked a thumb into one of the pockets of his waistcoat. "I'm sorry in a way," he said. "She was a very striking personality. Ten times the man the King is, if we're absolutely honest."

Cathcart pondered the question. "Maybe," he said at last. "But the time has gone when we could afford a striking personality on the throne. The first duty of the King is to be dull as ditchwater. Wouldn't you say?"

"I suppose," Blackrock said. "She was uncomfortable to have around, but she was stimulating."

"Well, now we must pray for a soporific successor."

The bees and the traffic hummed, the tennis match concluded, the girl in the bikini folded her towel and left, the gardener turned off the sprinkler, but the two old friends and colleagues remained in the gardens for more than an hour.

It was a fitting day for a funeral.

All along the Mall spectators had held a candlelight vigil and camped, curled in sleeping bags to make sure of a good view of the procession, and at 8:45 as Henderson walked to work they were eating breakfast. Above them, banners hung limply from the flagpoles and the rain slanted across grey pavements, dampening the spirits of the populace still further, if such a thing were possible. Henderson was profoundly depressed. Privately he had resolved that he would be handing in his resignation as soon as palace life reverted to something approaching normal. He was deeply saddened by the Queen's death, but over and above the tragedy there was an idea eating away at him, a grim suspicion which he could hardly formulate. Remembering Caroline's admonition to him, he had quietly taken her diaries from the safe and prepared to send them to her friend, Joanne. Before doing so he had read them through, and what he read made him uncomfortable. He had not realized the extent of her despair and her altruism, had not fully understood her desire to do good or her hatred and suspicion of the authorities as exemplified by Sir Evelyn Blackrock. Was he imagining it, or was there a hint of hypocrisy in Sir Evelyn's grief? He knew the two of them had been at odds for the past three years . . .

And then, this morning he had a letter, a letter with an East German postmark. It was unsigned and it said, simply, "She was not killed by the BRA. Look nearer home. More follows. A friend." He had not shown the letter to anyone. He did not know what it meant. But it disturbed him.

When he arrived at his room he found a message saying that the King wanted him. He swallowed hard. Interviews with the King since Caroline's death had been heartrendingly lugubrious affairs. His Majesty was given to punctuating the conversation with long silent stares during which his eyes became moist and he had trouble keeping his mouth still. He was drinking more than he should. "I blame myself," he said more than once. He should never have abandoned her, should never have ignored her so, should never, perhaps, have married her and exposed her to such risks . . .

Henderson found him sitting at his desk, already wearing the full dress uniform of an Admiral of the Fleet, the most funereal of his military outfits. He was writing a letter.

"Ah Henderson," he said with a pathetic attempt at cheerfulness and efficiency.

"You sent for me, sir."

"Yes," he smiled wearily, "and do you know, I can't for the life of me remember what it was about."

"Oh."

"Never mind," he said, "it's strange isn't it? Your first big job for us was the wedding."

"That's right, sir."

There was a long silence. "Dental records," the King said at last. "They identified her from dental records. All the bastards left were her teeth. Christ! Can you imagine that?"

Henderson said nothing. There was nothing to say. The King apologized. "Everything under control?" he asked in a perfunctory fashion. Henderson assured him it was. The apparatus was supremely well equipped to deal with occasions such as this. All over London the traditional cogs in the wheel of British panoply and pomp would be oiling themselves in readiness for the ceremony. At the College of Arms, Garter Principal King of Arms would be struggling into his tabard and mustering his heralds of York and Somerset, Richmond and Windsor. At Westminster the Dean would be in his canonicals casting a final eye over his clergy, and in Horse Guards the General Officer Commanding London Division would be flicking dust from the deep shiny black of his toecaps and wondering if security would hold. Sergeant at Arms, Black Rod, the Lord High Chancellor, the Lord President of the Council, the Earl Marshal, the Lord Great Chamberlain and all the other officers of state would be preparing to pay their last respects to the woman whose death, by a frightful paradox, was going to make another five years of this sort of thing possible after all.

"The people love us again," the King said bitterly, cutting into his thoughts. "It seems from the opinion polls that we are to be spared socialism after all."

"Yes," Henderson said, "Her Majesty's death has had that effect."

This time the King did not reply, but simply sat staring fixedly at a point somewhere above Henderson's head. After a minute or two Henderson coughed apologetically, muttered and withdrew. But the King did not move.

At eleven-fifteen the gun carriage started to roll across the palace courtyard, hauled by men of the Royal Navy in their old-fashioned blue uniforms with stiff white hats and webbing. The coffin itself was draped in not one but two flags, the Union Jack of her adopted nation and the Stars and Stripes of her native land. Immediately behind, one of the palace grooms led Piñero, the grey gelding she had ridden sometimes on parade. In the stirrups a pair of empty riding boots faced backward, a reminder, if one were needed, of the demise that was being commemorated. Next came the widower King, sword clanking at his side, face as grey as the steel-hued sky above, as he marched in time to the slow tramp of the sailors ahead. A pace behind him, flanked by Secret Service agents, walked the dead Queen's father, Henry Knight, in heavy black coat and tall silk top hat, and the President of the United States and her husband. Behind them, an escort of the First Battalion of the Scots Guards, their arms reversed in tribute and their band and pipers playing the hauntingly mournful lament, "The Flowers of the Forest." It was a somber sight, but it had a grandeur too, that melancholy cortege, as the processioners swayed in time to the muffled drumbeat and moved slowly down a Mall thick with mourners whose bare heads were bowed in tearful salute. Above the West front of Buckingham Palace, the Royal Standard hung limply at half-mast, a salute which was echoed throughout the city and the country and indeed the world.

Everywhere flags were at half-mast, and the television cameras made the most of this symbol of loss that transcended nations and languages, sending the pictures bouncing around the globe by satellite from Canberra to Khartoum, Ottawa to Austria and Manchester to Mongolia. It made heart-stirring television, as commentators, voices muted in the broadcaster's equivalent of the muffled drum, described the event in lachrymose detail, as if there would be no end to the tears, from that first moment when the coffin appeared through the palace gates, through the Abbey service to that final public scene at Waterloo Station when the pallbearers loaded the coffin onto the special train which was to take it to Windsor and the private interment at the royal mausoleum at Frognal. A hastily edited version was shown that evening for those very few Britons who had not sat through the live broadcast, and it was quickly turned into an hour-long special film. It was, said senior TV men, the best funeral since Winston Churchill's, and the film would go on to win many prizes.

"Impressive, don't you agree?" said Sir Evelyn Blackrock, as the final credits rolled. He turned off the videotape machine, drew back the curtains and stood staring thoughtfully out over the rolling parkland to the high wall which enclosed it and separated it from the moors beyond. This was a very secure house. There were signs on the moors warning of mines and unexploded bombs, and they were not fooling. There *was* a minefield out there. The house had first been used for the debriefing of Hitler's deputy, Rudolf Hess, after he had flown mysteriously to Britain in World War II. It had been Ministry of Defense property ever since, though its precise function was a closely and effectively guarded secret. Blackrock turned to face the bed, where a young woman, face heavily bandaged, lay back against a bank of pillows. "So," he said, "you had quite a send-off. Not a dry eye in the country. And thanks to our efforts an absolutely whopping victory for Prime Minister Potter and the Conservatives. So your husband and the children are secure for a while yet. And I think you'll agree that you haven't come out of it too badly yourself. You knew, didn't you, that queenship was a mistake almost as soon as you embarked on it? And thanks, I may say, to my own good offices you're alive and well. Or as well as could be expected."

"You never did like me." Caroline had trouble talking. Her face hurt terribly. She had no idea what they had done to her; her face had been swathed in bandages since the operation, so she could only guess. Blackrock shrugged. "I can't blame you for thinking that," he said, "though it doesn't happen to be true. It was never anything personal. On a purely personal level I never felt the slightest animosity, but it very quickly became clear to me that you were not good for the country or for the monarchy."

"What makes you think you're entitled to decide that?"

Blackrock appeared to consider the question and then decided to ignore it. "The photographs were the last straw," he said, "though I'm running away with myself. You don't, of course, know about the photographs yet."

She shook her head, and winced at the further discomfort this caused her. Her mind was reeling. Perhaps she *was* dead. Maybe this was hell.

"That silly, silly outing to the Otley Rock Festival." Blackrock looked genuinely regretful. "That was a set-up. It was a trap. A man called Schnabel, alias Smith, alias God knows what else, engineered it. The girl Samantha worked for him. And your friend Locke—though I have to admit he had second thoughts and expressed real contrition. He died, by the way, car crash. Pity." He paused. "Everything was photographed. This chap Schnabel had tipped off a photographer and he followed you all around the rock festival. Some of the pictures were simply mischievous but others were rather more . . . should, I say, revealing. Night photography is very good these days. Infrared and all that. The detail in the night shots was really rather remarkable."

Caroline said nothing. There was nothing to say. She felt more wretched than at any time since her abduction.

"You're an intelligent woman," Blackrock said, "and so you will understand that we could not risk those photographs achieving any currency. We had to move fast and, reluctantly, we had to face the fact that only your immediate 'elimination' would render those pictures harmless. Besides which, I'm bound to admit that your death did have its attractions. The electorate was most upset. It had a wonderfully unifying effect. Which, happily, was translated into an overall Conservative majority of sixty seats."

"Does my husband know?"

"His Majesty knows nothing." Blackrock put on a menacing expression. "Nor should he. He never saw the photographs, which I am happy to say I destroyed personally."

"But," she faltered and put a hand to the bandages at her temple. "My death, I mean . . . he thinks I really am dead."

"Oh yes." Blackrock smiled, a thin glacial flick of the lips. "Much better that way. You'll be glad . . ." he spoke without a trace of irony, "to hear that he has been inconsolable. So much so that I begin to fear that he may go into the sort of decline and retreat that poor Queen Victoria indulged herself in after the death of her beloved Albert. However, if you'll forgive the cliché, time does have a habit of healing even the most terrible wounds. In due course I have every hope that your children will have a suitable *English* stepmother."

"Why didn't you kill me?" she asked, whispering, "I'd be better off dead."

"I ask myself that," he said smiling again, more gently this time, "my principal collaborator thinks me squeamish, but I prefer the word 'scrupulous.' Perhaps it's just sentiment. I know you must think me impossibly malevolent, but I am not a gratuitously cruel or callous man. So both of you are wrong about me. It seemed to me that it was possible to enjoy the benefits of your removal while, at the same time, mitigating its grosser and more irreversible elements."

He looked at his watch. "I don't have very much longer," he said, "and this is the last contact we shall have, so listen carefully. When those bandages come off you won't recognize yourself. The surgeon responsible is the best there is so you will still, we all hope, be an extremely attractive and personable young woman. But unrecognizable. Your pigmentation has been changed too. When everything has healed you will be taken from here to Glasgow International Airport and put on a flight to what I can best describe as a safe place, a much safer place than this one, as a matter of fact. I don't think you'll find it wholly disagreeable. Tropical climate. Small island, so you'll be quite near the beach. I've given instructions that the security shall be as unobtrusive as possible. The whole installation keeps a very low profile. You won't of course be allowed to communicate with the outside world, but you will be allowed books, even newspapers I think, though I'm leaving that to the authorities on the spot. And there'll be no need to see anything of the other patients."

"Patients?" she asked, not believing any of this nightmare, not *wanting* to believe it.

"It's a mental institution. Of a rather interesting kind. The staff has been told that you're suffering from delusions of a somewhat, how shall we say, colorful nature."

"Life imprisonment," she said bitterly.

"If you wish." He frowned, wondering for the hundredth time about the scruples that had made him keep her alive. How much easier it would have been to have done as Cathcart supposed he had—and killed her properly. But at the back of his mind, only half acknowledged, had been fear of Cathcart's being found out. Then, if she was really dead, he too would be guilty of regicide. The worst kind of treason, punishable by death. This way, he had her up his sleeve. A trump card. No one could say he was a murderer if he was able to produce a living "victim." And he would be able to. At the drop of a hat. Then let Cathcart explain his two bombings while he played savior. He was not going to go the way of Dusty Fanshawe and the photographer and Julian Locke . . .

"You have me to thank that you're even alive," he went on, "although I don't expect you to understand that now. But you will. And you'll realize that the plastic surgery is for your own protection. You have worse enemies than me in the world, believe me. So don't make it any harder on yourself than necessary. If you start trying to convince people you're the rightful Queen of England you'll no more be believed than the Grand Duchess Anastasia."

"I have you to thank, all right, you sonofabitch." Caroline's head sagged in a forlorn gesture of helplessness. Thank God, she thought to herself, he could not see her tears beneath the bandages.

Six months later, Maurice Henderson left his job with the Royal Family. The King was sad to see him go, Blackrock less so. Blackrock thought the man was soft, and too suspicious. Not to put too fine a point on it, Blackrock had a hunch that Henderson was skeptical about the Queen's murder. Nevertheless he was confident that his tracks had been sufficiently well covered, through several layers of cutouts and intermediaries. Besides, it had all worked out for the best. The King was still disconsolate, but Blackrock was sure he would get over it. More importantly, the country was back on the right tack. An extreme right tack. The left were in utter disarray. The Atlantic alliance had stood firm. Communism had been held at bay. And, though hardly anyone realized, or ever would, it was all due to Sir Evelyn Blackrock.

The euphoria he was forced to keep to himself made him marginally less careful than was his wont. He did not know that Henderson had the Queen's diaries, or what those diaries said about him. He did not realize that Schnabel had succeeded in making contact with Henderson, or that Henderson had been in touch with Joanne Hollis. He knew none of this, perhaps because he would not have wanted to.

The day after Henderson left royal service he called the American Embassy in Grosvenor Square, where he saw a man who gave his name as "Perkins." Although as Perkins listened he did not tell Henderson as much, he and his agency had been harboring independently some suspicions of their own. These had been reinforced by some highly peculiar intelligence reports which had come their way from a well-placed source in the Indian Ocean. The British, Perkins thought, were uncharacteristically smug about their high-security psychiatric ward five hundred miles east-southeast of Mauritius. They evidently thought everyone believed their cover story—that it was no more and no less than a satellite tracking station on a tiny atoll miles from nowhere. Their source had reported a new arrival whose provenance seemed oddly suspect. Coupled with their own inquiries at *Gossip Magazine* and in East Berlin, it began to seem curiouser and curiouser. Their contacts in British Intelligence were not as good as they had once been, but Henderson's visit was something of a clincher. That evening Perkins drove to one of the U.S. Air Force bases in East Anglia and took a military jet transport to Andrews Air Force Base outside Washington, D.C. Henderson went with him.

Of this Blackrock knew nothing. Neither did Cathcart, nor even the King.

A week later, somehow, Washington had photographs of the woman on St. Hubert's Island. They were inconclusive.

A week after that they acquired a handwriting sample. It looked good enough to act on. Henderson recognized it. So did Joanne Hollis. Their opinions were endorsed by two independent experts. Perkins and his superiors made a report to the White House, where the Chief of Staff took it directly to the

President. The President, aghast, summoned her National Security Advisor and the directors of Central Intelligence, the National Security Agency and the Defense Intelligence Agency; she took confidential soundings. Normally, of course, she would have conferred with the Brits discreetly but directly, especially now that they had installed this new hard-line government pledged to stand firm against the Soviets and the Warsaw Pact forces. But, as the President's advisers explained painstakingly, the problem here was that Queen Caroline appeared to be—impossible though this all was—a victim of the Brits themselves. Or of *some* Brits. There had been a conspiracy involving, so it seemed, the chief secretary to the British King, and an influential British Cabinet Minister . . .

The President wanted to know whether the British King was involved. Her advisers said no, categorically. She wanted to know whether Prime Minister Potter could be involved. Again the consensus was "no," although this time less categorically so.

Finally the President asked if there was any way of establishing contact on this subject with King and Prime Minister without alerting the conspirators. The experts said that, unhappily, in their opinion there was not. In their opinion, though, it should be remembered that Queen Caroline had been an American citizen, and although she might have forfeited her *de jure* privileges by marrying into the English royal house, the United States had some moral duties where she was concerned. Also it could be to the advantage of the U.S.A. to engineer her return, if such a thing was possible.

"Is it possible?" the President asked.

When there was no answer, she turned to her military aide, a Navy commander. "Get me the Chairman of the Joint Chiefs of Staff," she said.

Two weeks later the American Ambassador in London requested an audience with His Majesty the King at precisely 1500 hours Greenwich Mean Time the following Thursday.

The time was important and it was confidential. Since the request had to be made through Blackrock, the Ambassador could not say what it was about. Indeed he did not know himself. He had simply been told that at five minutes past three that afternoon, a telephone call would be put through to him at Buckingham Palace. In reality the call would be for the King, but for some reason that the Ambassador knew better than to ask Washington, this was the only way in which the call was certain to get through direct to the King, person to person. That, evidently, was vital, and vitally secret.

Of this Blackrock knew nothing.

Early that morning a small U.S. Navy amphibious task force appeared suddenly off the shores of St. Hubert's Island and took it over without a shot being fired. All outgoing radio frequencies from the hospital compound had been monitored by an electronics warfare ship since before dawn, and no transmissions were heard to leave the island.

By the time the U.S. Ambassador arrived at the palace, the telephone links were in place and only the final connections at the London end had to be made. The King and Blackrock still knew nothing of what was to come, but thousands of miles away the woman who once was Queen Caroline looked at the telephone in the Admiral's cabin and felt herself gripped by icy apprehension.

To say that this was the most difficult moment of her life fell short of what she felt now. Since the marines had arrived at dawn she had rehearsed this speech a hundred times. It was still not right. It would never be right. There simply were no precedents for coming back from the dead like this . . .

She was alone now and waiting. Somewhere else on the vast nuclear aircraft-carrier were Maurice Henderson and Joanne. She owed a lot to them, she realized, but even *their* meeting had been awkward. How much more so was this telephone reunion with her husband. "Oh God!" she whispered to herself. "Please help me this time."

She looked up at the clock and saw the seconds ticking toward the moment she longed for and yet dreaded.

The telephone rang. For a moment she hesitated. It rang again. She swallowed hard and picked it up.

Halfway across the world the American Ambassador put his hand over the receiver and passed it across to the King. "In fact . . . it's for you, sir," he said.

And downstairs, Blackrock, monitoring the call in his office, put his hand to his neck as he began to feel apprehensive stirrings of his own.